That's What Friends Are For

DIANE GREENWOOD MUIR

Cover Design Photography: Maxim M. Muir

Don't miss any books in Diane Greenwood Muir's

Bellingwood Series

Diane publishes a new book in this series
on the 25th of March, June, September, and December.
Short stories are published between those dates
and vignettes are written and published each month
in the newsletter.

Journals

(Paperback only)
Find Joy — A Gratitude Journal
Books are Life — A Reading Journal
Capture Your Memories — A Journal

Re-told Bible Stories

(Kindle only)
Abiding Love — the story of Ruth
Abiding Grace — the story of the Prodigal Son

You can find a list of all published works
at nammynools.com

CONTENTS

ACKNOWLEDGMENTS

Summer is finally at an end. It's the most difficult season of the year for me to work. Why? I have no idea. Well, except for heat, humidity, and other miseries it delivers to me. I'm definitely a winter gal. As long as I have four strong walls around me and supplies set in so that I don't have to rush out in a snowstorm, bring it all on.

I'm excited about the new family that moved in across the street from Polly and Henry. Sometimes you uncover a character who is filled with energy and you can hardly wait to bring them to life.

Characters are a big part of what makes writing so much fun. I'm often asked who my characters are taken from. My friends? My family? Myself? Well, yes, no, and maybe. I pour my personality into the books. I can hardly help myself - there's no one I know better. Though I pick up bits and pieces from people I know, it's more about telling their stories than relating their personality. Some stories do come from my life - though I might exaggerate them.

My characters have grown into themselves and become more than I imagined when I first began writing these stories. Characters who were originally introduced as minor players have become more important as the stories progress, and some whom I assumed would have a prominent place in Polly's life are supporting players, living lives that don't always intersect with hers. Just as the people in our lives move in and out, these characters live out their lives whether we pay attention or not. It's kind of fun to watch. It's even more fun to write about them.

I am grateful for those who help bring these books to publication. Before you see these stories, a fantastic group of brilliant and insightful people offers their time and expertise to me. Thank you to: Diane Wendt, Carol Greenwood, Alice Stewart, Eileen Adickes, Fran Neff, Max Muir, Linda Baker, Linda Watson, Nancy Quist, Rebecca Bauman, and Judy Tew.

Spend time with us at facebook.com/pollygiller.

CHAPTER ONE

"I just need to pick up a few things," Polly said. "I'll be back for my online order."

Barb smiled at her from behind the customer service desk. "Will you need help out with it?"

Before Polly could respond, Barb glanced at her computer. "Oh, I guess you will," she said with a laugh.

Polly's grocery orders rarely filled only one cart. She hated grocery shopping. Not only did she have to come back at least once because she'd forgotten something important, pushing two carts through the store was ridiculous. Once she figured out this whole online ordering thing, life was much better. Feeding eleven people every day was not something to be taken lightly.

When she'd placed her order late last night, she'd been remiss in not asking Elijah and his brothers if there was anything they wanted. It was her own fault. She'd heard them talking but hadn't put it all together. They wanted to make Snickerdoodles and molasses cookies for their friends at the nursing home. How did she not have cream of tartar in the pantry? Everyone had cream of tartar sitting around. And to top it off, she was out of molasses.

They could have gone to the grocery store in Bellingwood, but while she was here, she might as well pick up what they needed. The animals wouldn't hate it if she wandered down the pet aisle looking for cat and dog toys, either.

"I only need a few extra things," Polly said. "It shouldn't take more than ten minutes."

"I'll ask Annette to gather your order," Barb replied with a smile. "We'll be ready for you."

Polly nodded. She'd brought a cart in with her and pushed it forward while peering at the overhead signs, trying to decide where to go first.

Her attention snapped back to her surroundings when she heard an 'oomph' as the cart made contact with soft flesh.

"I'm sorry," Polly cried, looking in shock at the young man she'd thumped. He'd been bent over, placing a heavy bag of dog food into the bottom of his cart.

"It's no problem, ma'am," he said as he stood up. He patted his hip. "No damage."

"I am so sorry. I wasn't paying any attention. Are you sure you're okay?"

"It's cool. I'm fine. I'll tell Darth that though the run to the store was only ten parsecs, I encountered enemy ships and sustained minor damage."

She laughed. "Darth?"

"Yeah," he shrugged. "My little brother named him. He's a big black Great Dane. It seemed to fit. Except the dumb dog is no Sith Lord. He's more like Jabba the Hut, a slug that sits on top of you."

"Well, you tell Darth that at my house, we are part of the Resistance, not the Empire. Luke, Leia, Obiwan, and Han live with me. We are the enemy."

He laughed. "Nice."

The boy couldn't be much older than Rebecca and was built like a wrestler — thick and well-muscled. He wasn't tall, but more than made up for his height, carrying himself with a powerful demeanor. It seemed strange to Polly that she'd never seen him before. She would have noticed this good-looking young man.

"I am sorry," she said again. "Get an extra hug from your dog for your trouble."

He nodded as Polly walked away and into the depths of the store. She shook her head at herself. "From here on out, pay attention, you dope. No more damaging cute young men. Rebecca might like to meet them."

This school year was going to be a new experience for Rebecca. She and Andrew had broken up a month ago, not long after she returned from her trip to the East Coast with Beryl Watson. Things had been a bit edgy between the two kids even before she left. He wasn't happy with the fact that she had other things she planned to do with her life. She wasn't happy with the fact that he didn't understand how she needed freedom and independence. When Rebecca got back to Bellingwood, he'd been sullen for a week and refused to come over to the house. He had grudgingly accepted the cool Boston Public Library delivery bag that she'd purchased for him, but hadn't been enthusiastic in his gratitude. An infuriated Polly tried to talk to him, but he wanted nothing to do with that.

She'd spoken to Sylvie, who told Polly to let him be what he was ... an adolescent who was making strange choices.

The last month had been uncomfortable and odd. Rebecca had cried a lot that first week. He was not only her boyfriend, but one of her best friends and she had confided in him things that no one else knew. She missed that part of their relationship the most. Andrew was the boy who had brought Rebecca and Polly together. He had seen something in that little girl that she'd barely seen in herself and encouraged her to be all she wanted to be. Whatever had happened to make him set her aside, he wasn't talking about it.

Kayla had heard that he was chatting online with another girl, a Tawnya Mastering from Boone. That news had wrecked Rebecca again.

Polly was grateful this happened during the summer rather than in the middle of the school year. She'd known these painful times would be coming for Rebecca. She wasn't dumb enough to think that the girl would get through high school without angst and heartbreak. Polly also wasn't surprised that the two kids had broken up. They'd fallen together because for so long there had been no one else. When Kayla came into their small group, she'd accepted their relationship as it was. But Rebecca had discovered more of herself this last year and began making new friends. Dierdre Adams and Libby Francis spent quite a bit of time with Kayla and Rebecca, either at the Bell House, at Dierdre's new house, or at Libby's — whose parents had put a large above-ground pool in this summer. Even though the Francis' lived on a farm east of town, quite a few kids from their class found their way out to play in the pool.

Polly had offered to get in the middle of the mess with Andrew and Rebecca. In fact, she'd talked to Henry about just doing so without permission, but he told her to leave it alone. That wasn't surprising. Henry hadn't wanted those two to 'be' together at this point anyway. He wanted them to experience more life before they settled into a forever-relationship.

What Polly most wanted to do was pop Andrew upside the back of the head. The thing was, he was such a good kid. If he didn't want to be with Rebecca, then the two of them needed to figure out how to be friends. He'd come to the Bell House a couple of times to babysit for the little boys when everyone else had things going on and Polly didn't want to lose that connection. The boys loved him and he was a big part of this family. But life was filled with change and Polly couldn't control it all, no matter how hard she tried. She hated that the kids had to go through this, but how would they ever learn to deal with what life handed them if they didn't start now? All she could do was offer comfort and love.

~~~

When she arrived home, she smiled. Her four boys were standing with Cat on the front sidewalk, staring at a large moving van parked in front of the house across the street.

4

Calvin and Chris Dexter had moved to a small town in Southeast Iowa in early July because he'd gotten a new job. Their house was sold a week later, but it had taken nearly a month for the family to arrive. Today was apparently the day.

She rolled the window down. "Been out here long?"

Cat shook her head. "The van arrived fifteen minutes ago and they're waiting for someone to get here with keys. I offered to make some calls. I guess the family got into town late last night. Talk about timing."

"I have groceries, boys," Polly said. "Will you help me carry things inside?"

All four boys gave her a stricken look and then glanced at the moving van.

"You won't miss much," she replied. "Especially if you hurry."

"Do you think they have kids our age?" Elijah asked.

Polly hoped so. They'd been devastated when the Dexters moved away — just when summer was kicking off. But it wasn't so bad in the end. It took more effort than walking across the street, but between Elva Johnson's four kids and Dierdre Adams' little brothers, the house and yard were generally full of activity. The kids loved camping out in the shed. When it got too warm, they moved to the lower level and wandered through the tunnel into the basement of the house. There was plenty of fun to be had.

"We'll see," she said. "I suspect we'll meet them all today. Help me unload, then you can come back out. I bought what you need to make cookies."

Elijah jumped up and down, patting the side of the Suburban. He turned to Cat. "Can we make cookies today?"

"I thought you wanted to watch the moving van get unloaded," Cat said.

The summer had been a time of wild growth, especially for Noah. He'd grown four inches and would be in fifth grade this fall. How was this happening? Elijah would be going into fourth grade, JaRon into first grade, and Caleb would begin third grade.

Caleb and JaRon's mother wasn't making any effort to clean up. Though she made noise about wanting to get her babies back, she was unable to stabilize herself enough to move forward. That was so hard for Polly to accept. She wanted to help the young woman — to give her a safe place to clean up and make her life work again, but there was no way she had the capacity for that. She had asked Mrs. Tally, the Child Services representative about Cassidy, the little girl Caleb remembered was their sister. To everyone's surprise, there was no record of the child in their system. Caleb and JaRon didn't remember much else, other than that she'd been born. When the kids got back into school this fall, Polly thought she might do some more investigating on her own. She had no idea where to even begin, but there had to be something out there.

Bag after bag of groceries went into the house and as she did every time it happened, Polly watched them pile up on the counters and on the island. The next part was no fun either.

Noah dropped a bag in front of the pantry door. "That's cat treats," he said. "Everything else is here."

"Nothing left in the Suburban?" Polly asked.

He smiled at her. "Unless you put a big bag of candy bars in the front seat."

"No candy bars," she said with a laugh. "Nice try, though."

"Can we go back outside?" Elijah asked.

"Is the moving van being unloaded?"

"Not yet."

"Then you four can help me put groceries away. You know the drill."

He heaved a dramatic sigh and opened a bag. Every time he made those sounds, Polly remembered Rebecca's dramatic sighs of disbelief when she was asked to do something she didn't want to do. It was right about this age, too. Before long, the boys had spread the contents of the grocery bags around the kitchen. Things that belonged in the pantry were placed just inside the door, things that went in the refrigerator were put on the island counter top and things that went into the cupboards went onto the counter along the south wall. The items they were unsure of were placed on the counter beside the coffee maker.

6

Polly and Cat were in charge of putting things away on shelves and into the refrigerator. For the most part, none of the boys could reach the upper cupboards, but when she'd started this process with them, she found groceries in the strangest places. Cheese slices had landed in the pantry and unopened ketchup bottles were in the refrigerator. Those had been fairly minor and kind of understandable. She hadn't been able to figure out why the cat treats ended up in the freezer. The only thing she could think was that someone had been distracted. Or … one of them had been playing a prank.

"Now?" Elijah asked impatiently. He gestured around the room. "Haven't we done enough?"

Polly tried hard not to snort with laughter. "For now. Thank you very much. Be sure to let me know what you find out."

His eyes lit up and he shivered his shoulders. "I will. Come on, guys. Let's go." He led the parade out through the back door.

Obiwan and Han made an attempt to follow, but Polly clicked her tongue and said, "Obiwan."

The two dogs came back in and sat down. She opened a new container of treats and gave one to each of them. "Good boys. You don't need to be involved today. Maybe later."

"Do you know anything about the new neighbors?" Cat asked Polly.

She and Hayden had gotten back from their honeymoon last weekend. They'd gone to Niagara Falls and then up into Maine. Polly's family had spent a great deal of time on the East Coast this summer. The thing was, she was thrilled for them. She didn't miss Boston. Right now, she was the happiest she'd ever been in her life.

Rebecca had called every night while she'd been away, telling stories of her adventures with Beryl. They'd met important people in the art world out there, impressing the heck out of the girl. True to her word, Drea Renaldi had taken a couple of days off and showed Rebecca the sights, giving Beryl time to meet with her agent and gallery owners. She'd taken them both to her mother's home for dinner one night and the whole family had shown up.

7

Rebecca was deeply and passionately in love with Jon. It didn't matter that he was twenty years older, she had a huge crush on him. Mama Renaldi had been everything Polly described and, as Rebecca told the story, Beryl had been on her best behavior.

Polly smiled at Cat. "The husband, Kirk, is Deb Waters' son. Henry knew him in high school. He left right away and joined the Marines. Been career military, but he lost a leg last year and now he's gotta move on."

"That's too bad."

Polly shrugged. "If he's Henry's age, that means he's been in the service for nearly twenty years. It has to be hard to have that happen this late in the game. Henry hasn't seen him in years."

Rebecca came down the back steps. "They're finally moving in?" She went over to the pantry and picked up two grocery bags before walking in.

"Yeah. What do you think?"

"I think it would be nice if we knew more. Why didn't you ask better questions?" Rebecca stuck her head out of the door and grinned at Polly.

"I don't know. I'm so ashamed," Polly replied. "Hey, heads-up."

Rebecca held up the two bags of groceries and gave her a look of panic.

With an evil grin, Polly tossed a container of mixed nuts across the room, then dropped her head as it caromed off the door to the foyer.

"Not even close," Rebecca said. "I don't know why I was worried. When will you stop throwing things?"

"Just about the time that I figure out how to aim. While I was at the grocery store, I ran into this cute boy about your age."

"A what?" Rebecca came back out into the kitchen, still holding a bag of groceries. "Where? And ran into? What does that mean?"

"I rammed my cart into him at the grocery store. He was bent over and didn't see me, so he couldn't escape."

"A cute boy and my mom runs into him. That's just perfect," Rebecca said with the same dramatic sigh that Polly had heard for years. "I'm single again and the only way I can find dates is to have my mom hit them. Fan. Tastic."

Cat chuckled. She handed Polly two canisters of biscuits.

"What's his name?" Rebecca yelled out.

"I didn't ask. I do know that he has a Great Dane named Darth and at least one younger brother," Polly said.

Rebecca came back out with the two plastic bags and jammed them into the bag that was filling up with other empties. "How is that helpful to me?"

"It's not," Polly said with a short laugh. "When school starts, I'll walk down the halls with you until I recognize him. Maybe I can run into him again."

"They're here!" Elijah yelled out, coming into the porch. "And there are kids our age. They have a dog. This huge thing. You have to come see it." He stood in the doorway between the kitchen and the porch. "Come on!"

"You go," Polly said. "We'll meet them later. They need to be able to concentrate on moving in today."

"No," he whined. "You have to see this dog. You won't believe it. It's taller than me." He ran over and grabbed Polly's hand. "Please. Come see it."

She laughed and let him pull her out onto the porch. "One of these days, young man, your cute face isn't going to get you everything you want."

Elijah batted his eyes at her. "It won't?" His cute face burst into a smile. "Come on."

They went outside and he pulled her across the yard. Chaos had erupted across the street. Cars were parked along the road since they couldn't get into the driveway with the moving van there. Three young children, who most likely would be in at least one of her kids' classes were running back and forth from a minivan to the house. Then she saw a big black Great Dane chasing the kids.

She took a breath.

And released it when the young man she'd rammed with her grocery cart stepped out from behind the moving van.

He yelled for Darth to come to him and glanced at her. A look of confusion passed across his face and then he grinned and waved. With his hand on the big dog's collar, he strode toward her and put his hand out. "You must be Ms. Giller. Grandma told me that you lived here, and Dad said he knows your husband. I'm Justin Waters."

Within seconds, his three younger siblings had followed him across the street.

"I am," Polly said. "I didn't think I'd ever see you again. I'm still sorry for running into you."

"I can't believe it was you."

She nodded. "It's always me. Introduce me to your family."

"This is Nathan, Lara, and Abby."

"I was a surprise," Abby said proudly.

"Were you," Polly replied. "I like surprises."

"Mom says she does too."

"These are my boys," Polly said. She patted their shoulders as she introduced them. "This is Caleb and Noah, Elijah and JaRon. Boys, did you hear what he called his dog?"

They all looked at her.

Nathan put his hand on the big dog's back. "His name is Darth."

"Like Vader?" Noah asked, his eyes big. "That's cool. Our dogs are Obiwan and Han."

"And our cats are Luke and Leia," JaRon said. "We love *Star Wars*."

"So do we," Lara said. "I watch it all the time."

CHAPTER TWO

Coming out from behind the moving van, a harried woman was followed by a girl about Rebecca's age. The woman was in her late thirties and had straight dark hair that hung just below her shoulders. Parted just off to one side, she wore it with sharp bangs. About Polly's height, she was maybe a little thicker all over. Her hands were strong and other than a thin gold band on her wedding finger, she wore no jewelry. She wore jean shorts that came down past her mid-thigh, a blue tank top with the words *Queen of All I Survey* on the front, and well-worn leather flip flops on her feet.

"There you are," the woman said. "I thought we agreed y'all wouldn't bother the neighbors until I had an opportunity to introduce myself." She gave her children a mock scowl and rolled her eyes. "I'm sorry if they interrupted your day. They know better. Don't you all have assigned tasks to complete?"

The three younger children nodded. "Yes, ma'am," they said and headed back to the house.

"Mom," Justin said. "This is the lady from the grocery store. I told you about her dogs, Obiwan and Han? She's Polly Giller!"

Polly laughed at that and put her hand out. "I am ..." she nodded toward Justin, "... Polly Giller. Welcome to the neighborhood."

The woman glanced at her son and then at Polly. "Are you kidding me? You meet one person and it's our new neighbor?" She reached out to take Polly's hand. "I'm Andrea Waters." She pronounced her first name with the emphasis on the second syllable. She had a touch of a southern accent in her voice. Not much, just enough to tell Polly that she hadn't grown up in Iowa.

"Hmm," said Polly. "I don't often hear that name pronounced that way. One of my best friends is called Drea."

"That's what my daddy called me," Andrea said. "He was the only one, though. Mama insisted that I be Andrea." She waved Justin away. "You go on, too. Make sure your father ..." She shook her head. "Just. You know."

He nodded. "It's nice to meet you, Ms. Giller."

"This is Marigold Lucille." Andrea touched her daughter's shoulder as she grinned.

"Mom," the girl said with great annoyance. "Why do you do that to me?"

"Because I'm your mother and I can. Be polite."

The girl put her hand out and as Polly took it, she said, "Cilla. I had to name myself something interesting. Marigold Lucille," she said derisively. "Who does that to a little girl?"

Polly laughed out loud. "It's quite an interesting name." She let her voice trail off. "Isn't it?"

"My grandmothers on both sides insisted that I use their names for the first girl," Andrea said. "I assumed we'd call her Mari or Goldie, but when Justin heard her name, he picked up on Cilla and it's been that ever since." She patted her daughter's shoulders. "He's the one who named you and you know it."

"It sounds better when I tell the story my way," Cilla said. She turned to Polly. "Grandma says you have a daughter my age. Is she home today?"

Polly blinked. "She sure is. Do you have time to meet her?"

Cilla looked at her mother. "Please?"

"Don't bother them very long," Andrea said. She stroked her daughter's reddish gold hair. That had to come from the Waters' side of the family. Louis Waters, the girl's grandfather was a redhead. "You are going to have a lot of work to do keeping us all organized when the van is unpacked."

"I know, right?" the girl said. She smiled at Polly. "I've labeled every room, pinned tags on all the furniture, made sure boxes were marked before they went in the van, and they still aren't getting it right. Even now, I'm sure the entire house is devolving into chaos and destruction."

Andrea laughed. "She's my brilliant drama queen."

"Mother!"

With her hands up in a gesture of surrender, Andrea laughed. "Don't forget that I am the mother," she said. "Half hour. Don't bother them any longer than that."

"We're fine," Polly said. "Our biggest entertainment today is watching you move in."

"You're sure?"

Polly nodded.

Andrea looked down at the four little boys standing beside Polly. "Would you like to come over and help my terrible trio? They're in charge of making sure any boxes that don't arrive in the correct room end up where they belong." Then she flinched and looked up at Polly. "I'm sorry. I should have asked you first."

The four excited faces looking at Polly made her chuckle. "How about they don't spend much more than a half hour with you, either. That way they won't get underfoot while you're trying to get moved in."

"Perfect," Andrea said. "It will be just like Rudolph Abel and Gary Powers in Berlin." She turned and gestured for the four boys to precede her across the street. Halfway there, she stopped, turned to Polly and drew a line on the pavement with her foot. "One half hour. We'll meet in the middle. I'll release yours and you'll release mine." With a grin, she turned and followed the boys to her house.

"She's so weird," Cilla said. "She loves World War II and Cold

War spy novels and movies."

"I think it's awesome," Polly replied. "What do you love?"

"Making Mother crazy," Cilla retorted immediately. "That and drama. I really am her drama queen. It's pretty much my life. Grandma says that the new school has some fairly decent productions. I'm here to take that up a notch." She put her foot on the first step. "They won't know what hit 'em."

Polly shook her head. She was sure that they wouldn't. She pushed the door open and went inside, surprised there were no dogs or people in her kitchen. She hadn't been gone that long. Then she saw a streak fly across the backyard through the glass doors.

Henry had finally knocked the wall out and put sliding glass doors in on the back wall of the kitchen. Once this heat finally quit searing her world, Polly was going to put paving stones in to make a patio. Things weren't so bad today, but the forecast promised more heat soon and she didn't think that starting a job and not finishing for weeks would work for her, so she'd wait.

"I'll bet they're out back with the dogs," she said. "This way."

"This place is huge," Cilla said. "And what a great kitchen. Mom would love this. She'd set her office up back here, so she could keep an eye on everything."

They'd also knocked out the wall between the kitchen and the stairway. She was happy with this space. Two comfortable sofas and three overstuffed chairs with big ottomans later, it had become one of her favorite places in the house. The kids loved to hang out here when they had time, and there was always traffic coming through from the upstairs. She could curl up with her coffee and a book in the early morning, dogs and cats gathered around her on the sofas and chairs and wait for the kids to come down to start their day.

She pushed the sliding glass door open and looked outside. "Rebecca? Are you out here?"

"Over here," Rebecca said, waving idly from the back porch. She was sitting in one of the rockers with her back to the patio and Polly. "Did you meet that cute boy? What's his name?"

"Uhhh," Polly said. "His sister is here to meet you. She's in your grade at school."

The rocker came to a sudden stop. There was some muttering and Polly was sure she heard a curse word, then Cat's laughter.

"I'll be right there."

Cilla laughed out loud. "I like her already. But Justin's heart was broken by a girl last year." She shrugged. "I dunno. Maybe he's ready to meet someone new. I've never let him near any of my girlfriends, but seriously. I was in junior high. He shouldn't be dating a junior high girl. That's just not right. He's going to be a senior, for heaven's sake. Yes, I know, last year I was a freshman, but still. We were children."

Polly gestured for Cilla to head back into the kitchen. "She'll be coming down the hall. Would you like something to drink? There's iced tea in the fridge."

"Sweet tea?" Cilla asked.

The last person who asked Polly for sweet tea was Aaron Merritt's sister from Atlanta.

"I have sugar," Polly said.

"No, that's okay. I'm fine." Cilla turned at the sound of footsteps. She moved forward and waited.

Rebecca came into the room, shaking her head. "I'm so sorry. That was embarrassing. I'm Rebecca."

"I'm Cilla. So, is it Rebecca or Rebs or Becky or what?"

"Rebecca."

The girls stood and looked at each other. It was only a few seconds of silence, but Polly chewed on her lower lip. "Do you two girls want to tell each other about yourselves or should I start talking about the little that I know of Cilla and the huge amount I know of Rebecca. Your choice."

Rebecca laughed. "She's kind of pushy."

"Pushy?" Cilla asked. "Good grief. Let me tell you about pushy. One time my mother drove me to the house of the boy who'd asked me out on a date because she wasn't going to let me go without meeting his mother. She didn't even call first and it was like a week before the date even happened. She just walked me right up to the front door, knocked, and then made the woman promise that her son wouldn't mess with me."

Both Polly and Rebecca burst out laughing.

"You've got to be kidding?" Rebecca asked. "At least you haven't done that, Polly."

"You haven't dated anyone I didn't know," Polly said.

"You call her Polly?" Cilla asked.

"Yeah. My mom died, and Polly adopted me. I knew her as Polly for a long time before that, so how could I change?"

"That makes sense."

Cat came into the room, peering in first. "You okay, Rebecca?"

Rebecca smiled at her. "I'm good. This is Cilla. Cilla, this is my …" She stopped. "I still don't know what to call you."

"Just Cat." The older girl put her hand out. "It's nice to meet you, Cilla."

"Grandma said you had a lot of people living here," Cilla said to Polly. "She tried to count, but said she forgot how many."

"Eleven," Rebecca said. "Most of the time. There are always a million more people in and out. You'll have to meet my friends, Kayla, Dierdre, Libby, and …" she gulped back Andrew's name and gave Polly a stricken look. It still wasn't over for her.

Maybe Polly would have to step in. Those two kids needed each other's friendship, but how in the world would they ever get past the fact that they'd tried to be more than that and it was over? She had no idea. That was completely new territory for her.

"I'd love to meet them," Cilla said. "The more people I meet before school starts the better, I say. I hate going into a new building without knowing anyone. And I've done that so many times, it's just crazy. But you get to know people in a hurry. I like meeting new people. So do you want to meet my cute brother?"

Rebecca dropped her head as she shook it. "I want to die."

"Nah. He is cute. He doesn't think so, but he is. I'll never tell him that, though. Give him a big head and everything? The last thing I need is Justin wandering around the house thinking he's all that. There only needs to be one of us in the family and I'm already competing with Mom. The rotten thing is, she's the boss and isn't afraid to remind me of it, every hour of the day if necessary. I keep telling her that I'll be in charge of her wheelchair when she gets old. But that doesn't work because Abby comes up and tells Mom that she'll take care of her because she's the youngest. And she looooves Mom." Cilla drew the word out as she rolled her eyes. "Little suck-up."

"How old is Abby?" Cat asked.

"She's six. Gonna be in first grade."

"And how old is your brother?" Rebecca asked.

"Justin? He's seventeen." Cilla nodded. "Yeah, there's eleven years there. Mom said that Dad saw her hips and married her fast so she could start tossing out babies for him."

Polly and Cat both laughed out loud.

"She said that every time he came home, he knocked her up and just because he's home for good now, he'd better not think more kids are happening. She's done. He even knocked her up before he went into boot camp." Cilla laughed and stepped back enough to make sure her audience could all see her. "Knocked up. Isn't that the weirdest phrase for getting pregnant? I mean, how does knocking ..." she lifted her closed fist and rapped on an imaginary door, "... mean, you know, the act of getting someone pregnant?" She turned to Polly. "Mom says I can't use the F-word. It's just a word. It's kind of a cool word and it has so many great uses. Think of the fantastic consonant sounds in that word. F and K. Those are strong consonants, so if you have to spit out an invective, it takes on so much power and gives you command over it. When a pretty girl with a southern drawl snarls up her lips and spits it out, there ain't no one that won't cower at her feet." Cilla gave them a knowing grin. "And then as a descriptive. Is there anyone that doesn't know what it means when you say that? Such a great word. I could go on and on."

She glanced to each face and smiled. "I did it, didn't I?"

"What?" Rebecca asked.

"Went too far. I said too much. Just opened my mouth and started talking. Nobody ever knows how to shut me up. Don't even try," she said as she shook her head. "I'll ignore you. When I realize that I've been going on and on, I'll finally stop and admit it. So … your turn."

"I don't know what to say," Rebecca said.

"What is your favorite thing to do?"

Rebecca's eyes lit with joy. "I'm an artist."

"No way," Cilla said. "You're a creative, too?" She looked at Polly. "That's what they call us, you know."

"Okay," Polly replied with a laugh.

"What do you art?" Cilla asked. "Do you paint, sculpt, draw, what?"

"I can show you. Do you have time?" Rebecca asked, already heading for the back steps.

Cilla looked at Polly. "What time is the transfer?"

"Ten minutes," Polly said, checking the clock on the wall of the kitchen. "We probably don't want to be late. I'd hate to imagine the consequences."

"Yeah. She might keep yours and make you keep me." Cilla ran to catch up to Rebecca. "Do you get lost in this big house?" she asked, their voices fading away as they headed up the steps.

Cat dropped into one of the seats at the island. "What just happened?"

"A force of nature. That girl is the first person I've ever met who might just give Rebecca a run for her money."

"Cilla would probably question that idiom, too," Cat said.

Polly peered at her, then blinked. "Run for the money? You're probably right."

"Did you meet her mother?"

"I've met everyone but her dad. They seem like a nice family. Five kids, though. I can't believe that house is big enough to hold them."

The Dexters had four children. Polly had never been upstairs, but from what she could see of the windows, there were only four bedrooms up there. She'd been on the main floor many times. It was a nice-size home and there was an extra room, she supposed. Chris had it set up as a play room for the kids. Long ago, it would have been used as a parlor or sitting room. Polly had never been down to the basement, so she didn't know if it was finished or not.

"Can you imagine raising five kids with your husband gone all the time?" Cat asked.

Polly hitched in a breath. "Uh, no. Single parents are amazing. Sylvie blows me away. It never occurred to her that she was anything other than their mom. It wasn't about being a single mom, it was about raising her boys to be their best selves. If she had to do it alone, that was just the way it was. I don't think I could do that. And Elva? How scary that had to have been. She barely knew her brother, her husband didn't care about their kids, and she had no idea what to do next. But she did something."

"And now look at her," Cat replied.

"Yeah. I guess that Andrea Waters did what she had to do. There wasn't any other option, so she just did it."

They heard voices in the foyer, and soon, Rebecca and Cilla walked into the kitchen.

"This house is incredible," Cilla said. "When I get tired of my brothers and sisters, can I come over here?"

Polly looked at Rebecca who was smiling warmly at Cilla. That was enough of a signal. "Any time, Cilla. Any time."

"She totally did the *Gone with the Wind* walk down the staircase in the foyer," Rebecca said.

"That room is just begging for plays and dramatic presentations," Cilla said, waving grandly toward the foyer. "The upstairs landing? So awesome. Tell me you use it for something other than car racing."

The tracks had gone up not long after Hayden and Cat's wedding at the end of May. When the days were much too hot to play outside, and the kids wanted to do something other than play in the basement and tunnel, they spent time in the big foyer. Between indoor soccer and the racetrack all over the place, there was plenty to keep them busy.

"You should have seen Cat's wedding," Rebecca said. "It was beautiful. Her father escorted her down the steps and she was wearing a beautiful white gown. Like an angel." Rebecca's voice grew dreamy. "I want my wedding in there someday." She huffed. "If I ever find someone worthwhile to marry."

"You can have Justin," Cilla said. She pointed to the clock as Rebecca looked at her in shock. "Is it time for the transfer?"

Polly laughed. "I'll escort you."

"What transfer?" Rebecca asked.

"My mother's a little weird. Come watch," Cilla said. She headed for the porch and after she opened the door and got to the bottom of the steps, she turned to Polly. "Stay close behind me. If you want to put your hand at my back like you have a gun, that wouldn't be a bad idea. Make sure Mom knows you mean business." She put her hands up in the air and took a step forward. When Polly hesitated, she said, "Come on. You know you want to."

Polly laughed and put her index finger against the small of Cilla's back. "Okay, but don't make any sudden moves. You don't want to lose your life today. Let's take this nice and easy."

Cat and Rebecca laughed as they followed behind them. When Cilla passed the hedges and arrived at the sidewalk, she sighed and dropped her arms. "She's late. What a way to louse up my dramatic entrance. I hate it when she does this to me."

CHAPTER THREE

As Polly sat on the sofa looking out into the back yard, she wondered what today would bring. The Waters' hadn't stayed late at their new home. They'd gone back out to Louis and Deb's home for the night and would be back today to start unpacking. She hadn't met Andrea's husband, Kirk, and Henry had gotten home after the family left, so they'd probably all meet today. Since it was Saturday, she hoped Henry would be around.

He was working in the office this morning. It was hers during the week, but evenings and weekends he took over. Heath and Hayden were on their way out to the bed and breakfast. Once classes started, the boys wouldn't have much extra time to work.

Shelly was now working at the bakery with Sylvie. They'd talked about her working as a barista in the coffee shop, but Shelly wasn't ready to talk to people who might pepper her with questions about her experiences. Camille agreed. There were plenty of busybodies who would have no hesitation asking the poor girl to serve up intimate details along with a cup of coffee. People seemed to have no sense these days and thought that everybody else's business belonged to the whole world.

Marta was the perfect person to work with Shelly. She had an innate sense of how to talk with the girl, giving her support when she needed it and yet, avoided conversations that made Shelly uncomfortable. She also insisted that Shelly work hard to finish her high school equivalency. While Rebecca had offered to assist, it was Marta who spent time with Shelly, both at the coffee shop and at the library. Sylvie told Polly that the two were perfect together. Shelly had been making some noise about helping with set design and props at the community theater this fall. Marta told her that if she passed the first of her tests by the time auditions happened, she'd let her participate.

It never ceased to amaze Polly that there were so many wonderful people in the world. Shelly was absolutely in love with Marta and the world that was opening up to her because of this friendship. She couldn't wait to get up in the morning to go to work, and when she got home she had new things to talk about at dinner.

Cat came down the stairs with a load of laundry. "The boys are cleaning their rooms. Before we make cookies this morning, they're sweeping the floors and dusting windows and door frames."

"Rebecca's gonna love that," Polly said. She followed Cat into the kitchen and stopped at the coffee maker for another cup.

"Caleb and Noah will be cleaning the stairs in the foyer. I told them if there was any grumbling, we'd be dusting the library today, too."

Polly laughed out loud. "You're a girl after my own heart."

"They'll dust it on Monday anyway," Cat said. "Having four helpers for an hour every day makes cleaning this place much easier."

"That's what I always thought. I bought breakfast pizzas yesterday. How does that sound?"

Cat came back through the door. "Wonderful. I didn't know what we were going to eat this morning."

Having Cat shoulder some of the responsibility for caring for the four little boys, as well as keeping the Bell House clean had been a wonderful decision. By the time she was finished with college, the boys would be older and wouldn't require so much hands-on attention. She and Hayden had turned the rooms over the kitchen into a cozy apartment.

Sometimes Polly worried that the new couple didn't have enough privacy or the opportunity to get their feet wet out in the real world with an apartment of their own. However, she couldn't help but be thankful for their help around this place.

Henry walked into the kitchen and gave Cat a distracted nod as he headed for the coffee pot.

"What's up?" Polly asked.

He looked at her in confusion. "Nothing. Why?"

"You aren't all here."

Henry shook his head. "Too many numbers floating around. What are we doing about breakfast?"

Polly touched his hand and gave him a smile. "Eleven. Seven. Two."

"What?" Henry frowned.

"Just giving you some more random numbers. Sorry. I'm going to put a few breakfast pizzas in the oven. Does that sound good?"

"One of these days you need to make your homemade breakfast pizza again," he said with a smile. "You haven't done that in years."

She rolled her eyes. "I've gotten all about the easy, haven't I. Maybe next weekend." Hopefully he'd forget by then.

Cat had unwrapped two pizzas and put them into the oven, then set the timer. "The boys are cleaning upstairs. They'll think this is a nice reward for their hard work."

"You're doing a great job with them this summer," Henry said. He sat down on a stool at the island. "We appreciate it." He chuckled and tipped his mug at Polly. "We also appreciate the cleaning you do around here. No more desperate last-minute scrubbing before company shows up."

"Hey!" Polly said. Then she laughed. "Okay. He's not wrong. I can get more done in one hour of desperation than I'll do all week long." She shook her head. "Though with Cat keeping everyone motivated, I've done more cleaning this summer than ever before."

"Did she ever tell you about the apartment?" Henry asked.

Cat looked confused and Polly scowled at him.

"I came home early from visiting my parents in Arizona to surprise her …"

Polly threw a towel across the island. He didn't even flinch as it sailed past him and hit the floor.

"It would have been cleaner if you'd come home when I expected you."

"Admit it. You were a slob."

She simpered at Cat. "I was a slob. When kids moved in, I had to get my act together. Poor Rebecca started cleaning toilets because I knew I couldn't keep up by myself. I was confident that her snarky mouth would get her in trouble often enough to maintain some semblance of cleanliness in those bathrooms."

The sounds of four boys running down the back steps stopped their conversation.

"They're back!" Elijah yelled as the four ran past them to the side door.

Polly looked at Cat. "How do they even know that?"

"Because I opened my door to go to the bathroom. They all wanted to see the cats. The next thing I knew, they were all excited about the neighbors being back and I chased them out of my room. Little buggers."

All three adults turned to see a bleary-eyed Rebecca standing there with her cat, Wonder, in her arms.

"Good morning," Polly said. "Aren't you the happy one today."

"It's seven o'clock on a Saturday morning. Why am I even down here?" Rebecca asked.

"To get a little love and attention?" Henry asked. He walked over and gave her a hug.

The girl stood as stiff as a board.

"What?" he asked.

"I prefer sleep to love and attention. I was up late last night."

"Doing what?"

"I couldn't turn my brain off, so I read a book." She sniffed. "I read the whole book. All the way through. Then I still couldn't sleep, so I tried to do some sketches. Beryl and I are meeting at the coffee shop today. She wants me to work on faces. There are tons of faces up there. But I thought that if I could practice, maybe that would put me to sleep. It didn't."

"What time did you finally fall asleep?" Polly asked.

"It was, like, two-thirty."

"I'm sorry," Cat said.

Rebecca frowned. "What did you do?"

"I asked the boys to clean up there this morning. If I'd known you were up so late, I would have brought them downstairs."

Rebecca huffed a laugh. "Like that would have mattered. They're all over the house in the morning. Sometimes I wish I had their energy. Oh, to be young again. Is it okay if I go back to bed? I don't have to meet Beryl until eleven. Will you wake me up at ten thirty if you don't hear me?"

"I'll check on you," Cat said, after she saw Polly nod.

"Thank you. I don't need breakfast. Don't save anything for me." Rebecca turned back and headed upstairs.

Polly chuckled. "She thought we'd save something for her? She never eats breakfast with us on Saturday."

"I feel bad about the boys bothering her," Cat said. "We could have worked in another part of the house."

"Don't worry," Polly said. "We all live here and she understands that."

"What do you suppose kept her up so late?" Henry asked. "I know she's a night owl, but she's not usually that bad."

"I don't know," Polly said. "It could be a million things. Band camp starts next week, she's excited about Cilla moving in next door, she's still upset about Andrew. Who knows? I'll talk to her later."

~~~

When Polly and Rebecca left to go to the coffee shop, Cat was busy making cookies with the four boys. They'd run over to say hello to the new kids across the street, but Cat had chased them down, reminding them that they had chores to finish if they wanted to make cookies and head to the nursing home. It had been the right thing to do anyway. Chaos reigned at the Waters' house, with everyone including the grandparents moving things around. Polly's boys didn't need to be part of that.

"What do you think about the new neighbors?" Rebecca asked Polly.

"Ummm, they're fine?" Polly gave Rebecca a curious glance. "Why do you ask?"

"I was just thinking about that big family moving into that house. We haven't even seen the dad yet."

Polly chuckled. "Other than a few minutes yesterday, we haven't seen Andrea either. They have to be pretty busy trying to set things up."

"Do you think you'll be friends with her?"

"Probably?" Polly looked at Rebecca again. "What are you trying to ask me here?"

Rebecca waved her hand. "Nothing. I'm just making conversation. How long do you think I should wait before I introduce Cilla to Kayla and everybody else? She's kind of different. Do you think my friends will like her?"

"Do you like her?"

Polly pulled into a parking spot down the street from Sweet Beans and turned to look at Rebecca. The girl's eyes were laughing as a slow grin came to her lips.

"I think she's awesome. If she's that pushy with everyone, she's kind of ..." Rebecca hesitated, looking for the right word. She turned to Polly. "People are either going to like her or hate her."

"Polarizing?"

"Yeah. That's it." Rebecca slumped. "I miss Andrew. He always had the right words."

Polly put her hand on Rebecca's knee. "I'm sorry."

"It's fine that he doesn't want to be my boyfriend." Rebecca turned to Polly, trying to reassure her. "I mean it. Sometimes I wondered if we were meant to be together that way. But he's been my best friend for years and it's weird that he just went away. It's like part of me went with him. I keep trying to make it be okay. I love my friends and you guys and I love all the things that I do, but then I think about telling him something silly just to get his reaction and I can't call because it's gotten so weird." She turned her body to Polly and leaned against the door. "Before school let out, we talked about doing this illustrated story. Last night I found the sketches. I love doing those creative things with him. Not only is part of me gone, but part of the creative me went away when he did, too. I just want my friend back."

"Have you told him that?"

Rebecca slowly shook her head as she looked at her lap. "No. It sounds so pathetic. If he wants to date other girls, I shouldn't get in his way. I heard Henry telling you that now is the time we're supposed to be trying out new relationships and all that. High school is about learning new things and finding out how we want to live our lives. It isn't supposed to be the beginning of a lifetime commitment." She looked up. "I totally get that. It makes total sense. But this is awful."

Polly took in a deep breath. "A couple of things to think about. First, talk to him."

"I know," Rebecca said, pursing her lips. "Second?"

"It might not work out that you two are friends."

"But why?"

"Think about how close you've been."

"That's my whole problem. I have been."

"Imagine how you'd feel if you had a new boyfriend whose best friend was a girl and they were still as close as they were when they were going together." Polly chuckled. "That was a horrible sentence, but think about it. Everyone in town and in high school knows that you and Andrew were inseparable. There isn't a girl alive who will believe that you want nothing more than to be his friend."

"That's her problem, not mine."

"What about a boy that you start dating? Is it fair to expect him to believe that you and Andrew will never be more than friends?"

"If that's what we are, there won't be anything more."

"Honey, that isn't reality. Even when you were in fourth grade, Andrew thought of you as his girlfriend. You were never just friends."

Rebecca rolled her eyes and leaned her head against the door frame. "So you're saying I've lost my best friend and there's nothing I can do about it."

"What I'm going to say next is going to make you angry, but that's just the way it's going to be."

"Go ahead."

"The things you experience while you're in high school are temporary. I know it feels like your world has fallen apart, but this next year you will meet new friends and you'll experience new things with your old friends. You're going to date boys and you'll break up with them. Some friends might move out of town, while interesting and wonderful people will come into your life. Next summer at this time, the conversation we're having right now won't even be part of your memory. You and Andrew will have settled into a relationship that is comfortable for you, but he might not be the person you count on." Polly held her hand up when Rebecca took a breath to speak. "I'm not saying that the two of you couldn't end up back together. Who knows what the future holds? Right now, though, you need to count on the fact that today looks nothing like the future. You'll get over this ..."

"Are you sure?" Rebecca's small voice interrupted her.

Polly took Rebecca's hand in hers. "I am certain. I'm so certain that I'll make you a deal. If, by Thanksgiving, you still feel that you are lost without Andrew in your everyday life, I will ..." She bit her lip as she thought.

"Pay for another trip with Beryl?"

"No, because we help with that anyway. I want this to be really out there. How about I will clean your room for a month?"

Rebecca laughed. "You're not worried, are you?"

Polly shook her head as she laughed. "Nope."

Rebecca took out her phone and typed furiously.

"What are you doing?"

"I just put a reminder in my calendar for Thanksgiving Day. I don't want to think about it until then, but I want to remember what you said. Because if I'm still this sad in November, I'm going to need you to clean my room for a month."

"That's my girl. I know this is hard and I wish I could snap my fingers and make it better."

"I wish my feelings would just quit being so touchy."

"You may not want to hear it, but you're better now than you were."

There had been a few bleak days after the breakup. Polly had held Rebecca while she sobbed and then held her again when she fell apart the next time. One evening, the little boys brought flowers in from outside, which had made Rebecca cry even more.

"Do you think so?"

"I know so. Do you cry yourself to sleep now?"

Rebecca shook her head. "No, but sometimes I go back and forth between mad and sad so fast I get a headache."

"There are a lot of emotions to manage while you work your way through this."

"At least he isn't dead."

Polly snapped her head up to look at Rebecca.

"I mean. At least he's here for me to be mad at. I was mad at Mom when she died and it wasn't fair because she wasn't around." Rebecca's eyes filled with tears.

"Oh, honey." Polly lifted herself out of her seat and reached across the console as Rebecca fell into her arms. They held on to each other as Rebecca shook with sobs.

"I'm sorry," Rebecca blubbered. "I don't know why I went there." She pulled back from Polly and opened the glove compartment to search for a tissue. "It's like I was looking for a reason to cry."

"That's okay," Polly said. She kept her hand on Rebecca's knee. "It's been a while since we've done this."

Rebecca chuckled and wiped her cheeks before blowing her nose. "Crying in the truck? Yeah. I didn't think I'd ever need to do that again. I'm just a hot mess."

"You're my hot mess and I love you."

"I'd better get inside before Beryl lights up our phones with panicked texts," Rebecca said. "How bad do I look?"

"You'll be fine."

"That wasn't an answer." Rebecca grinned at her. "Oh well, it isn't like I have a boy that I'm trying to impress. Am I right?" She gave her head a shake and opened the Suburban's door, then jumped out. She opened the back door and picked up her carry case. "Are you coming in?"

Polly had her hand on her door and gave Rebecca a look. "You're kidding, right? You think I'd miss an opportunity to visit my favorite place on earth?"

"Just checking."

They walked past the thrift shop and the quilt shop, both of which seemed to be busy this morning. The downtown area continued to grow as small businesses opened in empty spaces. There were hints of a barbecue restaurant opening next to the grocery store. Henry was waiting with bated breath for that one.

She opened the door to Sweet Beans and smiled at the familiar scents of coffee and baked goods.

"You always do that," Rebecca said.

"Do what?"

"Open the door and sniff. We all watch and wait, you know."

"Come on."

"I'm not kidding. It's a thing. Everyone knows you do it."

"About time the two of you showed up." Beryl frowned at Rebecca, then at Polly. "What did you do to her? Did you make her cry? I'll beat you up for that. She's my favorite girl." The older woman put her arm protectively around Rebecca's shoulder.

"Yeah. She's got my back," Rebecca said. "You have to be good to me."

"Whatever. You two are spending too much time together. I need coffee to handle both of you at once." Polly brushed her thumb across Rebecca's cheek. "You be good. Is Kayla coming over later?"

Rebecca nodded. "She's meeting me here. We'll walk home. I can't wait to introduce her to Cilla."

"Who's Cilla?" Beryl asked as the two headed for a table she'd claimed.

The woman was so good for Rebecca. Polly was incredibly grateful for the people who showed up in the lives of her kids. She wandered up to the front counter. Gayla Livingston stepped forward.

"Hi, Ms. Giller. What can I make for you?"

"A large cold brew," Polly said. "Is Shelly in the back?"

The girl's eyes went wide. "Yeah. Sylvie's there too. She had to come in this morning. Marta had an accident last night and can't work."

Polly frowned. "An accident? Is she hurt?"

Gayla shrugged. "I don't know. We've been busy, so I haven't had time to talk to them except for orders."

"I'll go back and check." Polly dropped a few bills in the tip jar, took her coffee, and headed for the kitchen. Marta, Shelly, and another young woman, Rita Smithson, usually handled Saturdays without Sylvie these days. Rita had been a godsend. She and her husband moved into Bellingwood in early June and she'd applied for the job. She had some training — mostly in a small delicatessen in Pennsylvania, but she learned quickly and last month, Sylvie started taking more days away from the bakery. Granted, she usually had a wedding cake or two to set up, but Rita and Shelly were learning that process as well. Soon Sylvie would feel as if she could take entire weekends off and her world wouldn't fall apart around her.

Polly stood in the doorway and waited as the three women bustled around. Shelly was the first to see her there.

"Polly, did you hear about Marta?"

"Yeah. What happened?"

CHAPTER FOUR

Nodding her permission, Sylvie gave a quick smile to Shelly who walked out into the hallway with Polly.

"She fell down her back outside steps. That's what she told Sylvie. She's scraped up and she messed up her left wrist. How is she supposed to take care of her dad if she's hurt like that?"

Polly frowned. She'd forgotten that Marta cared for her father who had Alzheimer's. "Surely some of her helpers are there."

"But you know her. She'll try to do everything herself." Shelly shrugged. "Just like she'll probably try to come back to work next week. I wish I could help. What can I do?"

"I'm not sure. I'll give her a call."

Shelly moved Polly further from the doorway. "Would it be weird if I offered to spend a couple of nights with her?"

"I don't think that's weird at all. Are you sure?"

"Yeah. It's not like I have anything else to do and Marta could help me study in the evenings. It would only be for two or three nights, don't you think? Maybe that would be good for me. See if I can sleep in a new place and not freak out. If I can't do it, then I can't do it, but I feel safe with Marta."

"I know you do," Polly said with a smile, putting her hand on Shelly's arm. "You've been doing well with her. I think the world of her, too. She's a wonderful woman."

"You wouldn't care if I offered?"

"That would be terrific. I can pick you up when you're finished here today and then after you pack a bag, I'll take you to her house."

Shelly glanced at Sylvie, took her phone out, then glanced at Sylvie again. "Can you wait a minute? Let me ask Mrs. Donovan if I can make a call. We're busy today."

"Go ahead," Polly said with a smile. She loved that Shelly was so respectful of her job. She'd come far this summer. Polly chalked a lot of that up to Grey's work with her, but Shelly was resilient. There was also the fact that she lived with a family full of people who regularly faced their own demons. Elijah, as light-hearted as he was, had a tender spot for people in pain. But he didn't let them stay in their pain. He was always doing or saying something silly immediately following a touching moment. Never contrived or set up, it was just his perfect, honest innocence. She worried that he'd lose that someday but so far, he was holding on.

Shelly came back out into the hallway with a smile. "Mrs. Donovan says it's a good idea, too. I'm going to call Marta. She has to let me help her." She wandered toward the back door and Polly leaned against the wall of the hallway.

Sylvie stepped into the doorway. "Everything okay?"

"Yeah. I just didn't want to bother you. Both Shelly and Gayla told me how busy you are."

"It's just one of those days," Sylvie said. "We'll get through it. I'm sorry for Marta. She was beside herself when she called me last night. That poor woman never wants to let anyone down."

"Did she say what happened?"

Sylvie shook her head. "Just that she fell. I didn't think to ask why. She was waiting for one of her nurses to come stay at the house and for another friend who would take her down to Boone. I offered to drive her, but she wanted me to go to sleep so I could get up this morning."

"She's just awesome," Polly said.

Shelly came back toward them, a huge smile on her face. "She said yes, that she'd like the help, and I'm going to learn how to sew."

"Sew?"

"She has these costumes to finish, and she can't do it with her arm in a sling. It's not hard. Just gotta sew a straight line."

"Have you ever sewn anything before?" Sylvie asked.

"No." Shelly gave a slow shrug. "But I think I can do it. I won't be as good as you, Polly, but it should be okay, right?"

"Absolutely," Polly said. "If you want to sew things at home, you just have to let me know. I'd love to show you how to use my machine. If I can learn it, anyone can."

"Marta is a great seamstress," Sylvie said. "She'll be a good teacher. I wish I knew how to sew."

"We should take classes next door," Polly said. "I'm always ready to take another class with those women. I learn so much."

Sylvie huffed. "Whatever. You're great. Once you started sewing, it was like you always knew how. I've seen your curtains and those cute stuffed animals you made for the boys."

"She made me some cool pillowcases too," Shelly said.

"Yeah, yeah, yeah." Polly waved at the bakery. "Poor Rita is in there working her butt off while you two yak it up with me. Go back to work. I'll be here when you're finished, Shelly."

Shelly hugged Polly. "Thank you. I'm excited." She danced her way back in and pulled a tall rack over to where Rita was bagging up loaves of bread.

"She's going to be okay," Sylvie said. "It's nice to see her come into herself."

"I appreciate your patience with her."

"She wants to be a good worker and to please me. Mostly it's been about giving her confidence. She won't go out into the main shop yet. Rita and Marta do all the running, but we all understand that she doesn't want to encounter anyone she might know. I figure the more people she becomes acquainted with on a one-to-one basis, the easier it will be for her."

Polly shuddered. "Can you imagine worrying about whether or not you might meet someone who'd been a client?"

Sylvie's eyes shot up. "I hadn't even thought of that. Oh, blech. How awful." She looked in at Shelly, who was laughing with Rita as they stacked bread loaves onto trays. "That poor thing."

"That's why I'm so thankful she's working out well here. She has a job, makes some money, and doesn't have to see a bunch of people every day."

"She's protected back here. Just us and delivery guys. She met them slowly and though she doesn't engage with them, at least she doesn't hide any longer."

"I'm thankful that you gave her a chance." Polly reached out to hug her friend. "I'll let you go. Tell Shelly I'll pick her up at the back door."

Polly walked back through the coffee shop, waved at Beryl and Rebecca, who were hovered over Rebecca's sketch pad as they discussed something. She got a barely perceptible nod from her daughter as she went past them on the way out to her Suburban.

When she turned onto Beech Street, Polly peered ahead, trying to see what the activity was in front of her house. Since the street was blocked with cars and people, most of whom she recognized, Polly came a stop in the middle of the street and got out.

Henry was the first to see her and waved. "Come here, Polly. You have to see this."

She lifted her eyebrows. He was about to talk to her about that old car. She could tell that right off. The four little boys were all standing around the front of the red car, looking inside the engine compartment. She recognized Louis Waters and his grandson Justin, who was standing beside someone who was bent over inside. She realized that had to be his father, Kirk. One leg on his jeans had been hemmed off at the knee, nothing was there below it. A wheelchair sat off to the side.

"What am I looking at?" Polly asked.

Four male faces turned to her in surprise. One of them was her husband. He shouldn't be surprised. He was aware of how little she knew about cars. Her brain moved as fast as it could. The car was from the seventies. She'd seen enough of them in magazines he had lying around the house. It had a long front end and looked kind of flashy. "Mustang?" she asked.

Henry chuckled. "I love her anyway," he said. "Kirk, meet my wife, Polly. Polly, this is Kirk Waters and this, my dear, is a Camaro Z28."

Kirk steadied himself on the car and hopped toward her, then grabbed his son's arm while putting his other hand out. "Nice to meet you, Ms. Giller. Right? Not Mrs. Sturtz?"

"I can be Mrs. Sturtz," she said with a smile. "Most people just call me Polly. You should do that. This is your car?"

He grinned at his son. "It's Justin's now. We still have some work to do on it. It's been sittin' in Dad's garage for years. I started rebuilding it when I was in high school, but didn't get a chance to finish it. Justin's going to need some wheels. He thinks these will be just fine."

"I called Nate," Henry said. "He's chomping at the bit to put this up on the rack in his workshop."

"So now you're going to get to work out there?" Polly asked. "Finally?"

He smiled at her. "You wouldn't care if we went over this afternoon?"

"Not at all."

"Can we go?" Elijah asked.

Polly glanced at Henry. He flinched, only enough so she could see it.

"Not this afternoon," Polly replied. "Why don't you invite Nathan, Lara, and Abby over to play. Maybe you should see if Rose would like to come, too."

"Aww, I want to go," he said with a whine.

"Not today," Henry said, putting his hand on Elijah's shoulder. "No whining."

Elijah opened his mouth to say something else, took one look at Henry and closed his mouth in a hurry. Just like that, he came up with another idea. "You guys haven't seen the tunnel yet. Can I show them the tunnel?"

This time Polly looked at Kirk. "It's fine with me, unless your kids have responsibilities inside."

He gave a short laugh. "Mom and Andrea would probably be thrilled to have them out of the house. They'll get more work done. But that's a lot of kids. Are you sure?"

"It isn't anything new for us. There are plenty of things to keep them busy and they can't hurt anything. We have a volleyball net out back and soccer goals. They'll stay busy. I'm glad to feed them lunch if you boys want to take off now."

Kirk hopped over to his wheelchair and landed in it with a whoomph. "I've had my prosthesis on so much the last few days, my stump was hurting."

His father had watched the entire thing and quietly took a breath. She watched him push aside the pain he felt for his son. "You want to ride with me out to the Mikkels place? Henry can go out in the Camaro with Justin."

"Maybe Henry should drive it." Kirk gave his son a wicked grin. "It might be too much of a car for my city boy."

"Dad!" Justin protested.

"I'll take my truck," Henry said. "But one of these days when it's purring like a kitten, I'd like to borrow it to take my girl for a quick drive." He winked at Polly. "This one has a little more spunk in it than my T-bird."

"You still have that?" Kirk asked.

Henry nodded. "I couldn't give it up. It's the car that impressed Polly enough to marry me."

"What?" she asked. "It was not."

"Oh, come on," he said. "You know you love it. And it makes a good story. Let me have this one."

"You guys and your cars. I think you find more romance in them than you do in us."

Andrea Waters came out of the front door, holding empty boxes in both hands. "Get that car out of the street, y'all," she yelled at them. "We are not doing a road rally here today."

"Do you need us?" Kirk asked.

She frowned at him. "And what exactly do you mean by that?"

Polly could have sworn she saw the man gulp, but he forged ahead. "Thought we'd take the car over to this garage that one of Henry's buddies has. Put it up on the rack. See what's going on underneath. Kinda make a plan. Polly said the young'uns can go play at her house so they're out of your way."

"You thought that would be a good idea? Leave the unpackin' to me and your mama?"

"And Cilla?" he asked.

Polly heard a door open and close and saw Mona Bright and her daughter, Rose, come out on their front stoop.

"Mona," she called. "Have you met the Waters' yet?"

"Whew," Kirk said under his breath. "Saved by the neighbors."

Andrea dropped the boxes onto the ground and walked across the yard toward Polly. "These men ..." She pointed at each one of them. "They ain't so dumb. That one of mine has figured out how to get out of unpacking boxes for years now. Don't know why I thought this move would be any different." She waggled her finger at Louis. "I thought you'd be more help."

"Who, me?" he asked with a laugh. "Deb will tell you I'm lousy help."

"Yes, she probably will." Andrea strode over to Polly and hooked her arm. "Introduce me to my neighbor, will you?"

Polly blinked. She couldn't help herself and laughed out loud. "Andrea, this is Mona Bright and her daughter, Rose. Rose, aren't you going to be in third grade this year?"

The little girl nodded and Polly turned back toward the cluster of people around the car. "Elijah, would you come here a minute?"

He ran over to see what she wanted. "Honey, would you introduce Rose to your new friends?"

"Sure!" Elijah reached out and took Rose's hand. "Come on. This is going to be the best place to live ever."

Andrea had released Polly and walked up the stoop to put her hand out. "It's nice to meet you, Mrs. Bright. My kids are a little loud, but they're polite and respectful most of the time."

"Rose is pretty quiet," Mona said. "But she's getting better with

Polly's kids around. She'd gotten to know the Dexter kids. I think she misses Julia. I was glad to see you had a couple of little girls."

"Lara will be in fourth grade and Abby in first. They'll have a lot of years to spend together." Andrea turned back to the street. "They're truly going to leave me this afternoon, aren't they? Damned boys. Here I thought I'd at least get a week's worth of work out of them before they took off on me. Can't believe Henry has a buddy with a garage. That would just figure, wouldn't it? That car has been sitting in storage for nearly twenty years and its first day out, it attracts a crowd."

Mona gave Polly a wide-eyed stare.

"I have some time this afternoon," Polly said. "Cat is taking the boys down to the nursing home at some point. I know the residents would love to get to know your three, too."

Andrea gave her a questioning look. "The nursing home?"

Polly pointed. "It's right down there. My boys love those people and they're getting used to having kids around. They've always got treats and games around for them. I'll ask Cat, but I don't think she'd mind adding a few more to the herd."

"Maybe Nathan. The girls need to work in their room. Justin and Louis put up their loft beds this morning." She gave Polly a gentle push. "Don't think I don't want the girls to hang out with your boys, it's just that they got a bit snitty with their grandma last night and now they must make their room spic and span sooner rather than later. Poor Natty-boy has a tiny little storage closet for a room. They're going to turn it into a castle tower or something insane, but for now, he's stuck sleeping on the couch."

"Natty-boy?"

Andrea shook her head. "Cilla named him. He'll answer to Nathan, but he's decided that Nate isn't a moniker he'd like."

"One of my horses is named Nat."

"No kidding," Andrea said with a grin. "Hey, Nat. There's a horse in town named after you."

"Noah told me!" he yelled back at her. "Can I go see him?"

"Are these the horses down by the old school?" Andrea asked. "Deb told me about your rescues."

Polly nodded. "Four big Percherons and a couple of donkeys."

"Nat seems like an odd name for a horse."

"Nat and Nan, Demi and …"

Before Polly could finish, Andrea pushed at her again. "Daisy? Is that true? From the Alcott books?"

"Yeah," Polly said. "I didn't name them, but yeah."

"That's why Cilla called him Nat. She loved those books. Ah, hell," Andrea slapped her hand across her mouth. "Sorry. Anyway, I think she still does." She turned back to Mona Bright, still standing in silence. "We should have a block party one of these nights so we can get to know everyone. Once I find my ice cream freezer, we'll make ice cream. I make a mean batch of brownies, too. I'll bet we've got a few grills up and down these streets. Haul everyone out of their houses, put brats and burgers on the grills and make it a party." She laughed. "My kids aren't allowed in the house much. I work from home, so they find plenty to keep them busy. I won't have kids stuck to the television or those electronic babysitters." She glanced at Mona again, then at Polly. "I'm opinionated and loud. I apologize. I don't even know you and am making annoying comments. Trust me, you'll find plenty wrong with my parenting. I don't have any right to declare that my ways are the best ways for anybody else. They're just my ways and my poor benighted children have to put up with them."

She waved at Mona. "If you ever need anything, knock on my door. Someone's always there. But then, I'm sure you're already great friends with Polly. You don't need me butting into your business. I should probably release the hordes to go do their thing. Notice those boys are waiting for me to tell them it's okay? Yeah. That will last only so long. Kirk's torn between feeling guilty for not helping and desperately wanting to play with his toy."

Polly chuckled. This woman was a character.

"Mrs. Bright?" Andrea stopped and turned back. "Your little girl can help mine put their room together while the boys take off and visit the old folks. Unless you'd rather she come home."

Mona didn't know what to say to that. The Brights weren't terribly social, no matter how hard Polly tried to get them to come over. Rose had tailed along every so often with the Dexter kids, but they'd shut themselves away again after the Dexters left town.

"Maybe another time," Mona said.

"That's fine," Andrea replied. "Just know that she's welcome in our house any time."

"Thank you."

"What are your plans for lunch, boys?" Andrea asked, striding up to her son. She took his arm and leaned in.

"We were just talking about that," Henry replied. "You shouldn't have to cook for us."

"I wasn't planning to. I kinda thought maybe y'all would bring back food for us to eat. We're the ones doing all the work. Unpacking the boxes, raising your kids. You know … the tough stuff."

Polly snorted with laughter.

"Well, we can get something for you."

"He's so easy," Andrea said to Polly.

"He doesn't know you yet," Kirk said. He spun his chair. "We're going to the diner. The boys are going to have sandwiches at Polly's house before they go to the nursing home. You can take care of yourself and the rest of your posse."

"Wanna be in my posse, Polly?" Andrea asked.

"Sure. I probably have easier access to food than you do, though."

"Bet me. I programmed the number for that pizza place last night. They deliver, right?"

"Pizzazz? Absolutely."

"And you know what kind of pizza is the best?"

"I do."

"We're covered, then. You boys go do whatever it is that you think is right. We'll be working and eating pizza. Taking care of the home front while you play." Andrea winked at Polly. "You had no idea what was moving in across the street from you, did you?"

"Nope. I could never have guessed."

CHAPTER FIVE

Thankful when the last platter of grilled chicken was set onto her big dining room table, Polly dropped into a seat. Looking around, she was surprised that there was nobody extra seated with them. The only person missing was Shelly, who was spending the next few days helping out at Marta's house.

Shelly was so excited at this opportunity, she'd practically vibrated herself out of the Suburban when Polly dropped her off this afternoon. All summer long, as she studied and worked toward passing her high school equivalency tests, she talked about becoming a nurse. This dream was a big deal for the girl. She volunteered at the care center on her days off, willing to do anything that was needed. She had a lot of work ahead, but if nothing more than her passion and energy carried her through, she'd achieve her goal.

Cat put a piece of chicken on JaRon's plate and passed the platter to Polly, who breathed a deep sigh of contentment.

"What's that sound for?" Henry asked.

"It's good to have everyone here in the same place," Polly replied. "I miss Shelly, but I'm weary, and I'm glad to have my family all together in the same place at the same time."

"You're getting old," Rebecca said, putting a cheddar biscuit onto Caleb's plate before handing it to Heath.

"Probably. Today felt like a million people were everywhere doing everything. And every single one of you was off doing something I wasn't involved in, so ..." Polly smiled. "You know what this means, don't you?"

The four little boys looked at her curiously, Heath frowned, Hayden grinned, and Rebecca rolled her eyes.

"Yep. You have to tell me what you did today. I want to hear all about it. JaRon, we'll start with you. What fun thing happened to you today?"

He was working to cut off a piece of chicken and Cat reached over to help him. "Go ahead," she said. "Tell her about Mr. Cooper."

His eyes grew big. "I helped Mr. Cooper paint an airplane. I just did the big parts. He's making a model."

Caleb nodded. "I helped too."

"How big is the plane?" Henry asked.

He smiled at Polly as the boys described their day at the nursing home. Nat Waters had gone along. He'd been a little leery at first, according to Cat, but no one could be in Elijah's presence for long without relaxing and having fun.

Cat was such a gem. The work she'd done with these boys this summer was life-changing for them. She'd taken time to work with Caleb on his vocabulary skills and using full sentences to express himself. Some of his lazy speech patterns were beginning to disappear and she'd spent hours studying different ways to help him pronounce hard consonants. He wasn't there yet but since a speech therapist came to the school every week, Polly and Henry hoped his success would only continue.

As the conversation wound down, Cat put her hand on Hayden's arm. "I have an announcement."

"You're pregnant," Rebecca said with a gasp.

"Really?" Heath stared at the two of them. "When are you due?"

Cat glared at Rebecca. "I'm not pregnant. Don't you dare start that rumor. No. Not pregnant." She frowned around the table. "All of you get that out of your heads. No babies. Not right now. No, this is completely different. I'm changing my major. It's going to take some extra time, but that's okay. Hayden and I have talked about this and it's because of you four." She pointed at the four young boys. "This has been an extraordinary summer for me and I discovered a passion I didn't realize I had. As much as I love what I've learned, I want to teach at the elementary level rather than high school or college courses in journalism and linguistics. I'm talking to my advisor on Monday. There will be a lot of work as I transition, but I can't ignore this."

"I wish you could be my teacher," Caleb said. "I like you."

"I like you too," she replied. "You are part of the reason I want to do this. Who knows, maybe in a couple of years I can at least do my student teaching in Bellingwood."

"Congratulations, Cat," Polly said. "I believe you'll be a fantastic teacher. You're great with our kids."

"You're going to be Mrs. Harvey," Elijah said with a grin. "That will be weird because we know your first name."

Polly laughed. "I remember when I found out that my first-grade teacher had a first name. She was always Mrs. Samuels to me. It was sometime in the spring. I remember because I was wearing a little dress the day I heard another teacher call her Geneva. Suddenly she was a real person, not just my teacher. She had two names just like everyone else. That was a big moment for me."

"But you never called her anything but Mrs. Samuels, did you?" Noah asked.

"No," Polly replied. "That was unacceptable, and you boys aren't to ever call your teachers anything but what they tell you to call them, right?"

He nodded, then looked at Rebecca. "What did you do today?"

"I drew people's faces," she said, deadpan. Then she smiled at him. "It was kinda fun. Beryl ..." She looked at Polly. "I mean, Ms. Watson and I sat at the coffee shop drawing different people's faces today. It's interesting to look at how sharp or flat their cheekbones are and to think about how their ears are shaped. I gave away a bunch of things when they saw that I was drawing them. Then Kayla came over and we walked all the way back to the hotel. It was hot out." She looked at Polly. "Beryl is going to give me my bag later. She put it in her car since I was walking today."

Beryl had insisted that Rebecca call her by her first name. After all they had done together this year, that was the relationship they had, but Rebecca knew the boys still called her Ms. Watson. It was an interesting balance for the girl, but she tried.

"Sky was getting down and dirty in the basement," Rebecca said. "He wants to see about finishing it so there's more room. He said he was going to talk to you next week, Polly. Like maybe a man cave and a game room. Or a place where Kayla could have parties sometimes. Especially if they're going to live there for a while."

Polly glanced at Henry and he shrugged. "There's no reason that shouldn't be finished. It was used for storage for so many years, nobody ever thought about using it for anything else. No matter how hard we worked, it was never what you'd call clean."

"That's what Sky said. He was all over it this morning. When Kayla and I got there, he was measuring and planning. He said that if there's enough room, he'd even think about building another bedroom so Kayla didn't have to be upstairs with them. Wouldn't that be cool? Just like her own apartment. Except not really. Kinda like you and Hayden, Cat. Your own apartment, but no kitchen. Do you think you could put a bathroom in that basement, Henry?" Rebecca turned on him.

He nodded. "I know there's water down there. Pipes and drains are in the northwest corner." Henry looked at Polly. "Do you have your phone? Make a note for me to call Skylar on Monday or Tuesday. If he's planning on staying in that job, the least we could do is upgrade the living space for them. That kitchen is tiny. It was fine for Grey, but it's not big enough for a family."

"Really?" Rebecca asked.

Henry looked at her. "You keep this to yourself. Let me talk to Skylar. Don't be sticking your nose into it."

"I stuck my nose in and told you about it." Rebecca bit her upper lip as soon as the words were out of her mouth. "Sorry. That was rude. I'll let you talk to him."

"Thank you." Henry nodded slowly. "How are things out at the B&B, boys?"

Hayden stretched his upper shoulders and neck. "Good. I want to be through with the major construction before classes start back up if we can. Yeah, Heath?"

His brother nodded. "It's one thing to have us all working together out there, but I don't know about leaving some of that to Jason and Dick. Dick's doing good and Jason's learning, but neither of them ..." He shook his head. "No, they're doing really good. Those two rooms you're putting in the attic will be pretty, but that's a lot of work to finish it. Once we get done up there, we'll get going on the new windows. Then we can start painting. It's going to be such a great place when it's done. All old-fashioned and stuff. I think all those windows and that cool wood stove will be great in the dining room."

Hayden grinned at his brother. "You just love this stuff, don't you?"

"Don't you?"

"No, buddy, I don't. I like working with you and I don't mind the work. It's good money and all, but you love seeing those bare walls, knowing something is going to come of it."

"I can see it happening in front of me," Heath said. He chuckled. "I think I like demolition as much as construction, though. It was fun knocking that wall out to make the big dining room."

They'd decided to enclose part of the back porch with windows and opened up a portion of it to the old dining room, giving it a big, expansive feeling. When they opened up the side of the house, that had been worrisome for everyone. It was in that week that torrential rains soaked the county. But they got through it and though there was plastic sheeting everywhere, it would soon be finished.

"It's been fun working with Jason again, too," Heath said. "He feels kinda weird about not going to college. Like he thinks maybe he made a mistake what with everyone else going away in a few weeks. I told him that he can go whenever he wants to go and if he doesn't want to, that's cool, too. I didn't think I'd ever want to go to college and I'm actually looking forward to seeing everyone again. It's not as bad as I thought it would be."

"Do you think he really is having second thoughts or does he just feel left out?" Polly asked.

"Second thoughts. At least that's like fifty or sixty percent of it. But he made a decision and he's going to stick with it. Maybe next year. He's kinda worried that after the work at the B&B is done, he won't find another job."

Jason was working at Sycamore House with Eliseo, at the stables with Elva, and at the B&B. He had very little free time, which drove his brother crazy since most of the chores at home had fallen on him. When Polly thought about it, she grinned. Served the little brat right. Andrew'd had it pretty easy over the last few years, spending his time with Rebecca and Kayla. He'd done the absolute minimum work at home to keep his mother off his back. He was a good kid, but he was old enough to take responsibility around the house. He couldn't count on his brother being there forever.

"There are always more jobs," Polly said. "For that matter, if we're starting a relatively big project in the caretaker's basement at the hotel, he could probably pick up some hours there as soon as we know what we're doing."

"I doubt that Skylar will want to wait until we're finished at the B&B," Henry said. "Not if he's already digging around."

"Does he have any construction background?" she asked.

He shrugged. "I don't know. We'll talk about that."

"I don't want him doing a little bit here and there. If we decide to build out the basement, I want it done well and I want it done right. New electricity, make sure it looks good. We haven't invested all that time and money down there to do a half-baked job."

Henry raised his eyebrows. "I know. I've got this."

"It's only three months until Jason and Heath will be free. They only just moved in a couple of months ago. He can wait that long."

If it was possible, Henry's eyebrows went up a little further. "I'll talk to him."

"I just want it to be nice."

"It will be."

Rebecca had watched the two of them, her eyes darting back and forth as they discussed it. In fact, the entire table had grown silent.

"I'm sorry," Polly said. "I'm exhausted. You're right. How was your day at Nate's?"

Henry beamed. "We had a great time. Nate had fun showing the guys his garage and his cars. They're leaving the Camaro there. Kirk and Justin will be going over to work on it. I don't think they could believe Nate's equipment. Everything they need is right there and he's so glad someone will use it, he's beside himself. Then we showed them the Woodies. That set off a whole different conversation. Nate's ready to get started on those again." He shook his head. "I don't know if I have time. Maybe Nate was just excited about it because Kirk and his dad love working on cars. I don't know how he'll find the time either, but he says we're going to find a way. Louis said that when he was younger, he had a '34 Ford Coupe hotrod. He had to sell it when they had kids. Man, I wish he hadn't. I'd love seeing that around town. He built that thing out all by himself. It had a 331 Chrysler Hemi in it."

"Surely you saw it around town," Polly said, laughing at herself. She couldn't even get a picture of what he was talking about into her head, much less make sense of the words.

He shook his head. "I don't remember it. Dad probably would. He'd have thought that was cool. I think it's great that Justin is helping his dad restore this Camaro, though." Henry grinned and looked pointedly at Rebecca. "You don't get to ride in it."

"Why not?"

"Because it's fast and dangerous for little girls. That's why not. Boys in Camaros aren't to be trusted. When you're thirty-five, maybe."

"Whatever. It's not like he even noticed me."

"When did you see him?" Polly asked her.

"Yesterday when you and Mrs. Waters were exchanging kids in the middle of the road. That was weird, by the way."

"It was weird. But it was hilarious. She is really something. Such a bright woman. I mean, who thinks of having a spy trade in the middle of a street in Bellingwood, Iowa?"

"Evidently, Mrs. Waters does," Hayden said. "You didn't tell us about that."

"Her daughter for the boys."

"Did you talk to Cilla today?" Rebecca asked.

"Yeah. She wondered what you were doing. I helped them unpack the kitchen and dining room. The girls were upstairs working in their own rooms while I was there."

Rebecca frowned. "They aren't making Mr. Waters go up those steps every night, are they?"

"No. They're turning the family room at the back of the house into the master bedroom. It will be nice when they're finished, but they have a lot of work to do. I think we'll be seeing a lot of Kirk's parents there in the next few weeks. She wants to knock out some walls on the main level and open it up. I told her that you could at least tell her if they were load-bearing so she didn't have to worry." Polly aimed that at Henry. "But I didn't offer your construction help. In fact, I pretty much told her you were buried at work. She said Justin's a good worker and he works well with his grandfather."

"Kirk can do it," Henry said.

"If she lets him. She's worries about him. Doesn't think a year is long enough for him to be completely recovered." Polly glanced around the table and realized that the boys were paying attention. "You boys know that you have to take your showers tonight, right? I'm not yelling and screaming at you in the morning."

"Right," Caleb said. "We have to go to church tomorrow."

"You don't like going to church?" Heath asked.

"It's okay."

Polly wasn't going to deal with that conversation. Her kids were up and down with what they liked and disliked every week. They didn't all warrant an argument or discussion. He'd get up tomorrow morning and go to church with them no matter what. If there was a problem she needed to know about, it would come up sooner or later.

"We should clear the table and put food away first," Cat said. "It's your turn to scrape plates, JaRon. Noah and Elijah, you're on table-clearing duty. Caleb, you'll help me with the dishwasher."

"I like Saturdays," Rebecca said, sitting back in her chair. "The one night I don't have to do dishes."

"You hardly ever do dishes," Elijah said as he picked up her plate.

Rebecca poked his cheek with her finger. "More than you do."

"Nuh uh. I'm always helping. You only sometimes help."

"Bet me."

He stuck his tongue out at her and spun to head for the kitchen, silverware clattering to the floor as it flipped off the plate. "Look what you made me do," he accused Rebecca, his face hot.

She sat up and creased her forehead. "I'm sorry." Then she bent to pick up what had fallen. "I didn't mean to make you mad." She put the silverware back onto the plate and he stomped out of the room.

"What was that?" Rebecca mouthed to Polly.

Polly lifted her shoulders. "I don't know. Just boy stuff. He doesn't like missing out on conversations any more than you do."

"Can I call Dierdre?" Rebecca asked.

"Text her first and see if her Mom is okay with you two talking tonight. If not, you have laundry to manage. Your room is getting out of control again."

Rebecca rolled her eyes. "I guess I can do both. I don't know what I'm going to wear on Monday. I need more choices."

"That's such a surprise." Polly laughed and then she groaned.

Last year, Stephanie and Sylvie had traded off most of the early morning driving to Boone for marching band. Stephanie still wasn't driving, though she had finally set aside her walker for a cane. The girl was doing better every day. Polly and Sylvie hadn't talked at all about getting Andrew and Rebecca to school this fall. They'd done everything together last year. Traveling was always a group activity. Was he going to be part of that?

"You were right," she muttered to Henry as they headed down the hall to the office.

"Those are words I like to hear. But what is it this time?"

"Andrew and Rebecca should never have become a couple. This breakup is going to kill me."

"At least you have your priorities straight. It's all about me being right and things being difficult for you."

"Don't you forget it."

"Tell me the rest of what Andrea said about her husband not being well."

"She's worried that he's pushing it too fast. She doesn't know me well enough to tell me every intimate detail, but she isn't shy about talking, that's for sure. He insists he's fine and thinks that hard work and perseverance will take him through this. She's says he's ignoring the fact that he lost part of his body. He had to talk to a therapist when he was recovering, but as soon as he could get out of that, he did. Sometimes his pain is bad, too. He's got painkillers and she didn't say it, but she's worried about him getting off those. I don't think this is going to be an easy road for them."

"He seemed upbeat and happy today," Henry said. "I didn't even question whether that was real or put on."

CHAPTER SIX

"Painful. This is just painful," Rebecca moaned from the front passenger seat. "When I get old, I want a job where I can work my own hours and sleep all morning if I want to. Why does the world even exist before ten o'clock?"

"You just need coffee," Cilla said. "Loads and loads of coffee."

Rebecca turned. "I'm not allowed. Not until I'm thirty-five. I can't do anything until I'm thirty-five. Why won't they let me sleep until I'm thirty-five?"

Cilla chuckled behind Polly. "I'm not allowed either, but what Mama Waters doesn't know won't hurt me. Tell me what the clarinet section is like here. I was ready to take first chair last year until we moved. How much murder and mayhem must I commit in order to secure the top spot?"

"Are you kidding me?" Rebecca asked. "That's where I am, but in the flute section. You're that good? The best player graduated in May, but there's some competition. And you know us small town kids, we are threatened by outsiders." She grinned. "I have a girl coming up behind me that thinks she's going to give me trouble, but I've got her number. I'm better."

"Rebecca," Polly said warningly.

"What? I am."

"That's fine. But be careful. Humility is a better way to act in public. You and I both know that the more bragging you do, the bigger target you create."

"Impressive," Cilla said. "Monday morning wisdom and it's not even seven o'clock yet."

Polly laughed as she pulled into the Sycamore Inn parking lot. Kayla was waiting outside and when she saw Cilla sitting in the seat behind Polly, ran around to the other side and got in.

"Good morning, Kayla," Polly said. "How are you?"

"I'm fine." She peered at Cilla and then at Polly.

Polly gave a raised eyebrow to Rebecca.

"What?" Rebecca asked.

"You're supposed to introduce us," Cilla said.

"Oh! I didn't even think. Sorry. Cilla, this is my best friend, Kayla Johnson. Kayla, this is Cilla Waters. I told you about her. She lives across the street from me."

Kayla nodded shyly at Cilla. "You're in band, too? That's cool."

"Band geeks are the best," Cilla said. "Okay, next to theater geeks. But still, the best. We're going to have a great year. We should plan a party for the last football game, maybe a kegger and get drunk and do panty raids on the football players."

Polly let out a cackle. "Count me in. I'll drive the getaway vehicle."

"We could put the whole band in here," Cilla said. "You live at the hotel? That seems interesting. Is it?"

Kayla frowned. "I suppose. Interesting people show up, but they're always involved in themselves and don't pay attention to me. Since Skylar is running the place and Stephanie oversees him, and they're like, my parents, I'm hopefully going to work the front desk when I learn the software. Wouldn't that be cool?"

"Does no one call their parents mom and dad around here?" Cilla asked. "Is this a thing in Iowa or something?"

Rebecca laughed. "That's funny. Stephanie is Kayla's older sister. But she's just like her mom."

Cilla gave her a long, slow nod. "That makes sense, I guess. See, it isn't smart for me to make assumptions about people. Who's Skylar, then?"

"Stephanie's boyfriend. He manages the hotel and Stephanie is the assistant to Jeff Lyndsay, who is Polly's property manager. That's what you call him, right?"

"It works," Polly said. "He oversees everything for me."

"We're picking Libby Francis up, too," Rebecca said. "She's another friend. Dierdre Adams isn't in band. She's cool. You'll meet her when school starts. Are you riding the bus?"

"Justin said he would only drive me to school if the situation were dire," Cilla said.

"We won't ride the bus in the mornings because of band practice. Polly did you talk to Mrs. Waters about that?"

"I haven't talked to her about school stuff yet other than getting Cilla to band camp this week."

"When do you get your license, Cilla?" Rebecca asked. "I don't get mine until May. Andrew ..." She stopped. "Never mind."

"It's kind of weird not having him go to band with us," Kayla said quietly.

"Who's Andrew?"

"He and Rebecca have been together for like nearly five years. Even before I moved into town," Kayla responded. "He broke up with her a month ago or something. Jerk."

"I'm glad you told me," Cilla said. "I'd hate to have met him and thought he was a nice guy, then come to find out he messed with the only person who knows me and likes me. I'll stick right there with you, Rebecca. If you say he's a jerk, he's a jerk."

Polly tried not to chuckle, but she slipped a glance at Rebecca, who stared straight ahead.

"He's not really a jerk," Rebecca said. "Just stupid. Boys are so stupid."

"I live with one of the stupidest," Cilla said. "Now what about those two cute older brothers of yours. That Hayden, he's married to Cat, right?"

Rebecca nodded and smiled at Polly.

"And Heath is his brother?" She sat forward. "Do you just take everyone in, Miss Polly?"

"I do if they need me," Polly replied. "I've been lucky to be able to have pretty wonderful kids in my life."

"And no one else is related to those two. I mean, like blood-related?" Cilla asked.

Rebecca turned to look at her. "No, it's just them."

"Is Heath dating anyone?"

Rebecca touched Polly's arm. "Have you heard about him dating anybody? I haven't."

"Not that I know of," Polly said.

"Hmmm," Cilla mused as she sat back in her seat. "I wonder what he'd think of a precocious fifteen-year-old."

"Statutory," Polly muttered.

"What was that?"

Polly chuckled. "Nothing. He's a little old for you."

"I know. The good ones always are. Mama would have my head if I tried to date a college boy. She tries to make me believe that Daddy is the one who would be angry, but he's a mooshie sweetie pie when it comes to me."

"Use your power for good," Polly said.

"I'm an adolescent girl. That's asking a lot of me," Cilla replied with a laugh. "Aren't we expected to be conniving and filled with angst at this age?"

Polly grinned at Rebecca.

Rebecca sighed. "I know. I know." She pointed at her chest. "Angst-filled here. I can't get away with conniving. It's like Polly always knows and then I'm stuck cleaning a bathroom."

"It's been a while since you've had to do that," Kayla said. "What happened?"

"Polly gets mad at the boys more than she does me."

"Or maybe you're growing up," Polly said.

"I really, really hate cleaning toilets." Rebecca turned to look at Cilla. "That's, like, the worst punishment she could have ever given me and she gave it to me all the time."

Cilla laughed. It was a musical sound that made everyone in

the Suburban smile. "Mama makes me clean my sisters' room. From the top to the bottom. One day she even made me climb up on a step stool and wash the top of their window frames. Disgusting. How do little girls get dirt up there? I don't think it's fair that I should have to clean their room and they don't have to clean mine when they get in trouble."

"Do you want them in your room?" Kayla asked.

"Well," Cilla said agreeably. "You're right, there. They'd be into everything. As it is, I have to lock my journals up in a box and hide them in the back corner under my bed. No. Wait. I'm hiding those from Mama. I would be tossed into a bottomless pit if she ever read what I wrote in my journals. I'm sure I've already told you. I'm a bit of a drama queen. It occurs to me that it might be good for the soul to dream about the unattainable cute boy who lives across the street in his beautiful palace. Do you think he'd be willing to dream about me the same way? Maybe I could turn it into a *West Side Story* love affair. Our parents don't understand our love and in the end, I die for him." She'd reached her arm toward the front as she lifted her voice. "We could write dance numbers and songs and dramatic death scenes." Dropping her arm back into her lap, Cilla sat forward again. "What do you think, Miss Polly? Is Bellingwood ready for a *Romeo and Juliet* story to happen in their midst?"

"Is anyone ever ready for you?"

Cilla laughed again. "I like you. I'll bet there aren't very many people who intimidate you, are there?"

"Your mother." But Polly kept those words to herself as she pulled into the driveway at Libby Francis's house.

Libby came dashing out of the back door and climbed into the seat behind Kayla. "Are you Cilla?" she asked. "Rebecca told us she had a new neighbor. I'm Libby. She said you had a cute big brother. Is he in band?"

Cilla turned. "Hello there. No, Justin isn't in band. He used to be, but the band director his freshman year said something rude about him playing the oboe. At least that's the story I got. He just quit. He's busy with football and wrestling, though I don't think he's going out for football here since he's a senior and we just got to town." She shrugged. "I don't know. If I can ignore him, I do. He's just a boy." She tapped Rebecca on the shoulder. "And boys are stupid, right?"

"Speaking of stupid boys," Libby said. "Rebecca, you aren't going to believe what I heard last night. I was going to call you, but then I remembered you don't have your phone with you all the time. I wondered if Andrew would be in the car this morning, but since he's not, I'll bet I know who he's with. You won't even believe it."

"What?" Rebecca asked flatly. "What won't I believe?"

"Who he's dating now."

"Someone new? Already?" Kayla asked.

"Yeah. So, that girl from Boone, Tawnya? She started going with someone who lives there and blew Andrew off. But you won't even believe who he's going with now."

"Who!" Rebecca said, sounding exasperated.

"You won't believe it," Libby said again. "Maddy Spotter."

Polly watched Rebecca deflate. She reached across the console to touch her arm. Rebecca pulled away, hunching toward the door, her face growing darker and angrier with every mile.

"He fu …" Rebecca stopped and looked at Polly, her lips curled up in a snarl. "Sorry. But he knows how I feel about her. I had one year of peace without that little bitch in my face. Then he breaks up with me and promptly starts going with her? I hate him. I hate him, I hate him, I hate him."

"What?" Cilla asked quietly. "Who's this Maddy-shrew?"

"You remember that flute player Rebecca told you she competes with?" Polly asked, trying to give Rebecca enough time to gather her wits. "Madison Spotter."

"I dated her brother last year. He's okay," Kayla said. "But Maddy has it out for Rebecca. She probably went after Andrew as soon as she found out that they broke up. They don't live very far from Andrew's house either. I'll bet she walked over and threw herself at him. He probably didn't have a choice. He wouldn't do that to you on purpose, Rebecca. He's not that mean."

"Yeah, but he's stupid," Rebecca said. "I can't believe I have to go to band today and watch the two of them fawn all over each other. Can you give me an excuse or something, Polly?"

Polly slowly shook her head. "I'm sorry. I know this stinks, but you need to go kick some butt today. You're going to be the leader of your section, and you'll be stronger than you think. You have to be."

"Never let 'em see you sweat," Cilla said. "Besides, look at your crew. We're awesome. We've got your back. If you want me to, I'll trip her when she marches close to a mud puddle. I'm new and innocent. I don't know anyone. Why would I do that intentionally?"

"Seriously. Use your power for good, young woman," Polly said with a forced laugh. She knew this was just high school stuff and in three years it would all be behind them, but it still hurt to watch Rebecca suffer through so much pain.

Things in the Suburban went silent as she drove into Boone and wound her way through town to the high school. When she pulled to a stop to let them out, Rebecca didn't move.

"I don't want to go in," she said.

"You have to," Polly replied.

Kayla put her hand on Rebecca's shoulder. "We'll be right there with you."

Rebecca turned pained eyes on Polly. "Please don't make me. It's too hard."

"I'm sorry, honey. I can't take this one away from you. You have to go in and you have to face him. You have to do your very best today. Show Madison Spotter that you are stronger than the stuff she's trying to throw at you. Because you are. You are strong."

"I'm tired of being strong. Can't I just once give up and lie down? They got me where they want me. I don't have anything left. I give up."

"No you don't," Cilla said. "Not today. We're going to kick butt and take names. Because there ain't no boy out there who can have control over us. We are strong and brave and beautiful."

Rebecca shrugged and rolled her eyes. "I'm not getting out of this, am I."

"I'm sorry," Polly said. "When you get home tonight, I'll tell you how much I love you and listen while you scream and rage about what a jerk Andrew is. Then we'll go eat ice cream or popcorn and talk trash about Maddy Spotter. How's that?"

"Not enough, but if I have to, I have to." Rebecca pushed her door open. "This is the worst thing I've ever had to face. The absolute worst."

"Come on, girls," Cilla said, opening her door. "She's not doing this alone. Am I right?" She got out of the Suburban and started to sing. *"What doesn't kill you makes you stronger. Stand a little taller. Doesn't mean I'm lonely when I'm alone ..."*

Before she got too far, Kayla and Libby had joined in, singing at the top of their lungs. *"What doesn't kill you makes a fighter. Footsteps even lighter. Doesn't mean I'm over cause you're gone."*

They were singing together by the time they got to Rebecca's door.

"Come on," Cilla said. "We've got you."

Rebecca's eyes were filled with tears when she smiled at Polly. "See you later?"

"I'll be here."

Polly watched them walk to the school, carrying their instruments, with their arms hooked together. Well, that was really something. Rebecca had always been the strongest of her friends. Kayla was there to comfort her, but never to take charge when Rebecca needed strength. Suddenly, Rebecca's girlfriends were a team. For a single moment, she envied them this time together. Passions ran so deep at this age. Whether it was boyfriends or girlfriends, there was nothing rational about the relationships they were building. She would have given anything to be able to take Rebecca home and wrap her up in a soft, safe blanket. But that wasn't what was needed, no matter how much she wanted it. For Rebecca to face everything that would come at her in the future, she needed the strength that came from handling rough moments like today. But to have three girlfriends walk through it with you? A girl just couldn't ask for much more.

Before she left the parking lot, Polly pulled out her phone and swiped a call open.

"Good morning, dear. How are you?"

"I'm okay. I just wanted to call you and tell you how much I appreciate your friendship. Thank you."

"Polly, that's the best way to start a Monday morning," Lydia said. "Thank you. What made you think of me?"

"I just dropped Rebecca and her friends off at band camp and was reminded about how important friends are. What does your week look like?"

"I'm still trying to get things back in order. I was a very bad Lydia and didn't put the house back together after we packed for our trip. I'm paying for it now. Mother always told me to be sure to clean the house before I went away. She was right. It's terrible to come back to a house in chaos when you're exhausted."

Lydia and Aaron had just returned from a trip to Atlanta to visit their son, Jim, and his girlfriend, Kate. Since Aaron's sister also lived there, they'd taken two weeks to make the trip. Lydia had done exactly what she planned to do and packed everything they'd stored for Jim and delivered it to him. She'd been dedicated to that task this summer, making a quick trip to Minnesota to deliver things to their daughter, Sandy, in early July. A load of things had been unceremoniously dropped on their son, Dan, and even Marilyn in Dayton had a few boxes delivered to her. The only one who had yet to get a visit from her parents was Jill. That would come later.

"Do you have time for lunch this week? I missed you while you were gone."

"I sure do. Shall I call the girls?"

"Yes, please. Any and all of them. We can even eat at Sweet Beans if that means Sylvie might join us."

"I heard Marta was hurt. Does that mean Sylvie's working more hours?"

"Yeah. That's probably right. Shelly is staying with Marta for a few days to help her out."

"That's so nice. I'm glad to see that girl find her way. Oh, and Deb Waters told me yesterday that her son is home and that he moved in across the street from you. Have you met him yet?"

Polly laughed out loud. "Kirk Waters is the least interesting person who moved into that house and he's the one who lost his leg. Lydia, the women in his life are incredible. Andrea is brassy, brilliant, pushy, loud, and hilarious. She will compete with Beryl for crazy lady in my life. She has a daughter who is Rebecca's age and they are on track to become best friends. Cilla is as witty and wild as her mother and it seems she's talented and bright, too. Our neighborhood just got a fresh infusion of crazy. I can't wait to see what happens."

"I can hardly wait to meet this family. When are you going to have a party?"

"Maybe this weekend. How does that sound?"

"What a week," Lydia said. "I get to have lunch with you and a party at your house. I'm glad I came home."

"I'm glad you did, too," Polly replied. "Was there a concern that you wouldn't?"

"No. I'm just being silly. We had a wonderful time. Jim's girlfriend, Kate, is the sweetest thing. I wish they didn't live so far away, but they're happy and we got a chance to meet some of their friends. I always enjoy seeing my kids surrounded by good people. Now, what days are you free for lunch?"

"Any day should be fine. Rebecca is busy all week in Boone, Cat is spending time with the boys, and Shelly is either working or will be with Marta. I can get away for lunch, no matter where I'm working."

"How are things going at the hotel now that Skylar is managing it."

"Very well. The biggest thing is that I think he's enjoying it. He's also much more relaxed now that he and Stephanie can be in the same place. He's almost back to the boy I met when he walked into Sweet Beans the first time. A little older, a little more mature, but he'll shed that someday."

Lydia laughed. "When he turns fifty maybe? We gotta cut loose just to remind ourselves that we're still alive. Speaking of cutting loose, I'll call Beryl and find out when she's free. Can I send you a text?"

"That would be wonderful. I love you, Lydia. I am glad you're home."

"This has been the perfect way to start my day. Thank you for calling. I love you, too."

CHAPTER SEVEN

In case Rebecca was still a mess, Polly braced herself for an oncoming emotional breakdown. She didn't know what to expect when she picked up the girls in Boone. There hadn't been any phone calls or texts, but between marching practice on the field and music practice in the building, there couldn't have been any free time.

Polly had spent most of her day buried deep in accounts. When had she become so stinking proficient at that garbage? It wasn't that difficult. At least she came up with positive numbers. They were pouring more money than she expected into the renovation at the bed and breakfast, but that would pay for itself over the next few years. Sycamore Inn was busy nearly all the time these days. Skylar was a very different manager than Grey. While Grey had done a terrific job, Skylar was much more passionate about making the inn a great place to stay. He was having a fantastic time, greeting guests and getting to know them.

It was fun to watch June Livengood with him. She couldn't help herself and treated him like a young boy, but he knew exactly what to do and flirted outrageously with the woman. To hear Stephanie tell stories, he was even worse with June's mother and aunt, who invited the young couple and Kayla over for dinner as often as they could get away with it. Skylar's network had brought more employees to Sycamore Inn, making it easier on everyone. Nick Arthur still worked the evening shift, but they'd added three part-time people on weekends and two others during the week. For the first time, they weren't stretched thin. There was so much more energy now. Both Polly and Jeff were thrilled with how this had worked out.

She sat in her air-conditioned Suburban waiting for the girls to come out of the school. At least they were marching in the morning before the heat of the day took over. When she looked up, she saw Rebecca and her friends racing across the parking lot, laughing and bumping into each other. There was no hint of pain on Rebecca's face. Polly relaxed. The day had gone better than she expected, then. Why was it that she took so much of Rebecca's pain on herself? The hardest thing was, that while she had worried all day, Rebecca had obviously gotten through it with little stress. Good for her. Polly needed to learn to be okay with her daughter's life being what it was.

"Can I spend the night at Libby's?" Rebecca asked as she opened the door. "We already asked Mrs. Francis. She said she'd take us tomorrow morning. No problem. Cilla called her mom and Kayla's already called Stephanie. Is that okay?"

Rebecca gave Polly a tentative look. She knew that she wasn't supposed to ask permission to do things with her friends — in front of her friends. Those were conversations she was supposed to have with Polly alone.

"Why didn't you call me?"

"Because I was busy. I'm sorry. Can I?"

Polly pulled out of her parking spot, then headed for the street. "Did you have a good day?"

"It was a blast. It's so different being a sophomore. All these scared little freshmen who don't know anything. They don't know where to go or where to sit or even where the bathroom is." Rebecca turned around. "Were we like that last year?"

Kayla put her hand up. "I was. I was so scared. If you hadn't been there, I might never have gone to school. That building was big. But it's not so big now. It's just school."

"You didn't act scared, Cilla," Rebecca said. "How was your day?"

"I was with you guys. I just acted like I knew where we were going since you were already going there," Cilla said with a laugh.

As the three girls in the back chattered, Rebecca reached over and touched Polly's arm. "Can I go?"

Polly gave her a nod. "We'll talk about it later, though."

"I'm sorry," Rebecca mouthed. "It was a crazy day and I totally didn't even pull my phone out ever. Can you believe it?"

"Nope. I totally can't believe it," Polly said with a laugh. "How was it seeing Andrew?"

Rebecca shrugged. "I guess it was okay. At least he didn't drape himself all over Maddy. They ate lunch together, but it could have been worse. She tried to get pushy with me, but I just acted like she wasn't even there."

"Really?"

"Yeah. She asked me dumb questions and I ignored her. If she asked something important, I'd answer, but otherwise ..." Rebecca showed Polly her palm. "Not even part of my space."

"That's one way of dealing with it. Did Andrew try to talk to you?"

"No. He's being all popular boy or something, hanging out with these guys he never wanted anything to do with before. It's like he has something to prove. That's cool, though. We're going down different paths now. I'm going to be fine." She turned in her seat. "Cause I got my girls. Uh huh?"

"Uh huh," the three responded.

"We're going to rule the school," Cilla said.

Polly hadn't intended to shuttle kids to their homes and then out to Libby's house, but she dropped Kayla at the hotel, then drove to her neighborhood, telling the girls to be sure they didn't pack for a week. It was only an overnight. Rebecca had rolled her eyes at that before running in to pack a bag and beg one of the boys to care for her cats that evening. She didn't have to beg very hard. She'd discovered that a payment of a dollar per cat got plenty of volunteers.

While Polly waited in the Suburban for both girls to return — Libby had chosen to run inside with Rebecca rather than sit with Polly — she sent a text to Henry. *"Rebecca's out for tonight. Going to Libby's house. I think Cat and Hayden are doing some movie thing with the boys. Heath can fend for himself. Wanna take me out on a date? Like, out of town even?"*

She waited and waited for a response, then finally put her phone down. That just meant he was busy. He wouldn't ignore an invitation like that. She looked up in her rear-view mirror at the Waters' house. The siding was still a mess. The Dexters had never done anything with that. So many houses on this street were run down. There wasn't much money here. How could you spend money on fixing the outside of your house when you were barely making payments on it and keeping food on the table? She'd heard so many nasty comments from people who thought that maybe since she and Henry had renovated the Bell House, some of the lazy people down here might finally fix up their own houses. She hated hearing those types of things. How can you judge when you don't know what's going on inside the home? Mona Bright had nothing, but she had made a nice, clean home for Rose and the little girl was happy and safe. It might not look beautiful on the outside, in fact, it didn't even look beautiful on the inside, but it was theirs. No beautiful paint job, but a lot of love. That's what mattered.

Cilla was the first to return to the Suburban. She jumped in behind Polly. "I'm the first one?"

"Yes, you are. Did you bring a swim suit?"

"I can't believe she has a swimming pool. That's awesome. Mom said Lara and Abby were spending the night at Grandma's and Natty-boy is hanging out at your house. She's going to make Dad take her out. We've lived in town for less than a week and we're already spreading out. She's so happy. Grandma told us we struck gold when a house opened up across the street from you. The outside needs a lot of work. Well, the inside does, too, but Mom says she has a family full of strong backs to make it better. I told her the first thing we had to replace was the bathroom upstairs. It's old and decrepit. I'm worried that if too many of us stand in there at one time, the floor will collapse, but then, why would we all be in there at the same time? That's just gross. I don't take very much time in the bathroom. When you grow up in base housing, there are never enough bathrooms. You either hurry or get yelled at. It won't be a big deal to have all five of us using the same bathroom. At least Mom and Dad won't be up there using it, too. There was one house where we only had one bathroom and that was downstairs. Mornings were ugly. You had to schedule time to use the toilet and forget about putting your makeup on in there. Ridiculous. There they are."

Libby and Rebecca came out of the house, each of them carrying a tote bag.

"What did you pack?" Polly asked Rebecca when she got into the car. "Two bags? Why? Just why?"

"Leave me alone. It's not my fault. Kayla wanted to borrow a pair of shoes for tomorrow."

~~~

Heath, Hayden, and Cat, with a great deal of help from five small boys, put up the screen canopy in the back yard. With a white sheet at one end, it was the perfect place for the kids to watch movies outside. Polly made big batches of popcorn and a pan of brownies and then Hayden cooked hotdogs on the grill. The boys were in heaven. Polly had a pile of blankets and quilts that weren't used for anything other than picnics and play, and they settled in for a fun evening.

Andrea Waters had offered to help with them, but Cat sent her home. Adding one small boy wasn't going to create extra chaos.

Henry had driven home in his Thunderbird. That brought Kirk and Justin outside to look in and around the vehicle. Polly almost felt bad for not inviting Kirk and Andrea to go out for dinner with them, but not bad enough to do anything about it. She wanted to spend her evening with Henry.

When he came inside to get cleaned up, Polly was already dressed, wearing a bright green pair of capri pants and a flowery tank top.

"Whoa," he said. "Who are you?"

"What?" She spun around.

"You always look nice, but you never wear bright colors when we go out. Uh, what's going on?"

"Rebecca said I needed more color in my wardrobe. I don't know if I agree with her, but I like this. It's kind of cute."

He kissed her on the nose. "You're adorable. I'm going to take a quick shower and then I'll be ready to go."

"Can I watch?"

He shook his head. "Whatever. How was Rebecca's day?"

She'd told him about the meltdown this morning.

"Apparently, it went better than I expected. I worried about her all day and when she came out this afternoon, she was just fine. Like nothing bad had happened all day. Why did I worry?"

"That's what moms do," he replied.

She followed him into the bathroom and sat down on the edge of their jacuzzi while he was in the shower.

"When I was in college," Henry said from the shower, "I called Mom one night in an absolute panic about something or other. I don't even remember what it was. By the time she talked me down, I was fine. I went to bed and then to classes the next day. I didn't think another thing about it. That next night? I got a freaked out call from her. She was really worried. It hadn't occurred to me that I needed to tell her I was fine. I was fine when we hung up the night before, but I guess I didn't say so. All I needed was for her to listen to me. I guess I passed my stress off and she picked it up. I learned after that to let her know that I was okay. I didn't mean to leave it like that. Who knew?"

"Sometimes being a parent is hard," Polly said. "I'm going to like having Cilla in Rebecca's life. That girl took charge today and gave her a little additional bit of backbone. Rebecca lost all of that when she and Andrew broke up. Kayla's wonderful, but she doesn't have that kind of confidence and strength. Libby is too caught up in her own spinny little head to think about Rebecca, and Dierdre … well, she's Dierdre. If push came to shove, she'd be there, but right now she doesn't trust anyone. At least that's what it looks like."

He stepped out of the shower and grabbed a towel. "Why do you suppose that is? You don't think there's anything wrong at home?"

"No," Polly said. "Her parents are pretty normal. The little kids are normal. I think Dierdre has some things she needs to figure out. At some point she's going to need to talk to her parents."

"What do you mean?"

"That she's gay."

"You're sure?"

Polly stared at him. "You're not?"

"You believe her parents aren't seeing it?"

"I think they're seeing a messed-up daughter who is in the middle of adolescent hell and they don't know exactly what her trigger is."

"How do you think they'll handle it? You know them better than I do."

"I only know Michelle. If Dierdre would just talk to her mother, they'd be great, but I'd say this hasn't even occurred to Michelle yet."

"What does Rebecca say?"

"That Dierdre is gay and doesn't want to talk about it with anyone."

"Tell me you aren't getting involved."

"I'm not getting involved. I don't know any of them well enough to stick my nose in that far. I told Rebecca that if Dierdre ever wants to talk to me, though, she can."

"So you are getting involved."

"Not on purpose."

"Can I wear shorts tonight?"

"Sure. Where are we going?"

"I don't know. Let's head to Ames and see what sounds exciting. Surely we can find something other than fast food in that city."

While he dressed, Polly walked over to look out the window into the back yard. The dogs were snuggled in with the boys. She could almost hear their laughter. "I think it's awesome that Cat wants to teach little ones."

"She's good for our four. I love that you and I get to go out by ourselves every once in a while. Do we need to check on them before we leave?"

Polly smirked. "No. I'm just going to send Cat a text that we're heading out. That way we won't get caught up in the good-byes. We'll check in on them when we get home."

He held the door open for her to get into the car. The sky was still blue, puffy white clouds hung in place. It was a nice evening to be out. Polly rolled down her window and took a deep breath, contented that her world was in place.

"Rats," she said under her breath.

Henry had heard her. "What. Did we forget someone?"

"No. I just jinxed my week."

"What do you mean?"

"I thought about how everything was going well. That will teach me to feel all happy and content."

"Nothing's happened yet."

"Drive only on main highways and streets tonight. Don't veer off. Don't get lost. Don't go anywhere that there aren't a ton of people. I am not finding a body. I'm not getting involved in a mystery. Nothing. Stay on target. Stay on target."

He pulled onto the highway. "Less than a half hour to Ames. Can we make it?"

"Maybe I'll just lean my head back and close my eyes. If I tell you to take any road other than a main thoroughfare, ignore me. I don't want to look into empty parking lots. Nothing. Just get me to Ames. And we're not going to Hickory Park for barbecue either. Just so we're clear."

"Aaron's home, right?"

"See. Right there. You be quiet. Yes, he's home, but it's not because I need him to be there. Nothing is going to happen. Not tonight, not tomorrow. Not at all." Polly wiggled her fingers.

"What is that about?"

"I'm ridding myself of bad energy. Wiggling it right out of me."

Henry reached up and brought her left hand down, holding it in his. "Here, take some of my energy. It's all good. I promise."

"I'm a weirdo, aren't I."

"A little, but I still love you."

They traveled in silence and Polly relaxed as they drove past fields of corn and soybeans. "It's so strange," she said. "I've been back here for six years now and I'm still entranced by these immense fields. I love watching things grow." She laughed. "But don't think for a minute that I'll ever be able to keep flowers alive. If Eliseo and Sam Gardner didn't show up on a regular basis, we'd have brown grass and dead things in all the beds around the house. Do you know that man told me to keep my filthy hands off his babies?"

"What man?"

"Sam. I killed one plant last year and now he's threatening me."

"Honey, you killed a hosta. Those are hardy plants and will live through practically anything."

"Whatever. He was still mean to me."

"But you're glad he comes over. Right?"

"Well," she said with a giggle. "Yes."

He drove past the western edge of Ames and pointed. "Look. The lights of Ames. We made it. No detours, nothing bad."

"I'm holding out hope, then. Where shall we go?"

"There's that new place on Duff, just south of Lincoln Way. Wanna try it?"

She nodded and shrugged. "Sure. Pork Tenderloin?"

"I don't think so. More like burgers and wings."

"How can it be an Iowa restaurant without a tenderloin?"

"I have no idea, but why do you care when one of the best is served at Joe's?"

Polly squeezed his hand. "You're right. I'm just being a dope. It's so nice to be out of Bellingwood and doing something with you and no kids."

Henry found a parking place and put his hand on Polly's. "Wait for me."

"Yeah, yeah, yeah. I can open my own door."

He took a deep breath. "You are much too independent for this chivalrous old man. Just wait a heartbeat, please?"

Polly sat back and waited for him to come around, then opened the door and took his hand as he helped her stand up. "This place looks like it might be loud."

"You can stare into my eyes all night. We don't need to talk. If we have to say something and it's that loud, you can text me."

"You're ridiculous," she said with a laugh.

They went in the front door and the host greeted them. Polly was surprised they could get a table without waiting. But then, it was a Monday evening in the summer and most of the college kids had yet to return to the city. The noise level wasn't bad at all. She could enjoy her evening with Henry. As the host led them through to their table, her eyes landed on the familiar face of Jeff Lyndsay, who looked like he was there with a date.

Polly tugged on Henry's arm. "Jeff is here."

"Where?"

Because she was feeling exceptionally ornery, Polly pointed. "Right there."

Jeff rolled his eyes at her and shook his head, then beckoned for them to come over. "What are you two doing out? Did the inmates release their jailers for the night?"

"We left them in the gentle care of the associate wardens. How was your day?" Polly asked. Jeff usually took Sundays and Mondays off. He'd gotten better about staying away from Sycamore House when he wasn't scheduled and she wondered if this might be the reason why.

He smiled. "I had a very nice day. What about you?"

"You don't care," she said. "You're just being polite. Are you going to introduce us or am I going to have to embarrass you?"

Jeff laughed out loud. He looked at the host, who was watching them, waiting for Polly and Henry to pay attention and be seated. "We haven't ordered yet. Do you want to just seat them at our table? I'll take responsibility for their actions."

The young host looked at Henry for permission.

"If it's okay with them, I think this might make a very entertaining evening," Henry said.

CHAPTER EIGHT

"Tell me you're sure about this," Polly said to Jeff. "We don't want to bother you."

He glared at her. "If you don't join us, you'll be staring over here all night, wondering who I'm sitting with and conjuring up all manner of scenarios and possibilities. Then, you'll find reasons to come speak to me, hoping that I'll spill some tidbit of information for you to take back to Henry, and the two of you will hash it over, tear it apart and put it back together, a mere shell of its former truth. I believe it would be much easier if I just invite you to join us."

She turned to the host. "Evidently, we're joining them."

Jeff's friend moved around the corner of the table so Polly and Henry could sit beside each other.

"Good," Polly said. "He's right across from me now. I can judge what kind of a person he is."

Jeff turned to his friend. "She doesn't judge, she's just snippy."

"Your server will be right over," the host said and left them.

"Thank goodness he's gone," Polly said. "Now we can get down to business. Jeff, you should wear your old jeans to work tomorrow. Eliseo needs some extra help in the barn and I volunteered you for the job. He was surprised because he knows how much you hate the muck and the dirt, but he's desperate. So, yeah?"

Jeff rolled his eyes. "I'll get right on that. Polly, this is Adam Epperson. Adam, this is Polly Giller and Henry Sturtz."

"Oh," Adam said. He put his hand out to shake Henry's. "It's nice to meet you."

He was about to stand, when suddenly their server was beside him. She put her hand on his shoulder. "I'm sorry."

"It's okay," he said, sitting back down. "I'll be polite later."

"Nice," Polly said with a small laugh.

After the young woman left with their drink orders, Polly turned on Jeff. "How well should I get to know Adam, here?"

He looked at her in shock. "What do you mean by that?"

"I don't know. What do I mean by that?"

"We're dating," Adam said. "We have been for a while. Since the cat's out of the bag, I'd say that it's safe to get to know me well."

"Good," she responded. "You know I have questions, right?"

He chuckled. "I'd assume so. Jeff has told me a great deal about you."

Polly gripped Jeff's hand. "I see how important I am to you. You've told me nothing. Last I heard you weren't interested in dating."

Jeff pulled his hand away. "Henry. I'd feel much safer if the two of us left them here to talk about me. Do you want to go somewhere else for dinner?"

"No, sir," Henry said. "I don't get a lot of entertainment in my life. This should be great fun."

"Then I need alcohol. Would anyone at the table be offended if I order a bottle or two of wine? I'll be the one drinking the first bottle."

"You have to work tomorrow," Polly said. "I won't be quite so understanding when Kristen calls me to come over and step in for you."

"I intend for you to drink as much as I do," Jeff said.

"Yes, but I can hold it better."

"Doubtful."

"You wanna try it, big boy?" Polly asked.

Henry put his hand out. "It's Monday evening. You've already jinxed the week. Don't you think you should be careful?"

"She what?" Jeff asked. He turned to Adam. "Don't get in a car with this lady. She'll take you to bad, bad places."

"You've told me," Adam said. "But you're a scaredy-cat. I'm not afraid."

"You will be," Polly retorted. "Oh, you will be."

The two young men frowned at her.

"What?" Jeff asked.

Henry shook his head. *Star Wars*. Ignore her. I swear we didn't drink anything before we got in the car tonight."

"He drove his T-bird," Polly said. "That means he can't drink. He'd be scared of wrecking it."

"A new one or a classic," Adam asked.

"1955."

"No way. Those are beautiful. It's here? Right now?"

"Just outside."

"I'd love to see it."

"Let's go. We can leave these two here alone, can't we?"

"Hey," Polly said. "Not until we've ordered. I'm hungry."

Their server returned with their soft drinks and Jeff grabbed her arm. "I need a bottle of wine. Do you have anything from Secret Woods?" He grinned at Polly. "I always ask. They never do. But I can't help myself."

"Actually, we do," the young woman said.

Jeff blinked. "A bottle of the dry white, then. Is that okay? Glasses for everyone."

She took their meal order and before Polly could say anything else, Adam and Henry were up and gone from the table.

"He was serious about seeing the car," Polly said.

Jeff chuckled. "I had no idea he liked classic cars. That's something new for me."

"All right, spill. How long have you two been dating?"

Jeff considered her question. "About six months."

"Six months? Are you kidding me? How have you been dating for six months and none of us knew about it." Then she stopped and looked at him. "Six months. That's about the time you stopped working every single day of the week. That's when you started taking your days off as days off."

"Maybe. I'll get back to normal someday. Don't worry."

"I was just glad you felt like the businesses were healthy enough that you could be gone for a couple of days every week. It didn't even occur to me that you had another agenda. Where did you meet him?"

"Believe it or not, in Bellingwood."

"Is he from there? I've never seen him in town."

"No. He lives in Slater. He was at a meeting at Sycamore House and we struck up a conversation after it was over. He gave me his business card and then we met for lunch and it's just been …" he paused, "… nice."

"So nice that you couldn't tell us about it?"

Jeff shook his head slowly. "You and your nosy friends get pushy about people's personal lives. I wasn't ready to serve myself up for that."

"We do get nosy," Polly said with a grin. "But you know it's because we love you."

"Kind of like how you knew that when your friends were pushing you to marry Henry?"

"Exactly like that," she said, laughing out loud. "How serious is this thing?"

"I don't know. I think it's pretty serious."

"Have you met each other's families?"

"Lord, no," Jeff exclaimed. "Well, that's not true. He's in business with his father, so I've met his parents. But I'm not introducing him to my mother until there are no other options. You've met the woman. Why would I subject him to that?"

"What kind of business?"

"They own a sign company."

"Billboards, that kind of sign?"

"More like business signs, both indoor and outdoor, vehicle wraps, trade show displays, that kind of thing."

"That's cool. What does Adam do?"

"Everything. He has a graphic design degree and then a master's degree in business."

"Kinda hot stuff," Polly said. "Does he like it?"

"Yeah. He does."

"Well, he's adorable."

"You be good."

"I'm not kidding. He's cute."

Adam looked like the boy next door, blond hair neatly trimmed, blue eyes, maybe five-foot-nine. He wore glasses and was dressed casually this evening in a button-down shirt that hung over long blue shorts.

"I think so," Jeff said. "He's interesting, too. He likes different music than I do."

"What does that mean?"

Jeff laughed. "Country. He likes country music. There. I said it. He's taking me to Shania Twain and I'm taking him to Dave Matthews."

Polly took his hand again. "I won't tease you too much. I'm happy that you're enjoying yourself. What does he think of Luna?"

"They're disgusting together. She is totally enamored with him. When he comes to the apartment, she runs circles around him in her excitement, then as soon as he sits down, flops over on her back for a tummy rub. I don't even get that kind of attention from the dumb dog."

"Liar," Polly said. "I've seen her do that to you if you walk in the door after having been gone for only a few minutes."

"Well, that response should be all mine. I'm her daddy."

Polly looked up as Henry and Adam came back to the table.

"Did you get the scoop?" Henry asked her. "We gave you as much time as we could. Was it enough for a good grilling?"

She glanced between the two men. "Are you kidding me?"

Adam shook his head. "Not kidding you. As soon as we were introduced, I knew I needed to get out of the way so you could get all the details. Henry's car was just a good excuse. It's also a fabulous car. One of these days I'm coming to Bellingwood so I can take it for a drive."

"There are several great cars in Bellingwood you should see," Polly said. "If Jeff hadn't been hiding you from us, you could have come to the car show during Bellingwood Days." She grinned at Jeff. "I might have lied to you about the teasing. I can hardly help myself."

"That isn't surprising. I'll live with it."

"So now that the secret is out, do I have to keep it?" Polly asked. "You know that will kill me."

Jeff looked at Adam, who shrugged, then turned back to Polly. "It wasn't a secret. I just wasn't talking about it."

"And you weren't inviting him to any of the events in Bellingwood." Polly counted on her fingers. "You two were dating when you came to Jason's graduation party at my house and you didn't bring him. There were all of these things that you came to alone." She leaned into the table. "Weren't you offended by that, Adam?"

Adam bit his upper lip. "No?"

"Why not. He shouldn't be hiding you. You're adorable."

"Adorable," Adam said with a sigh. "Why do I always get the adorable tag. Not gorgeous. Not handsome. Not the strong descriptives of beauty, but adorable. I told Mom that I was going to get a nose job and lose this button nose, but it's hers and she was insulted, so I put up with it. And the dimples. Nothing can be done about the dimples. I'm always going to be adorable. It's a curse."

"Oh, the suffering," Jeff said. "I'm sorry you have to live with that."

"Adam and his father own a sign company," Polly said to Henry.

He perked up. "Really."

Adam nodded. "Do you need something?"

"We need a lot of something. The company we were using went out of business last year and I've never taken the time to find someone else. Do you have a business card on you? I'd love to get pricing on several different things." He looked at Polly. "Dad and I have talked about putting up a new sign at the shop, too."

"That would be great," she said. "Use bright neon lights so we can turn it on at night and annoy the neighbors." Then she turned to Jeff. "Is this who did the wrap for the catering van?"

He shook his head. "No. We used a company in Ames. It was before I met Adam."

"What about the logo and sign for the bed and breakfast?"

"Okay. I'll discuss it with him and bring you a proposal."

"He's right here."

Jeff rolled his eyes and shook his head, then looked up as the server returned with their food.

"Bottle of wine?" he asked.

"I'm sorry," she said. "I completely forgot about it. That should have been here long ago. I'll be right back." She turned, then turned back. "No. Sorry. Food first. I'm scattered tonight and I'm so sorry."

"We're fine. Everything okay?"

The girl closed her eyes, then nodded. "I apologize. It's fine. I'll take care of everything. And the wine is on me."

"No, no, no," Adam said. "Don't do that."

She served the food and apologized again before walking away.

"I want to ask her what's wrong and make her tell me," Polly said. "She isn't focused on her work. Her mind is somewhere else and I don't think it's anyplace good. Did you see her eyes? She was ready to cry."

Jeff turned to Adam. "This is what Polly does. Before we leave this evening, we'll know exactly what Lissa's problem is and Polly will be halfway to fixing it."

"Lissa?" Adam asked.

"Our server?" Jeff frowned. "Didn't you hear her introduce herself earlier?"

Adam looked at Henry and Polly, both of whom shrugged. They hadn't heard it either.

"Am I dreaming? Did I make that up?" Jeff asked.

The server returned with a bottle of wine from Secret Woods and four glasses. She opened it and poured.

"Is your name Lissa?" Jeff asked.

She nodded with a small smile.

"See," he said. "I told you. I pay attention when people are introduced to me."

Lissa gave him another smile. "I am sorry about forgetting this. Let me pay for it."

"Not on your life," Jeff said. "We've all had our days when things get past us."

She nodded and took a breath. "It is definitely one of those days. Let me know if you need anything else."

"Jeff told me about your big horses, Polly. Whatever made you do that?" Adam asked.

"I couldn't not do it," she replied. "At the time it felt like there was no one else around who would give them a safe place to come back to good health. Doc Ogden asked if I would and how could I say no? I figured if he had thought there was anyone else that would have been able to care for them, he would have asked them instead of me."

"And the donkeys?"

"I'm a sucker for a good rescue," Polly said. "If I can help, I will. Fortunately, the right people come into my life and help make it all work out. Kind of like Jeff, here. I had no intention of turning Sycamore House into what it has become, but he showed up and told me I'd be a fool not to hire him. He was right, though he tossed my world upside down. I just wanted to have a quiet little place where we had a few parties once in a while. Next thing I knew, we were hosting large events, talking a friend into becoming a certified chef, hiring more employees and then everything exploded. When I look back, I realize it couldn't have happened any other way, but it still surprises me sometimes. I blame Jeff for most of it. The rest I blame on Henry."

"Hey. I didn't do anything."

"No? You're the one who wanted to rescue the hotel. It was your family who wanted to do the bed and breakfast and you're the one who said we could renovate the Bell House. Without you, I'd still be at Sycamore House, living in my little apartment."

"I don't think so," Henry said. "You kept rescuing people and inviting them to live with us. You needed a big house."

She nodded. "And sometimes I still worry that it might not be enough room."

They talked and ate and drank wine and then talked some more. Polly knew they were taking up a table for far too long, but she wasn't willing to end the evening. Adam Epperson was a fun and interesting young man and they were enjoying themselves. Jeff had called Lissa over and ordered another bottle of wine, one that he and Polly shared between them. He tried to justify it by asserting he was supporting a local business, but the truth was, he was having fun.

Finally, Polly stood up.

Henry looked at her. "Are we leaving?"

"No," she said as she gripped the chair so she didn't weave. "But I need to use the bathroom. Please be here when I return, okay?"

"I think you're safe. Go on," he said. "Do you need help?"

"I'm not that drunk. Just a little tipsy. Remind me to take a large glass of water to bed with us tonight."

"She'll drink it," Henry said to Adam. "It's not some weird sex game. I promise."

Polly walked away and looked around for the bathroom.

"Back that way, ma'am," a young man at the bar said to her.

"Thank you. I was lost." She headed the way he pointed and was relieved to find the door. She needed to stop drinking right now or things were going to be rough tomorrow morning. At least she didn't have to get up to take the girls to Boone.

When she opened the door, she heard quiet sobbing coming from one of the stalls. Now, that put her into an awkward position. Polly hated talking to someone through a closed stall door, even if they did need help. First things first, though, or she'd be no good to anyone. As she washed her hands a few minutes later, the sobbing had subsided, and the stall door opened. Their server, Lissa, exited, toilet tissue in her hands as she dabbed her eyes.

"You aren't okay," Polly said.

Lissa shook her head and tears filled her eyes again. "I'm so sorry. You must think I'm some silly drama queen. I shouldn't be doing this where I work. I know better."

"What happened?"

"I lost everything."

"Everything?"

"Not everything. I have my clothes, but I've lost everything else. I don't know what I'm going to do next. I don't have a place to sleep tonight, except for my car. At least it's not freezing outside or something. I don't know what to do. I keep trying to come up with some great idea, but I'm just lost."

"What do you mean, you lost everything?"

"My roommate and her boyfriend decided that they wanted me out. They didn't give me any notice or time to find another place to live. This morning when I was in the shower, she threw my clothes into garbage bags and put them outside the front door. When I asked why, she told me that her boyfriend hated me, and she didn't like me very much either, so I was just out."

"He's been living with you two for a while?"

"No. That's the thing. He moved in two days ago. They only met, like, a week or two ago. She's weird. She's always been weird, but I didn't think she'd do anything like this. He stole money from me too." Lissa nodded. "That's probably why they wanted me out. I asked about the money last night. It was, like, two hundred dollars. And they stole my laptop. The only money I have on me is whatever I get from tips tonight. I could get a hotel room, but then what will I do tomorrow night?"

"Can you call family?"

Lissa shook her head. "They don't have any money. It isn't like they can send me anything. Mom's got mouths to feed. I was trying to save up so I could go to school here, but that isn't going to happen this year."

"Where are you from?"

"It doesn't matter," Lissa said. "This isn't your problem. I'm sorry. I shouldn't have said anything. You just caught me when I was down."

Polly put her hand on the girl's arm. "I know you have no idea who I am and have no reason to trust me, but I can help you."

Lissa pulled back. "Yeah. No. I'm not looking for help."

"I understand," Polly said. "But I can help you." She took out a business card. "This is who I am. At that table with me is my husband, Henry. The cute curly dark-haired man is my operations director, Jeff. He manages our properties in Bellingwood, and the other man is his boyfriend. We're just normal people. But the weird thing about me is that I end up talking to people who need a hand to get out of bad situations. I know it sounds crazy and weird, but it's true. I can't convince you of that, especially when you're scared and alone, but I can help. If what you want is a safe place to stay tonight, drive to Bellingwood. Do you have a pen?"

Lissa took a pen out of her apron pocket.

"Give me back that business card," Polly said. She took it from Lissa and put the hotel phone number on the back, along with her personal cell phone number. "The top number is the hotel that I own. I know they have rooms available tonight. I will call the manager and give him your name. If you can get yourself to Bellingwood, you can stay there on me. If it takes several days for you to figure things out, I'm fine with that. Ask people in Bellingwood about me, then call my cell phone and tell me that you'll let me help you. There is no reason for you to be alone and scared. There are good people in the world."

"I don't know what to say."

"Say that you'll trust me enough to drive to Bellingwood. Sycamore Inn is right there on the highway. Nick Arthur is working the night shift. He'll be looking for you. You will be safe. That's what is important. Deal?"

"Okay."

"I'm serious, Lissa."

"Thank you. I can't believe you'd do this for me."

"Lissa, I would do this for anyone. Wouldn't you?"

"I don't know. It's never come up."

Polly chuckled. "It comes up for me all the time. I've learned to just go with it. Now wash your face and finish your shift." She took twenty dollars out and handed it to Lissa.

The girl tried to protest, but Polly pushed it at her. "If you need gas to get to Bellingwood, use this. Save your tips for other things you'll need."

"Thank you so much."

"Call me tomorrow." Polly gave Lissa a smile and walked out of the bathroom and back to her seat.

"Everything okay?" Henry asked. "You were gone a long time. I was starting to worry."

"If I tell you what I was doing, you will all laugh at me," Polly said.

"What now?" Jeff asked.

"Lissa may be staying at the hotel tonight. I need to call over there and make a reservation for her."

"Of course she is," he responded. "Should I figure out where we can employ her?"

"That's up to her. First, I need her to trust me enough to come to Bellingwood. After that, we'll see where it goes."

"She's alone and in trouble?" Adam asked.

"Got kicked out of her apartment by a strange roommate. All she has is her car and her clothes. She thought she was sleeping in her car tonight. Not if I can help it."

Henry took Polly's hand. "And that folks, is my wife."

CHAPTER NINE

Yawning, Polly took another drink from her coffee cup before logging into the hotel management software. She'd called Nick to let him know that the Lissa might show up and to comp the room. Hopefully the girl had taken Polly up on her offer of a safe place to sleep.

The little boys were already in bed when she and Henry got home. The evening spent with Jeff and Adam was fun. She liked Adam and he seemed to like Jeff. That was all she could ask for, right?

It felt strange to walk into such a quiet house. Cat and Hayden were in their apartment and Heath was in the family room, playing video games. Polly didn't realize how much extra noise Rebecca and Shelly made when they were home. She'd gone into each room to check on the boys, but only Caleb had come awake enough to realize she was there. He turned over after she gave him a quick kiss and was back to sleep before she left the room.

Cat had the Suburban today. She was taking the boys to spend the morning with Marie. After lunch they were going out to Elva's place to play with the Johnson kids. As long as Polly didn't have kids to cart around, she didn't mind driving Cat's little car. Now was the time she would like to have that Woody finished. It would be much more fun to drive that around Bellingwood. Having more people interested in restoring cars might get Nate and Henry off their keisters. She'd wait and see.

Once she was logged in, Polly scanned through the names of last night's guests at Sycamore Inn and took a deep breath when she saw that Lissa Keenan had checked in at ten-forty-five. She opened her phone and called the hotel's number.

"Sycamore Inn. This is June, how may I help you?"

"Hi June, this is Polly. Is Skylar around this morning?"

"He certainly is. I'll transfer you to him."

Polly waited and soon Skylar came on the phone.

"Well, Madame Boss Lady. What's up in the wide world of Polly Giller today?"

"Just checking in. I called Nick last night about a guest and I see she checked in."

"Yeah. He left a note for me. What's up?"

"She suddenly became homeless yesterday and I wanted to give her a little space to figure things out."

"Someone you know?"

Polly chuckled to herself. "She was our server at the restaurant."

"I see," he said, his tone a bit mocking. "She was your server and you discovered that she'd suddenly become homeless and so you offered to help her. Why am I not surprised by this?"

"Because you know and love me?"

"I do. You're right. How long is she staying?"

"Well ..."

"Okay. I get it. She's here until you find her a better place to live. No problem. We'll make her comfortable. You're kind of a crazy woman, Polly Giller."

"I know. I can't help myself. I gave her my cell phone number. If she asks about me, be kind. I want her to trust me so that we can move past her being homeless to something a little more stable."

"Can do. Be nice to the new girl so Polly can save her."

"You be good, Mister Man," Polly said.

"I try so hard, but I fail so miserably. Say, have you heard what I want to do in the basement under the apartment here?"

"Yeah. Henry and I haven't had time to talk about it yet."

"Oh." He sounded disappointed. "Okay."

"No. That's not it," she said. "It's a great idea, but we want to do it right. He doesn't have crews who can work on it right now, and until the bed and breakfast is finished, we won't have extra help. When the weather gets colder and we've had our Grand Opening out there, we'll have time to renovate that and make it nice."

"I can do some of the work."

"Have you ever done any construction work, Skylar?"

He laughed. "I painted a bedroom once. But I was in high school and I'd guess that lime green and black striped walls aren't what you'd consider construction work."

"You have got to be kidding me."

"Nope. I was a problem child. At least that's what they told me on a regular basis."

"Why don't you begin taking good measurements down there and sketch out what you'd like to see happen. What are you thinking?"

"Maybe a rec room with a big screen television. I don't know. Ping pong. I don't think we can get a pool table down there. I was thinking about putting in another bedroom so Kayla could have her own place, but then it hit me."

"What?"

"There's only that outside entrance, so that won't work. But, you know, now that Grey isn't living here, when he starts working with the kids on the hockey rink, it might be nice to have a place they can warm up, go to the bathroom, have snacks."

"That's a good idea."

"The other thing is that if we ever have a tornado come through, I'd like to have the place finished so guests could hide and wait it out."

"The weather has gotten a little raucous in Iowa lately," Polly said. "That actually changes how we look at this. I need to talk to Henry. Maybe we do this sooner rather than later."

"We go down there now with tornado warnings, but it isn't a pleasant stay," he replied. "It could be so much better."

"I'm glad you said that to me. Now I can't think of anything other than finishing in a hurry."

Skylar chuckled. "We're perfectly safe in the basement without it being renovated. I don't think anyone is looking for plush accommodations to wait out a tornado warning, but it would be nice."

"Yep. I'll talk to Henry. If you want us to do anything in the apartment to make it nicer for Stephanie and Kayla, let me know."

"They're settling in. I'm just along as the muscle, you know."

"Uh huh. I can't believe that. You not offering an opinion?"

"But my opinions don't matter," he said with a laugh. "No, they're making a nice home here and I'm learning how to cook."

"What?"

"Yeah. We take turns. It was Stephanie's idea. Do you have any idea how frugal that girl is? She won't let us go out to eat if we can cook a meal at home. She keeps telling me it's so much healthier. Believe it or not, we feed Nick nearly every evening too because Stephanie can't stand the idea of that poor boy not getting home cooked meals." He sighed. "It's a tough life I'm leading, Polly, a really tough life. I don't know if I can keep up."

"Sounds like it. You start measuring the basement and we'll make plans."

"Thanks. And Polly?"

"Yeah?"

"I know I've said this a hundred times, but I feel like there might be at least a hundred more. Thank you for this opportunity. My soul was being sucked out with every pair of socks or shorts I sold. Girls with more money than sense complained because a sweater's hue didn't match her pants perfectly. Are you kidding me? And the rich ones who tried to sneak clothes out — why? Why would you do that? It's like they thought they were experienced jewel thieves."

"People steal towels and things from the rooms at the hotel. I know. I sign the checks for new stuff every month."

He laughed out loud at that one. "Yes, they do. I had a fellow ask me to help him carry his suitcase out to his car the other day. Buddy, why? Why did you have to jam it closed like that? It popped open and two pillows popped out. He just looked at them and at me, shrugged, and tried to jam them back in the suitcase. I had to ask if he wanted to be that blatant about theft. He thought maybe he should leave them with me."

"You are perfect for this job, Skylar. At least you see the humor in it."

"I don't think Grey did. He was too serious. He's such a nice man, but I think this job was about to strangle him. Whenever he talked about theft it emotionally wounded him that people would steal from us. He's just so full of empathy."

"He never said anything."

"Well, he wouldn't, now, would he?"

"I guess."

"Will I see you tomorrow morning?"

"Do you want to?"

"Only if you bring me something wonderful from Sweet Beans."

She laughed. That was their deal now. After all the times that he'd served her, he took great pleasure in allowing her to bring him his coffee. "Any preferences?"

"Surprise me."

"I'll see you in the morning."

She put her phone down and smiled. When Skylar left Sweet Beans, it had nearly killed her. She loved seeing him up there. He was such a light-hearted young man and took joy in his job. She would do nearly anything to help him maintain that joy at the hotel. He'd been miserable while selling clothes, but he had been doing his best to grow up. She hoped he'd find a way to make this job all that it could be for him.

Polly worked through the rest of the morning and was surprised at how swiftly time passed. The next time she looked at her phone it was one o'clock. Obiwan lifted his head and looked at her as she stretched before standing up.

"Would the two of you like to go outside?" Polly asked. She opened the door to the back porch and walked out with Obiwan and Han. This was not one of those beautiful days. The humidity was high and the temperature was warm enough to be uncomfortable. She hoped the kids at band camp weren't too miserable. Oh, what was she thinking. Misery was what you did when you were at high school band camp. That way you'd have something to complain about for decades. She remembered marching on the field, learning patterns, and praying for it to be over before she collapsed from exhaustion. All of those days of practice, though, would prepare you for a Friday evening performance that made you proud. She watched the dogs chase each other, then went inside and headed for the kitchen. Now that she thought about it, she was hungry. There wouldn't be any leftovers. Heath pretty much took care of those. That boy was a one-man eating machine, and he was still lanky. Someday he would thicken out, but it hadn't happened yet.

Polly looked forward to the day Heath finally came into himself. He was still so unsure about who he was and what the future looked like. While confident that he wanted to work with Henry in the family business, Heath saw himself as an assistant or Henry's helper. Henry tried to get him to take more responsibility, but Heath wasn't comfortable with that yet. He wasn't ready to take risks, to lead out and do things on his own, even with encouragement. He worked hard, he'd made good grades last year, and he was as reliable as could be, but Polly wanted more for him. He had a couple of friends that he'd do things with, but he was more comfortable coming home in the evenings and spending time with his brother and Cat, or hanging out with the little boys. He adored those boys and they thought the sun rose and set on him.

She wondered when he would work up the courage to be interested in a girl. Hayden had dated all through college and from the sounds of it, had also been popular in high school. That might have had something to do with his basketball career, but still, he was comfortable around everyone. With all that Heath had faced after his parents' death, he'd never felt safe engaging with people his own age. Jason Donovan was only a year younger than Heath and though the two worked together and their families did things together, Heath never initiated things with Jason.

That was another young man that Polly worried about. He had a nice girlfriend in Mel, but she was heading to college in Cedar Falls next week. The friends they spent time with were all leaving for college as well. Scar and Kent weren't going to be around, leaving Jason very much alone. He worried about money and becoming a responsible young man who could take care of his mother, but had no idea how to make that happen. He knew better than to think that working part-time jobs for Eliseo and Polly would be enough to carry him through, but he was floundering when it came to deciding what came next. Sylvie was in no hurry for him to leave the nest. She still saw him as her little boy, though he was far from that. That young man had grown so much since Polly first met him. He was big and strong ... and gentle as a lamb.

Even Eliseo was frustrated with Jason's lack of commitment to a future. He'd tried to talk to Sylvie, but she wasn't ready to force the issue. When Eliseo tried to talk to Jason, the boy shut down. His girlfriend, Mel, told him over and over that he could do anything he wanted to do. Jason was so afraid of not meeting everyone's expectations and turning out like his father, he was spinning in circles. There wasn't a thing Polly could do to help, except keep him busy until he made some decisions.

With Jason hiding from the reality of growing up and Andrew breaking away from Polly's family, Polly was doing her best to hold onto her friendship with Sylvie. They avoided conversations about Sylvie's boys now where before those two were an easy focal point. Sylvie didn't know how to deal with Andrew and his behavior. He was usually so smart as well as considerate of other people, but this summer he'd become more self-centered. He wasn't reading or writing like he had been — his life was now spent going out with friends who had their drivers licenses and could get them out of town. He wasn't doing anything wrong, at least not overtly, so it wasn't as if Sylvie could tell him to straighten up and fly right. If his grades fell this next year she'd have something to say, but the truth was she was thrilled to see him making new friends. Rebecca and Kayla were unimpressed with the people Andrew was choosing to spend time with, but Sylvie ignored that fact. She was sorry that he'd hurt Rebecca, but told Polly that some of that was just high school kid stuff and they had to find their way through it. Polly knew that. It was what she preached at home, too. It was still hard to watch it happen and know that Sylvie wasn't going to expect her son to be the sweet little boy he'd been for years.

Polly just hoped Andrew didn't stray too far. He didn't have the same experiences with his father that his brother did. Jason worried about being the product of Anthony Donovan and was constantly on guard.

"Being a parent stinks sometimes," Polly said to no one in particular. She walked over to the glass doors leading to the backyard from the kitchen. Luke and Leia were curled up in a sunbeam that happened to land on one of the sofas every day about this time. "At least you two are here for me."

A procession of cars, led by a hearse, drove into the cemetery.

"I wonder who died," she said and dropped down onto the sofa. Luke stretched out, reaching toward her with his front paws. He wasn't going to move from where he was comfortable, but he'd at least acknowledge her presence.

Her stomach growled. "That's why I'm out here," Polly said. "What's for lunch?" She stood up again and headed for the refrigerator, sure she could find something in there to eat. Just as she pulled the door open, she heard pounding at her side door.

"Miss Polly! Miss Polly!"

She ran to the door and pulled it open.

Nat Waters stood there with his hand lifted to pound again.

"What's up, Nat? Come in."

"Can you come over? Mom's hurt."

She didn't even think, just pulled the door shut behind her and headed down the steps with him. "What happened?"

"Mom was trying to put up these heavy shelves in the garage and it all came falling down on her. Dad and Justin aren't home." The little boy was in a panic and Polly followed him into the garage.

Whatever sets of shelving Andrea Waters had been working on had collapsed all around the woman. Heavy pieces of plywood and metal supports were in heaps.

"Andrea?" Polly called out.

"Yeah. I'm here. I'm a damned idiot, but I'm here. I think I'm okay."

The woman shifted a piece of plywood and looked up at Polly from the floor of the garage. She had a few scrapes on her face and blood on her forearm, but she was moving.

"How fast did you get to me?" Polly asked Nat.

"I heard it go down and Mom wouldn't answer me," he said.

"It knocked the wind out of me. He was gone before I could catch my breath," Andrea said. She held her hand out to Polly. "Kirk is going to yell at me."

Polly helped her stand up. "Yeah. I get that. I want to yell at you."

"Okay," Andrea said. "Fifty bucks if you'll help me get this put up before they come home this afternoon."

Polly laughed. "I don't usually do this kind of work. I hope I'm useful, but yeah, I can help."

"Maybe I slow down and start at the bottom this time," Andrea said. "I didn't think I was a dumb female, but if my husband sees what I did, I'm not going to live this down." She turned on her son. "And you will be sleeping in the bathtub if you tell him."

He shook his head. "I won't say anything. I promise."

She rolled her eyes at Polly. "He'll talk as soon as Kirk asks what we did today. The boy has no discretion."

Polly and Andrea dug in to set up the shelving units. It was more difficult than Polly could have imagined. They finally had the thing put together and shoved against the back wall when she heard barking.

"I left the dogs outside," Polly said.

"Can Nat take them in? I'd love to unpack some of these boxes and get this garage opened up. Seriously. I'm up to a hundred bucks now. I'm desperate for help."

Polly laughed. "Nat, if you'd like to let them inside, that would be great. Did you see where the pantry was?"

He nodded.

"Right inside the door on the floor is a canister of dog treats. Each dog gets one. They'll love you forever."

"I'm gonna love you forever," Andrea said, lifting a box up to a shelf. "Go on, Natty-boy. Take care of Miss Polly's dogs. We'll be here when you get back."

Nat took off across the street.

"Where's Darth?" Polly asked.

"With Justin and Kirk. The girls are still out at their grandmother's house. I thought that Natty and I could get a lot done today. I wouldn't have been able to do this without you, though. Tell me, how do you like having pushy neighbors living across the street from you? I'll bet I'm like no one else you know."

"You'd be right there," Polly replied, opening another box. "At least you aren't boring."

Andrea whispered, "Like that poor woman next door? What am I going to do with her? She's scared of her own shadow and she's scaring her little girl, too. That's no way to live."

"Fear is the mind-killer," Polly said.

"I will face my fear," Andrea responded. "I will allow it to pass over me and through me. Where the fear has gone, there will be nothing. Only I will remain."

"No way," Polly responded. "You're a *Dune* fan?"

"Yeah. I'm a fan. Books have always been my haven."

"I was a librarian before I moved to Bellingwood."

"You're kidding me. Really?"

"Yeah. In Boston. When I came back to Iowa, that just wasn't my world any longer. I have books, though. Plenty of books."

95

"My books are in boxes out at Louis and Deb's house," Andrea said. "I haven't had the courage to bring them here yet. I don't know where I'd put them. They'll probably be out there for years before I find a home for them. Maybe I'll hire Henry to build another room or two onto this house. Either that or I'll start kicking kids out when they turn eighteen. What was I thinking having five kids?" Then she laughed. "But look at me talking to you. How many kids do you have over there?"

"More than five," Polly said. "We'll just leave it at that."

They looked up as a minivan pulled into Polly's driveway.

"Who's that?" Andrea asked.

"The girls are home. That's Libby Francis's mother."

"I guess I should introduce myself."

"I'll introduce you. How about that?" Polly put her hand on Andrea's back and walked out onto the driveway.

Kayla, Cilla, and Rebecca got out of the van and turned to see them. Libby's mother backed up and turned, the driver's side of the van facing Polly and Andrea.

"Mary, this is Andrea Waters, Cilla's mother. Andrea, this is Mary Francis."

"Thanks so much for taking my daughter," Andrea said, putting her hand out. "I hope she wasn't any trouble."

"She's a nice girl," Mary Francis said. "We enjoyed having her. Has Polly told you where we live yet?"

"No, but I'll get it before tomorrow morning. We'll be there bright and early to pick Libby up."

"It's good to meet you," Mary said. "Libby has a date with her dentist. I need to hurry."

"Thanks again," Andrea said.

The girls waited until Mary and Libby had driven away, then crossed the street.

"Mom, you look like you fell down and bumped your head," Cilla said.

Andrea rubbed her forehead. "Oh, crap. I did. I need to clean up before your dad comes home. How was your day?"

"Kinda weird. There was this man who, like, watched us from

the stands while we were marching this morning. I swear he looked familiar, but I couldn't see him very well. He had a hoodie on. It was kinda creepy, wasn't it?" Cilla turned to Kayla and Rebecca for affirmation.

"Like?" Andrea asked. "Valley-girl talk on day two of band camp? You can lose that lazy speech right now."

"I'm sorry. But it was still creepy. I asked some of the other people if he was related to them and nobody knew him. I don't want to say that he followed us to Bellingwood, but he might have."

Andrea frowned, then turned to Polly, something dark and frightened in her visage.

"What are you thinking?" Polly asked.

"Nothing. It's nothing."

Nat had come out of Polly's house. He smiled when he saw his sister. "The shelves in the garage fell down on Mom. Polly helped her rebuild them."

Andrea laughed. "What did I tell you? The boy can't keep a secret to save his life. I'll let you go now. I've held you hostage long enough. Thank you for helping me this afternoon and don't worry, I'm good for the hundred dollars."

Polly shook her head. "Are you finished? With all of us we could get those boxes unpacked and on shelves in no time. What do you think, girls?" she asked Rebecca and Kayla.

"We'll help," Rebecca said. "I'm already a sweaty mess. Might as well destroy these clothes for the day."

CHAPTER TEN

Polly finished at Sycamore Inn, and then ran home to let the dogs outside for a few minutes before heading up to Sweet Beans. With Lydia gone for two weeks Polly hadn't spent time with Beryl either. She'd seen Andy a few times while out walking with the dogs, but otherwise, hadn't made much contact. She missed her friends.

She pulled into the driveway at the Bell House and opened the door of Cat's car. It sounded like there were hundreds of kids playing in the back yard. She'd thought Cat was taking the boys off on another adventure this morning, so was surprised to see the Suburban still in place. When she got to the back yard, she grinned. Every child in the neighborhood was here. They'd hooked up the garden hose to a slip and slide along the back fence while another hose went from the pump behind the garage to a sprinkler they'd set near the gazebo where Cat sat out of the sun.

"Polly!" JaRon yelled, running toward her. "It's too hot to do anything else today, so we're watering the yard."

"Are you having fun?"

He nodded and ran away as her other boys gathered around.

"Cat is making us move around so we get the whole yard watered," Noah announced. "She doesn't think the hose will reach around to the other side of the house, though. But that's okay. We shouldn't get the volleyball net wet, right?"

"Whatever she says," Polly replied. "Are you having a good morning?"

He nodded. "We're going swimming this afternoon. Mrs. Waters said it was okay if Nat, Lara, and Abby go with us. I think Rose might get to go, too."

Elijah grabbed her hand. "I asked if we could call some other friends, but Cat said this was enough."

"Isn't it?"

He shrugged. "It's never enough. More is always better."

Nat yelled as he skidded down the slip and slide, careening from side to side. Her boys turned to see what the commotion was and then they were gone in a flash. Polly waved at Cat, who got up to come over toward her.

"It was just too hot to do anything else," Cat said. "Mrs. Waters had the slip and slide. She said she just unpacked it. We have the perfect yard and I thought it would be fine back by the fence line. I didn't want to send too much water into the ground over the tunnel."

Polly sent her eyes heavenward. "I never would have thought about that. Good call. They look like they're having fun."

"Two spigots makes this easy. Aren't you supposed to be having lunch?"

"I was just going to let the dogs out."

"They went inside about ten minutes ago. I wiped them down first. Don't worry."

"I wasn't worried. Thank you for this. Do you need anything?"

Cat wrinkled her forehead. "No. I'm packing everyone up for the swimming pool. We should be good to go."

"You're a natural, Cat. I can't wait to see you in the classroom."

"I doubt it will be just like this, but I'm excited about it. The kids want me to observe their classrooms this year. Do you think their teachers would allow me to do that?"

"Most of the teachers I know at the elementary school would love that. They'd probably put you to work."

"That would be great. Maybe you could introduce me after school starts."

Polly laughed. "I'd be glad to."

A happy scream came from the slip and slide and they both turned to see Rose flying down it, her limbs flailing as the water took her.

"I'd better keep an eye on them," Cat said.

Polly watched a few more minutes and then turned to go back to the car. She wasn't needed here. This idea of having a nanny in the house was wonderful. Or maybe it was just Cat who was wonderful. She saw these kids as her own family and loved spending time with them. As she looked in her rear-view mirror to back out, she saw Andrea Waters waving from her driveway. Polly backed up and turned so she could talk to the woman.

"What's up?"

"I needed to tell you how sorry I was for putting you to work yesterday."

"Sorry? I was glad to help."

"No, I was upset because I'd been stupid and I wanted to get those shelves up before Kirk saw what I'd done. My poor old useless brains saw themselves spilled on the concrete floor and they frightened my weak heart. I should never have done that. Thank you for understanding."

"Andrea, it was fine," Polly replied. "We got the work done, you didn't hurt yourself too badly, and I got to see your garage junk. Now, if you'll let me unpack more of the boxes in your house, I'll know everything about you."

"I wanted you to know that I'm not actually that scatterbrained or pushy ..." She hesitated long enough for Polly to lift her eyebrows. "Okay, I'm a pushy broad. Even I heard the lie. But not when it comes to asking people to help me. Your family has been terrific. I've lived in a thousand places and I've never moved in beside someone who gave my kids a safe place to play. I can't believe that I actually have peace and quiet so I can work. The house is coming together, Kirk is more relaxed than I've seen him in years, and my kids have friends. Thank you."

"I'm glad you've moved in, too," Polly said. "This is going to be fun."

"Or crazy. I'll pick the girls up this afternoon. Who's got it tomorrow?"

"Me again. Stephanie Armstrong's car isn't big enough and she's just started driving again after a bad car accident last year."

"She works for you, right?"

Polly nodded. "Over at Sycamore House."

"Does everyone in town work for you?"

With a waggle of her eyebrows, Polly grinned. "If they know what's good for them. I'm kidding. Henry and I have a several businesses. We like to remodel and restore buildings. He has the skills and I have that wonderful nagging quality he's come to love and adore."

"I'll let you go do whatever you were heading out to do, but I did want to tell you that I'm not quite as crazy as the person you saw yesterday. Believe me?"

"Until you bring her back for an encore," Polly said. She waved as she drove off. It had seemed strange yesterday, but she'd also known the panic that came from everything falling apart on you when you thought you had it all together. Andrea hadn't lived in Bellingwood for a week and her family was scattered in every direction. Even when Polly moved into town, she'd had several months to get her feet under her before the town swept her up into its busyness.

She found a space to park on the west side of Sweet Beans. It was hot today. She'd worked up a small sweat before she got to the front door, but as soon as she opened it, the jangle of the bell and the familiar sights, scents, and sounds greeted her. The air-conditioned air was a nice touch, too.

"Boo!"

Polly turned on Beryl, who had come up behind her. "Why do you do that to me?"

"I don't dare do it to the old ladies," Beryl said. "They might have heart attacks and die on me. We don't want that, do we? Why are you so late?"

"Chatty neighbors."

Beryl turned up her nose. "We don't like those."

"Not chatty neighbors like yours," Polly said. "I have a new neighbor. Deb Waters' daughter-in-law is a hoot. I'm going to love her. She might give you a run for the money when it comes to the crazy."

"Well, now, how am I supposed to like her? I'm the only one allowed to live outside the box in this town."

"She has her own well-defined box," Polly said. "It just happens to be uniquely shaped." She sat down across from Lydia. "You have a tan. I thought you were visiting your family. It looks like you went to the beach."

"No beaches. Just summer gardening," Lydia said with a smile.

"Because you forgot your hat," Beryl said.

Lydia nodded. "I've accused Aaron of packing it up in one of the kids' boxes. I can't find the thing anywhere. When we moved their belongings out of the house, I expected we'd have more room. Nothing has changed. I've driven all over the country depositing box after box on doorsteps and I still have as much stuff as I ever had. It's not fair."

"Move to a smaller house," Andy said. "That did it for me."

"I'm never moving," Lydia replied. "Never. They can haul my dead body out and then set fire to the place. I won't care anymore. But until then, I'm staying put."

"Does that mean we aren't going to move to a retirement community together?" Beryl asked. "I was kind of looking forward to playing pranks on old people."

Lydia clamped her fingers to her thumb in front of Beryl's face. "Hush your mouth. Enough of that. I'm not moving. There will be no more conversation about this. Period. The end."

Beryl slid a glance to Polly. "I just found a new hot button. This is months of free entertainment for me."

"You're horrible," Polly said. "Should we order lunch? I'm hungry."

"This place needs a liquor license and a wine bar." Beryl stood up, then offered Lydia her arm. "Need some help, old lady?"

"I'm not old. There is no retirement home. I will kick your behind into the next county, then kick it back again so Aaron can pick you up and take you home."

The bell on the front door jangled and Polly looked up. "Excuse me," she said. "I'll be right back."

The women behind her were whispering at each other about who had just come in.

"Lissa, how are you?" Polly said, walking over to greet the young woman. "Are you doing okay at the hotel?"

Lissa Keenan nodded and gave her a small smile, relief in her face. "It's been one thing after another. I lost my job last night."

"Why?"

"They said it's because they have too many employees, but Melody told me that my roommate showed up with some of my things and told everyone I'd stolen money from her. I don't know why she's messing with me unless it's because of Bryce hitting on me all the time." She shook her head. "I didn't expect to see you up here. The lady at the hotel said they were looking for baristas. I thought maybe I'd apply here and look for another job, too. I won't stay at the hotel very long, just until I can find someplace to stay." She gave a deep sigh and her eyes shone with tears. "What's going on with me? I didn't do anything wrong."

"Have you eaten anything?" Polly asked.

Lissa shook her head. "I didn't even get supper at the restaurant last night. He let me go and told me I had to leave. I usually get to eat during my shift. I guess I had a croissant this morning in the lobby."

"Let me buy you lunch. Did you ask people about me?"

The girl's eyes lit up. "The lady at the hotel said you were awesome. Well, she said you were really nice and helped a lot of people. But I don't expect anything more. I just came in to see about a job. Might as well see if I can find something since I'm here."

"Have you ever worked as a barista?"

Lissa shook her head. "But it's just learning how to make coffee. I've worked as a server. Oh, you already know that."

They'd made their way to the front counter where Polly's friends were talking to Camille.

Lydia turned. "Who's this?" she asked.

"This is Lissa," Polly said. "Camille, she'd like to apply for a job, but first we need lunch." Polly pointed to the chalkboard with the brightly lettered lunch menu. "I'm partial to their chicken salad, but it's all very good."

"It smells wonderful in here. I forgot how good a bakery smells. My uncle owned one. I used to work for him when I was in high school."

Camille tilted her head as she glanced at Polly.

"What did you do for him?"

"Whatever he needed. But he died and they sold it. Then I graduated and, well … here I am."

"Let Sylvie know," Polly said to Camille with a smile. She pointed at the menu again. "What kind of sandwich would you like?"

Lissa ordered a turkey sandwich and seemed surprised to find herself escorted back to the table with Polly and her friends.

"How do you know Polly?" Andy asked Lissa.

"She kinda …" Lissa stopped, "found me. The lady at the hotel says she's done this before."

Beryl cackled. "That's our Polly. Always looking to find people. Where did she find you?"

Lissa told them an abbreviated version of the meal on Monday evening. Lydia raised her eye when the girl described Polly's dinner companions. Polly shrugged.

"Hi, Polly," Shelly said, coming up behind her.

Polly turned to look up. "Hello, stranger. How's life in the big ole world? Do you miss me?"

Shelly chuckled. "Kinda, but it's fun at Marta's house. She totally needs me to help with her and her dad. Do you care if I stay longer? I told her I'd ask. It's working out good. Mrs. Donovan picks me up in the morning and brings me to work and since Rita comes in the afternoons to help, she gives me a ride back. I'm working tons of hours. It's gonna be great money. Marta says if I save enough, I might be able to buy a car. But first I have to get my driver's license. She's going to help me study for that too."

"You're really digging in," Polly said. "What does your dad say about a car?"

"He says he'd buy it and I should save money for insurance and stuff like that. I don't know what to do. I have all these people telling me things. Who knows what's right? I'm just going to keep working and studying. Marta says I'll figure it out as I go. If you plan too much, things will go awry anyway, so you have to be flexible." Shelly looked around the table. "Are you Lissa?"

Lissa nodded.

"I'm supposed to see if you're finished and then take you back to meet Mrs. Donovan in the bakery. She's looking for more help, too. Maybe you want to work there and up front. I don't want to work up front, so I just work in the bakery. It's a pretty good job. If you worked as a server, you're probably more comfortable with customers than I am." She sent a glance to Polly. "I don't want to meet anyone. Ever."

Lissa swallowed the bite she'd put in her mouth, then took a drink of her water. "Right now's okay?"

"If you're ready. We had a lady hurt herself and Mrs. Donovan is working all these extra hours. She's nice to work for and never asks you to do anything she won't do. Is it okay to take her, Polly?"

Polly looked at Lissa, then pointed at the sandwich. "Up to you. If I leave before you're back, I'll have Camille wrap this up for you."

"Thank you," Lissa said. She picked up her purse and stood to follow Shelly. "This is crazy. Thank you."

"What just happened here?" Beryl asked. She'd barely had time to eat anything on her plate.

Polly laughed. "I don't even have to rescue them anymore. All I do is bring them into Bellingwood and the town does the rest."

"But she can't stay at the hotel forever," Andy said.

"She can stay for a few more days. That won't hurt anyone."

"What do you know about her?"

Polly took a breath. "Just that she was living with a rotten roommate who kicked her out with no notice. There's every probability that she's one of those girls who doesn't have a firm grasp of life and when things can go wrong, they will. I don't know where she's from or why she was in Ames, except that she wanted to go to school there. She has no money, but she does have a car."

"What's the license plate on the car say?" Lydia asked.

Polly glared at the woman. "I don't know. That seems like an obvious clue though, doesn't it?" She laughed. "Why didn't I think of that?"

"You might be a private investigator," Beryl said, "but Lydia's been married to the sheriff for a long time. She's got the goods."

"I don't suppose it matters," Lydia said. "I'm just being snoopy. Why should I care where she's from?"

"Sometimes we can't help ourselves," Andy said. She turned on Polly. "Speaking of being snoopy. You met Lissa when you were having dinner with who?" She looked at Beryl and Lydia. "Who? Whom? Which?"

Lydia laughed. "Grammar or information. Which is more important?"

"Information," Beryl said, turning to Polly. "Jeff was on a date? You and Henry went with them?"

"How did you know it was Jeff?" Polly asked. "Or a date?"

Beryl nodded toward the kitchen. "I assumed it was you and Henry. She said you were with your assistant and his date. That's enough to get my curiosity up. Was it Jeff?"

Polly nodded. "But I'm not talking about it. That story is for Jeff to share."

"Yeah, right." Beryl said. "I guess I won't tell you about Esther Haney's new car because she crashed the old car into a ditch."

"She did?" Lydia asked in surprise. "I didn't know that. Was she hurt?"

Beryl rolled her eyes. "I didn't say it was true. It was just a possible story. You know, to get the girl to talk."

Lydia shook her head. "You're awful. If Polly doesn't think she should tell us about Jeff and his date, that's her business. You know we'll find out sooner or later."

"I like the sooner rather than the later," Beryl said. "What if Esther Haney drives her car over me while I'm walking to my front door? Then I'll never know."

"Who is Esther Haney?" Polly asked, peering at Beryl.

"Busybody neighbor who lives across the street from me. I'm pretty sure she parks her rocking chair just out of sight of the front window so she can watch the neighborhood. I wouldn't be surprised if the woman has binoculars or even a telescope hiding in that house. She knows everything that's going on and she has an opinion about each person who lives within ten miles of Bellingwood."

"She's not that bad," Lydia said. "She's just lonely. Maybe you should cross the street and invite her to lunch sometimes. That would give her something to do."

Beryl blinked. "Are you talking to me?"

Lydia put her hands on both sides of her mouth, opening to an 'O' shape. "What was I saying? I must have lost my mind. But she is lonely. Her kids don't come home often and her last sister died two years ago. She has no one to get her out of the house. What else is the poor woman to do?"

"If I didn't have you all, I might be like that," Andy said quietly.

Scooting her chair around the table, Beryl flung an arm over Andy's shoulders. "You never have to worry, sweat-pea. I'll never allow you to turn into a nosy busybody. I promise."

CHAPTER ELEVEN

Once she realized Lissa's interview with Sylvie was going to be longer than she wanted to wait, Polly took the sandwich up to the counter and asked Camille to wrap it. She also asked Camille to add a second sandwich, bags of potato chips, some rolls and butter, as well as some fruit. She could at least feed the girl this evening. Hoping that things were going well between Lissa and Sylvie, Polly left the bag with Camille and headed out. She could have spent all afternoon with her friends, but Andy was working at the library and Beryl was antsy to get back to her studio. She'd landed more work while traveling with Rebecca this summer and was eager to stay on task.

If Beryl had her way, she'd never leave her studio, except to sleep and cuddle her cats. She loved her friends, but the woman's work was what gave her intense satisfaction. Polly could make no sense of that. Her life was better when she was surrounded by people — lots of people. She was grateful for moments of quiet that landed every once in a while, but even then, all she needed was a few minutes of rest and she was ready to get back at it. Lydia felt the same way. As long as she was with her friends and family, she was happy. But not Beryl. That woman was happier in solitude.

Polly was getting back into Cat's car when her phone rang. Henry. "Hello there, hotstuff. What's my favorite wood man doing today?"

He chuckled. "With a come-on like that, I'll meet you at home in fifteen minutes."

"I'm on my way."

"No, really. Are you busy?"

"I was headed to Sycamore House. What's up?"

"Could you stop by the shop? Hayden's trying to finish the moldings in one of the bedrooms and two were missing from the box. Len found them, but he and Doug have a big job they're trying to finish."

"Sure."

"I'm not stopping you from anything important?"

"If they can wait ten extra minutes, I'll go sign the checks that need to be mailed and then head their way. Will that work?"

"You're the best."

"Don't you ever forget it. How are you?"

"It's not a bad day. Met with Larry Welch. Think we're going to get the contract."

Polly hesitated. This conversation meant that he thought he'd told her about the job. She didn't have a clue as to who Larry Welch might be. "That's awesome. When will it start?" Maybe he'd give her a few hints.

"If the money's approved, we'll dig in two weeks."

"That seems fast."

"They want to be in by the first of the year. This is a big deal for Bellingwood."

Now she was stumped. How had she missed something that was a big deal for Bellingwood? "Okay. I give. I must not have been paying attention when you told me about this. Who is Larry Welch and what job are you bidding on?"

He laughed out loud. "I knew you weren't listening to me the other night. I told you all about it on the way home from dinner in

109

Ames, but your mind was a million miles away. Even when I asked if you'd heard me and you said yes, I knew you didn't mean it."

"I'm sorry," she said. "I'm a horrible wife. Tell me?"

"Larry's a developer out of Ames. There's a group that wants to put up a small retail space out east of town on the highway. It will just be six bays, but they already have three commitments."

"What kind of commitments?"

"I shouldn't tell you. They aren't making any announcements until everything is signed and ready to go."

"Seriously?"

"I'm just that dumb, aren't I. Should've kept my mouth shut in the first place, but this is exciting. If it all goes through, they're also putting another convenience store and gas station out there."

"That would be nice," Polly said. "This one in town is always busy. Luckily Boone isn't that far away. We could use two more of those. So, what are the commitments?"

"Yeah, you didn't let me get away with that. It looks like an upscale bar and grill at one end, a salon/spa at the other end, and then they have a home decor shop that is someone local. I don't know who, though."

"Why wouldn't they come into one of the downtown spaces?" Polly asked. "We have so many left here to fill." She growled. "Always with the new, never with the renovations. These people."

"These people pay me good money," he reminded her.

"Yeah, yeah, yeah," she said with a laugh. "Let me get going and tell Len I'll be there soon."

"Thanks, dear."

"What?"

"I hear other people call you dear and thought I'd try it. That was awful."

"Lydia calls me dear. She's the only who can get away with it. Never say that word to me again. It sounds creepy from you."

He laughed. "I love you, dear." And with that, he ended the call.

Polly swiped to open a text. *Bite me.*

"*Any time*," he replied.

Yeah, that conversation could go south in a hurry. She put the phone on the passenger seat and backed out of the parking space. It never failed. That man made her feel so good, she couldn't help but smile.

She pulled up in front of Sycamore House and waved at Eliseo, who was in the pasture playing with the donkeys and a couple of big red balls. They were bouncing and kicking them around, chasing and playing. The horses were across the creek in the other pasture — she could see Demi through the trees. What a life she'd started here in Bellingwood.

Polly went inside, and before she turned to head into the office, stopped as she heard sounds coming from all over the building. Someone was speaking in the auditorium, the sounds of people laughing came down the stairs and, when the door to the classrooms opened, she heard more talking and laughter in there. She missed being part of the everyday action here sometimes. Then there were the days she was thankful Jeff, Stephanie, and Rachel took care of the problem guests.

She walked through the main door to the office and smiled at Kristen. "Busy place here today."

"It will be like this all week," Kristen said. She pushed a folder across the table. "Jeff ran uptown and Stephanie's in the kitchen."

"This is fine," Polly said. "I need to keep moving." She pointed at a check. "We should just buy a new freezer. This thing keeps giving Rachel fits. Tell Jeff I said so."

Kristen laughed. "Rachel would love you. Jeff says two more months, though."

Polly shrugged. "He's the boss."

"I thought you were." Kristen gave her a knowing grin.

"Funny. He's the one who knows best. How's that?"

"I'm sorry we brought you in for this today. Since you aren't having your staff meeting tomorrow and this one needs to go out tonight, Jeff said to call."

"No problem at all. I kind of like coming over here when it's crazy busy like this."

Kristen looked at her. "I heard the newspaper is getting bought."

The Bellingwood newspaper was the absolute worst. No one paid any attention to it — the thing came out every other week and rarely carried news of interest. It was mostly an advertising piece, but Polly and Jeff refused to have anything to do with it because it was so poorly produced. The editors couldn't spell to save their lives and their grammar was atrocious. It was just embarrassing. The previous owners had operated a small printing shop as well as the newspaper, but the man who bought it the year before Polly came to town, closed the print shop and operated the newspaper with his wife.

"That's interesting," Polly said. "Who's buying it?"

"Somebody from out of town, maybe. Nobody knows who. It's just that Annabelle down there is, like, packing their stuff. I heard they're selling their house, too."

"See what I miss by not working here every day?" Polly asked with a grin.

"There's always something."

Polly put the pen down on top of the stack of checks and pushed it back toward Kristen. "I need to run. I'll see you later."

Kristen gathered the checks and sorted them out into whatever organizational thing she had going on as Polly headed for the front door.

"Polly!"

She turned to see Stephanie walking without her cane. She wasn't walking very fast, but she was doing it.

"Hey there. No cane."

"Yeah. I'm confident here and at home. If I have to go a long way, though, I need it. You were here to sign checks? You can't stay?"

"No, I need to get going. I talked to Skylar yesterday."

"He told me. Thanks for making sure Kayla gets to school for this band camp thing. She says your new neighbor girl is really nice." Stephanie stopped in front of her. "I think she might be a little jealous that what's her name, Cilla? Yeah. That she's living across the street from Rebecca. But I told her that there's no reason they can't have lots of friends. She used to worry about Dierdre and Libby, too, but they're all friends now. It's no big deal. I know we don't have a fancy house like you, but Skylar and I thought that maybe some night you and Henry and Rebecca could come over. After all you've done for us, we'd love to make dinner for you. I wish I could say we'd invite your whole family, but I don't know where we'd put them." Stephanie laughed. "That's a lot of people."

"We'd love to," Polly said. "Just the three of us. I'd like that. You figure out a time when you aren't swamped here and let me know."

"Jeff said he saw you in Ames the other night."

Polly had just put her foot forward to walk away, then stopped in surprise. "Henry and I had an opportunity to go out by ourselves and we grabbed it. We went to that new burgers and wings place on Duff."

"Skylar took me and Kayla there a couple of weeks ago. It was okay. I'd go again."

"That's what I thought." Polly waited just a moment to see if Stephanie would say anything more about Jeff. She couldn't tell whether Stephanie knew he was serious about someone or not. "I need to head out to the bed and breakfast on an errand for Henry. Call or text me about dinner, okay?"

"Thanks, Polly." Stephanie walked away, slowly and steadily. She would probably always walk with a slight limp, but everyone was just grateful she was in good shape.

Polly headed for the shop. When she opened the front door, Len pointed at a box sitting on a work bench. He and Doug were both running machines and the sound in the place was deafening. She waved at him, picked up the box and headed back out to her car. If she hurried, she could get this errand completed and still get home before the kids landed. One or two more hours of quiet and she'd be nearly caught up in the office.

As she headed north out of town, Polly took a long breath. The hardest part of renovation was this part right here. They were so close to being finished at the B&B, but far enough out that she couldn't get a solid grasp of the timeline. She was tired of this not being done. Not that anyone was slacking off; it was just time to move forward. She'd been sitting on this property long enough. The landscaping was absolutely lush and gorgeous. The outside would be finished in the next few weeks, but there were so many rooms to decorate. She, Jeff, Marie, Judy, and anyone else who wanted to be involved needed to decide on appliances. Lydia would help decorate bedrooms, but there was still plenty of time. Judy wasn't interested in decorating at all. If she needed to, she'd help, but that wasn't one of her talents. Polly couldn't wait to see some of these rooms finished. Then they'd be able to stand in the rooms and talk about wainscoting or wallpaper, paint colors, trims, door and window casings, on and on. Yeah, she hated this in-between part. She was ready to get moving.

Dick Mercer was sitting on the steps of the front porch with a glass of something in one hand. He stood when Polly drove in, then came down the steps and approached her car.

"Are you waiting for me?" Polly asked, after she rolled the window down.

"I told those boys that I'm an old man and I needed a break. They work hard." He grinned. "But they're good boys and they're doing good work. I don't have to hardly sit on them at all to get them to do what I want."

"Maybe you should sit on them more often," she replied.

"Betty wouldn't like it. You know she flirts with those young boys, makes them cookies. This morning, she brought over homemade donuts. She's never made donuts for me and I put up with her snoring." He shook his head. "It just isn't right."

"You live a rough life, Dick Mercer."

He tipped his baseball cap. "Yes ma'am, I do. Did you bring us some mouldings? Len cut rosettes for one of the rooms. That's the one I'm decorating."

"You're decorating a room?" Polly raised an eyebrow.

"Yes I am. Pretty rosettes on the door frame and some of Bill's pretty crown molding. I told him we should use the same on a chair rail, but he informed me that until you decided on paints and such, I had to wait. But this room is the Dick Mercer special. I guarantee it will be your most popular room. If it's not, I'll …" He thought for a moment. "I won't do anything. I can't even come up with a good idea. But I figure with all the time I've put into this old place, the least I can do is fancy up one of the rooms."

"Why not more than one?" Polly asked.

He leaned down and whispered. "Because my boring brother-in-law thinks that things should be neat and tidy. Old fuddy-duddy."

"That's where Henry gets it," she replied with a laugh.

"When you take over and start decorating, don't you listen to that man. You do what you want. He gets away with telling me that I have to be careful of things because you might not like them. I'm telling you right now. If you don't like what I do, you take me aside and whisper your concerns. Don't let him know, okay?"

"I promise," Polly said. She unflapped the box with the rosettes that Len had for her. They were beautiful. "But if this is the work you're doing in that room, I'm going to love it."

"Thought you would," he said with a grin. "You're welcome to come in, but it's loud and dusty. It's getting better, but we aren't there yet."

"I'll wait until it's not quite as loud," Polly said. She patted his hand, then handed him the box. "We're going to make this place a glorious success. Even the Dick Mercer room will be successful."

"I know it will, sweet girl. I know it will." He patted the top of her car. "Be careful on your drive home. I like having you around."

She watched him head back to the front porch. He was such a good guy.

Polly drove around the driveway and headed back out. She was going to have some quiet time at the house. Before she turned onto the road, she checked her phone. Cat was taking the kids to the swimming pool, Rebecca was in Boone, Henry was busy, and Shelly was heading back to Marta's house. Not a one of them had any reason to need her. She almost felt a little lost. Strange days.

She laughed as she turned onto the road to head south back into Bellingwood.

If she had to start her new life after Boston all over again, would she still have made the same decisions? She definitely would have married Henry, but she might have allowed herself to do that earlier. She hadn't been prepared to give up her freedom right after she got to Bellingwood. It wasn't like she'd never experienced it, though. Before she met Joey, she'd been free as a bird, enjoying her job and her friends. Why in the world had she ever allowed him to take so many liberties with her? She shook her head. No sense re-hashing things that were long since finished.

As Polly considered each of the people she'd brought into her home, there was no one she'd have chosen to miss out on. She remembered something she'd read about C.S. Lewis and his friends. He not only loved them as friends, but as a group of friends together. He loved the responses and insight that each gave another's conversation. If one were missing from the group, they all missed out on that additional depth. That's how she felt about her family. Each person brought something interesting and unique to the mix and she couldn't imagine living without that. It was hard for her to think about any of them leaving and moving on, but it would happen and new people would come in. Just like Cat.

Because Heath had shown up in her garage one night, Polly got to know him, Hayden, and now here was this wonderful young woman who made it easier for Polly to take care of four young boys who needed so much love and attention. All four had thrived this summer, learning new ways to communicate with each other. Cat took cues from Polly and worked with Caleb on proper speech patterns and how to address people. He still had a ways to go, but she had him reading out loud to his brother at night. He'd come so far.

She drove into her driveway and turned the car off. Then she curled her upper lip. She hated that garage. Not only was it ugly sitting beside their beautiful home and nicely groomed lawn, it was practically useless. They'd build a decent workshop for Henry and Heath, but that thing was coming down next summer, come hell or high water.

Polly waited for her dogs to express their ecstasy at her return. She picked up the mail and walked back to the office, flipping through the junk and the envelopes. Nothing interesting today. She dropped everything on the desk and then went into the foyer and ran up the steps. If she wasn't going out again, there was a comfortable t-shirt and pair of shorts waiting for her. She heard water running and rolled her eyes. Getting those little boys to remember to turn off the faucet in their bathroom was a constant struggle. The cats loved it, but not while everyone was gone.

She was surprised when she opened their bathroom door and the faucets were off. As she turned, she yelped in shock.

"It's just me," Heath said. "I didn't mean to scare you."

"I didn't see your truck." Then Polly realized he was holding his right hand in a bloody towel. "What happened?"

"I'm okay."

"Uhhh." She felt her knees wobble. "Seriously. What happened."

"Polly, are you still with me?"

She shook her head and turned away, stumbling into her bedroom. She was a terrible mom. Heath could bleed to death in front of her and she wouldn't be able to help him. Polly sat down in Henry's chair and dropped her head between her knees. "What did you do?"

"I sliced it on a piece of metal. Rio dropped me off here because it kinda hurt. My truck's in Boone. Hay says he'll take me down to get it later."

"Do you need stitches?"

Heath didn't reply.

Polly looked up, saw the bloody towel and dropped her head again. "Answer me. Do you need stitches?"

"I doubt it."

"Right. Okay. Come with me." She marched out of the room in front of him and without waiting to see whether he would follow, headed down the hall to the back steps. "You'd better be following me, Heath Harvey. I can't look at you, but I expect you to obey."

"I'm right here. Where are we going?"

"You'll see. Keep coming." Polly walked out of the house and across the street. She knocked on the front door of the Waters' house.

"What are you doing, Polly?" Heath asked.

"I'm guessing you need stitches, but before I put you in the car, I'm getting a second opinion."

Andrea Waters came to the door and looked at them, perplexed. "Hi Polly. What's up?"

"This is Heath. He cut his hand. You know that conversation we had earlier? I need you to look at it and tell me if he needs stitches."

Andrea threw her head back and laughed. "Now I love you even more. Come on in. Heath, we're going back to the kitchen. Heck, I can stitch you up myself if need be."

Polly glanced at his face. That scared him. She held back a laugh. "Didn't see that coming, did you? Go on," she said. "I'll just be here waiting for you, not watching you bleed."

CHAPTER TWELVE

"Lord above, that's a bad cut," Andrea said, coming back out with Heath.

He was as pale as Polly had ever seen him.

"He needs stitches?"

Andrea nodded. "I'd say, yes. Should have gone straight to the emergency room. I cleaned it out and wrapped it. Since I need to pick up the girls, I can drop him off and then go back for him."

Polly pursed her lips in thought. "Heath, where did you leave your truck?"

"At that house we're building on the west side of Boone."

"Close to the high school?"

He nodded.

"If you'd take us both, I can pick up his truck," Polly said.

"I'm glad to." Andrea tossed her keys to Polly. "Go ahead. I need two minutes."

Polly took Heath's arm, glad that Andrea had put a new wrap on his hand. "You okay?"

He shook his head and wobbled on his feet. "I think I'm going to puke."

"Not in here, you aren't." She led him to the front door and helped him down the steps. "She made it hurt?"

His eyes rolled up in his head and then he shook it, trying to clear the fog. "So bad. She got right down to business. I thought I was going to pass out."

"Sit on the step here," Polly said. "Put your head between your legs."

Heath obeyed and took in a few deep breaths while Polly rubbed his shoulders.

They were still in the same position when Andrea came outside.

"You okay?" she asked.

Heath nodded and stood up slowly. "Yeah."

"He'll thank you later," Polly said with a grin.

"That is a nasty slice. He'll have a pretty scar to attract tough women." Andrea accepted her van keys from Polly and pressed the fob to unlock it. "You'll need to direct me to the hospital."

Polly walked beside Heath and when she opened the front door, he shook his head, nodding at the back. He had more color, but still looked as if he was holding himself together by sheer force of will.

Once they were in and belted up, Andrea backed out of her driveway and headed for the highway. "Kirk and Justin are at your friend's garage again today," she said. "Justin insists he wants to drive that car to school on his first day. I told him that there isn't a mother out there who would let her daughter get in that thing for a date. I certainly wouldn't."

"It never occurred to me that the car defined the man," Polly said. She gave Andrea a smirk. "Does it, though?"

"Only in his dreams. However, it might have defined his father before the Army tamed him. He liked everything to be fast. His cars, his life, his women. Before five kids slowed me down, I kept up. I don't know what he's going to do when this car is out of the garage, though. He's spent the last year in rehabilitation, every day focused on being independent again. There was always some goal in front of him. Then we had to make the move and that kept him busy. Now he's got the car, but that's short-term. I'd hoped that living close to his parents would help, but after just being here these few short days, I see where he got it. Those two never sit still. If it isn't one thing, it's another. I thought Deb would be a great grandmotherly type of a person. Don't get me wrong, she's wonderful with the kids, but she doesn't have time to watch them day after day."

Andrea took a breath, then turned to Polly. "Do you have any idea how long it's been since I've done things with a woman my age? How long since I've had a girlfriend? I hate to scare you, but the minute I set eyes on you, I knew you were going to be my friend. I hope that's okay. Do you think I'm weird?"

"It's a little weird." Polly grinned when Andrea turned surprised eyes on her. "You asked. How many people in your life have you decided were going to be your friend?"

"None."

"So, it's weird. But it's also perfect and it's okay. I like your family and we're going to have great fun living across the street from each other. I think that us being friends is exactly what both of us have been looking for. We didn't know we needed it, but when it showed up, we realized what we were missing." They'd arrived on the outskirts of Boone and she pointed to the street ahead of them. "Just keep going on this road to the hospital."

At the next stop sign, Andrea turned to look at Heath. "He might be asleep. I don't know how. The pain has to be killing him."

"Not asleep," Heath muttered.

"Will you forgive me for the pain I caused you?" she asked, turning to Polly with a grin.

"Later."

Both women laughed.

Polly focused on guiding Andrea through town and to the hospital emergency room. Andrea pulled up in front of the doors. "Do you want me to wait? I have a few minutes before the girls expect me. If not, I can come back with them and we can take you over to the truck."

"I can do this by myself," Heath said.

"If you have a few minutes, let me take him in and start the check-in process," Polly said. "They'll probably make him wait and the last place I want to be is in the room with him while they stitch him up."

"Please, no," Heath said. "You'd pass out, fall, and bump your head. I don't want to explain that to Henry." He opened the van door.

Polly nodded. "Neither do I."

"Just come tell me if I should stay or go." Andrea pointed to a parking space. "That is my parking spot. There are many like it, but this one is mine."

Even Heath laughed out loud at that one.

"I'll be right back," Polly said.

She walked beside Heath as they entered through the main doors. A woman behind the counter glanced at them and returned to her work. Polly shook her head. Always so busy. The two stood, waiting, until the woman looked back up.

"My son has cut himself and needs stitches," Polly said.

The woman pushed a clipboard to them. "Fill this out. Bring it back."

"Good thing you didn't cut off a limb," Polly said to Heath. She'd filled these forms out more often than she liked to admit, so hurried through it and, motioning for Heath to stay where he was, returned to the counter.

"We'll call him," the woman said.

Polly put on her nicest, warmest smile. "Thank you. I appreciate it." When she returned to Heath, she said. "They'll call you." Then she pointed at a door. "From there. If you aren't here when I get back, I'll just wait. Send someone out for me if they admit you."

He looked at her in shock. "What?"

"Well, you know, just in case they discover that you're missing half of your brain or something." She bent over and gave him a quick hug. "It will be fine. You'll get stitches. They'll give you a pill to make the pain go away and some antibiotics. You've had a tetanus shot, so no worries there. Can I have your truck keys? I'll be right back."

He nodded, then tried to reach into his pants pocket across his body with his good hand. He looked at her pathetically and stood up.

Polly reached in and took the keys from him. She couldn't help herself and gave him another hug. "You'll be fine. I won't take long."

She headed for the door and turned back. Her big, grown boy looked so young and small sitting there by himself, cradling his hand. She hated to leave him, but she'd be back. There was no way she dared sit in the room while they stitched him up, so this was just as well. If they'd only taken him right in, she wouldn't feel bad about leaving.

With a quick shake of her head, she went through the doors and back outside to Andrea's van.

"How is he?" Andrea asked.

"He's a nineteen-year-old boy and yet I feel like I left my toddler alone in that waiting room with no one to protect him."

"I doubt if you'll ever get past that. How long has Heath lived with you?"

"Three years? Four years?" Polly shook her head. "Time goes by so fast. One minute I was a single girl, looking for a place to call home, and the next I was married with kids coming out of every nook and cranny." She pointed again. "You'll want to turn here." Then she laughed. "I have no idea where you're taking me. Let me call Henry. Just head up here and turn left at Mamie Eisenhower. At this point, I'm aiming for the high school."

Polly took out her phone and placed the call.

"Hey there," he said. "Have you seen Heath?"

"You mean my poor little boy who is sitting by himself in the emergency room? Would you tell those developer friends of yours that we need an emergency clinic in Bellingwood?"

"I'll get on that. He was hurt that badly?"

"I can't be sure," Polly said.

He laughed. "You didn't look at it?"

"No, I made Andrea do it. That's why I'm calling you. She drove us to Boone so I can get his truck, but I don't know where I'm going. Where's the house you're building down here?"

"You're at the high school?"

"Almost." She pointed at the street where she wanted Andrea to turn north.

Henry gave her directions as well as the address, and then asked, "How bad was the cut?"

"How bad was it?" Polly asked Andrea.

"It was deep and long. I saw muscle."

Polly shuddered and swallowed. "How about I don't talk about this with you now," she said to Henry. "Okay?"

"Got it. Bad enough. I'll see you later."

"You don't do blood, do you?" Andrea said when Polly put her phone back in her pocket.

"Not if you want me to remain upright. I'm glad you were available. I'm not sure what I'd have done."

"You'd have managed. You're a mom."

Polly pointed at Heath's truck and her heart sank. She hadn't driven this thing since the day Joey and his serial killer friend had stolen it. She'd sworn to never drive it again.

"What's up?" Andrea asked.

"That's the truck," Polly said.

"I assumed. New construction. Lone pickup. But you reacted."

"It's my old truck. A serial killer stole it from me and posed girls in it trying to get my attention. I swore I'd never drive it again."

Andrea stopped beside the pickup, then turned slowly to look at Polly. "I'm sorry, what?"

"You heard me. Life in Polly Giller's world can be scary. I'm warning you. That friendship you think is such a great idea? I'm not your normal girlfriend. I know Deb has to have told you about me."

"She said something, but it sounded so ridiculous."

"That I find dead bodies? Not so ridiculous. That psycho killers tend to end up in my periphery? Again, not ridiculous."

"And you're okay with that?"

Polly shrugged. "I don't have a choice. I can either lose my mind or deal with it. People need to know that their loved ones have been found. I do the finding. Better me than anyone else, I guess. I don't melt down, I don't scream, I don't throw tantrums. I just call my friend, the local sheriff."

She didn't want to drive that truck, but there was no other choice. It was only a truck. It didn't carry any memories itself, they were all in her head and she could manage those as well as she managed everything else.

"Can I help you?" Andrea asked.

"No. Just steeling myself. In my head, I know that it's just a truck." She gave herself another shake. "I'm good. Go get the girls. Tell Rebecca we'll be home after a while."

"I'll keep an eye on them. You're sure?"

"I'm sure."

"What about I wait until you get that thing started."

Polly opened the door and stepped out of the van, then turned back and smiled. "Thanks. I'll be fine, though."

She made her way over to the truck and opened the front door. It smelled like Heath. He'd put in new seat covers and she smiled at his coveralls and boots in the passenger seat. This wasn't her old truck. It was his. With a wave at Andrea, she climbed in, adjusted the seat, put the key in the ignition, and started it up. She really was fine. Hopefully Heath would be nearly finished when she got back to the hospital and they could head home. Tonight, he would get whatever he wanted for supper.

~~~

As Polly and Heath drove through Boone, Polly ended up pulling over when sheriff's vehicles roared past her, sirens whining and screaming.

"I wonder what happened?" she asked.

They'd gotten to the north end of town when she saw more emergency vehicles.

"That's kinda weird," he said. "I hope it's no one we know."

"I'm not there," Polly replied. "At least no one has died."

"Yet."

"Stop it. They gave you a pain killer. You're high."

He chuckled. "Not really, but that's okay."

"How are you feeling?"

"About the same as the last three times you asked. I'll be all right."

She shot him a glare. "Fine. I was going to offer you your heart's desire for supper. We'd even go out if that's what you wanted. I'm taking it all back."

"I don't need anything special. I was the one who hurt myself. It isn't like I rescued puppies."

Polly laughed out loud. "You can still have whatever you want. The little boys will need to hear all about your afternoon, too." She slowed as she came upon the emergency vehicles. "I wonder what happened."

As she started to go around, she slammed the brakes on and threw the truck into park.

"Isn't that Mrs. Waters' van?" Heath asked in shock. He opened his truck door.

Polly was already out. She ran across the highway where she found Stu Decker walking Rebecca up and out of the ditch. Tab Hudson was with Kayla and Libby Francis.

Rebecca looked at Polly, her eyes wide in surprise. "I was just thinking about how I wished you were here. Are you real?"

Polly looked at Stu. "Is she hurt?"

"I don't think so," he said. "The driver is banged up, but the girls are all fine. They're just a little unsteady. They had a wild ride."

"What happened?" Polly asked.

Rebecca looked at Stu and when he released her, she ran into Polly's open arms. "It was awful. Somebody tried to run us off the road. Mrs. Waters was awesome. She just kept trying to slow down, but then he'd weave in front of her, cutting her off. He did it over and over. Finally, he smacked the front of the van really hard. She was on the shoulder and lost control. We went into the ditch. The asshole drove down and smacked her side of the car again, but then he drove off. I called 911 when it all started."

"Good for you. Did any of you see the driver?"

Kayla came over to them and Polly pulled her in as well.

"He had a hoodie on and we couldn't see his face," Kayla said.

"How are you doing, Libby?" Polly asked.

Libby's face was white and she shook where she stood.

"Can I put them in my truck?" Polly asked Stu.

"Why don't we let the EMTs check them. I don't think there's anything wrong, but I want to be sure. Can you pull your truck over?"

Polly looked back. "Oh. Yeah. We need to make some calls, too. Do you girls all have your phones?"

Libby nodded.

"Call your mom, Libby. She should be here."

Libby nodded again and allowed herself to be led to the ambulance.

"Rebecca, make sure she calls. I'll be right back."

She heard Rebecca asking Heath about his hand as she got into the truck to pull ahead of the accident. They were close to a farmhouse, so Polly pulled in and sat in her truck, taking deep breaths. A woman came out of the side door and waved at her.

Polly opened the truck door. "I'm sorry. I won't stay long."

"Do you know the folks in that accident?"

"My neighbor was driving my daughter and some friends back to Bellingwood from Boone. They were run off the road."

"I heard the commotion, but didn't get upstairs from the basement in time to see what happened. I called 911. Is everyone okay?"

"Yes."

"Was it a drunk driver, do you suppose?" the woman asked.

Polly shook her head. "I don't know. They're still trying to get information out of the girls."

"If you need someplace safe for the girls to sit, they're welcome here. I can put up a pitcher of lemonade in just a flash."

"Thank you." Polly took out a business card. "I'm Polly Giller."

"Why, yes you are," the woman replied. "I met you at one of the Christmas events in town. You own that Sycamore House, don't you? Aren't you involved in that coffee shop they put downtown? I keep telling Harold that we need to check it out. He gets busy, you know. We don't just flit into town like we used to. I've got my little business in the basement. I paint ceramic pieces and sell them online. It's not a big business, but it keeps me busy and adds a little something extra to the bottom line. Maybe one of these days I'll get out and stop in for coffee."

Polly smiled and looked back toward the hubbub on the highway. Cars were slowing, people were gawking, and she'd managed to find herself a very talkative new friend. "Do you have a business card?"

"I do," the woman said. "Millie Tempel. I'll go inside and get one for you."

"I'm going down to check on my daughter. Just put it on the seat of the truck. Thank you for letting me park here."

"Anything I can do to help," Millie replied. She put her hand out. "It's very nice to meet you, Ms. Giller."

"And you, too." Polly shook the woman's hand, then headed back down the highway. Now she had two kids to worry about tonight. Well, four kids and a neighbor, but who was counting?

CHAPTER THIRTEEN

Looking toward the accident as she walked, Polly saw that two more sheriff's department vehicles had joined the chaos. Deputy Will Kellar was directing traffic and Polly's friend, Tab Hudson, was talking to the four high school girls.

High school girls. Just thinking about them being in their second year of high school was enough to give Polly the willies. No. She wasn't thinking about that right now. She needed to focus on the matter at hand.

Heath was standing off to the side and as Polly walked over to join him, she realized that Cilla Waters had turned herself so she could glance at him whenever she wasn't being asked a direct question.

"You have an admirer," Polly whispered.

He frowned at her. "What?"

"Cilla."

"Stop it. She's Rebecca's age. That would be like dating my little sister."

"I'm not saying you should do anything about it. Just bask in the glow."

"You're weird."

She laughed. "You've told me that before."

Tab walked over to Polly, followed by the four girls. "What are you doing here? Everyone is alive and safe."

"That's right," Polly said. "I had nothing to do with this. Heath and I were headed back to Bellingwood, and we realized the car in the ditch belonged to Andrea, which meant my kids were in it. I stopped. Do you have any idea who did this to her?"

"The description of the vehicle is similar to a truck that was reported stolen, so for all we know, it could be the second cousin to the man in the moon. The girls didn't see anything. Let me tell you, when the 911 operator heard that it was Rebecca on the phone, she scrambled everyone. I'm surprised Aaron isn't here yet. Do you have the Suburban?"

Polly shook her head. "Cat has it. She's transporting my other batch of kids today. I'm driving Heath's truck."

Tab scowled. "Seriously?"

"A girl's got to do what a girl's got to do. Especially when her kids need her."

"Unless there's blood involved," Heath said. He held his hand out so Tab could see it. "Had to get stitches. Mrs. Waters drove us down."

"That makes more sense," Tab said. "So, weird question. You aren't involved in anything that could set someone after Rebecca and her friends, are you?"

"What?" Polly asked, her eyebrows rising as her voice went up.

"Look, you're standing right here in front of me. Tell me the last time you were at a crime scene and not involved."

Heath nudged Polly. "Go on. Tell her."

From behind Tab, Kayla and Rebecca both giggled.

"I'm not involved in nothing, no how," Polly said. She leaned to the side to deliver a scowl to Rebecca. "How's Andrea? She's not still in the van, is she?"

Tab stepped to the side and looked down into the ditch. "She's coming up now. She says she's fine, but they want to check her out. The door was destroyed, her airbag went off, and her seatbelt jammed. They went slow just to make sure. I'm guessing they'll insist she go to the hospital."

"What?" Cilla asked. "Mom? I thought she was okay."

"I'm fine, baby," Andrea said from the gurney. "I really am. They're not hauling me away."

"Ma'am," the paramedic said, "we can't be sure of that."

She glared up at him. "Don't make me get all rough on you. I'll let you check me out, but then you're going to let me go home."

He looked at his partner. "She doesn't have to go," the young woman said. "You know that."

Polly walked over to them. "You made Heath get stitches. Are you going to fight them on this?"

"I'm fine," Andrea said. "I didn't bump my head. I ache from the hit, but that idiot didn't make contact with my body."

"You have scrapes and bruises on your face," Polly said. "Apparently you did bump your head."

Andrea glared. "You're not helping."

"I can be all up in your face about this," Polly retorted. "There's very little blood involved. So there."

"Polly," Andrea said quietly as she reached out to take Polly's hand. "I have to go home. I can't leave Kirk alone with the kids. He needs so much from me right now and I'm not asking any of my children to help him. Not yet. He needs them to see him as a strong man. It will kill him to show weakness."

She wanted to tell Andrea that the kids would love him just as much, maybe even more, if he showed them who he truly was, but that wasn't her business. Kirk Waters was likely dealing with post-traumatic stress to the point that making a decision that Polly Giller believed to be best, might not be the best thing for him. All she could do was support the family.

"I'll do whatever you need me to do," Polly said. "If you want me to take your kids overnight, I can do that. We have plenty of room." She chuckled. "We should set a couple of tents up in the foyer and let them have a sleepover."

"Justin and Cilla could help you," Andrea said, almost pleading with her.

"Will you be honest with me about your injuries?" Polly asked. "Tell me if something is wrong? You won't do your husband any good if you push too hard and end up hospitalized anyway."

Andrea nodded. "I'll try. Mostly, I just ignore my own aches and pains. I'm a tough old broad."

Polly squeezed her hand. "Yes you are. Let's get you home and go from there. Hopefully Libby's mom will be here soon to pick her up." She nodded back toward Tab Hudson. "The deputies will want a statement."

"While I waited for them to pry the door open and get me out, I told them everything I know. There's nothing more."

"Tab?" Polly turned to look for her friend. "These are all friends of mine, Andrea."

The woman rolled her eyes. "I guess if you're always in the middle of it, you'd make friends with the local peace officers."

"What's up, Polly?"

"I can't get everyone back to Bellingwood in my truck."

"We'll make sure they get home safe. Stu is gathering their personal items from the van. I can take some of the girls. Mrs. Waters, are you heading to Boone?"

"Not on your life," Andrea said. She put out her hand. "Polly says you're a friend. Andrea is my name."

"Tab Hudson. Are you sure about refusing medical help?"

"I don't need medical help. I swear to you. I just need to ..."

"Relax," Polly interrupted. "They'll bring paperwork for you to sign and then you can get out of here. Tab, Andrea and her daughter, Cilla live right across the street from me. And of course, Kayla is coming to my house."

"I figured that one. A single stop. I like it. How would you like to do this?"

"Rebecca and Kayla can come with me, I guess," Polly said. "I'm not sure Andrea wants to climb up into the pickup."

"Then I'll get to know your new neighbor." Tab shot Polly a grin. "I should probably let her know a few things about you. She needs to be as careful navigating around your life as she was navigating around an idiot driver today."

Andrea sat up on the gurney and winced. She glared at Polly again. "I'm fine. Where's that paperwork I'm supposed to sign?"

~~~

Polly, Henry, Cat, and Hayden sat at the island in the kitchen listening to the sounds of laughter, squealing, giggling, and yelling come from the foyer. The doors were all propped open and the noise was intense. Rather than cook, they'd ordered pizza. Polly marveled at how often she could feed that to her kids and they never tired of it. She'd asked Rebecca and Cilla to take charge of the younger kids. They weren't thrilled with the idea, but no one complained. Cat looked exhausted, but part of that was just from being outside in the sunshine all day today. Her normally brown skin had darkened quite a bit this summer, only adding to her beauty. Because Hayden spent so much time indoors working on the bed and breakfast, the contrast in their skin color was much more pronounced than usual.

"Heath isn't going to have any trouble with his hand, is he?" Hayden asked her. "I didn't want to ask about it at dinner, just in case it was bad news."

"He'll be fine. The metal missed his tendons. It just went deep." Polly grimaced. "I don't want to think about it. Thank goodness Andrea was across the street, otherwise I might have made Heath climb into the trunk to ride down to Boone." She turned on Henry. "I'm telling ya, we need an emergency clinic in Bellingwood. Make that happen."

He laughed and sat back, pointing at his chest. "Me? How am I supposed to make that happen?"

"You have connections with all those developers. Tell them you want one. Now."

"Talk to your buddy, Jeff," Henry replied. "He knows more of the movers and shakers in this town than I do." Then he frowned. "Why don't we have one?"

"People just figure they'll go to Boone," she said. "I'm tired of taking little things to Boone. Doctor Mason is a great doctor, but he's so busy nowadays, he can hardly find time to see the kids for their annual physicals. I keep telling him he needs to bring on a partner and expand his practice. It's like it doesn't even register. The man still behaves as if Bellingwood is dying rather than growing, even with the increase in his business." She shook her head. "Sal should ask her father if he knows of any young doctors who would like a small-town practice."

"And leave Boston?" Henry asked. "Not likely."

"The two of us came to Bellingwood. Why wouldn't a young doctor want this life?"

"Because the money wouldn't be the same as in Boston?"

Polly nodded. "And neither would the stress." She took another slice of pizza from the box in front of her and nibbled at the end. "I'm not hungry. I should go across the street and check on Andrea and Kirk. It scares me to death that she got a concussion today or something even worse and refused to admit it. I made her promise to be honest with me, but I don't know if she was." She looked around the kitchen. "What could I take over that they might need?"

Cat laughed out loud. "This is what I love about you, Polly."

"What?"

"I would never say that out loud."

"Say what?"

"That I was looking for something so I could surreptitiously check on them. I'd dream it up all on my own and try to get away with it without anyone else knowing. Not you. You just say it like it is."

"If I were going to say it like it is, I'd just walk over and tell her I was checking on them." Polly turned to Henry. "Come on. You're going with me."

"Me? Why am I involved?" He was already standing up from the stool. "I swear. The things I get into because I'm married to you."

She winked at him and took his hand. When they got outside, she started laughing out loud.

"Now what?" he asked.

"You get into me," she said, snorting with laughter.

"What?"

"You said, 'the things I get into because I'm married to you.' You get into me. Get it? I couldn't say anything in front of the kids, but I thought I was going to choke."

He shook his head. "I have no words for your dirty mind. So what's our excuse for visiting?"

"Just checking on them. Andrea bumped her head. I want to make sure she'll live through the night. It's my prerogative as a nosy neighbor."

"And we don't even have a casserole."

"I know, right?"

They heard a deep bark as they walked up the sidewalk.

"That's what we'll offer," Polly said.

"What?"

"To walk Darth."

"Didn't the boys do that before supper?"

"You wouldn't expect to go all night long before using the bathroom, would you?"

"I could."

Polly shook her head at him as she reached for the doorbell.

The inside door opened and Kirk was there in his wheelchair. "Polly. Henry. Is everything okay?"

"I just wanted to check on Andrea," Polly said, her hand on the handle of the screen door. "How's she feeling?"

Kirk rolled back and gestured for them to come in. "Things are still a mess. I'm sorry. I can't believe how chaotic life has been. We've lived here a week and can't seem to get through the boxes. Who has time? And now this. Andrea is fit to be tied. She's never taken so long to get a house in order. But then, this house needed more work than others, too." He frowned. "I figured she'd hear you. She's just back in her office. Andrea?" he called out.

"Right back here?" Polly asked, pointing to the room she was sure had been turned into Andrea's office. "You talk to Henry about cars. I'll check on her." Polly slipped past him and walked down the hallway.

"Andrea?" she asked softly. "Are you in here?"

She was sure she heard snuffling, so she tapped on the door. "It's me. Polly. Can I come in?"

"Just a minute."

Polly didn't want to wait, but she exercised patience and soon the door opened. Andrea grabbed her arm, dragged her in, and closed the door. "I don't want him to know I've been crying."

"Oh, honey," Polly said. She reached out to hug Andrea, but the woman backed away.

"No. You'll just make it worse. Today was so overwhelming."

"You don't think he'll know you've been crying?" Polly asked. "Have you looked at yourself? You look worse than Rebecca does and she's one of the splotchiest weepers I've ever met."

"When Kirk was in the hospital, I used to wait until I got out to the car and then I'd sit and sob for five or ten minutes. After I got it all out, I drove home. The drive usually took about a half hour and by the time I got there, no one could tell I'd been a wreck." Andrea pointed to a pretty little stuffed chair sitting beside her desk. "I'll straighten up in a few minutes."

Polly sat. "Do you mean to tell me that no one in your family has ever seen you cry?"

"Sometimes. When we watch sad movies or things like that, but not when I'm worried about them. Especially now. I've always had to be strong. Kirk's never been around, so I just was. My kids need to know that I can handle anything." She thumped her fist on her desk. "And damn it, I can. I think this is just because I got scared today and I hurt like the dickens. I was so terrified that something awful would happen to those girls. They were all calm and smart. Rebecca was calling 911 even as everything started. Did you teach her that?"

"I didn't teach it to her, but she's been around enough trauma and catastrophes that it's probably the first thing that comes to mind now. And besides, she knows every member of the Bellingwood Police Department and the Boone County Sheriff's Department, some of them as close friends. If she's scared enough and they can help, she knows they will."

"That has to be comforting. For her as well as for you."

"They're just good people," Polly said.

Andrea heaved a shuddering breath. "So are you. I can't tell you how strange it is for me to trust someone like this. I don't do this. Ever."

Polly reached out and put her hand on Andrea's knee. "I'm safe. I promise."

"I know that."

"One of these days I should tell you the story of the day four women in town showed up at my front door and told me they were going to be my friends."

"Here, in Bellingwood? Is that what happens when you move in? You become friendly to the point of insisting?"

Polly laughed. "First of all, you're the one who insisted. I don't know if that's how it works, but it's a good way to live, don't you think?"

"That's one of the reasons I agreed to move back here. Louis and Deb have mentioned it over the years. They hinted that maybe when Kirk retired, he should come back to Iowa. When everything fell apart, we talked about what possibilities we had for next steps. He wanted to come home. When he talked about Bellingwood in such glowing terms, I assumed he was just romanticizing it, especially since he'd spent so long in the military dealing with so many awful situations. You know, remembering only the good. I figured he just needed to think that there was somewhere safe and beautiful when all around him was death and destruction. But I don't know. I'm beginning to think he wasn't making it up."

"Bellingwood is filled with people who aren't very nice. It's just like any other small town. The gossip mills work overtime, everyone knows about your life, and people stick their noses in your business when they shouldn't. But then you get to know them and you listen to their stories and understand the life they've dealt with. You don't have to like their behavior, but if you pay attention, at least it makes sense. There are small towns all throughout the Midwest just like this one."

"And I know there are the same small towns all over the country," Andrea said. "I've just never experienced them for myself. Kirk tried to tell me. And then you showed up."

"Well," Polly said with a laugh. "I have a tendency to do that."

"Yeah, why are you here this evening?"

"Checking on you. I tried to come up with a good reason to visit, but I decided to just own it. I was worried, I wanted to know how you were doing, so I dragged Henry across the street with me. If nothing else, we were going to offer to walk Darth for you."

"I took him out a little while ago. He'll be fine until morning."

"See. I look good and didn't have to do the work."

"How are my kids?"

"Justin is playing a video game with Heath in the family room. Cilla and Rebecca have been put in charge of the mob and the mob is having the time of their lives."

"Your friend, Tab, invited me to join you all for pizza on Sunday nights. She says there's a group of women who meet up town and leave their families to fend for themselves. Is it every Sunday?"

"Whenever we can. There are enough of us now that we don't all show up every Sunday, but yeah. Whenever you want to join us, you can. I know that it's just before the week starts, but by then, there's not much else you can do. Monday is coming whether you like it or not."

"Most of my Sunday nights during the school year are spent making sure that kids have all of their projects done and clean clothes for the week."

"Make Cilla do that," Polly said. "At least once or twice a month."

"We'll see. It would be nice to get out and meet more people." Andrea stood up. "How do I look?"

"Surprisingly normal."

"Thanks. I think." She touched her forehead. "How bad is the bruise?"

"Red and bumpy." Polly reached for Andrea's cheek. "That cut looks like it should have a stitch or two."

"Whatever. Scars make me look strong."

"I think you're strong enough. Are you sure you don't hurt anywhere else?"

"I ache. I'll probably moan and groan when I get out of bed in the morning. Now I just need to figure out what we're going to do about a vehicle. Deb said we could borrow hers until we get this handled. It's just always something."

"Let me know if I can help. I'm taking the girls to Boone again tomorrow morning, so I'll talk to you when I'm home."

"Thank you again, Polly. I promise to be back to my normal acerbic self real soon."

CHAPTER FOURTEEN

"You're late." Sal waved at Polly from a booth at Sweet Beans. "I'm running out of time. Mrs. Dobley has already been with the kids for an hour. I told her I wouldn't be gone long."

Polly tipped her head. "Did I know we were meeting?"

Sal grinned and pointed at the bench across from her. "No, but you always show up on Thursday to take Shelly to her appointment. And you always give yourself enough time to drink coffee and have a muffin."

Polly grimaced. "I'm that predictable?"

"Yeah. Isn't it boring?"

"You have no idea. That scares me enough that I'm going to change up my patterns. I can't have this." She slumped her shoulders. "But I really want coffee and a blueberry muffin. I'll change things up tomorrow. How are the boys?"

"They're good. I want to hear about your new neighbors. What are they like?"

"You've already heard about my new neighbors? How?"

"I don't know. It might have been Mark or maybe it was somebody talking about it here." Sal leaned in and lowered her voice. "I heard she's a real loudmouth and he's totally whipped. He lost a leg in combat and she won't let him out of her sight. They have five kids and the oldest is this punk who drives a fast car and the next one is a snotty high school girl. There wasn't much they had to say about the three youngest kids."

Polly nodded slowly. "That's about right. Just a sec, I need to get my coffee."

"Wait. I'm right about this?" Sal jumped out of her seat to follow Polly to the counter. "I figured you were going to tell me that it was all gossip and they were a sweet and wonderful family. Or maybe you don't know them yet. Have you even met them?"

"I just want a large iced coffee," Polly told Gayla. "And one of the blueberry muffins." She smiled at Sal. "I said that you were right. Doesn't that make you happy?"

"You're messing with me."

"Wait. You didn't hear that the woman had Rebecca in her van yesterday and ran off the road? Maybe she drinks. Maybe that's what happened. She nearly killed Rebecca and Kayla and their other friend, Libby Francis."

"Did that really happen?" Sal asked, her mouth agape. "She nearly killed your daughter and you're standing here all calm? Tell me you took her out."

Polly smiled at Gayla when she handed her the glass of coffee and a plate with the muffin on it.

"Of course I did," Polly said.

"I knew it. I knew you wouldn't put up with that crap."

Sal followed Polly back to her seat. "So, you've met her."

"Uh huh."

"And you let your daughter get in her car?"

"Uh huh." Polly started to peel back the paper wrapper, then grinned up at Sal and patted it instead. "I love these muffins."

"You're messing with me."

"Uh huh."

"Why would you do that? You know I don't get enough adult interaction. Two dogs, two little boys, an old lady, and a husband whose good looks are only surpassed by his talent for falling in cow crap. That's what I have to stimulate my mind. I need to live vicariously through someone. It might as well be you."

Polly frowned. "Do you even hear yourself? This is not the Sal Kahane I know and love."

"I know." Sal bowed her head in shame. "I couldn't believe those words came out of my mouth even when I was speaking. I need to get out of town. Just for a day. I need to go out with people my own age and do exciting things, even if those exciting things are shopping for baby clothes and school supplies."

"School supplies?"

"Yeah. The PTA is looking for people to adopt a classroom. Sounds like there are some kids who need extra help with their lists. Your flute-playing friend, Jeanie Dykstra, was in here talking to her sister-in-law and a bunch of the ladies from the quilt shop the other day about it. I told them to sign me up. I can either order it all online or I could beg you to take me shopping."

Jeanie Dykstra and Polly had first gotten to know each other when they played together in the summer band a few years ago. Jeanie was also the boys' piano teacher. Her sister-in-law, Jen, opened the quilt shop next door to Sweet Beans. Polly never ceased to be amazed at how small her little town really was. Everyone was connected to everyone else.

"We can go to Ames any time you want," Polly said. "Why don't you ask Rebecca and Kayla to babysit if you don't want Mrs. Dobley to spend a whole day with the boys."

"She's fine. She'd love to spend the day with them. Alexander adores her and that woman can get Theodore to sleep like no one else, even me. There have been a few nights that I almost called her at two in the morning to ask her to come over. Mark won't let me."

"You love your boys."

"Yes I do. Absolutely. But I'm ready to be a person for just a few hours."

"A person?"

"A not-a-mommy person. I don't want to do it very long. Only a few hours."

"You decide when you can escape, and we'll go to Ames. We'll eat at an adult restaurant and go to adult stores and you can buy things for your babies."

"Now, tell me about your neighbor. Did she really have an accident with Rebecca in her car?"

"Yeah. Someone tried to run them off the road. Rebecca says that it was because Andrea was such a good driver that nothing bad happened. They were all fine."

"Andrea? That's her name? Like your friend in Boston?"

"I know," Polly said with a smile. "You're the only person that put that together."

"The girl with the gorgeous brothers. I'll never forget her." Sal grinned. "Or her brothers. Tell me more about your neighbor, though."

"She is a loudmouth," Polly said. "She's the sassiest, brassiest woman this side of …" She chuckled. "… you. She raised the kids herself because Kirk was gone so much, so she's tough. She's bright and well-read, her kids are interesting and funny, she's having to come to grips with a new life where her husband isn't the big, strong soldier but now has post-traumatic stress and is missing a leg. They moved off military bases where she was comfortable in how things worked to a small town hundreds of miles away from anything familiar. They're fitting seven people into a house that's probably built to house four or five, and neither of them leave the house to go to work. His parents live here in Bellingwood, so at least she has that support system."

"Who are his parents?"

"Louis and Deb Waters."

"I know them."

Polly peered at her.

Sal waved her off. "I know people."

"Their oldest daughter, Cilla, is full of spit and vinegar."

"That's not what you wanted to say."

Polly laughed. "It's polite. She's fantastic. I hope that she and Rebecca become good friends. She is bright and confident and she'll challenge that girl of mine."

"Rebecca needs that."

"No kidding."

"How old is Andrea?"

"Hmm," Polly said. "Justin is maybe seventeen. She's probably our age or a little older."

"Do you think she'd want to go shopping?"

"With us?"

"Yeah. Will I like her?"

"You'd better."

"When can I meet her?"

"Tab invited her to come to Pizzazz on Sunday night. Is that soon enough?"

"You're going to make me wait until Sunday? We should go out to dinner. Invite the Mikkels's. Invite Sylvie and Eliseo. Invite Tab and JJ. Heck, we could do dinner at Davey's and then go over to Secret Woods later. What about Saturday?"

Polly's first thought was to say no. She didn't know if Kirk would be prepared to do much with people in town, but then she stopped herself. That wasn't her deal. If they didn't want to go, they'd say so. And besides, he already knew Nate and Henry. Mark was easy to talk to and JJ was, well, JJ.

"Sure. I'll ask her," Polly said. "Maybe we should have a party at the house."

"Look. I want to meet them, but even more, I want to do something fun. Please?"

The pleading look on Sal's face made Polly laugh. "Absolutely. I'll talk to Henry and then I'll ask Andrea if she'd like to meet some of my crazy friends."

"Do you suppose she drinks coffee?"

"Yeah, why?"

"Because you need to bring her up here, too."

"I should always ask," Polly said, "But if she works from home during the day, I suspect she won't be quite as flexible as you and I are about it. She might actually be committed to working full-time."

"That's rubbish. Flexibility is a good thing."

"So is respecting someone's boundaries."

"Because you're so good at that."

"I try," Polly protested. "Give me a break."

Shelly took that moment to walk up to their table. "Hi, Polly. Hi, Mrs. Ogden."

"Is it that time?" Polly asked.

Shelly nodded.

"The car's out front. I'll be right there." Polly stood up and crossed to Sal's side to give her a hug. "Ask Sylvie about Saturday night. I'll call Joss and Tab."

"You don't want to talk to Sylvie?"

"You're right here," Polly said. "I've got to go." She grabbed up her coffee and headed for the front door, thankful that she didn't have to explain how uncomfortable things had gotten with Sylvie since Andrew and Rebecca had broken up. Both tried to act as if nothing was wrong, but at the same time, neither was ready to confront reality. The thing was, all of the adults were just as thankful that the two weren't going to have a chance to get hot and heavy with each other. They needed to be older.

The loss of that friendship was the most difficult. Andrew was either being a jerk or, more likely, he had no idea what his behavior was doing to Rebecca. There was no way they could have avoided this situation. Telling the two kids not to allow their friendship to grow into a relationship was ridiculous. Telling them they couldn't break up was even more ridiculous. Helping them figure out how to be friends again was going to be difficult and it might take more than a few months or even a couple of years. This stuff gave Polly a headache.

She got in the car and patted Shelly's knee. "I miss you. How are things at Marta's house?"

"I love it there," Shelly said. "We study every night. She says she's learning things, too. And she's remembering things she learned forever ago. One night we sewed. I learned how to sew, Polly. Last night, she showed me how to cut fabric out to make a quilt. She says that if I make a nice quilt top, she'll help me quilt it before Christmas. And she also told me that if you agreed, she'd teach me how to drive so I can get my driver's license. Could we go get me a learner's permit sometime?"

"Of course we can," Polly said. "You're having fun."

"Marta says it's nice to have someone with energy in the house again. It's just been her and her dad for so long that she forgot what it's like to talk to a real person at night. She either sews or hangs out online. Since I'm there, she's sewing, but having fun, too. Do you care if I stay for a little longer? I'm really helping her."

"That's fine. I'm glad you're having fun."

"Don't get me wrong. I love your family, but it's always so busy and crazy there. Sometimes, Marta and I just sit in the quiet and work. I study or take practice tests and she sews or reads. She loves to cook and bake, too. I learned how to make a German Chocolate cake the other day. It's different than with Sylvie. This is like, personal baking. We baked the cake in two pans. One for us and we took the other one to her neighbor, an old guy who lives by himself. Marta kind of takes care of him, too. He doesn't have Alzheimer's like her dad, but she keeps an eye on him."

"That's wonderful, Shelly. You stay as long as the two of you are okay with it."

"Lissa started working this morning."

"She did? That was fast."

"Mrs. Donovan said we needed someone right now and as long as she was ready to work, she might as well."

"How's that going?"

"She's pretty good. When I started, I didn't know anything either. Mrs. Donovan has to be patient. But when I listen to her tell Lissa things, it's like I'm learning it again. She's said a couple of things that I'd forgotten she told me. Lissa says she doesn't know where she's going to live. Maybe if I stay with Marta, she could come live with you in my old room."

"Let's not make any decisions about that right now," Polly said. "You didn't mention that, did you?"

"Oh no," Shelly said. "I wouldn't say anything. I don't even know how long Marta wants me to stay there. I just thought it would be nice for her."

"We need to wait and see," Polly said. She pulled into the driveway of a home on the north side of Bellingwood, not far from the baseball fields. It had been a purely serendipitous find for Grey and Nan. A big old house with an exterior entrance to a second-floor apartment as well as a walk-out finished basement. Nan was living in the apartment and Grey had his office set up in the basement. He hired Henry to put a sidewalk along the side of the house and planned to cover it at some point. If the weather was awful, his clients could always enter through the main door, but he was hoping to avoid that as much as possible.

Nan was working outside in a small garden she'd planted when they moved in several weeks ago. She looked up and waved when Polly parked the car. "Hi there. Shelly, you can go on around. Grey's waiting for you."

Shelly bounced off, light on her feet.

"She looks happy," Nan said. She tugged the gloves from her hands.

"I think she is," Polly replied. "How are you?"

"I'm good. Grey told me that I'm not allowed to sit inside and work all day. I'm under orders to spend at least a half hour every day messing with these plants. He doesn't understand that I shorten their lives every time I touch them. I've called Mom so many times to help me rescue something, she just laughs when she sees my phone number come up."

"How are the two of you liking this house?"

Nan looked up at it. "It's a beautiful old house. I think Grey is happy with his purchase. It feels a little strange having his practice in his home, but that's probably just me. I'm used to office buildings and cubicles. I'm trying to get used to creating my own business without the benefit of noisy secretaries or coworkers, too. It's wonderful, but I never thought of myself as a person who would work from home. If we don't have any clients, I can sit in my apartment and work without even getting out of my pajamas." She grinned. "I could get used to this."

"You're going to get so busy that you won't have time to get used to it."

The young woman nodded. "I hope so. There are some businesses that could use a marketing strategy. Heck, before we know it, I might be the one who needs an assistant. Mrs. Dykstra at the quilt shop called the other day. We're having coffee tomorrow morning. She wants help with advertising and building a website. If we can get her online, she could grow. I met with the owner of Smoking Hot last week. He wants me to design their new menu and expand their website, too. I didn't know so many people needed help with websites."

"What about JJ out at Secret Woods?"

Nan nodded. "I'm working for him as well. He wants to introduce a new line of fruit-based wines next spring, so we're going to build a marketing plan for that. I have plenty of research to do. There are a lot of wineries in Iowa. We just need to find the right place for him to land with the new wines."

"It sounds like you're digging in."

"Can you believe it? Six months ago, I thought I was going to waste away on my parents' ranch. Now I'm living in Iowa and things are taking off." She sat down on the front steps. "I thought I was coming out here to help Grey start his practice. It never occurred to me that it would be a bigger deal than that personally. I'm going to do everything I can for him, but now I see that I need to do my thing for me as well."

"He agrees with that, right?"

"He does. If he needs to hire a manager for his practice, he'll find someone. We're both small enough right now, that isn't a problem. And he's helping me connect with people around town. We're taking care of each other." She chuckled. "Except I need to get better about taking care of his house. That man can't decorate to save his life. You saw his apartment at the hotel. He moved in and just left it like it was. That's what he did here, too. He bought a bed and a dresser, then he bought a recliner and a television set. I convinced him that he needed a kitchen table and chairs. I don't want to push too hard. He's trying to be frugal, but at some point he needs more furniture and to hang paintings on the walls, on and on. He comes up to my apartment for dinner all the time.

That's probably because I've decorated it and it feels homey. Silly man. One of these days I'll be too busy to do that for him, so we'd better get it done now."

"I'm glad you're here, Nan," Polly said. "He needed you to show up and spur him forward. I wonder how long he would have stayed at the hotel."

"He was getting antsy, but yeah, he needed a kick in the pants. I'm glad I'm here, too. It's nice being able to talk to him face to face whenever I want. I feel so free."

"Yeah?"

Nan nodded. "I still shut down sometimes, but nobody in town knows what happened to me except your family and Grey. People don't look at me like I'm a victim. I'm just a person. If they do find out what happened, they see me as I am now, not like when I got home and was a complete wreck. I have a long way to go, but this is a good place to be."

"I'm so glad you're here. Any time you need a girl's view, call me."

Nan stood up. "I will. Oh, and do you want me to take Shelly back to the coffee shop? I have to get some groceries. I could do it then."

"That's not necessary. I can come back for her."

"No, if you don't mind, I'll do this. He doesn't have any more clients until later today, so I can leave for a while."

"Thank you, then," Polly said. "That would be great."

"It's nice to see you."

"Really, Nan. Call any time."

CHAPTER FIFTEEN

Slowing as she drove down Elm Street toward the main part of town, Polly peered at the young man on the sidewalk. It looked like Andrew, but that made no sense. He was supposed to be in Boone at band camp. It was Andrew. He was at least six blocks from home, so she slowed and rolled down the car window.

"Hey there, handsome. Wha'cha doin'?"

He glanced at her, offered a small wave, and kept walking.

She nearly drove off, but decided that one dumb young man didn't get to play games with her. He could get away with messing with her daughter, but she and Andrew went too far back for this garbage. Polly slowed even further to match his pace.

"Yo, Andrew. Whazzup?"

He shrugged, looked straight ahead and continued to walk.

Polly almost choked with laughter. Was he dumb enough to think that he could get away with this?

"People want to know," she said. "Why aren't you in Boone with the rest of the band?"

Andrew gave her another shrug.

"Did you skip out today?" Polly asked. "Does your mother

know? Because I'm just the person to call and check. You do know that, right?"

He hesitated and then nodded as he continued to walk. Polly sped up toward the corner he was approaching, then turned in front of where he would cross the street. She reached over and threw open the car door.

"Want a ride? I have puppies. No wait … candy. I have candy. And air conditioning. Come on, little boy. Don 'cha wanna ride with the crazy lady?" Polly watched his lips start to turn into a smile, but he refused to make eye contact. When he got to the street, he walked around her car.

"Now you're just annoying me." Polly put the car in park, opened her car door and got out.

That threw him. He stood in place when she stepped in front of him, then mumbled, "Excuse me," and tried to continue around her.

"No you don't, Andrew Donovan," Polly said. "I don't know what's gotten into you, but you don't get to behave this way with me. Get in the car."

"I'm busy," he said, still trying to step around her.

"You can try to get past me," Polly replied. "You can try to ignore me. You can try to avoid me. But guess what you can't do?"

He shook his head and started walking.

Polly walked along beside him. "You can't get rid of me. This is a small town, buster. I can find you anywhere."

He whirled on her. "Why are you bothering me? I've got things to do and I'm not interested in having a conversation with you. Leave me alone."

She was stunned enough by his attack that he had time to take off again, achieving some distance between them. It was hot outside and sweat was already trickling down her back. Polly got into the car, checked for traffic, backed out onto Elm Street, and drove down beside him again.

"I don't want to threaten you," Polly said through the open window, "but I expect you to get into this car right now. You know better than to treat me this way. I'm ashamed of your behavior and you should be, too."

Andrew stopped, turned and bent over to look into her car. "Why don't you understand that I have better things to do than to spend time talking to you?"

She had no idea who this was. This Andrew sounded more and more like his father than he did the young man she'd watched grow up. It made her feel sick inside.

"In. The. Car." Polly said. "I don't care what you have to do or who you think you are, but the very last thing in the world you get to do is speak to me this way. Get in this car immediately. Don't whine at me, don't argue with me, just do it."

"Oh, for God's sake," he spat. He stomped his feet as he walked toward her. Wrenching the car door open, he sat down in the passenger seat and crossed his arms. "What?"

"Close the car door."

With a huff and a dramatic shake of his head, Andrew slammed the car door closed.

"Where were you heading?"

"Home."

"Why were you walking?"

"None of your business."

It took everything inside Polly not to scream curses at him, shake him, or even spank his bottom. Though that last was ridiculous, she wanted to do something to shock him, but she knew better. What didn't need to happen right now, though, was to give him permission to escalate his ... whatever it was he had going on. She wanted to react as badly as he was, but she curbed her tongue. It wasn't easy. Man, it wasn't easy.

"Why aren't you in Boone?"

"Prior commitments," he said.

"I see. Your mother knows you're here?"

"Why do you care?" he asked, frowning at her. "It's none of your business. Whatever Mom and I decide is right for me, that's our business. I'm not part of your life anymore, don't pretend that I am."

"What?"

"You heard me."

"You're right," Polly said. "I heard you. But I don't think I understand you. What do you mean that you're not part of my life?"

"I know you and Henry didn't want me dating your precious, wonderful daughter. Now that we're no longer together, at last you don't have to worry about me in your life."

"What in the world are you talking about?"

"Don't try to tell me that Henry and you liked me dating Rebecca. Please, I know better."

"Is that why you broke up with her?"

"That, and it was time for me to see what else was out there in the world. Little Miss Priss Pants and her girlfriends think they're all that and they just aren't. There are other nice girls in our school. I don't need to be tied to one girl. I can date whoever I want. I can be friends with whoever I want. I don't need her and I don't need you."

"Wow," Polly said. "That's a whole lot of mad going on right there. Don't you think you might be overdoing it?"

"Yeah. That's what you always do, try to make it seem like it's all my fault. You and that daughter of yours are just alike. You think you're smarter and better than everyone else. Well, you're not. Neither of you are. I'm my own person. If I want to be mad about something, I can. I don't need your permission, I don't need your approval, and I don't need you to think that you can just talk me out of it."

"Have you talked to anybody about how mad you are at us? Your mom? Jason? Eliseo?"

He blew out a breath. "Whatever. You have them all buffaloed, too. They think you're Polly Perfect. I talk to my friends."

She shook her head. "I don't know that I have ever been quite as disappointed in someone as I am in you right now."

"Is that supposed to shame me? Make me feel all bad about the way I'm talking to you? Like I'm supposed to be so respectful of you or something? I guess what goes around comes around."

"Andrew Donovan," Polly said, grimacing. "What in the world has happened to you?"

"Nothing's happened to me. My eyes have been opened wide. I see through you now, you know."

"Who did this eye-opening trick for you?"

"My friends. People who treat me like I'm a real human being, not some puppet that just goes along with everything they say."

"Do these friends have names?"

"Nobody you'd think is important."

"Actually," Polly said, "if someone is telling you that I'm yanking your chain or disrespecting you or that I'm Miss Polly Perfect, or a liar or any of these horrible things, I do think they're important. How long have you known me, Andrew?"

"Way too long, that's for sure. I can't believe I was so gullible."

"Gullible. I see."

"You've taken in everyone. I don't know how you did it, but you did. But not me. Not any longer. I see you for who you truly are?"

"And who's that?"

"You just want ..." He paused, trying to form the sentence.

"What do I want, Andrew?"

He shrugged. "You want everybody to agree with you and do things your way. It doesn't matter if people see things differently, they have to agree with you."

"Do you really believe that?"

"Yes. It's the truth."

"Whose truth? Who is telling you those things about me?"

"People know these things. There are lots of people in Bellingwood that know about you. You and your family, you're all trying to control this town. You think that if you throw enough money out there, people will just bow to you and do what you want."

"And what good is that going to do me?" Polly asked. She was struggling now. This conversation made her want to cry. Who was corrupting this beautiful young man into thinking such vile things about her? Then she swallowed.

154

"Give you power, so you can hold it over our heads," he said. "You get to do whatever you want in town and no one can stop you."

"Andrew, are you talking to your father?" Polly asked quietly.

"No," he snapped. But the answer came too quickly and he looked away.

"Does Jason know that Anthony is communicating with you? Does your mother know?"

"I'm not. Stop implying that I am."

"Are you lying to me now?"

"See! That's what I'm saying. You think you know everything and if people don't agree, then you accuse them of lying."

"Are you?"

He threw his hands up in the air. "What would be so awful if I was? I'm not saying I am. I have other friends. But why can't I talk to my own father? I should be allowed to see him."

"Of course you should," she said, keeping her voice as quiet and as contained as she could. "Is he the one telling you bad things about me?"

"A lot of people don't like you."

"I'm sure of that," Polly said. "I've made people angry and I've made people jealous. I can't help it if they don't like me because I'm my own person."

"That's not the only reason."

"What else have I done to make people angry?"

"You walk around like you're more important than anyone else. You flaunt your money."

"I do, do I?" she said with a sigh. "While I wear my diamond tiara and designer clothing, ride in my chauffeur-driven limousine and have my butler open the front door to the hundreds of exclusive guests I invite to the house. Oh wait, that used to include you, but now that you've uncovered my hidden motives, you're much too good for me." She put her hand up. "I'm sorry. That was underhanded. After practically living with me and my family for the last five years, you actually believe that I'm as awful as you are saying?"

"I don't think you're as special as you think you are."

"The only reason I'm special," Polly said, "is because of the people who love me. Without them, my life wouldn't be worth anything. You're one of those people, Andrew. I can't understand why you've allowed someone to corrupt your thinking ..."

"No one corrupted my thinking," he protested. "I just finally ..." He flung one hand to the side. "Whatever. I told you I didn't want to talk to you about this. You're the last person I wanted to have this discussion with."

"Have you told your mother how you feel about me?"

"Hell, no," he said, not even flinching at using the curse word in front of her. "She still thinks you're God's gift to Bellingwood."

"Because she's my friend."

"No, because she wants to be like you. To have everything you have. A fancy house, a fancy job, some man. She thinks that's a big damned deal."

"Getting kind of risqué with your language there, bub. I can't imagine Sylvie would let you get away with that."

"She's not around that much anymore to even care. Now that Jason's out of high school, she's busy with everyone else. She doesn't care what I do or where I go. As long as I'm not in her hair, she could care less."

"Couldn't."

"Huh?"

"She couldn't care less. That's the proper use of the phrase."

"Seriously?"

"We've spent five years playing the grammar game, I see no reason to stop now."

He shook his head in disbelief. "You don't get it, do you?"

"What am I supposed to get?"

"I'm done with you. I don't want to play grammar games, I don't want to have a relationship with you. I know who you are and I'm finished with you and your whole family."

Polly turned in the seat to look at him. She reached out to touch his leg and he pulled away, so she put her hand on his shoulder. The boy didn't know what to do with that, but she ignored his discomfort. "Here's the deal. I know who you are, too. This behavior and attitude I'm seeing right now? It's not really you."

When he started to argue, she put her other hand up to stop him. "I understand that you believe this is the real and true you. I don't know who has been feeding you this garbage you're spewing, but if you spend time truly thinking about it with an open mind, and not a mind that is set on finding the bad in me and my family and my friends, you'll discover what truth is. Truth never alienates, sweetie. Truth encompasses people." She smiled. "I have a favorite saying. In fact, I can't believe I haven't found this to put on one of my walls. It's from a man named Edwin Markham. *'He drew a circle that shut me out. Heretic, rebel, a thing to flout. But love and I had the wit to win. We drew a circle and took him in.'* See, you're prepared to shut people out of your life because one man who is angry and twisted and bitter is lying to you. He wants you on his side. He wants you to feel the same anger and bitterness that he feels so he isn't quite as alone."

"You're talking about my dad, but it isn't only him."

"No, but I'm guessing he's at the root of much that you're spouting. Then you managed to talk about it to people who need to feel justified in their own bitterness and jealousy. They jumped right up on your pity party bandwagon."

"Like who?"

"I'm guessing Maddy Spotter."

He recoiled, then tried to recover by shifting in his seat. "What's she got to do with it?"

"You know how she and Rebecca feel about each other. You knew that long before Maddy called once she heard you weren't dating Rebecca anymore, right? Rebecca confided that in you. But Maddy would be the perfect person for you to pour out your frustration and anger at Rebecca. She'd love to hear all of that. I suspect she ate it up and encouraged you even more, saying negative things about us, things that you took in because they justified your own bad behavior."

"She's not a bad person."

"Fine, she's not a bad person. But you are, aren't you?"

"What?"

"You deliberately drove the wedge between her and Rebecca deeper just to serve your own interests. You wanted someone else to be as angry at Rebecca as you are. How many intimate things have you told Maddy about Rebecca? Things that Rebecca trusted you with, things that you know because of the friendship the two of you built over all those years?"

"Maddy is my girlfriend now. She has a right to know about my past."

"Does she have a right to know about Rebecca's?"

"So what if I tell her things? I need to talk about my life to someone. She's the only one who listens to me."

Polly snapped her finger at his shoulder. "Because you've cut everyone else out of your life. I find it hard to believe that you are so dense. I thought you were smarter than this."

"I'm as smart as Rebecca," he muttered.

"When it comes to behaving like a moron, I'd have to agree."

He snapped his head to up to peer at her.

She shrugged. "Rebecca's made dumb decisions because she goes off half-cocked without talking to anyone else. She gets herself all worked up and thinks that she knows better. You know how that has worked out for her in the past. And just so we're clear, it won't work out any better for you. This lousy snotty attitude that you've managed to pick up is ugly on you. It isn't cool, it doesn't make you a better person, and it won't encourage people to like you. It will only alienate you from the people who have always loved you." She rubbed his shoulder this time. "It doesn't mean we'll love you any less. You also know how I feel about that. My love for you doesn't stop because you make me angry or act like a jerk, but if you won't let me love you, then it separates us. I will fight that as hard as I can, I promise. I'm not letting you go. You are much too wonderful."

He huffed another breath. "I gotta go. Are you done yet?"

Polly grabbed his shoulder to stop him. "I want you to understand that your mother is one of my closest friends. When you get out of this car, I'm calling her."

Andrew looked stricken.

"You'd like to beg me not to, wouldn't you, but you don't dare because you've lost any credibility with me, right? There was a time not so long ago that you could have asked that favor of me and I might have considered it because of our relationship, but you've severed that. It's on you, Andrew. I love you and I will do my best to protect you from the stupidity that you bring down on yourself, but I can't do it alone and neither can your mother. If the bulk of this is coming from your father, you managed to choose to side with the one person who has done more to wound that wonderful woman than anyone else in the world. Consider that as you're listening to him spew hateful garbage."

"He's never said a bad word about her to me."

"He doesn't have to. He's corrupting your understanding of what love and goodness is. If you listen to him long enough, you'll begin to alter your way of looking at the world. You'll see only darkness and ugliness and believe the absolute worst about people rather than look for their goodness. If he can destroy that part of you, that will hurt your mother more than any of the physical blows he rained down on her years ago. You know what? I won't allow her to be blind-sided by that. She'll face it knowing what is happening and she'll know that she has my support along with anyone else who knows who your father is."

"You just don't know anything," he said and opened the car door. "I'll walk from here."

"I love you, Andrew."

He slammed the car door shut and walked away from her. Polly sagged. She didn't want to make this call. For the last few weeks, though, Sylvie had been avoiding her. She'd not come out for Sunday evening pizza and even though they spoke at Sweet Beans, it wasn't like it should be. Sylvie was caught up in the ugliness that Andrew was spreading throughout his life, even though she probably didn't realize what was happening. Oh good heavens, Polly didn't want to be the one to talk to her. But there was no one else. She swiped the call open.

CHAPTER SIXTEEN

No answer. Polly put the phone down on the passenger seat. This was the wrong time of the day anyway. Things were too busy for Sylvie at work. Polly was so frustrated she wanted to scream. In the entire time she'd known that boy, he had never treated her with disrespect and he had never once walked away without resolving a disagreement.

The problem with Andrew was that he was so stinking bright. He could argue a point as well as anyone. His mind was quick and he was articulate. Up until this summer, he'd been loving and caring, his playfulness and positive outlook a strong part of his personality. Whatever had happened to him had completely altered that. Gone were his positive attributes, and unless the kid had some terrible physical problem that no one had yet identified, the biggest influence on Andrew had to be his father. Even a snotty little girl like Maddy Spotter wouldn't have that much of an impact on him.

Polly wasn't ready to go home. Cat had the boys again today. They were heading to the cemetery to help Charlie with some cleanup he wanted to finish. He'd been trimming and clearing bushes and when Cat asked how they could help, he thought that having extra hands haul debris for him would be great.

It had been a long time since Polly had landed at the barn because her heart hurt, but today, that's where she wanted to be.

Polly crossed the highway and drove past Sycamore House, then turned in just before the barn and parked. She looked at what she was wearing and didn't care. There would be time to change before she headed to Boone to pick up the girls. Clothes were easily washed and her work boots were already here.

Polly waved at Eliseo, who was crossing the bridge at the far corner of the pasture. Tom and Huck saw her first and ran around the side of the barn to get to her. When she went inside, rather than go through the gate, those smart boys made a dash for Demi's stall door, the fastest way to get inside. She greeted them both as they barreled toward her.

"I don't have anything for you," she said as Huck pushed his nose into her side. "I'll give you love and attention. I have plenty of that."

The two animals crowded her as she walked back to the tack room.

"I have nothing. I'm sorry," Polly repeated, pushing Tom back and away. "Quit begging."

He honked at her and she laughed. "Okay, okay. When Eliseo gets here, I'll ask permission." She rubbed his nose. "But if he tells me no, you're going to have to live with it."

She was sitting on a bench, pulling on her left boot when Eliseo walked into the room.

"Hey, Polly."

"Hey."

"What are you doing here at this hour?"

She shrugged. "I needed a few minutes with animals that didn't talk back."

"You might have come to the wrong place," he said with a laugh. "Especially with these two. They get more and more attitude every day. The horses are in the other pasture. Do you want to ride Demi?"

"No, I should have called if I wanted to do that."

"I can make it happen."

"No, really. I might wander over and hang out with him for a few minutes, though."

"He'd be glad to see you. I can walk with you and get you up on his back."

She wasn't quite as comfortable riding bareback, but she'd done it often enough. Eliseo always had something new for her to learn and get comfortable with. She drew the line at jumping, but he'd worked with her on different courses, always asking her to become more comfortable giving commands to Demi and trusting that he would obey.

"It's okay." She stood and stamped her feet into the boots. "Is there anything I can help you with today? I have time."

He shook his head. "Everyone is happy and content. We're doing good."

"Thanks." Polly hugged Tom, who had stayed next to her. He didn't try to pull away. "They were begging for treats."

"They don't need anything. They're just beggars."

"That's what I told them. I'm going to head out. I'll be back after a while."

He nodded and she walked out of the barn and headed across the pasture. When she got to the gate leading to the bridge, she stopped. "You two go on back. You aren't coming with me."

Tom looked at her like she'd lost her mind as she waved him away.

"I know," Polly said. "Roughest life ever. You never get anything. Go on back now." She slipped through the gate and pulled it closed, heart nearly breaking at the two forlorn donkeys watching her leave them behind.

"I'm not looking at you any longer," Polly said. She crossed the wooden bridge, thankful that they'd gone ahead and purchased this land. When she opened the gate on the other side, she stopped and looked around. The corn in Dan Severt's field was high and tassels were waving in the wind. She'd heard that the weather had been nearly perfect this year and it was possible corn might come out early. She was used to harvest happening in October, sometimes with bad weather, going out as late as the middle of November. One year there had been a few holdouts that didn't get the last of their beans in until early December. But to think about harvest beginning in late August or September was crazy. She laughed at herself. Polly Giller, Boston librarian, thinking about harvest-time in Iowa. That was just about as crazy as it could get.

The sound of four immense horses running toward you was enough to put any girl on the defensive. She knew they wouldn't trample her; they were just coming to say hello, but she took a step back and caught her breath.

"Hello there," she said. "I was thinking about how the four of you have taken care of me over the years when things fall apart. I could use a hug."

Demi was her boy. He came up to her and pushed at her shoulder. "I'm glad to see you, too," Polly said. "What would you do with a fifteen-year-old boy who's lost his mind and is acting like his abusive father?" Polly had tucked herself into Demi's neck and didn't know which of the other three nickered, but she nodded. "Me too. It's not a good look on him. It took all I had not to yell and throw a fit. I still wasn't over it when I got here, but I'm getting better." She wrapped her arms around Demi as he nuzzled her back with his nose.

A cough from behind her startled Polly.

Eliseo stood there with Demi's bridle and a step stool. "Maybe you should ride him. He'll take better care of you that way. You know I'm right."

Her face flushed red. She hadn't expected him to show up while she was baring her soul to her horses. "How much did you hear?"

"It's Andrew, right?"

"We just had a …" She looked for the right words. "It wasn't a fight, but it was close. He's changed this summer."

Eliseo nodded. "I've seen it. We've all seen it, but until Sylvie is ready to do something, I can't speak to it."

"He has to be spending time with his father," Polly said. "This behavior is Anthony's. Andrew wouldn't learn it anywhere else."

"Bad attitudes can show up without any prompting or help from outside sources."

"But not Andrew. Not my boy. He's sweet and kind and loving. He'd rather make people laugh than upset them. But the boy today was insulting and rude. He had no problem challenging me or refusing to care what terrible things he said. If it isn't an outside influence, I'd tell Sylvie that she needs to have him evaluated for either drug use or some other psychological breakdown."

Eliseo flinched. He wasn't able to show his emotions on his face, but his body reacted to the big emotions. Polly often missed subtleties in his reactions, but not the big stuff.

"You don't think it's drugs, do you?" he asked.

She shook her head. "I'd rather believe that it's Anthony, but until we know more, I don't think anything should be ruled out."

"This is Andrew we're talking about," Eliseo said. "I would never have considered drugs or a psychological problem with him in a million years. Both Sylvie and I assumed he was going through a period of raging hormonal imbalance that came about after he and Rebecca broke up."

"Does she know he wasn't at band camp today?" Polly asked.

The frown in his eyes came across clearly. "She didn't say anything. There's no reason for him to have missed."

"He told me he had other commitments. I found him walking about six blocks from his house." Polly took a breath. "Eliseo, it was the saddest thing. He was so cold and angry. He wants to hate me."

"Sylvie needs to know about this."

"I tried to call her," Polly said. "She didn't answer, but then, it's close to lunch. She's probably busy, but then, she hasn't spoken to me much at all this summer."

He nodded slowly, then walked over to Demi and patted the big horse on his shoulder. "She feels awkward around you, what with Andrew's behavior and all."

"That woman has never run from things that scare her."

"The fear of losing her friendship with you is bigger than her strength." With deft hands, he soon had Demi ready for Polly. He handed her the reins and snapped out the step ladder, then paced until he found a solid piece of ground. "Come on, get on up. Even if you only ride him for twenty minutes, you'll feel better. I know he will. He always behaves better after you've ridden him."

"I don't want to go out on the road," Polly said.

"That's fine. You have a couple of acres here, just ride around. Talk to Demi, let the others hear you, too. It's good for the soul. I'll be around. If you want help down, just yell for me."

"Thank you, Eliseo. You're good for me, too."

His eyes twinkled. "Have a good ride."

Daisy, Nat, and Nan followed Polly and Demi for a while, but they soon grew tired of that and fell to playing with each other, ignoring that she was still among them.

She didn't want to think about it any longer, so she leaned down to hug Demi, then sat back up and let him walk around the perimeter of the pasture.

When they arrived at the southwest corner, she looked off into Joss and Nate's land. This was the one small point where the two lots came together. No one was in the front yard. Nate had enclosed an area behind the house so they could let the kids run without worrying that they'd take off into the road, not that that was a real worry. The road they'd end up on was gravel and there was very little traffic. A half-mile away from their driveway entrance was the paved road that led past Sycamore House.

She wondered if Kirk and Justin Waters were in Nate's workshop today with the Camaro. Then she grinned as she wondered if threatening Henry with hiring those two to work on the Woodies would spur him into doing something. And she wondered if Nate and Kirk would become friends through this. Kirk was comfortable around Henry, but Nate was much more gregarious. She thought back to Henry's first exposure, when Nate had come off as a loud-mouthed, slick salesman, just to see their reaction. Kirk didn't seem like the type of person who would find that funny. Maybe she was wrong about him. She hadn't seen him in his own element.

Polly nudged Demi forward again. It felt so good to feel his muscles ripple down his body as he walked. There was such quiet and gentle strength in him and he never seemed to mind sharing that with her.

It infuriated Polly that she cared so much about how this kid treated her. She was an adult and supposed to be above it, especially when he wasn't in full control of his faculties. She knew that. She also knew that the only way to approach him was to avoid hurling anger back his way. She couldn't react with the visceral pain she felt. Had Andrew said these same things to Rebecca? She hadn't said much. The fact was, the two kids weren't talking now anyway. Those nights of Rebecca begging for time on her phone to talk to him were long gone. But if he'd said half of the nasty things to Rebecca that he'd said to Polly today, that would have wounded her daughter to the core. She wasn't used to being betrayed by those who cared about her.

She and Demi wandered back to where Eliseo had left the step stool. Polly swung off the horse, slid to the ground, and sat down on the stool, Demi's reins in her hand. "I'm sorry, Demi. I didn't mean to get you all dressed up today. I just wanted to spend a few minutes with you." She looked up at the sound of barking dogs. Khan and Kirk came tearing across the field to her. "Hi there, guys. Where were you earlier?"

Eliseo's familiar clicking slowed them as they came close to Polly and Demi.

"They were sleeping in the office," Eliseo said. "I saw you come back around and thought you might be ready for me. You got down on your own."

She grinned. "I know, right? I'm pretty proud of myself."

He took the reins from her. "I just talked to Sylvie. She said you aren't answering your phone."

Polly stood and patted her pockets. "Shoot. I left it in the car."

"Good enough," he said. "You needed this then."

"How long have I been out here."

"Forty-five minutes."

She frowned and looked around the pasture. It wasn't that big. "You're kidding me, right?"

"No. Forty-five minutes. That's why I started watching for you." He slipped her a handful of the treats they kept on hand for the horses.

"Thank you, Eliseo." Polly didn't know what she would ever do without this man. She stood and approached Demi, then opened her hand, reveling in the sensation of his lips on her palm as he gently took her offering. "Thank you, Demi."

"I didn't tell her anything," Eliseo said. "If you want me to, I will, but I figure that the two of you need to work this out."

"You're right." Polly pointed out to the other end of the pasture. "Do you want me to help bring them in?"

"No. They get to play out here all day. Jason will help me tonight."

"How's he doing?" Polly asked.

Eliseo nodded. "He's trying to figure it out. He's in that terrible transition time, you know. He has an idea where he wants to be in five or ten years, but discovering the right path to get there is confusing. His fear of failure is stopping him from striking out and trying things. We've talked to him about that, but so far, he isn't there. He wants his life to be safe and solid."

"I understand that," she replied. "I thought I had it all figured out, too. You might not think that living in Boston was safe, but it was. I had a job, an apartment, and a few good friends. I thought that was enough. But wow, it wasn't nearly enough at all. It was good at the time, but life is so much better now. I hope he figures it out."

"So do I," Eliseo said. "So do I. He's such a good kid. He needs to quit worrying about what the adults in his life want for him and to stop thinking that his mother's future is his responsibility. He won't let that go."

"He's spent his entire life wanting to take care of her," Polly said. "For a time, he wanted to take care of me, too. He has a real sense of responsibility."

"I don't know how to help him with that."

She grinned. "Yes you do."

"I do?" Eliseo tilted his head in confusion.

"Sure you do. Marry his mother. That will release Jason."

Eliseo opened his mouth to speak, then closed it. He opened it again, then closed it. Finally, he walked around to the other side of Demi, out of her line of sight.

"Did I freak you out?" Polly asked, following him. She tried not to smile at the havoc her words had created in him.

"I'm not certain how I should respond," he said quietly. "Sylvie and I have talked about this."

"And the two of you are choosing not to get married now, because?"

"We don't feel like it is the right time."

"When is it going to be the right time? When one or the other of you is on your death bed in fifty years? Come on, Eliseo. Why is this so difficult? You love each other and want to be with each other, right?"

He nodded.

"Her boys love and respect you, too."

"She wants to wait until Andrew is out of high school."

"Because why? Jason graduated this year and he hasn't moved out of the house. Who's to say that either of the boys will be gone by then. What's the sense in waiting?"

"You don't pull any punches, do you?"

"Yeah, yeah, yeah. And I know, this is none of my business, but someone needs to kick your behind."

"That's what Ralph and Sam tell me. They think I'm being a fool."

"They're good men," Polly said. "They know you well. Sam Gardner would be nothing without his wife. Now, Ralph. I'm not sure what to think of him. But I'm pretty sure he's looking for a lady to move into that old house."

"That would be funny. He's such an old bachelor. But yes, he does enjoy the ladies. They like him, too."

"Listen to them," Polly said. "Stop being a stubborn mule."

He glared at her. At least that's what it looked like.

"Too far?" she asked with a grin.

"I heard you."

"Good. Now, can I help with anything here?"

Eliseo shook his head. "No, go ahead. I've got this and evidently, I have things to think about."

"Let me know if you want some help picking out a ring. I'm good at that." Polly whirled on her heels and headed back to the gate. She walked through, crossed the bridge and then opened and closed the gate on the other side. The donkeys ran toward her and followed her back to the barn.

"You two are my favorites. I saved something for each of you." Polly reached into her pocket and pulled out a couple of treats that she'd hidden from Demi. She gave the boys a hug and then ran through the barn to the front door and out to the car. Sure enough, the phone was right where she'd left it. There were several missed calls from Sylvie. She called back.

"Hi Polly," Sylvie said. "Eliseo said you were spending time with the horses. You usually do that on the spur of the moment when you're upset. What's going on?"

"We need to talk."

Sylvie groaned. "I'm so sorry, Polly. I've been a terrible friend. Do you have time right now? I want to work this all out with you. It was so uncomfortable when you were up here the other day. I know this is all on me."

"Yeah, it was a little uncomfortable, but I think I'm going to make it worse. Are you really free?"

"For about an hour. Can we do it in that time?"

"I have to go to Boone to get the girls, so that would be perfect. I might smell like a horse, though. Do you feel comfortable leaving the bakery?"

"Sure. Do you want to meet somewhere?"

"Why don't I pick you up? I'm leaving Sycamore House now."

"I'll meet you out back."

CHAPTER SEVENTEEN

Eventually, Sylvie walked down the steps from the back dock of Sweet Beans. When she climbed into Polly's car, she handed over an iced coffee. "Sorry it took so long. And I brought a peace offering."

Polly laughed. "You didn't need to do that. We're fine."

"No, we aren't fine. I've been a complete chicken-shit over this whole thing with Andrew. He's my good boy and I don't know what to think about his behavior. I didn't want to talk to you about it, because ..." Sylvie dropped her purse on the floor between her legs. "Because I feel like such a stupid failure. I have one son who can't figure out what he wants to do with his future and another son who has decided to reject his friends. It's like I don't know them anymore."

She opened the purse and took out a pair of wrapped sandwiches. "Since you were at the barn, did you eat anything?"

Polly shook her head. "I didn't feel like eating."

"Marta talked me into putting toasted almonds in the chicken salad. It's amazing. Do you want it on a croissant or a French roll?"

"Umm, French roll, please? That sounds amazing."

"Lettuce and tomato okay?"

"Perfect. Where shall we go?"

"I don't care if we sit right here," Sylvie said. "I just want to spend time with you, telling you how sorry I am for being a jerk."

"You aren't a jerk."

"I've been better. You are such a good friend and you've always loved my boys. I didn't want to admit that I don't like either one of them right now."

"What's going on with Jason?" With Sylvie's admissions, Polly hated the idea that she was going to have to make this worse for her. If she could avoid it for a few more minutes, they might be able to eat their lunch. Otherwise, Polly knew that even the best chicken salad sandwich would taste like stale bread.

"It isn't that bad. I just never expected him to be so ..." Sylvie searched for the right word. "I think he's scared, Polly. He's afraid of disappointing us, he's afraid of making a bad decision, he's afraid of failing. What happened to my boy? Did I raise him to be like this?"

"I think a lot of kids have trouble launching themselves. For some reason, it feels like they don't want to struggle through paying their dues, they want to be successful right out of the box. They don't realize that success and failure today doesn't define their future, it just builds their character so they *have* a future."

"Jason has always talked about taking care of me," Sylvie said. "Now that I'm taking care of myself, he doesn't know what to do. Who is he supposed to focus on?"

"Himself," Polly said. "Since we're having this discussion, though, I'd guess that he doesn't see it that way."

"I want him to get out of the house and figure out his life," Sylvie said. "But I'd hate for things to fall apart for him."

"What happened to you when you and Anthony divorced? Did you move back in with your mother?"

Sylvie frowned. "No. No way. That would have been like taking a step backward. I was going to make it on my own, no matter ..." She stopped. "Oh."

"Yeah. You didn't give yourself the option. You had to do it."

"But if Jason were going to college, he'd still live at the house. He'd have another four years before he had to figure things out on his own."

"If he were in college, he'd probably live on campus, not at home. But he made the choice not to go to college, right? And there are plenty of kids who had to figure out how to do college and live on their own. Hayden did it until we came along. He didn't have any other choice, either."

"What do I do with him? Kick him out? I can't do that. I have this big house and lots of room. I like having him live there." She slumped. "But if that means I'm coddling him and not pushing him to grow up, I don't want to be that mom."

Polly shrugged. "Make him pay rent. Give him a deadline for finding his own place. I know that he's talked about going to DMACC for a vet tech degree. If he does that, maybe you decide that he can live rent-free in the house until he's finished. His life has been pretty easy. He hasn't had to go look for a job. We've all taken care of him. What's he doing with all his money?"

"I don't know. Saving it, I guess." Sylvie shook her head. "I haven't had any financial discussions with him either. Wow. I'm failing him in so many ways. I was not prepared for him to graduate from high school. It happened so fast."

"Really?"

Sylvie shook her head. "No. This is all my fault. I got so caught up in building my own career and then I began spending more time with Eliseo. My boys were always so good, I just corrected bad behavior and let the rest go along without my input. Eliseo talked to me about it, too, but I didn't listen. He was so afraid of offending me by implying I wasn't raising my boys right, that he stopped. I'm such an idiot. Maybe I should move into an apartment and ask Eliseo to move into the house. He can finish raising those two." She gave Polly a weak smile. "Think he'd go for that?"

"I think he'd be thrilled to move in with you," Polly replied.

Sylvie blinked. "Did he say something?"

"No. He'd never betray you like that. But you're the one holding all the cards here. Maybe having Eliseo in the house would be good for your boys. He loves them as much as anyone."

"They love him, too," Sylvie said. "I'm so scared of another relationship falling apart, I won't even think about marrying him."

"Huh. Wonder where Jason got his fear of failure?" Polly bit her lip, waiting to see how that comment played.

Sylvie took another bite from her sandwich and reached back into her purse to pull out a can of pop. She snapped the top open and took a drink, then looked for a cup holder.

"Nothing?" Polly asked.

"You're right," Sylvie said. "This whole thing is on me. I've screwed him up."

"That's not the reaction I was hoping for."

"But it's true." Sylvie looked at her with tears in her eyes. "I'm so lost right now. I feel completely alone. If you hadn't called today, I don't know how long this would have gone on. I didn't have the courage to try to fix it. Everything is so overwhelming. I don't know how much more I can do."

"Oh, honey." Polly found a place for her coffee and sandwich and then turned to hug Sylvie, more difficult in this small car than in her Suburban, to be sure.

"When you moved into town, all of a sudden I felt as if there was someone else who loved my boys as much as I did. You are smart and practical and understood what I expected of them. It was the first time in my life that anyone else was part of my family."

"And I'm grateful to be there."

"I didn't feel so lonely. Then, life kept changing and I thought I was handling it all. The boys do well in school, Jason was happy with his small jobs, Andrew was happy and busy with Rebecca and your family. He was so easygoing. But I let it happen around me. It was easier to think that I'd done my job and the kids could take it on their own from there. They can't and I don't know how to dig back in and shake them up."

"You remember that Sylvie who knew she could do it on her own after the divorce? You're the same person."

"But I'm not," Sylvie protested. "I didn't have friends to rely on then. I didn't have Eliseo. And my boys needed me to be involved in every single aspect of their lives. I didn't think about myself, I just did the work. See, that's the other thing you gave me. You told me I could make my own future and you made me realize that the boys weren't going to be around forever, so I needed to prepare for a life without them. I withdrew the focus from them and did the work. I have no balance."

"You are the most balanced person I know," Polly said. "Being overwhelmed doesn't change that. It doesn't mean it's a forever thing. It's a right now thing. And right now, I'm here with you." She pointed at the time. "How are you for time?"

Sylvie blinked. "What?"

"Do you need to get back soon?"

"Oh. No." Her eyes brightened. "You won't believe it. Marta came in after you called. She still can't do much of the laborious work, but we have three young helpers and she can supervise. Man, can she supervise. She's wonderful. Not much gets past her. Heck, she's probably a better trainer than I am. Marta is patient, and she genuinely likes those girls. When she told me she couldn't stand one more minute of being stuck in the house, I nearly squealed with excitement. I just love that woman."

"She's been helping Shelly," Polly said. "I appreciate that. The girl needs more friends in Bellingwood."

"Even if they're old ladies like me and Marta?"

"Whatever it takes. How about Lissa. Is she working out?"

"She'll be okay. She's not quite as dedicated as Shelly is, but she's got a lot going on. She knows she can't stay at the hotel forever." Sylvie breathed out. "I still can't believe you're letting her stay there rent free."

"Yeah. Like Jason is with you. Apparently, I'm the pot and you're the kettle."

Sylvie turned. "Just before I came out, Marta caught me. She likes Lissa and wondered what I thought of her and Shelly moving into an apartment together. They're about the same age. It doesn't need to be forever, but it might be good for them. Shelly is much better than when she started with us. Maybe it's time for her to try a little independence. What do you think?"

"Hmm, I don't know," Polly said. "I'd not considered that." She grinned. "What about that second-floor apartment at Nora Worth's house? She'd keep an eye on those girls and wouldn't put up with much, but it would be safe. The rent isn't horrible. I'd be glad to foot the first and last month's rent, and the girls make enough working here they could afford it. How do you think they are together?"

"They're getting to know each other," Sylvie said. "It's slow, but you know, we work in a pretty small space, so you either get along or get out."

"We need to talk to Shelly first. She's the one I care about. If she's ready to try it, we go forward. If not, I'll set a time limit for Lissa at the hotel and she'll need to look for a place. Surely there are more girls her age looking for a roommate."

"We know a lot of young women," Sylvie said. She took a deep breath. "I know you want to talk about Andrew. Did he say something or do something to Rebecca this week at band camp? I've tried to stay far away from his strange choices regarding his love life. I thought that if I just let him work through it, he'd come around. But now you're here and you're going to ask me to confront him, aren't you?"

"It's not about Rebecca and Andrew," Polly said. "I guess that isn't completely true. There's an element of their relationship in this, but something else is going on with him."

"Go ahead," Sylvie said. "I'm ready."

"Did you know Andrew wasn't in Boone today?"

Sylvie frowned. "No? What do you mean he wasn't in Boone today? How do you know that? Did Rebecca send you a text or something?" She took out her phone and looked through it. "There's nothing here. What do you know that I don't know?"

"I picked him up this morning on my way back from taking Shelly to Grey's office. He was walking down Elm Street."

"He what?" Sylvie asked, the frown deepening.

"And Sylvie, he was horrible to me. I've never met this Andrew. He said awful things to me, accused me of things that made me sick, and acted like ..." Polly shook her head. "He acted and sounded like his father. Do you know if the two of them have spent any time together?"

Sylvie pulled back. "What? No! Anthony isn't supposed to be with those boys without supervision. He has no right. That can't be. He knows that I can make sure he never sees either of the boys until they're eighteen. What?"

Polly gulped back her own fear and laid out for Sylvie the entire interaction she'd had with Andrew earlier in the day. Throughout her tale, Sylvie's eyes went from horror to fear, from anger to sadness. By the time Polly finished, Sylvie had gone through most of the takeout napkins in the glove compartment.

"He was up with that Maddy Spotter," Sylvie said. "What were they doing? Her parents both work, so they aren't home, and Jason and I both left early. One of Andrew's friends was going to pick him up." She opened her phone again and started to compose a text, then stopped herself. "No. That's not what I want to do. I don't want him to have time to come up with excuses."

"I told him that I was going to talk to you."

"So he's already working on his excuses. Great. I'm going to kill that kid. He knows better than to talk to any adult the way he spoke to you. I didn't raise him to be rude, especially to someone who loves him as much as you do. That little, freakin' jerk." Sylvie slammed her fist on the dashboard. "He's not even a sophomore in high school yet. Is he having sex with this girl? Oh, I want to be sick. He doesn't know anything about keeping himself safe."

"He probably does," Polly said. "Kids talk."

"Do you think he and Rebecca were doing it?"

"No," Polly declared. "I don't. Rebecca would have told me by now. She can't keep anything to herself."

"Thank goodness. So whatever he's doing, it's new this summer." Sylvie grabbed Polly's arm. "I'm not supposed to have to deal with this stupidity. It's not fair."

Polly gave a half laugh. "You're right. It isn't fair. What can I do to help you?"

"Do you have time to take me to my house?"

"Sure. I need to pick the girls up, but I have time."

"I don't want Andrew to get away with lying to me because you aren't there to challenge him face to face. Am I being a scaredy-cat, making you come with me?"

"You aren't making me. I'm glad to. I'd like to see that little brat's face when the two of us show up."

"He thinks he's so smart," Sylvie said, her anger seething. "He gets all flirty and cutesy when he's caught and is so eloquent that he sweet-talks his way out of everything. Not today, bub. Not today." She pushed the car door open. "I need to go in and tell Marta where I'm going. Then, maybe it's best if I drive, too. That way you don't have to worry about bringing me back here. You can just leave when you're ready. But first, you'll need to stop me from killing him."

Polly nodded and took a long, deep breath after Sylvie closed the car door. That poor woman didn't need her youngest son to be a jerk. But she wasn't sitting around feeling sorry for herself. At the very least, Andrew's attitude set Sylvie's mothering tendencies afire. If Jason wasn't careful, this would erupt on him too. It was so easy to enable these kids. They were good kids. Her own kids were good kids. Roots to grow, wings to fly. How did you know when their roots had grown down deep enough and their wings were strong enough? Sylvie's lesson today was one that Polly didn't want to have to learn. She needed to pay attention.

Sylvie came flying out of the back door of Sweet Beans and went to her car. Her face was still set in anger and she roared out of her parking space. If the nerves that Polly felt in her stomach were any indication of what Sylvie must be dealing with, it was a surprise the woman wasn't violently ill.

"He's just a kid," Polly said out loud. "He's just a stupid kid."

While that was true, she cared about him as much as any of her own kids. She hated the idea of any more vitriol coming from his mouth. He'd feel terrible for those words one day and she'd give anything to stop it before he got himself into so much trouble he couldn't find a way out.

Sylvie pulled into her driveway and waved at Polly to join her, but tore for the back door. Padme raced out into the back yard as Polly opened the gate. She stopped for a minute to say hello to the dog and then hesitantly walked up the steps to the door. She listened, wondering if there'd be yelling, but still nothing. She opened the door, went inside and stood for a moment. Other than Sylvie calling for Andrew, the house was quiet.

"Where is he?" Sylvie asked. "Didn't you bring him home?"

"I dropped him off at the end of the block. He said he'd walk from there. And he came this way."

"I'm sorry to drag you over here. He's probably gone back to his little girlfriend's house, thinking he'll show up when he usually does after he's done in Boone. Polly, he's going to try to lie to my face. How long has this been going on behind my back? Who is this kid? He's not mine, that's for sure. If he's spending time with his father and lying to me, I will kill both of them."

"Do you want me to stay for a while?" Polly asked. "Maybe he'll be home soon."

"No. He won't come home until his normal time." Sylvie's face fell. "I hope he comes home. Do you think he'd do something even stupider? What if he called Anthony and asked his dad to pick him up? What if he never comes home?"

"That's not going to happen," Polly said.

"It could. I wouldn't put it past him. If those two have spent time together this summer, Andrew would …" Sylvie whirled and ran out of the kitchen. Her footsteps thudded up the stairs. She was looking to see if he'd taken his things.

This terrified Polly — that Andrew would go too far and wouldn't know how to return to himself.

"He packed a bag," Sylvie said. The utter defeat in her voice broke Polly's heart. "He took his clothes. He took some of his books. His charger is gone. There's no note. Nothing. I don't know what to do."

"You need to call him," Polly said.

Sylvie looked at her purse like she didn't know what it was. "Call him?"

"Call him. Text him. Then have Jason reach out. And you need to call Eliseo. Once you get your family gathered around, the three of you need to go get him. If you're worried about Anthony, call Tab or Aaron. One of them would go with you."

"What in the actual hell?" Sylvie asked. She dug in her purse and took out her phone. "We're a good family. This crap isn't supposed to happen. Anthony lives in Fort Dodge. What does Andrew think he's going to do up there?"

"He's not thinking. He's just reacting. He's made some terrible mistakes and he doesn't know how to fix them. Make the call." Polly pointed at Sylvie's phone.

She swiped the call and put it on speaker. It went straight to voicemail. "Andrew. Call me. I know what happened today. I also know that you've packed a bag and left. Nothing is too difficult to overcome, but we need you here. I need you here. You are my son and I love you. Call me." She shook her head. "I'll text him, too."

Polly sat down beside her. "I'm calling Eliseo."

With eyes that held too much sorrow for one person, Sylvie looked at her and nodded as she sent the text, and then made another call. "Jason?"

Polly walked into the living room and dialed Eliseo's phone.

"Hello, Polly. Are you feeling better after some time with Demi? Have you talked to Sylvie?"

"I'm at her house, Eliseo. You need to come over. Andrew ran away."

"He what?"

"He packed a bag. We're just getting started, but he's gone."

"What happened?" Eliseo slammed a door. "I'll be right there. Tell her I'll be right there." He was gone without waiting for Polly to answer his question.

She walked back into the kitchen, where Sylvie sat at her table, her head in her arms, quiet sobs shaking her shoulders.

"Do you want me to call Aaron? Andrew's a minor."

"Not yet. Let's see if he calls to tell me where he is, first."

"You know that we should call Lydia, Beryl, and Andy, though. Right?"

"Not yet," Sylvie said. "Just not yet."

"What did Jason say?"

"He's going to try to call his brother and see if he picks up. He'll call me back."

"Eliseo's on his way."

"I hate to bring him into this."

"Why? Because he loves you?"

"You're right, but it's always just been me and my boys."

"Your family is bigger than that, Sylvie."

"I know." Sylvie looked at her. "Do you remember the last time I worried about Anthony taking him? The jerk dropped him off outside of town. He isn't trustworthy. I don't know what he'll do with Andrew."

"Andrew is smart and he's older now. Anthony would never hurt him. All that man wants is for his sons to believe that he's the best father in the world."

"I hope not. I don't have much faith in anything right now. My little boy is gone."

"Do you have phone numbers for the Spotters? For Maddy, at least?"

Sylvie shook her head, then she looked up. "Wait. I have the cell phone bills. It's gotta be in there." She growled. "And I'll bet I find Anthony's phone number in there, too. He is going to be in a world of hurt."

Padme barked and Sylvie jumped up, looking out the window into the back yard. She sat back down. "It's Eliseo."

"That was fast."

A quick rap at the back door and Padme barreled in, jumping up and down beside Eliseo. He clicked his tongue against his teeth and she sat. Then he strode over to Sylvie, knelt beside her and took her into his arms. What had been quiet sobs before turned into loud weeping as she buried her face in his shoulder.

CHAPTER EIGHTEEN

Watching the clock was stressful. Polly needed to pick up the girls in Boone but didn't want to leave Sylvie. Jason walked in the back door, followed soon by his girlfriend, Mel. He had tried to reach his brother, but to no avail. The kid wasn't answering anyone's calls. Jason had also stopped by Maddy Spotter's house. Her brother, Joel, who was the same age as Andrew and had always been a friend, was home and he didn't know where anyone was. Jason had gotten Maddy's phone number from Joel. She wasn't answering either. He also had his father's phone number. Another phone that wasn't being answered.

Sylvie looked to be in shock. She was only answering questions that were put directly to her. Jason sat down beside her and the two of them worked on a list of names — friends that Andrew might be in contact with. The list wasn't all that long. For years, Polly would have been at the top, followed by Rebecca and Kayla.

Polly knelt beside Sylvie's chair. "I need to go get the girls. As soon as I drop them off, I'll be back. We can drive to Fort Dodge or I'll park my butt at Maddy's house until her parents come home. Whatever it takes, we'll find out what's going on."

Sylvie nodded absently. Then she focused. "Go get the girls. That's right. You have to do that. Don't worry about us. We'll be fine."

No she wouldn't, but Polly could only hope it wouldn't take long to find Andrew and bring him home. His mother already doubted her ability to raise her boys. This wasn't helping.

"I'm so sorry," Polly said. "I wish I didn't have to leave, but there's no one else."

Eliseo took Polly's arm and walked to the back door with her. "It's okay. We're here. Call before you come back. Things might have worked themselves out."

She nodded and gave him a quick hug. The drawn faces around Sylvie's kitchen table were heartbreaking. Polly wanted to fix it. She couldn't.

Polly drove home and transferred into her Suburban, then took off after sending a quick text to Cat that she'd changed cars. She was going to be late if she didn't push this. She sent another text to Rebecca, telling her that she was on the way, then focused on driving. She wanted to call Lydia, but Sylvie had specifically asked her not to. The thing was, Polly wanted someone to talk to and right now she had no one. Henry was busy and unless this spun into a huge problem, he didn't need to worry unnecessarily. She took a breath and tried to relax her shoulders. Every time she thought she had them back down where they belonged, she discovered that they were hovering near her ears again. What had Andrew done? The stupid, stupid kid.

She realized that she was pulling into the school's parking lot and had no idea what had happened for the last few minutes. She hated when that happened. At least most of her conscious mind was on target.

Kayla, Libby, and Rebecca saw her coming and walked out to meet the Suburban.

They got in and Rebecca frowned at Polly.

"Where's Cilla?" Polly asked. "Just late?"

"She's gone," Rebecca said.

"What do you mean, gone?"

"We think she was kidnapped," Kayla said.

Polly snapped her head around. "Kidnapped?"

"She didn't want to go with the guy, but he made her."

"When did this happen?"

Rebecca turned around to look at her friends. "Like two minutes ago. We were totally freaked out. I didn't know what to do. He drove up and yelled her name. I didn't know she knew anybody from around here. When I tried to ask her who it was, she looked kinda scared, but she went over to talk to him. Then, they started yelling, but not really loud, just angry. I couldn't hear what they said. Could you?" she asked Libby and Kayla.

They shook their heads.

"I tried," Kayla said. "But it wasn't like yelling-yelling. It was more like under-their-breath yelling. He pointed at us and she got in his car. Then he drove away."

"What kind of car?" Polly asked. She was already calling Aaron.

"It was blue," Libby said.

Kayla shook her head. "Well, kind of gray-blue."

"Polly?" Aaron said. "Don't tell me."

"I hope not, Aaron," Polly said. "The girls tell me that Cilla Waters took off with someone and she looked scared. I know I need to check with her mother, but Andrea would have told me if Cilla wasn't coming home with us."

"Where are you?"

"Sorry. I'm at the high school."

"It could just be a friend."

"The girls say that Cilla seemed scared of him. And Aaron, they haven't lived in Bellingwood a week. She doesn't know anyone well enough to drive off with them."

"That makes sense. She was scared of him? Did he manhandle her?"

"I'm not sure," Polly said.

"What did the girls see? Can they give me a description?"

Polly looked at Rebecca. "Can you sketch the person who took Cilla?"

"I didn't see his face very well. He mostly kept his back to us. He had blonde, kinda shaggy hair. Not long, but messy. He was wearing jeans and I didn't see his shoes. I think he had on a denim jacket over a shirt."

"But could you sketch what you saw?"

Rebecca nodded. "I guess. All of my stuff is at home, though."

"What about the other girls?" Aaron asked. "Did they see anything else?"

Polly turned to the back. "Did you girls see anything else about him that stands out?"

"No," Libby said. "I wasn't paying attention. I just figured it was somebody she knew. People are in and out of here all the time and Cilla has been really friendly. She's, like, outgoing and stuff. She talks to anyone."

Kayla shook her head, her eyes were filled with tears. "We should have stopped her."

"It happened too fast," Rebecca said.

"At least you were walking toward them," Kayla said. "I just froze."

"You went after them?"

"It seemed so weird. I don't know what I thought I was going to do, but I started after the car. He tore out of the parking lot. I was going to call you, but I knew you were on your way and I didn't want to upset you while you were driving."

"Call me anytime," Polly said. "Aaron? What do you want me to do?"

"Call her mother. Find out for sure what they know. Ask if this is tied to the person who ran them off the road. I'm on my way to Bellingwood."

"I'll take Libby home and see you at the house. Thanks."

Polly drove on through the lot to the exit, then headed out of town.

"You called Aaron," Rebecca said softly so that the girls in back couldn't hear her. "You never call him unless you find a ..."

"That's not how this is going to work," Polly said. "It can't. I didn't find anyone." She handed her phone over. "Here, Andrea's number is programmed in. Would you find it and make the call for me?"

Rebecca took her phone. "What are all of these calls to Andrew's number? Is something wrong?"

"That's another story. I'll tell you later."

"Did something happen?"

"Not right now," Polly said. "Later. Call Andrea."

"But you want to talk to her, right? You won't make me do it."

"Yeah. I'll talk to her."

Rebecca handed the phone back to Polly, who put it up to her ear. It rang three times and then Andrea picked it up. "Polly? Is everything okay?"

"Andrea," Polly said quietly. "Have you heard from Cilla?"

"No. She isn't with you?"

"The girls tell me that she left with someone."

"Who in the world would she leave with?" Andrea asked. "She doesn't know anyone well enough to get in their car. And besides, she knows she needs to come home tonight. She's watching the kids while Kirk and I head to Ames for a meeting. This makes no sense."

"They saw her get into a blue car with a young man who had blond, shaggy hair. Is that familiar to you?"

"What?" Andrea practically bellowed the word, then cried out, "No."

She ended the call.

Polly took the phone down and swallowed hard. "Rebecca, I want to leave this phone open. I don't know what happened to Andrea, but I need to talk to Henry. Would you call him on your phone?" She was close to tears. She could feel them welling up in her throat and behind her eyes. What she most wanted to do right now was stop the Suburban, curl up into a ball and sob. This was too much.

Rebecca handed her phone over and Polly took it, listening to it ring.

"Heya, little chickadee," Henry said. "Howzit?"

"Henry, where are you?"

"Polly. You're not Rebecca. I'm in Boone. What's up?"

"Too much. How much more day do you have?"

"Is something going on, Polly?" he asked, suddenly engaged in what she was asking.

"Yes."

"Are you taking the girls home?"

"Yeah."

"And you can't tell me in front of them?"

"Well, for one, Cilla isn't with us. Someone picked her up at the school."

"That seems odd."

"Andrea is pretty freaked out. I've talked to Aaron and he asked about the connection between this and the person who ran them off the road."

"Oh no."

"Yeah. My mind is spinning with possibilities. And ..." Polly paused.

"And there's something else?"

"Yeah."

"This is what you can't talk about."

"Yeah."

"Is it bad?"

"It's not good."

"Are our kids okay?"

Andrew was one of her kids and he wasn't okay. Polly knew Henry was asking about their immediate family, but it was hard to separate Andrew from that.

"As far as I know. I'm sorry."

"Do you need me?"

"More than I can say. But this might have been enough. I'll be fine. Finish your work and come home."

"Are you sure?"

"I just needed to hear your voice." And that was her reality. He calmed her when nothing else could.

"I'll finish as fast as I can. If you don't see me, call me when you're free of the girls."

"I love you, Henry," Polly said, choking back tears.

"I love you, too. Everything will work out."

"I hope so." She ended the call and handed the phone back to Rebecca, a little surprised that Andrea hadn't called back. "Libby?"

"Yes?"

"I'm taking you home. If something has happened with Cilla and Sheriff Merritt needs to speak to you, he'll call before he comes to your house, okay?"

"Weird things happen around you guys," Libby said. "My life was boring before I was friends with Rebecca."

Polly glanced at her daughter. "That's what my friends said about me when I moved to Bellingwood."

"Don't even go there," Rebecca said.

"I didn't. She did."

"The universe didn't just hear that. I can't be like you."

"You keep saying that." Polly pulled into the front of the hotel first. "Kayla, same goes. If Sheriff Merritt needs to ask you any questions about what you saw today, he'll call first. Don't be afraid. Just tell him what you know."

"I wish I could come home with you," Kayla said.

"Not this time. It's going to be crazy and I might not be able to get you home tonight. Let Stephanie and Skylar know what's going on."

Kayla opened the door. "Okay," she said resignedly. "I never get to know what's happening."

"Rebecca will call you later."

Polly waited until Kayla was inside the front door and then drove out of the parking lot, heading east toward Libby's house. She looked at her phone every once in a while, willing it to ring. Two women she cared for had no idea where their kids were. How was this even real?

"If Cilla's been kidnapped, do you think we'll have band tomorrow?" Libby asked.

"I suspect so. We're going to hope she isn't kidnapped or that nothing terrible has happened. This is probably just a misunderstanding," Polly said. "Your mother is planning to drive tomorrow, right?"

"Yeah. She wanted me to ask if it would be okay if we got pizza or something after we were done."

"That sounds great."

"Cool. Kayla is supposed to ask, too. I hope Cilla can come. She's a blast."

Polly drove into their farm and pulled up in front of the house, then waited for Libby to get out. The girl waved from her back door and went inside, and then Polly heaved a big sigh. "Life sucks," she said.

"What else is going on?" Rebecca asked.

"You can't even believe it. Andrew's missing, too."

"What? I wondered why he wasn't there today. Maddy wasn't either, so I just figured they were off together. He's been weird this week. It was awkward before, but this week he's like, gone off on his friends. No one wants to be with him." She grimaced. "Except Maddy. She's always hanging all over him. It's gross."

Polly pulled to the end of the driveway and took her phone up. Nothing yet from Andrea. She called Eliseo's phone.

"Hey, Polly. We've got no news yet. We're trying to figure out what's next."

"I think you need to call Aaron," she said. "Don't wait. If they can get a deputy up to Anthony's house or at least look for him, that might be the best thing."

"I've tried to tell Sylvie. She doesn't want to."

"She wants Anthony in jail if he's taken her son. You know she does. Tell her not to wait."

"I'll keep trying."

"I can't come over right now, Eliseo. The girl who just moved in across the street — Cilla? She wasn't there when I picked up the girls. Someone took her and this might be an actual kidnapping."

"Oh no," he said.

"I'm so sorry. I don't want to land this on Sylvie. The Waters' are brand new in town and now this. I don't know where I'm supposed to be."

"Be there for now," he said. "We're going to find Andrew, and this is going to work out."

"Call Aaron. Please," Polly said. She leaned her forehead against the steering wheel, a severe pain taking hold in the back of her head.

"You're right."

A buzz alerted her to another call coming in.

"I need to go, Eliseo. I'll be in touch."

"We're fine, Polly."

"Tell Sylvie I love her."

"I will and she knows."

Polly looked at her phone. It was Andrea. "Hi," she said. Along with the headache that was threatening to swamp her, suddenly her stomach roiled with tension. She didn't know how much more of this she could handle. It was one thing to have people attack her. It was another when families that she loved were in the middle of a hell they couldn't find their way out of. She was being torn between two catastrophes and couldn't find her way through them.

"I'm sorry for hanging up," Andrea said. "What can you tell me?"

"Sheriff Merritt is coming to Bellingwood. Do you think this young man was the same person who ran you off the road yesterday?"

"It must be. Oh, Polly. He's got my daughter."

"Who is it?" Polly turned onto the highway and headed back to Bellingwood. She couldn't just sit here any longer. If she couldn't be at Sylvie's to help her friend wait for something to break, she could at least be at the Waters' house. Sylvie had a support system, if only she would tap into it. Andrea and Kirk had his parents and no one else. That was the decision she had to make, but it was tearing her apart.

"I thought we'd left him behind. How did he find us so fast?"

"Tell me." Polly said as calmly as she could. Everything inside her wanted to explode.

"Polly?" Rebecca asked.

She shook herself and glanced at her daughter. "What?"

"You closed your eyes."

"I what?"

Andrea spoke. "What?"

"Just a minute," Polly said. She looked at Rebecca.

"You look really bad," Rebecca said.

Polly slowed the Suburban. "Can you drive this?"

"Home?"

"Yeah."

"Okay."

Rebecca had her driving permit and she'd driven a lot this last year. Whenever she could talk someone into letting her get behind the wheel, she grabbed the keys and ran for the driver's seat.

They were only three miles out of Bellingwood. Rebecca had driven further than that, but never when she was worried about someone else.

"Andrea," Polly said as she pulled off onto the shoulder of the highway. "I'll be right there. Has Aaron arrived yet?"

"The sheriff?"

"Yeah. I'm sorry. Aaron Merritt."

"He's coming here?"

"Yes. I called him in Boone as soon as the girls told me what happened."

"You ... you think we need the sheriff?"

Polly blinked, trying to clear her head. She lay her forehead on the steering wheel again. She wanted to vomit.

She turned to see Rebecca at the door beside her.

"Come on, Polly. Get into the other seat," Rebecca said.

Polly let her pull her from the Suburban and put her in the passenger seat. She fumbled for the phone and Rebecca took it.

"Andrea? This is Rebecca. Polly and I will be there in about five minutes. If Sheriff Merritt shows up before we do, he'll take good care of you. I have to go now, Polly needs me to drive for her. We'll be right there."

Rebecca pulled the seatbelt across Polly, who took it from her and snapped it into place. "What's wrong with me?" Polly asked.

"I think you're in shock."

"Don't let me throw up."

"If you throw up, you have to clean it up," Rebecca said. "Remember how bad that is and don't do it."

She got into the driver's seat, adjusted it, then checked the mirrors. Polly gave a wan smile at the fact that she followed the checklist. Then Rebecca picked up her own phone and made a call.

"You can't be on the phone and drive," Polly said.

"I'm not driving. Be quiet."

"Don't sass me."

"Sorry, but be quiet."

"Henry?" Rebecca said. "Polly needs you to come home as fast as you can. She's in bad shape. There's something bad going on with Andrew, and with Cilla. I think she's kinda falling apart because she had to pull over so I could drive."

There was a pause.

"Yeah. I've got it. I told her she couldn't throw up, but she wants to and she's all clammy and stuff. No, don't worry. It's only a couple of miles. We just dropped Libby off."

After another pause, Rebecca said, "I'll tell her. Thanks."

She put the phone down and turned to look at Polly. "He's coming home and says to tell you that you're strong and everything will be fine. Oh, and that he loves you."

Polly nodded. She didn't feel strong.

CHAPTER NINETEEN

"Not yet." Rebecca pulled into the driveway at the Bell House. Two sheriff's vehicles were parked across the street, one Polly recognized as Aaron Merritt's.

"What?"

"Come inside first," Rebecca said.

"I'm sorry," Polly said as she got out of the Suburban. "I shouldn't have fallen apart on you. I'm the mama."

Rebecca grinned at her. "You can be the mama again in ten minutes. When's the last time you had anything to eat?"

Polly thought back through her day. Sylvie had brought out an amazing chicken salad sandwich on a French roll, but it was probably still in the front seat of Cat's car. She'd been so worried about telling her friend what was happening with Andrew, she'd been unable to eat. Sylvie had eaten most of her own sandwich, but Polly's would be fodder for the compost heap. She'd purchased a blueberry muffin when she and Sal had coffee. Was that only this morning? So much had happened since then. Polly closed her eyes and could clearly see it still intact on the table when she left to take Shelly to her appointment with Grey.

"Does coffee count?"

"Any water?"

The two walked inside and Polly sat down at the island. "Ibuprofen and a tall glass of water, then."

Rebecca nodded and opened the cupboard where Polly stashed the ibuprofen. It was far out of the reach of the little boys, but Rebecca was at least as tall as Polly now. Maybe even taller.

"You're really beautiful," Polly said quietly.

Rebecca turned on her and set the bottle on the counter top. "What? Are you loopy or something?"

"Nope. Just thinking about how you've grown up."

"Two of my friends are missing and you're talking about my beauty?" She shook her head and drew a glass of water from the refrigerator door. "Ice?"

"No, better not. You've gotten so tall. Your mother would be beside herself at the amazing young woman you've turned into. And you hardly have to clean bathrooms these days. You're growing up."

"About time, don't you think?" Rebecca asked. She opened the refrigerator. "Before you face the rest of this day, you need to eat something. Would you like a sandwich?"

"There's a wonderful chicken salad sandwich in Cat's car," Polly said. "Speaking of which, where are Cat and the boys?"

"Probably at the nursing home. It's Thursday. Remember?"

"Thank goodness. I couldn't deal with them right now."

"Start with this." Rebecca slid a piece of cold pizza onto a napkin and across the counter top.

Polly stopped it before it slid past her. "Can't believe Heath left anything."

"Take a bite," Rebecca ordered. "You need your strength."

"You're kind of bossy."

"Learned it from the best." Rebecca turned and grinned at her. "How close am I to being in trouble?"

"Miles," Polly said. She took a bite and then, after chewing it a couple of times, opened her mouth to show it to her daughter.

"You're so gross."

"I'm so freaked out," Polly said. "I should be across the street with Andrea. I should be at Sylvie's house. I should be out looking for both of those kids. Where am I? I'm in my kitchen, making my daughter take care of me because I can't properly feed myself during the day."

The back door opened and Henry flew into the kitchen. He pulled up to a stop in front of Polly. "What are you doing here? I thought you'd be across the street. Why was Rebecca driving? What's going on?"

"Rebecca is feeding me."

"She hasn't eaten a thing all day. All she had was coffee," Rebecca said. "I thought she was either going to pass out or vomit after we left Libby's house. I made her get in the passenger seat."

He frowned at Polly. "This is new."

"What do you mean?"

"You melting down so someone else has to take care of you."

Polly burst into tears. "I'm sorry."

"I didn't mean anything by it," Henry said as he gathered her into his arms. "What in the world has been happening up here today?"

"Fight with Andrew," Polly spluttered. "Sylvie isn't a bad mom. Jason's going nowhere and now Cilla's gone too. Bad man took her. I don't know anything. I can't help them all."

"Of course you can't," he said, holding her close.

"Sylvie won't let me call Lydia, but Lydia needs to know. She can help. She can mobilize an army."

"So ignore Sylvie and call Lydia. What's going on with Cilla?"

Polly gestured with her head toward their house. "Aaron came. I called him, but I should be over there. Andrea is a wreck. You know what that's like."

He nodded and glanced at Rebecca. "But I also remember that we didn't want people around while we focused on where she might be. Give it a few minutes. She and Kirk need to have time to process this with Aaron. You think someone took her?"

Rebecca stepped forward and put a roast beef sandwich in front of Polly. "You need to eat that, too. We saw her get into a car with this guy." Her eyes got big. "I'll be right back." She ran out of the room and upstairs.

"Where's she going?" Henry asked.

"Probably to get her sketchbook. She promised Aaron to make a sketch of what she saw this afternoon. Cilla was taken just before I got there. If I'd been on time, this wouldn't have happened, Henry. But I was running late because I couldn't leave Sylvie. It was awful. She was such a mess. She feels like she failed Jason because he can't seem to figure out what he wants to do with his life and now Andrew is a little jackass. He wouldn't admit it to me, but every nasty word he speaks tells me he's spending time with his father this summer. The kid didn't have enough to do and he wasn't spending time with Rebecca, so he was completely available to Anthony's seduction. That man wanted so badly to influence his kids. Jason pushed him away. We all thought Andrew had done the same. We were wrong."

"When did you spend time with Andrew?"

"I was driving home from dropping Shelly off at Grey's and saw him walking on Elm Street. When I tried to talk to him, he was flat out rude to me."

"That was his first mistake."

"Right?" Polly said. "I followed him and kept trying to get him to talk to me. I've never had this much trouble with him in all the time I've known him. But he got meaner and meaner. He accused me of awful things, said more terrible things to me and never once relented. It's a problem that he's so damned smart. He can out-talk just about anyone when he's got a mind to."

"Sounds like someone else I know."

"I was so astonished at his behavior, I found it difficult to keep up. I gave it my best shot. He lied to me, his mother, everyone. Then I talked to Sylvie and she apologized for shutting me out of her life this summer. She thinks I didn't understand why. I did. I just hadn't had time to fix it."

"You've fixed it now."

"Because of this mess. Then we went to her house to confront Andrew. He was supposed to be at band camp today, not in

Bellingwood. When we got there, he was gone. She checked his room. He'd packed his things. He's not answering his phone, his little girlfriend, Maddy, isn't answering hers, and they can't reach Anthony either. Eliseo and Jason are with her, but she needs someone else to push her. Eliseo won't and Jason's her son. She needs me and if not me, Lydia."

"Can you be more helpful there or here with Andrea?" Henry asked her. He had taken a seat next to her but kept his hand on her knee. He pushed the sandwich toward her again. "Eat more of this. Rebecca said so."

Polly grinned. "I feel like I shouldn't laugh, but she's awesome. All pushy and bossy with me. I'm better. I got some ibuprofen in me, so my headache is calming." She held up the empty glass. "That was probably helpful, too. I don't feel like I'm going to pass out. Things were bad in the car. Too much emotion and I didn't have enough to hold up under it."

Rebecca came back into the room. "I tried to call Maddy," she said. "I was going to use her absence today as an excuse to talk to her, but she's still not answering her phone. Do you think she's with Andrew?"

"I don't know," Polly said. "If she isn't, she knows where he is and has been sworn to secrecy."

"Maddy Spotter?" Henry asked.

"Yeah, bitchface," Rebecca replied.

"She's with Andrew now?"

"Yeah. It's not enough that she wants my chair in band, but she has to take my boyfriend? Here's the deal, tootsie-pop, you can have the boy — he's a jerk, but I'm not giving up my chair. I worked hard to get there, so back up and slow your roll."

"You might need to work on your empathy," he said.

"Not with her. Unless we find out that she and Andrew were kidnapped by someone awful or she's been hurt, I have no sympathy for her. None at all."

"Got it." Henry pointed at the sandwich. "Two more bites."

Polly snarled. "You two are mean."

"But you're feeling better, right?" Rebecca asked.

"You're right. I am." She took another bite and then tugged her phone out of her back pocket. "I can't take it. I have to call Lydia."

"Call Sylvie first, just in case," Henry said. "Maybe she has other friends who have shown up to be with her."

Polly gave him a sideways glance. "Our Sylvie? She doesn't ask for help. You have to force it on her." She agreed with him, though, and made the call. It would have been easier to call Eliseo again, but Polly wanted to hear Sylvie's voice.

"Hello?" Sylvie said.

"You haven't heard anything yet, have you?" Polly asked.

"No. Nothing. Eliseo says I should call Aaron. I just keep thinking Andrew will come walking in the back door."

"I understand that."

"He's not going to, is he?"

"I don't think so. I'm sure he's safe, but he's dug this hole so deep he doesn't know how to crawl out of it."

"Just like his mother. When things go bad, the crisis has to come to a head before I acknowledge that I need help," Sylvie said. "Eliseo said something happened with your neighbor?"

"You don't need to worry about that."

"Tell me so I can quit thinking about my own problems."

"Their daughter, Cilla, who is Andrew and Rebecca's age may have been kidnapped."

"Oh, God, no," Sylvie groaned. "You poor thing."

"I'm mostly worried about you and Andrea. You two are under immense amounts of stress right now."

"But you take care of us. I'm so sorry you have to worry about my family when this is going on across the street from you. I am going to kill that man, and then I'm stringing Andrew up by his toenails until he figures out how to be a decent boy again."

"Sylvie, he's going to be fine."

"I hope so. Polly, what if we're totally wrong and something bad has happened to him? I couldn't live with myself."

"He packed his things. This is on him."

"What am I going to do?"

"Have you called the sheriff's office?"

"I keep meaning to, and then, I think he'll figure this out and call me. But he doesn't."

"If I were there, would I let you get away with that?"

Sylvie let out a small, strained chuckle. "No."

"Then I'm sending Lydia to you. She will make you eat something and do what is necessary to get him home. You need her."

"I hate that."

"But I'm right?"

"I still hate it."

"I love you."

"I love you, too. And I'm sorry that your neighbor is dealing with her daughter being taken. I wish I could help."

"Of course you do," Polly said with a smile. "I'm sure Lydia will be there soon."

"Tell her not to hurry. She has plenty of things to take care of in her own life."

"Call Marta. Ask her to be at the bakery in the morning, would you?"

"Oh yeah. I need to do that."

"I'll talk to you later."

Polly hung up, looked at her phone, and then at Henry. "I need to get across the street."

"One thing at a time. Call Lydia first."

Polly made the call. She was so weary of explaining this.

"Hello, dear," Lydia said. "What's up with you?"

"More than I can possibly describe, Lydia. I need you."

Lydia paused. "What can I do to help? I heard something on the scanner about your neighbor. Is Aaron there?"

"Yes. I think her daughter's been kidnapped."

"Oh my," Lydia said with a gasp. "Are you sure?"

"No. I'm not sure. I kind of fell apart this afternoon and I haven't been able to get over to their house yet. Rebecca, Kayla and Libby saw the girl go off with a man, but Cilla wasn't happy about it."

"She knew him?"

"It sounds like it, but did Aaron tell you her mother was run off the road yesterday?"

"Oh, honey. What can I do to help?"

"Could you go to Sylvie's house?"

"Sylvie? What does she have to do with this?"

"Andrew ran away. I think he's with Anthony."

"What?" Lydia's voice was sharp. "Sweet Andrew? With Anthony? He ran away? What is going on?"

"She needs to file a missing person report so they can track Anthony down. He's not supposed to have access to those boys without supervision, but I think he's been spending time with Andrew all summer. You know, he warned me at Jason's graduation party. I figured he was just being a blow-hard, but he knows the best way to get back at me and Sylvie, and Jason, for that matter, is to corrupt Andrew. It's worked. You wouldn't recognize that boy. He's rude and mean."

"Not Andrew. Oh, please, not Andrew. What does Sylvie need from me?"

"She thinks that this is just going to fix itself, but Andrew and Anthony aren't answering their phones. Neither is Andrew's little girlfriend, Maddy Spotter."

"Jake Spotter's girl? That has to be who it is. I know Shirley. I'll give her a call. If Maddy knows anything, Shirley will get on it. She should be home from work any time now."

"That would be awesome. Andrew has completely disconnected from most of his friends. No one knows where he might be."

"I'm proud of you," Lydia said.

"Why?"

"Because you called me for help rather than trying to handle this all by yourself. I'm taking a casserole out of the freezer and heading over right now. Our girl will be cared for tonight, you can be sure of that."

"Thank you, Lydia. I wanted to call you as soon as this happened. Just knowing you're there makes it better."

"I don't know what else I can do but feed her."

"Give her other options. Help her see outside the panic that she's in."

"I can certainly do that. Now, you take care of your neighbor and I'll take care of our girl."

"Thank you, Lydia."

"I love you, Polly."

Polly put the phone down. "I can release that one for now." She put her head in her hands. "I'm not ready to go across the street, but I know that I need to. It's going to be dark and sad and frightened and tense over there."

"You won't be alone," Henry said.

She looked at him. "You'll go with me?"

"That's why I'm here."

"I can't believe you left work early."

"Polly, you don't have to fix the world by yourself. Most of the time the only reason you're alone is because I don't know what's happening."

"I'm sorry."

He stepped down from his seat and moved in to hold her. "That's not what I'm trying to say. There is no reason to be sorry. You are generally deep in the middle of an emergency before you have time to ask for help. Today, you asked and I should have listened when you called. Instead, it took Rebecca's call to light a fire under my hiney. I'm the one who should apologize. I need to listen better, but that's beside the point, too. We're together in this. We're together in everything."

"Thank you for leaving work."

Henry shook his head. "I know that I often let my work take over our lives. It should be subordinate to us. I need to work on that." He turned to Rebecca. "Is it too much to ask you to stay here and direct the troops as they come in?"

"You want me to stay out of it? Cilla's my friend. I saw the guy who took her. You can't do that to me," Rebecca said, her voice tinged with a whine.

Polly grinned at him. "At least it was you who walked into that one and not me. Are you really going to ask that of her?"

"I guess not," Henry said with a sigh. "I have two women in my life who don't let me get away with being the boss of either of them. It isn't fair, but it's what I've got. I'll send a text to Hayden and ask him to keep the home fires burning tonight."

Polly finished the second glass of water that Rebecca had put in front of her. "Have I met my physical needs to your satisfaction, Madame Nurse?"

"Yes, ma'am," Rebecca said. "Thanks for letting me tag along. I promise to stay out of the way."

"If we ask you to leave," Henry said, stopping Rebecca before she got to the back door, "I need you to obey. I promise we won't ask unless we see that there's a very good reason. You may not understand why at the time, but I have to trust you."

Rebecca gave him a frown, then nodded. "I can't imagine why you would have to, but if you ask, I'll listen."

"Thank you." He took a deep breath, then held out his hand for Polly. "Are you ready?"

She put her hand in his. "Nope. Not at all."

The three of them walked across the street. A third sheriff's vehicle had arrived. This didn't look good.

Before Polly could knock on the door, Stu Decker pulled it open. "Hey, Polly."

"Hey, Stu. Can we come in?"

He glanced back into the living room. "Yeah. It's probably good that you're here. The Waters' need some support."

"Have they called Kirk's parents?"

"They picked up the three younger kids about ten minutes ago and took them home. It was for the best." He shook his head. "Mrs. Waters knew the little ones needed her. They didn't want to go either." He shook Henry's hand as they went past him and into the living room.

Kirk Waters was seated in a recliner. He leaned forward in an attempt to stand, but Henry crossed the room to him.

"Man, I'm so sorry that this is going on. Stay seated." Henry shook his hand, then went into the kitchen and brought a straight-backed chair in for himself. "I'm sorry."

Kirk dropped his head and clutched his hair, gripping it until his knuckles were white. "I'm so fucking useless. I should be out there looking for her, doing something, but here I sit."

"You wanna go, you say the word," Henry said. "I'll drive all over hell if that's where you want to go."

"I can't sit here much longer. I'm going to go out of my mind. You'll really take me out?"

"Absolutely. If the sheriff says you don't have to stay, we'll hit the road. I've got nothing but time for you."

Kirk's eyes filled with tears. "Yeah?"

"Oh yeah," Henry said. "Stu?"

"Sheriff Merritt is in the office with Deputy Kellar and Mrs. Waters. Let me make sure he doesn't need anything." Stu left the room.

Polly sat down on the sofa. "I'm sorry, Kirk. We're going to find her."

"Damned right we are. He can't have my girl. Justin?"

His son came in from the kitchen, his face drawn and his eyes red.

"Yeah, Dad?" his voice hopeful.

"Get my chair. Henry and I are headed out. You stay here with your mom, okay?"

"Sure." Justin turned back to the kitchen, his shoulders slumping.

"He wants to help," Polly said quietly.

Kirk gave a short nod. "He needs to help his mother. I can't. Those two have been taking care of this family for years. She trusts him more than she does me right now. He's a good kid."

Henry's brows furrowed as he looked at Polly.

She certainly didn't know the dynamics of this family when they were in crisis. Andrea Waters was definitely in charge, but she'd worried about Kirk's reaction when she'd ended up beneath those shelves in the garage. The strain of what they were facing today was different than bringing Kirk back to normal after he'd lost his leg. This time, neither of them were in control and after all those years apart, the two didn't know how to support each other.

Polly and Henry had been through enough of those to know that it was hard work to maintain a connection.

"Here ya go, Dad," Justin said, bringing the chair into the room. Henry moved back into the kitchen and stood aside while Kirk shifted his body into the wheelchair.

Stu Decker came back, followed by Andrea Waters. Aaron and Will Kellar trailed behind them.

"You want to leave us?" Andrea asked.

"I gotta do something other than sit here," Kirk said, pleading with her. "Henry will drive. I just gotta go look for her. You understand, don't you?"

"No," she said. "I need you. Justin needs you. Cilla needs you."

He closed his eyes. "Please, Andrea. I can't sit on my ass and feel useless. This guy has our girl. Just let me get out and feel like I'm doing something productive. Please."

Andrea's eyes flashed as she took in the people in her living room. She landed on Polly.

Polly nodded.

"Fine," she said. "Make sure you have your phone."

"It's right here." Kirk patted his pocket. "I'll check in. And you check in with me. Call me if you have anything."

Andrea stepped back to let him pass, then thought better of it and stepped forward to block him again. She reached down and hugged his neck. "I'm sorry."

"Thanks, babe. I just need …"

"I know. I understand."

CHAPTER TWENTY

"Everyone is gone." Andrea Waters stood at the front door as she watched her husband leave with Henry. She shook her head. "I've sent them away. My family is breaking apart. What have I done?"

The entire room was silent. What could possibly be the response to that?

Aaron Merritt tapped Will Kellar's arm. "Go on, Deputy."

"It will be live as soon as I'm in Boone," Will said. He made his way around Andrea and left.

"You go, too, Deputy," Aaron said to Stu. "I'll stay."

Stu nodded at Polly, then slipped out behind Will.

"Rebecca," Aaron said. "What do you have for me?" He pointed at her sketch pad.

"It isn't much," Rebecca said. "I drew everything I could remember. I can keep working on it."

Andrea reached across Rebecca and snatched the pad out of her hand, flipping through it until she landed on the last sketch. "I knew it. I was right. That's him. Scott Richards," she said slamming her index finger at the image. "That's him. How did he find us?"

Rebecca cringed at the fury rolling off Andrea and bolted for the sofa. When she sat down, Polly put her arm across Rebecca's lap and tucked her close.

"May I?" Aaron asked quietly. He took the pad from Andrea, looked at it, and then turned to Rebecca. "You did a nice job. And you captured the car as well." He nodded. "I was afraid of that."

"What?" Andrea asked.

"This car was reported stolen early this morning. He's shifting through vehicles quickly. We won't find them in this one. It's been seen." He looked at his phone and tapped the screen. "In fact, it's just been found."

"Where?" she asked, sounds of desperation filling her voice.

"Two blocks from the high school. I'm sure he ditched it right away and had another one ready to go."

"So that doesn't give us a single lead," Andrea moaned. She paced back and forth. "Justin, call your father and tell them to quit looking for a blue car. We don't know what he's driving now."

Justin nodded and went into the kitchen.

"Who is this Scott Richards?" Polly asked.

Andrea stopped. "A psychotic son of a bitch that should have been locked away. Would they listen when I told them he was stalking our family? No." She took a long, deep breath and exhaled slowly. "He was part of Kirk's unit. Everyone knew he was crazy, but they didn't know how bad it was. When the guys talked about their families, Scott was always there, looking at their pictures, listening to their stories, but he never had any of his own. He got too crazy even for the military and they sent him home. It was weak, but he'd been hurt and they got him out on a medical discharge. He started showing up at our homes. At first, it was nice to hear stories about Kirk. It kinda helped make the connection more real. Scott could tell a story and make you feel like you were right there, part of everything. None of us thought a thing about it. We knew he missed the guys, so all of us were fine with inviting him to dinner. You know, we thought we were just being family. It's what we do.

"Then Kirk lost his leg. He came back to the States and lived in the hospital. Scott spent some time with him there, but Kirk was so out of it, he didn't think anything was weird. Some of the other guys and their families were transferred to other bases, but Scott just stayed. I don't even know if he had a job. I was focused on Kirk and my own job and my kids. Scott was kind of always around. He wouldn't go away. Ever. Then one day he was creeping on Cilla."

Polly's eyes grew wide and she clutched Rebecca a little tighter.

"She got uncomfortable and said something to me. He hadn't hurt her, so I told him that unless I was home, he wasn't welcome. I mentioned it to Kirk and he came unglued. He had no idea that Scott had been spending that much time with us. That's when he told me that Scott wasn't right upstairs and that we needed to be careful." She shook her head. "Well, great. Like I could put that genie back in the bottle. I'd come home from the hospital and find him sitting in the empty lot across from our house. He freakin' had a pair of binoculars and he was right out there, watching like he wasn't doing anything wrong. I called the MPs that first night. They came by and rousted him, but that was all. The next day I discovered him in a neighbor's yard. Honestly, I think it got worse when I told him to go away. He wasn't going to be denied. Maybe if I'd allowed him to stay, he wouldn't have melted down."

"He was getting weirder and weirder before you stopped him, Mom," Justin said. "He showed up at school one day. It scared Lara."

"He what? You didn't tell me about that."

Justin stepped further into the room. "You were busy with Dad all the time. I talked to him and asked him to stop scaring the little kids."

"You did?"

He shrugged. "What was he going to do to me?"

"What did he say?"

"He just told me that he wouldn't hurt anyone and we were his only family. I told him that family didn't scare their sisters and brothers and he was scaring mine."

Rebecca sat forward, dislodging Polly's hand. "Did he stop?"

"Not really."

"He did when they finally picked him up and put him in the brig," Andrea said. "But that was only for six months. Then they kicked him off the base. But that didn't stop him from hanging out at Cilla and Justin's school. It took a while before we realized that he was even there. He'd gotten pretty good at hiding himself. For the most part, all he did was watch. Then, about six months ago, we started getting packages at the house filled with photographs he'd taken and we realized he was posting them online, too. He'd created a fake account and they couldn't link it back to him. The police gave a half-hearted try connecting him to it, but he hadn't hurt anyone, so there wasn't much they could do. People can take photos. Most of the pictures were of Cilla, but there were plenty of me with the kids when we were out. It's like he waited for us to leave the base and then followed us everywhere." She huffed a breath. "I have no idea how he could afford a car, but he must have had one. I never saw him and trust me, I looked. I don't know where he was living, I couldn't tell you anything more about him. All of a sudden, the packages and the online photos just stopped. There was nothing. I figured he must have gotten caught doing something else and tossed in jail again. I hoped it was for a long, long time. I knew we were moving to Bellingwood and figured it would be far enough away, he'd never find us. Maybe he'd move on."

Andrea dropped into an old, overstuffed chair and tucked her legs up underneath her. "We all breathed a sigh of relief when the moving company drove off with our things and we still hadn't heard from him. We took a long, slow trip, stopping to see the sights along the way. Kirk was doing great, the family was happy to see Deb and Louis, and we were excited about a new adventure." She gave Polly a smile. "Then we moved in across the street from you guys and you can't even believe the noisy happy kids I had those first few days. We had great neighbors with kids who were ready to play. We all thought we'd hit the jackpot."

"You did," Aaron said. "We love Polly and Henry and their family. They are as good a people as you'll ever know."

"I feel like I've brought horror to this wonderfully quaint little town," Andrea said.

Polly blinked, glared at Aaron and then looked at Andrea. "I know your in-laws have told you about me."

"Yeah." Andrea pointed to the sofa. "That's why I want you to sit right there. You aren't finding my daughter's body. She's coming home safe."

"Polly also finds people who are lost. They aren't always bodies," Rebecca said defensively. "She found me and my mom and she's found a bunch of other people who needed her to be right where she was. Polly says that her finding bodies is a good thing. They might be dead, but they needed to be found."

Andrea untucked her legs, sat up and reached out to touch Rebecca. "I'm sorry. I forgot about you and your mother. Deb told me that story, too. She told us the stories about all of your kids, Polly. Rebecca's right. That was a knee-jerk reaction."

"I get that from a lot of people. I don't blame them," Polly said. "I hate that this is my reputation, but at the same time, I'm glad it's me and not someone else. Poor Sheriff Merritt has to take my calls. His job is the hard one. I pass the problem off to him and his deputies. You're lucky to be in his county. He's a good man. What do you think this Scott Richards wants with Cilla?"

"I don't know for sure," Andrea said. "I can almost guarantee you that he won't call us looking for a ransom. He doesn't think that way. He wants a family. Kirk told me that Scott's family abandoned him when he was little. He went through a ton of foster families. When he aged out of the system, he went into the military. It was the only place he ever felt like he belonged."

"Scott told me one night that Cilla looked just like one of his foster moms," Justin said. "I totally forgot about that until right now. He said it was the only place he'd ever felt like they cared, but then they moved away because of her husband's job. They weren't prepared to adopt him. I think he said he was nine or ten years old. I'm sorry I never told you some of this stuff, Mom."

"How would you know it was important?" she asked. "He talked about a million things with us. My Cilla is bright. She'll

THAT'S WHAT FRIENDS ARE FOR

figure out how to handle him. Hopefully she's smart enough to figure out how to get away. Until then, I don't know what else we can do." Andrea turned to look out the window. "I understand why Kirk had to leave. I don't like it. I wish he were here, but I'm just being selfish." She looked up. "Justin, why don't you show Rebecca the Camaro. You and your dad have put so much work into it. If you want to take a ride, go ahead. Just don't be gone long."

Rebecca glanced up at Polly.

"Go ahead," Polly said. She squeezed Rebecca's knee. "Not too fast, though, okay? I know about those cars."

Neither of the kids protested, though it was obvious they didn't want to leave.

"Call if you find out anything," Rebecca said. "Right away."

"We will."

When the back door slammed shut, Andrea breathed a sigh of relief. "Justin always has to be the strong one. Kirk is trying to re-establish himself as the man of the household, but for so long that's been my job. I've made all the decisions for our family. He was too busy making decisions that kept his unit alive, so the least I could do was manage our family for him. Now he's lost. He's so messed up from constantly being on alert, and then he lost part of himself. He hates the idea of taking meds, but his doctors insist. When Kirk doesn't take them, he drops deep into a depression. It feeds itself from there. He feels useless and helpless. I'd hoped that when we got to Bellingwood where he was happy and safe, he'd find new ways to come out of himself. Maybe get a job, help his parents, find old friends, make new friends. Working out at the Mikkels' place on the Camaro with Justin was great. Every once in a while, I'd see an inkling of the old Kirk. Those two came home the other night and he and Justin beamed as they described their day. For the first time in a year, Justin looked at Kirk like he saw his dad again, not just a broken man he'd have to take care of for the rest of his life."

She sighed. "Then this happened. I don't know what this will do to my husband. I'm glad Henry was here. Kirk likes him a lot."

A quiet rap on the front door made them all jump.

"I've got it," Polly said, as she came to her feet. She walked over and opened the door to Andy Specek. "Hey, Andy."

"I'm not staying," Andy said, and held out a bag from Sweet Beans, along with a drink carrier. "Thought you all might need some sustenance."

"Andrea?" Polly said.

Andrea stepped up to the door.

"This is Andy Specek. She lives down there." Polly pointed behind her house. "She's one of my closest friends."

"It's nice to meet you, ma'am," Andrea said.

Andy nodded and offered a warm smile. "I'm so sorry for what you're facing this evening. I wanted to drop these off and run, so don't even think about inviting me in. When this is all over, we'll talk about how Polly managed to add yet another woman to her life with our same name. There are people in town who care about you even though you haven't met them yet. Know that." She nodded again. "I'm just on my way home from the library, so I'd best get going. Two dogs will be waiting for me. Take care."

With that, she was heading back down the steps and to her car.

"That was nice," Andrea said. "I can't believe she didn't stay."

"My friends have a sixth sense about that," Polly said. "Andy and Sheriff Merritt's wife have been friends forever. Wait until you meet Lydia." She choked back tears. "A more loving and generous woman you'll never know. She scooped me up when I moved to Bellingwood and ensured that I was never alone when I didn't want to be. And when I needed to be, she was nowhere to be found. We're lucky to have her in our midst."

With a small smile, Polly looked at Aaron. "And she calls him snook-ums."

"I was going to tell you something nice about Polly," Aaron said. "But I've forgotten what it was."

"Sheriff, I don't know what you can do here," Andrea said. "You surely have other matters that need your attention. We'll let you know if we hear anything. Until Cilla makes contact, I'm at a loss."

He looked down at his tablet. "We've been pinging her phone. It's not online. Deputy Kellar and Deputy Decker are running down the most recent car thefts and law enforcement has been alerted throughout the region. Your photograph of Cilla and the one you had of Mr. Richards are being circulated and the Amber Alert has gone out." He shuddered a breath. "Two Amber Alerts tonight. What's this world coming to?"

"Two?" Andrea asked.

Polly turned to Aaron. "Andrew Donovan?"

He nodded. "Deputy Hudson is with the Donovans right now."

"Who is Andrew Donovan?" Andrea asked.

Polly put her head in her hands and felt the tears come. "I'm sorry," she said. "I'll be better in a minute."

"Andrew is a close friend of Polly's family. He used to date Rebecca," Aaron said. He sat down beside Polly. "You know he's with his father. All we have to do is track that man down."

"I know," she said, sniffing back the tears. "You're right. I'm being ridiculous."

"My goodness, Polly." Andrea sat down on her other side, then snagged a box of tissues from the table in front of them. "You're having a terrible day."

"Because this is about me?" Polly asked through a pained laugh. "No, I'm just being emotional. I know what's going on with Andrew. It's not fun and it's going to be difficult on his family, but he's not in any danger. His father is a nasty-mouthed, abusive man and is trying to prove that he's a big deal in his kids' lives." She pointed at the drink carrier on the table in front of them. "One of those is for me. I just know it is. What's in the bag?"

Aaron stood up. "I'm going back to the office. I'll call before I leave and stop by before I go home." He handed Andrea a business card. "Polly has my number, but my personal cell phone number is on the back. No matter what time, day or night, call if you need me." Patting Polly's shoulder, he smiled at her. "She does. I will be here as fast as I can put my clothes on and get out the door."

"Thank you, Sheriff." Andrea stood and walked with him to the front door. "Thank you for everything."

"As soon as this is all over, we'll all meet in Polly's back yard for dinner and some homemade ice cream. That okay with you, Polly?"

"You know it is, Aaron."

"Thank you." Andrea held the door open and watched him walk away.

Polly had opened the bag and emptied it of its contents: chocolate muffins, lemon muffins, croissants, raspberry and blueberry scones, chocolate chip cookies, a half dozen sourdough rolls, napkins, butter, and plastic knives. "A little bit of everything. Can you eat?"

"I guess. It smells wonderful."

"Sylvie Donovan is the head baker at Sweet Beans," Polly said. "She's another one of my friends."

"Andrew's mother?"

Polly nodded. "I was with her this afternoon before I went to Boone."

"You poor thing."

"No, really. I'm doing fine. Talk to me."

Andrea looked at Polly, then looked away, peering at the cups in front of her. She picked up one marked as a dark roast and set it back down, then picked up a sourdough roll. She took her time, breaking the roll in half, then opening a pat of butter and spreading it on the roll. Before she could take a bite, she dropped it to the table and let out a muted wail.

Polly scooted closer to her and enveloped the woman, holding her as she sobbed and sobbed.

CHAPTER TWENTY-ONE

It felt eerie. The household was too subdued Friday morning. Polly's first cup of coffee still sat in front of her on the island. She'd barely touched it. Cat had gotten up with the little boys and taken them to Marie's house for the day. The thing was, Polly knew that those four little boys kept her grounded, but she didn't know where the day would take her. Rebecca was on her way to Boone with Libby and Kayla. She wasn't any too happy about that, wanting to stay beside Polly, just in case news came in about either Andrew or Cilla.

Polly had almost considered allowing her to stay home, but this last day was too important. She promised to get Rebecca if anything big unfolded.

Kirk and Henry returned at ten o'clock last night. They'd driven through all of Boone and most of the communities in the county. There had been nothing. Rebecca and Justin had come home earlier than that, bringing sub sandwiches with them. They had also spent time driving through the countryside, looking for any sign of Cilla.

Aaron had called just before Kirk and Henry came back.

They'd gone through the neighborhood where the blue car had been found and discovered Cilla's cell phone, crushed and destroyed.

Polly sent Rebecca home at midnight and Henry followed soon after. He was going to check in with his crews this morning and be back to do whatever Kirk needed him to do. Fortunately, Fridays were generally a cleanup day as the guys prepared for the next week's work.

Polly had stayed with Andrea until after two o'clock. She'd offered to leave several times, but Andrea wasn't ready to be alone. Kirk had gone into their bedroom, but the television was on, so he wasn't sleeping either.

The sky outside this morning reflected Polly's mood. Dark gray clouds threatened to unleash torrential storms on them today.

Her phone rang and Polly grabbed it up, hoping for good news. Why was Rebecca calling? "Hey, what's up?" Polly asked.

"Can you come get me?"

"Tell me why you're ducking out on this last day."

"Mr. Edelbrock says I should go home. The whole band is, like, depressed. He told me that I know my part just fine and I should be with you rather than here." Rebecca sighed. "I don't think I'm paying enough attention."

"You're sure?"

"Yeah. Do you mind?"

"No problem. I'll be right down. Say, is Maddy there today?"

"No, she didn't show up. Her friend, Aria Grossman says that Maddy is grounded from everything for three months because she skipped school yesterday and then didn't answer her phone or the front door when people were looking for Andrew."

"She doesn't know where he is?"

"He left with his dad. That's all she knew. Aria told me that when Jason went to her house, they were hiding in a neighbor's yard waiting for Anthony to pick Andrew up."

"Sounds like she'd better be grounded. I hope that means she's stuck at home. Sylvie will kill her if she sees her. I should call her this morning."

"Get on the road to come get me first, please?"

Polly smiled. "I'm on it."

Deb and Louis Waters had arrived early this morning with Nat, Lara, and Abby. Their car was still in the driveway, so she hoped they'd be there most of today. She sent a quick text to Andrea, *"Heading to Boone to pick Rebecca up. If you need me, call. If I don't hear from you, I'll call to check in later. I love you."*

She snagged the keys for Cat's car from the hook and headed outside. It even smelled like a storm. Before she backed out, she swiped to call Sylvie and set her phone on the console.

"Good morning, Polly," Sylvie said.

"How are you doing, sweetie?"

"I'm at work."

"You're what?"

"Yeah. So's Jason. We talked about it last night. There's nothing we can do sitting at home. Did you hear that we're sure he's with Anthony?"

"I just talked to Rebecca. One of Maddy's friends said that she finally talked."

"Yeah. Little whore-slut-bitch."

"Whoa."

"Sorry," Sylvie whispered. "I'm by the back door. No one else can hear me. If I ever get my hands on that little freak, I will …"

"You'll what."

"You're right. I'll do nothing. Except I might glare daggers at her and tell her that I think she's a selfish little twit."

"That sounds more like my Sylvie."

"Her mother called me last night, so apologetic. They had no idea what Maddy was doing. They didn't even know she was dating Andrew. Polly, I just want to be sick. I think my son learned too much from that girl. I mean, way too much."

"What do you mean?"

"Her mother found condoms. Condoms! I told her that she might consider taking Maddy to someone who could talk to her. There's no girl that needs to be sexually active at that age. She's just out of eighth grade. What in the hell?"

"What are you going to do about Andrew?"

"The minute I get him home, he's going to have an appointment with Grey. I'm not about to have a kid living in my home who won't talk to me. If not me, then Grey. We're going to find out exactly why he thinks that this behavior is appropriate. I refuse to act like it isn't happening."

"Do you believe Andrew is having sex?"

"I think he's a boy and he's curious. I think that if he wanted to rebel against me and found a girl who encouraged him to do things he'd never considered before in his life, he'd do it, just to find out what it was all about. And I know my genetic offspring well enough to know that if he liked it, he's smart enough to justify his behavior."

"I don't want my kids to grow up," Polly said.

"It's the worst. You don't think he and Rebecca ..." Sylvie's voice trailed off.

"I don't think so, but trust me, I'm going to ask that question again in about ten minutes. This is why I was so thankful that Kayla was always around."

"But kids find a way."

"I know." Polly shook her head. "No, I don't know, but I get it. Do you have a full house this morning?"

"Marta is coming in about ten thirty. She wants to talk to the girls about moving in together. Are you okay with that?"

"It's fine with me," Polly said. "I'm not her mother. I've just been a safe place for her to recover. She's been here nearly eight months and I think she's grown up quite nicely. Do they get along well?"

"Lissa and Shelly?"

"Yeah." Polly shook her head. Sylvie wasn't completely on task here, but she understood.

"Sorry," Sylvie said. "They're doing fine together. Nothing wonderful, but then, nothing uncomfortable or awkward either. The thing is, Shelly is still talking about how wonderful it is at Marta's house. I wonder if she thought that she'd get to stay there."

"I'm so thankful she's still seeing Grey. Do me a favor?"

"Anything."

"Let Shelly know she needs to talk to me before she makes any decisions. She needs to talk to her father about this, too. I understand that she's an adult, but she has responsibilities to us, just like we are responsible to each other."

"I'll do that. I know Marta is just trying to help these girls find their way. Her heart is as big as the ocean."

"I'm not upset at all," Polly said. "Shelly just needs to be reminded that she's part of a bigger family. Even though she's gaining her independence, it doesn't change anything. We still love her and want to know what's she's doing."

"Are we going to be taking care of kids who make bad decisions for the rest of our lives, Polly?"

Polly chuckled. "Yeah. That's why you need to get off your keister and do something about Eliseo."

"What? What does that have to do with this?"

"If you spend much more time waiting for your kids to be all grown up or out of the house or making good decisions, you're going to miss out on the fun that you two could be having. Don't waste time. Find some of that fun for yourself."

"Well, you're kinda bossy."

"I know. And I feel terrible about it."

"No you don't."

"Actually, I kind of do. People told me that I needed to quit thinking about being with Henry and just do it. I'll never admit that they were right. I needed to do things my own way, but at the same time, the minute I quit trying to manage the relationship and just allowed it to happen? We had fun. I'd created so many rules and unwarranted concerns around it that I was making the whole thing more difficult than it needed to be."

"You aren't trying to tell me I'm a control freak, are you?" Sylvie asked with a small laugh.

"I wouldn't dare. You'd beat me."

"Darn right I would. I'll think about what you said, though. He spent the night with us last night. It was so nice to have him there.

He's steady and strong and when I cried, he held me. He didn't try to get me to go to bed and sleep, he allowed me to manage my worry and grief on my own."

"Yeah, he'll get over that when you're married. You do have to kick them in the butt every once in a while to remind them who's in charge."

"Wait. Marriage? Who said anything about marriage?"

"Oops. Sorry. You're in control. Not me."

"You are a problem child. Have you heard anything more about Cilla Waters?"

Polly turned on the street leading to the high school. "Nothing yet. If Rebecca's up for it, I think we might wander around and look for her."

"Do you have a feeling?"

"Not really. I just want to be busy with something. I sat up with Andrea late last night, but her in-laws are there today. I don't much feel like sitting around the house and I can promise that my brain won't allow me to do any work. It is all over the place. These kids need to come home soon so we can all just calm down."

"No kidding. Well, let me know if you hear anything."

"You too. I love you, Sylvie."

"I love you, too. Thanks for calling."

Polly drove into the parking lot as Sylvie ended the call. The skies hadn't yet unleashed their torrent, so Rebecca was standing outside waiting for her.

"Perfect timing," she said as she climbed into the car. She turned and put her things in the back seat. "I just walked out to see if you were here."

"You're sure this is okay?" Polly asked.

"It's fine. I was useless there and I already have everything memorized."

"That doesn't surprise me."

"Everybody was talking about Andrew and then Cilla, too. They kept asking me all these questions. Like I know anything. I haven't talked to Andrew in forever. How should I know what's going on with him?"

"How much do you know?" Polly asked.

"What do you mean?"

"I'm about to ask you a very uncomfortable question. I expect honesty."

Rebecca swallowed. "How uncomfortable?"

"How sexually active were you and Andrew?"

Silence fell in the car.

"Wow, you just came right out and asked," Rebecca said.

"I want an answer and your silence is making me nervous."

"Don't worry. We didn't do anything all the way. I promise. Both of us knew you and Henry would kill us."

"That's the only reason?"

Rebecca shrugged. "Isn't it enough?"

Polly didn't have a good answer for that. "I would have liked you to think about the consequences for yourselves. For your future. Not just punishment from me."

"I guess we did. It's not something we spent a lot of time talking about. It's no big deal."

"Sex is no big deal?" Polly was starting to ramp up for a bigger conversation.

"No. Whether we did anything or not. I mean, yeah. It's ..." She turned to Polly. "This is awkward."

"Be prepared for it to get worse unless you talk to me."

"Great. Can't you just be happy that we didn't do anything?"

"No. What if you start dating someone who is a little stronger at encouraging you to have sex. What then?"

"It's my body. If I don't want to have sex with him, then it's not going to happen. That's all there is to it. No boy is going to tell me what I should or shouldn't do."

"That's the first part of a good answer."

"Look, I get it that sex is all about intimacy and there's a bigger picture than just one single moment in time. And I've heard all the talk from them at church about how it makes you one body and you shouldn't share that with anyone until you're prepared to be with that person for the rest of your life. And I know all the stuff about saving yourself for marriage."

"But?"

"There's no but. I get it all. I'm not in any hurry to be that involved with someone. Anyone. And I know that Henry teases me about being thirty-five or whatever. Here's what I'll tell you. High school is kind of a big deal for me. I want to be able to do a million things. I want to go places with Beryl and experience as much of the world as I can. I want to travel with her and I want to focus on my art. I want to graduate in the top ten percent of my class. I want to have my pick of colleges and get scholarships so I have the freedom to do all of that. If I screw up my life by getting pregnant or getting hung up with some guy that I can't keep my hands off, I won't be able to live my dream. At least not right away. I don't want to put those dreams on hold. I want to go do all of that."

Polly wasn't quite sure what to do with this information. They'd never talked about it in these terms before. "Good. You avoided the awkward."

"I can't guarantee I won't do something stupid," Rebecca said. "You and I both know that, but my dreams and goals are bigger than just one boy." She turned to Polly and grinned. "Or maybe several boys. Who knows? The world's my oyster."

"Yeah?"

"Justin Waters is really nice," Rebecca said. "I couldn't believe it when his mom told him to take me for a drive in his Camaro. And you let me! It was like you were throwing us together. And hello, I was okay with that."

"What did you two talk about?"

Rebecca shrugged. "Everything. We talked about school. He was asking about some of the different people he's already met. I think he has a pretty good handle on what people are like. Of course, we talked about Cilla. He feels like he should have seen this coming. That Scott guy was really creepy. Justin thought he was harmless, but still, creepy. We talked about him moving to Bellingwood. I want to introduce him to Jason and some of his friends. I think he'd like them. But then, most of them are off to college, so that won't help. He'll make friends at school. It's just going to be hard, him being a senior and everything. I wouldn't want to move to a new school my senior year. He says that Cilla is seriously talented. Like over-the-top. She's got this big, gorgeous singing voice. She took lessons and everything. And she loves acting. He says she wants to at least audition on Broadway someday. That's like her first goal. But what she really wants to do is own a production company that produces their own plays and musicals and stuff. Like, in a big theater? But she wants to do that after she's done everything else. Maybe I can design her sets and things."

"And Andrew could write the scripts."

Rebecca nodded. "I miss him so much. I wish he hadn't gotten so stupid. If we could have just figured out how to be friends again. I kinda think I'd be fine with him dating other girls. Well, except for Maddy. I know he chose her to make me mad." She flipped her head toward Polly. "Is that why you were asking me about sex? Because of her? Can you even believe it? She's not even in high school and everybody knows that she'll put out for nearly anybody if they just ask."

"Do you think they're having sex?"

"I can't believe Andrew would be that stupid. He knows who she is."

"Maybe that's why he wanted to date her."

"It doesn't sound like him." Rebecca flicked her hand at the wrist. "But, like anything he's done this summer sounds like him. I'd like to know what happened in his tiny little brain. It's like someone flipped a switch and a brand-new version of Andrew Donovan started walking around."

"Before you two broke up, how much did he talk about his father?"

"I don't know. Some, I guess."

"Were they seeing each other?"

She nodded. "A couple of times. It started maybe after graduation, but it was no big deal. His dad just wanted to get to know Andrew better."

"And when did this happen? Did Sylvie know?"

Silence.

"Did Andrew ever tell his mother that he was coming to our house and then meet up with his father?"

"Maybe?"

"And when things started falling apart yesterday, it didn't occur to you to tell me about this?"

"There wasn't really time," Rebecca whined. "We were so busy with Cilla and stuff."

"So if he was sneaking around behind his mother's back, it didn't occur to you that something might be wrong with that decision?"

"Like Andrew said, he should be able to see his father. Just because his mother doesn't like him, that doesn't mean Andrew shouldn't."

"You believe that the adults in your lives make bad decisions for you."

"Well."

"Go ahead."

"Sometimes you don't take our feelings into consideration."

"Really," Polly said. "You believe that? You and Andrew talked about this?"

"Yeah."

"You think that Sylvie just willy-nilly made a decision about Andrew's life without considering the long-term implications?"

"Well, when you put it that way."

"I know that we've talked about this before. Henry and I don't make decisions about your life because we want to control you or stop you from doing fun things. Neither does Sylvie. But we often have more history with a situation, and because we've been around a few years longer than you, we've got more experience."

"If you'd ever talk to us, we'd understand why you make those decisions."

"Really?" Polly slowly turned to her. "Really?"

"Yeah. If Sylvie would have talked to Andrew about why she didn't want him spending time with Anthony, he could have made a different decision."

"You don't think she ever talked to him," Polly said flatly. "You believe that Andrew was completely uninformed about who his father is. You honestly believe that Sylvie chose to keep them apart without supervision simply because she was trying to stop Andrew from spending time with Anthony?"

"Gahhh," Rebecca said. "That's not it. You make it sound so bad."

"Rebecca, Anthony has taken Andrew away from his mother. They aren't answering their phones. Andrew hid in someone's back yard with Maddy so he could run away with his father. He snuck around this summer and involved you in the lie. He turned into someone that no one recognizes and we don't like very much. He broke up with you and tried to blame it on you. Tell me what's not so bad about that?"

"Nothing. It's all bad. I'm sorry."

"That's not what I want," Polly said, drained by the conversation. "I don't want your apology. I want you to understand so you handle this better the next time. Those things that you want for yourself? Those goals and dreams you talked about a little while ago? I want those things for you and I will do everything I can to help you achieve them. Along the way, I'm going to make decisions for you that you disagree with. We'll try to talk about them, but if Henry and I decide something, you need to understand that we do so with your very best interests in mind. Sylvie has done that for her son and he refused to get on board with it. Now look what's happened."

"I can't let this happen to me, is what you're telling me."

"I don't think it will. I hope that you will always communicate with me."

"We talked about sex. That wasn't fun."

Polly chuckled. "We'll talk about more uncomfortable subjects over the next few years. I missed having my mother around for some of those conversations. Mary was wonderful, but sometimes I needed Mom."

The rain had started coming down on them when Polly left Boone. She was driving aimlessly as she spoke with Rebecca, wandering down the highway. Instead of turning to go to Bellingwood, she headed west.

"What would you like to do for lunch?" Polly asked.

"Just us? Like a restaurant?"

"Sure. I don't know where we'll find one unless we go back to Bellingwood."

"No. That's boring. We eat at those places all the time. Let's do something else."

"There's a barbecue place in Stratford."

"No. I don't want barbecue."

"There's a bar and grill over in Boxholm. It's not much farther."

"You don't want to go home, do you?"

"It's depressing there."

"I'm game if you are, then."

"They're supposed to have great pork tenderloins."

Rebecca laughed. "I should have known. Onward."

The rain had steadily grown stronger. With the strange storms that had ripped through Iowa this summer, Polly probably should have just gone on home, but she was out and hoped a little rain wouldn't hurt them.

She approached the hill that went down into the Des Moines River valley and took a breath. This was beautiful when it wasn't raining. She hoped Cat's car had good tires. It was a long way down and a long way back up the other side. As soon as she started down the hill, rain poured out of the sky, making it nearly impossible to see. She turned her wipers on as fast as they would go, but there was no way she was staying on the highway during this. She didn't know how long this rain would last. If she remembered right, there was a turnoff at the bottom of the hill, just on the other side of the river. Checking her rear-view mirror for any traffic, she slowed and breathed a sigh of relief when she saw the road she was looking for.

"We're just going to wait this out," she said.

"Thank goodness. This is scary."

Polly turned off the road and drove a little further to find a place to turn around. Since she was moving more slowly than while on the highway, visibility wasn't quite as bad and she finally found an access road that ran along the river. She turned into it, but refused to go much further in Cat's car. Had she been in her pickup, she might have considered it. Polly turned in. As she put it in reverse, she hesitated, seeing something white among the green trees in front of her. Her breath caught.

"What?" Rebecca asked.

Polly pointed.

Rebecca groaned. "Nooooooo."

Instead of backing up, Polly crept forward.

CHAPTER TWENTY-TWO

Gripping the dashboard as Polly drove ahead on the terrible path that called itself a road, Rebecca leaned forward to peer out. "It can't be, Polly. It just can't be. Why did you have to come over here to find someone? Just once couldn't we take a drive and end up where we'd planned?"

"I know, honey," Polly said. She kept both hands on the steering wheel; the road was muddy and filled with holes that tossed them forward and backward, side to side. Getting in was the easy part, getting out of here was going to be treacherous. "I can't see it anymore. How far up was it?"

"I didn't see what you saw," Rebecca said. "I'm useless. You just pointed over here somewhere. It's kind of like when you tell me to look at the deer in a field. I never see it. Everyone else does, but I never do. But I figure that since you're here, you must have seen something."

While the rain was still coming down, at least the pelting torrent that drove them off the main road had moved on. Polly turned the windshield wipers to a slower setting. At high speed, they'd been as difficult to see through as the sheeting water. And the sound of them flying across the glass agitated Polly as she tried to concentrate on the road while looking through the woods for a bit of white.

Then she saw something flutter. "There," she said. "Right through there."

"Where?" Rebecca asked. While she was looking in the general direction, she turned her head back and forth, searching for what Polly had seen.

Polly slowed and finally the car lurched to a stop in a pothole. If she had to call for a tow truck to get out of this place, she wasn't going to be happy. "I see it just through there. I'm going in, but you have to stay in the car."

"What if you need me? If it isn't safe for me, it might not be safe for you. Just call the sheriff. I don't want you to get hurt. I won't be able to even see you if you go into those woods."

"It isn't that far. Less than an few dozen yards. Please stay in the car and lock the doors after I leave. I need to know that you're safe. Keep your phone in your hand. If something happens to me, you'll have to call for more help." She pointed ahead to the river. "We're on the west side of the Des Moines river just east of Pilot Mound. Those directions should get Henry here to find you. Don't get out of the car, don't let anyone in. If you have to drive away, slide over and do that. No one will be upset that you're driving with only a permit."

"Now you're scaring me," Rebecca said.

"I'm sorry. I generally don't have to go this far away from you when I find someone. And if it's more than an accident ..."

"Like a murder?"

Polly sighed. "Okay, yes. I worry that the person who committed it might still be around. This is a perfect area to hide. They're way back in here and this road is never traveled."

"Where do you think the car is if the bad person is still around."

"I don't know," Polly said. "I just want you to be safe. Stay here, lock the doors, keep your phone handy."

"But you'll take your phone, won't you?"

Polly nodded and reached over to give Rebecca a hug. "It's going to be all right."

"Two of my friends are missing and you're about to go out into a storm to see if you've just found one of them. I don't know how it's supposed to be okay." Rebecca's voice cracked with emotion. She swiped a tear from her cheek.

Taking a moment, Polly sat back in her seat, then brushed Rebecca's hair back from her face. "I know this is hard for you. I wish with all my heart that you weren't here right now."

"It wouldn't be any easier if I got the news at home," Rebecca said. "And I guess it's better that it's you doing this than someone else who doesn't care. Be careful?"

"I'll be fine." Polly looked down at her light tan canvas shoes. "These will be a mess, but I'll be fine." She took a deep breath, opened the car door and stepped out into the soaking rain, then plunged into the deeply wooded area where she'd seen the white cloth.

She walked for about twenty yards, picking her way across the thick vegetation on the woodland floor. There was no path. This had been a mistake. Polly wasn't sure where she was going and though the leaves of the trees above her offered some protection, the steady rain still made it difficult to see. All she could do was count on the fact that she was supposed to be here and would find her way.

As she trudged deeper in among the trees, she shook her head. "Count on the fact that I'm supposed to be here?" she asked out loud. "What kind of witchery is this? Good heavens, Giller, you're starting to believe it. Stop being ridiculous."

But sure enough, after she'd walked another twenty or thirty yards, she lifted her head to look forward and saw something white behind a tree. How had she glimpsed that from the road? This poor person really needed to be found. Polly continued on, terrified of who it might be. From this perspective she couldn't tell if it was a male or female, youth or adult. She couldn't imagine telling Sylvie that she'd found Andrew today. The thought of that made her choke. Andrea didn't know her well enough to understand that what Polly did was part and parcel of who Polly was. She would be destroyed.

She picked up the pace, wanting to get this over as quickly as possible. When she rounded the tree, she stopped in her tracks, utterly surprised. She took out her phone, opened it to the photograph of Scott Richards that Andrea had given Sheriff Merritt and looked back and forth three times.

He'd been shot. Polly couldn't tell if he'd been shot while sitting here or not. She gathered her wits about her and looked around the immediate area to see if there'd been a scuffle or maybe even drag marks. There was broken vegetation leading deeper into the woods. It looked as if the brush had been trampled, but there were no drag marks. She looked down at her phone again and wasn't surprised to find that she had no cell reception. They were deep in the river valley and the hillside rose on both sides of the river. She was going to have to figure out how to get out of here in that car. Hopefully, it wasn't stuck too badly. And she was soaked to the skin.

Wait a minute. Where was Cilla if Scott Richards was dead? Who'd killed him? Polly looked around.

"Cilla?" she called out, then yelled louder. "Cilla Waters! It's me. Polly Giller. Are you here? Cilla!" she shouted.

Polly looked at the trampled brush and started that way. She couldn't imagine what had happened here, but if that poor girl were out here alone, someone needed to find her. She continued to shout Cilla's name as she pushed past brambles and brush, noting how much had been broken along this recently made path. They'd been gone just a little over twenty-four hours. How long had Cilla been alone? She couldn't possibly know where she was.

"Cilla!" she shouted again. "It's Polly Giller. Are you out here?"

Polly heard something, so stopped and stood as still as possible, then shouted again. "Cilla! It's Polly. Where are you?"

What sounded like a whimper came from ahead and with renewed hope, she rushed forward, continuing to call Cilla's name.

"Polly?" a small voice croaked, and Cilla Waters crawled out from underneath a fallen tree. The girl was covered in leaves and mud, and had been splattered with blood. Polly wasn't sure if she had a black eye, or if that side of her face had lain on the dirt floor of the woods. Cilla was holding a gun in her trembling hand.

"Come here, honey," Polly said, opening her arms.

Cilla dropped the gun and rushed to Polly, embracing her as she sobbed. "I shot him. Am I going to jail?"

"What happened?" Polly looked down at the gun that had fallen into a bed of muddy leaves.

"He dragged me in here, and said we had to wait until he could find another car. He had the gun tucked in his jeans in the back and when he turned around I grabbed it. I didn't want to shoot him, but he came after me. He hit me and he pushed me down and then ..." Cilla's face screwed up and she gasped, trying to breathe through her sobs. "Then he hit me again and he ripped my shirt, trying to get the gun away from me. He was sitting on top of me and all of a sudden ..." She clenched up and rubbed at her eyes, then panted heavily as she continued to speak. "It went off. I know enough about guns to know that he should have had the safety on. But somehow he flicked it and he was ... he was ... oh god, Polly. He was going to rape me. He said so, then he was going to kill me. He punched me in my breasts. It hurt so bad, Polly. I didn't know what to do. I tried to swing the gun at his face, but he blocked my arm and he grabbed my hand and then he tried to get it away. I wasn't going to give it up." She stopped and sank back down onto the ground.

Polly knelt beside her.

"And then it just happened. I didn't mean to. I swear I didn't mean to."

"What happened next?" Polly didn't care. The gun could lie there in the mud for all she cared. She was getting this girl out of here.

"And then he ran away, screaming that he was coming back to kill me."

"He didn't get very far," Polly said. "He's dead. You're safe."

"It's my fault, then," Cilla said. "I killed him. They're going to send me to jail for killing a man. I'm not even sixteen years old. I didn't ask for this. I didn't ask for any of this."

"Cilla, you aren't going to jail. The sheriff doesn't work that way. Yes, you'll have to answer questions about what happened here today." Polly put her arm under Cilla's shoulder and lifted the girl to a standing position. "We're walking out of here now. Rebecca's in the car waiting for me. She'll be so thankful to see you. Everyone has been worried."

"I'm sorry," Cilla said.

"There is nothing for you to be sorry about."

Cilla and Polly focused on getting out to the road. When they went past Scott Richards' body, Cilla stopped as if she wanted to see him. Polly released her arm. She understood. While she'd been able to confront Joey face to face, there was something important about being able to see that it was truly over.

"He said we were meant to be together," Cilla said, standing over her kidnapper.

Polly remembered those words, too. She gave a small shudder at the thought of Joey's insanity. She'd let the girl have whatever time she needed to deal with this. Before she faced the police and the worried tears and questions from her family, she needed to wrap her own mind around these last twenty-four hours.

A gentle rain continued to come down on them. It no longer mattered that they were wet. All that mattered was that Cilla was alive and safe.

When the girl came back over to Polly, her face was grim, but she was no longer manic.

"Are you ready?" Polly asked.

"It's going to be bad, isn't it?"

"It won't be easy. There are many questions to be asked and they will come from everywhere. Your family, your friends, the sheriff, his deputies. They'll probably ask you to speak to a lawyer and you'll have to answer the same questions over and over again. It will be frustrating at times, but Cilla, you need to remember that in the larger scheme of things, this is only a short moment in your life. Be patient with your family and friends. They won't understand what you've been through." Polly smiled. "Your father may be your best friend."

"Why's that?"

"Because he understands pain and loss on a very personal level. He understands that everyone around him wants things to be normal, even when they aren't … even when you believe they never will be again."

They could see the edge of the woods and Cat's car now.

Cilla stopped. "How do you know all of this?"

"Because I had my own Scott Richards. He kidnapped me, and along with a man who everyone thought should be helping him get better, killed several young women who looked like me. If you want to hear the whole story, someday when we both have time, I'll tell you. But today, your story is the one that needs to be told. You need to talk about this. Don't hold anything back. Don't try to protect yourself because you think people won't believe you. Don't think for a minute that people expect you to have done anything differently than you did. You were the only person who was there. Your decisions were right for what you were facing and what you knew. Do you understand what I'm saying?"

"I think so."

Polly took her hand and they emerged into the clearing. The rain had slowed to a sprinkle.

Rebecca jumped out of the car. "Cilla!" She ran around to greet them and opened her arms. Cilla released Polly's hand and fell into her friend.

Wondering if Cat was as prepared as she hoped, Polly went to the passenger door, ducked inside and snagged the keys from the ignition. She popped the unlock button and then went to the trunk and opened it, hoping that … yes, there was a blanket in a tote bag. Tucked in behind it, Polly found three more ratty looking blankets. They looked like something she'd carry in her truck to manage filthy dog paws. She grabbed it all up, threw one of the ratty blankets over the driver's seat and then moved the girls out of the way so she could throw another across the back seat.

"You girls climb in back, so you can stay together. Here, wrap this around Cilla so she doesn't get cold." Polly tossed the other blanket on the passenger seat and waited for the two girls to get in and settle. She glared at the tires which were covered in mud. "You will back out of here and you will be good. Hear me?"

"What, Polly?" Rebecca asked.

"Just talking to the tires." Polly sat down on the driver's seat, her feet still outside the car; she slipped one shoe off and then the other. What a muddy, muddy mess.

"How are things back there?" she asked, turning around.

Cilla nodded, huddled into the blanket that Rebecca kept tightly wrapped around her.

"She's shivering," Rebecca said.

"Probably some shock, and she's wet. Just keep her warm." Polly turned the ignition, letting the car run for a moment as she took a deep breath. Front wheel drive. Better to try to drive forward first. She shifted into gear and pressed on the gas, then breathed a sigh of relief when it surged out of the hole. She stopped, put it into reverse, then turned in her seat and backed out the way they had come in. When she hit the secondary road, she backed up, then drove forward toward the highway.

"Where did he put the car?" Polly asked.

"The fourth car he stole?" Cilla replied. "It's across the road over there. He made me walk. It's a good thing I was dressed for marching band. At least I had decent shoes on."

Polly turned toward Pilot Mound. When she got out of the valley, she checked for a signal and pulled off into a farm field entrance. "I'm calling the sheriff. Then you're calling your mother."

"I couldn't believe he destroyed my phone. He said we wouldn't need it where we were going. What did that even mean?" Cilla asked. "And he didn't have one. How is that real? How do you live without a cell phone?"

"Polly?" Aaron asked. "Where are you?"

"I'm just east of Pilot Mound."

"Oh no," he moaned. "Please don't tell me."

"Yeah." Then it hit her that he'd have no idea who she'd found and was as worried as Rebecca had been that she might find one of the kids. "I found Scott Richards' body and I found Cilla Waters. She's safe."

"She's alive?"

"Yeah."

"How did he die?"

"He was shot."

"By Cilla?"

"Yes and no."

"What does that mean?" He stopped himself. "No, don't tell me. I'll talk to her. I'm sure everyone will talk to her. Have you called her parents yet?"

"They're next."

"I'd love to tell you to take her on home, but wait until we're there."

Polly nodded and smiled. This was always hard on Aaron. He just wanted people to be safe and happy. "We'll be here. She's in the back seat of my car with Rebecca, wrapped up in a blanket."

"Good. That girl has been through it this last week. Let's hope it's the end of stress for her. Hold tight. We're on the way."

He ended the call and Polly scrolled through until she found Andrea's number. "It's right there, Cilla. Call your mom."

Rebecca took the phone from Polly and started the call, then held it to Cilla's ear. The girl was shivering so badly she couldn't make her fingers work.

In just a few moments, she said, "No, Mommy. It's me. Polly found me."

CHAPTER TWENTY-THREE

"Holy mackerel," Rebecca said as she and Polly stood in front of Cat's car in their driveway. "That is one filthy car." She swiped her finger along the front of the hood and came away with caked mud.

"You've a mastery of the understatement."

Rebecca turned to Polly. "You're not much better. You can't go in the house like that. You'll make a terrible mess all over the floors. And who will be expected to clean it up? Me, that's who."

"Who's the mama here, little missy?"

"Depends on the day and time."

Kirk and Andrea had shown up on the scene within a half hour of Cilla's phone call. Polly was grateful to leave the worry over the girl's conversation with law enforcement and the EMTs behind. It was one thing to walk her own family members through something like that, but she wasn't comfortable doing that for someone else's daughter. While they waited, though, she stayed close in case Cilla needed support.

Polly was always surprised at how the activity exploded once everyone arrived on the scene. One team found the last car Scott

Richards had stolen, and another had escorted Polly back into the woods. She'd shown them where to find the gun, though that had been more of an adventure than she expected. She'd gone into those woods driven by pure adrenaline the first time, knowing that she not only had to discover the dead body, but once she knew it wasn't Cilla, to find the girl. Fortunately, she didn't have to be any kind of a tracker to see the trampled brush that led back to the fallen tree where Cilla had hidden herself. When she came back out, a third team was working over the body of Scott Richards.

Deputy Kellar had asked her if she'd disturbed anything and much as she didn't want to give him the 'duh' look, she could barely help herself. How many times had they been through this together? But he was doing his job and she wasn't going to fight with him about it. The young man was a good guy, but for some reason, he and Polly had never warmed up to each other.

Andrea had a hard time letting go of her daughter's hand, but finally broke away when Polly returned from her latest excursion into the woods, to tell her over and over again how thankful she was. Kirk sat off to the side in his wheelchair, watching it all happen, stoic until Cilla had finally excused herself from the ambulance and gone to him. He'd raised his arms and she'd dropped into his lap, wrapping her arms around his neck.

Polly didn't know how to tell the two of them that from here on out, they would each understand the other better than ever before. She'd tried to explain to Cilla that her father would be the anchor she needed as she dealt with her emotions. Her mother would always be strong for her, but Kirk would know her trauma.

The two had wept while Polly and Andrea turned away, uncomfortable at watching such an intimate moment.

"He needs her," Andrea had said. "I hate to think that this experience is anything but evil, but good will come of it for those two."

Good. She understood.

Polly had put her arm around the other woman's waist and held her as the pandemonium continued around them.

Polly and Rebecca had answered questions, but it wasn't that difficult for them since they knew the sheriff's deputies so well. Stu Decker was probably the warmest man Polly knew and she was glad that he'd been involved with this from the beginning. The Waters family was in good hands with him. They had a long day ahead.

"We didn't get any lunch," Rebecca said, moving Polly toward the side door. "I'm starving."

"Me too. What should we do about that?"

"First, you need a shower."

Henry drove in and parked beside Cat's car. "I heard from Kirk," he said after rolling his window down. "Why didn't I hear from you?"

"Because I'm a terrible person," Polly replied. "We had to answer questions. I had to take them to the body and help find the gun Cilla dropped in the mud. I'm soaking wet and a muddy mess." She nudged Rebecca's shoulder. "Why didn't you tell me to call Henry?"

"Because I'm a terrible daughter."

He shook his head. "When will I get it through your heads that all I need to know is that you are okay? I blithely go through my days thinking that nothing abnormal could possibly be occurring in Bellingwood, when out of the blue, I get a call telling me that my wife has performed a miracle and found the first of our long-lost youth."

"That's me. Miracle Worker Polly."

Henry got out of the truck and looked at Cat's car as he walked past it. "We need to wash that."

"It might be a good job for the boys," Polly said. Weariness struck her in force. Instead of a shower, she wanted a long, hot bath.

He laughed at her. "I think we can run it through a car wash first. That's a lot of mud. Did you just get home?"

She nodded. "Yeah. I don't know when the Waters' will be back. Cilla might be held responsible for shooting the guy."

"But she didn't mean to," Rebecca said in protest.

"And that will be what it boils down to," Henry said. "You shouldn't worry. You know that Sheriff Merritt isn't out to get her."

Rebecca frowned, not ready to let it go. "It was his gun. He was going to hurt her. She's just lucky she got it before he did anything really bad. Do you know that he told her yesterday that if she didn't get in the car with him, he was going to shoot all of us?"

"All of who?" Henry asked, his forehead furrowing.

"Us," Rebecca said. "Me, Kayla, and Libby when we were at the school yesterday waiting for Polly. That's why Cilla left with him in the first place. He had the gun pointed right at us. I didn't see it because it was inside the car, but she said he was serious. If he was ready to shoot us to get her in the car, who knows what else he was going to do? She thought that she'd be able to get away. He had to sleep at some point, didn't he?"

Polly nodded.

"She said he was popping pills, too. She didn't know what he was taking, but he kept taking them. Then she worried that he'd never go to sleep so she could try to get away."

"He'd have crashed at some point," Henry said. "I'm sorry that she is going to have to live with the fact that she killed someone."

"I don't know how they do that in a war," Rebecca said quietly. "How do you turn it off that you've just killed a real person? That would have to hurt. You'd never be able to forget it."

Polly and Henry looked at each other. This was a conversation they'd never expected to have with her.

She looked up at Polly. "Seriously. You need to get out of those wet clothes. You're going to catch a cold or something."

"Yes, Mother," Polly said. "Do you see what I have to live with?"

Henry chuckled. "I'd bet on you in a flat-out mama-fight."

"Good. At least someone still respects my place in this family."

He walked ahead of them and opened the door to the porch. "You two stay right here. I'll go upstairs and bring down a couple of robes. Rebecca, is yours hanging on the back of your door?"

"I'm not that wet," Rebecca protested.

"Look at your feet." He pointed down. Her tennis shoes were mud-caked, and her legs had spatters of wet leaves and mud on them.

"Polly," Rebecca complained. "Look what you did to me. I was perfectly clean until I got in the car with you." She laughed. "I didn't realize it was this bad."

"Your robe?" Henry asked.

"Yes. I'm sorry. Hanging on my door." Rebecca toed off one shoe and then the other. She sat down on the floor and took her socks off, tossing the first one at Polly.

It hit Polly right in the face and clung there.

"That's gross," Polly said. She flung it back toward Rebecca, who caught it as it sailed over her head.

"I never worry about you hitting me with anything. When will you ever learn?"

In response, Polly knelt down beside her daughter and pulled her into a strong hug, rubbing herself across Rebecca's back.

"What are you doing, crazy lady?"

"Sharing my dirty, muddy self with you." Polly sat down beside Rebecca. "Cilla is going to need her friends for the next few weeks. You remember what it's like to come out of something like this."

"Never this bad," Rebecca said. "But yeah. I get it. She's going to want to talk about it and talk about it and talk about it."

"You did."

Rebecca grinned. "I also remember when you'd had enough and let me know that I'd crossed over into the drama. I'll bet Cilla is way worse. She's already pretty dramatic."

"For those of us on the outside, it's a fine line to walk. How long do we let you live in that moment? When does it move from healthy communication to twisted wallowing? You just have to be patient and pay attention."

"I can't believe that they moved in right across the street from us and then all this happened. Can you even believe that?"

"Kinda cool how it all worked out."

Turning so that she and Polly were facing each other, their knees touching, Rebecca reached out and took Polly's hand. "Sometimes I can't believe that you're my mom and I live this life. I know that I'm not always nice to you. I get snotty and I'm hard to get along with and all that. I don't say it often enough. I am so glad you took me in. You're like this really cool angel person who shows up when people need you. It doesn't scare you to help somebody. I don't get that all the time. How important it is? Yeah. Most people just ignore stuff going on around them. I don't ever want to be like most people. I want to be like you."

Polly turned her hands palms up, so Rebecca could clasp them. "Thank you. I am proud of you. I want to say something to you, but you can't take it out of context."

"Uh oh. What?"

"No. This is good. When you are hard to get along with and you get snotty because you don't think we're paying attention to you or you want to do something that we don't think you should do, I run into a conundrum. You see, I like that spunky spark in you. That is one of those things in you that makes you so unique and amazing."

"Yeah?" Rebecca's eyes sparkled.

"What I said. Don't take it out of context. This is another fine line I tread with you and with every single one of my kids. I never want that strength to go away. What I want is for you all to know when it is right to let it loose and when you need to rein it in out of respect for others. I love you to pieces, Rebecca. I'm proud of you and I think that the world will unfold at your feet."

"But?"

"Stop with the buts. No buts. You are an incredible young woman and there's no reason you can't do everything you set your heart on. I'm sorry that Andrew screwed with you this summer." Polly grinned. "Okay, here's a but. But I think that you are going to do just fine without him as your boyfriend. At least for now. If the two of you ever decide that you want to be together, it won't be because it was the easy thing to do, the safe relationship to have. You'll be together because you've fallen madly and desperately in love with each other. Don't be afraid of dating other boys and don't be afraid of loving them. You're going to get hurt again if you do. It won't be pretty, but it won't be the end of the world either and you will be a stronger person because of it. Learning how to love and how to be loved is the most glorious experience you'll ever have."

Rebecca nodded and sat there quietly. Then she looked at Polly and grinned. "See. You really are this cool angel person. I do try to be good and think about the things I say and do. It gets so hard sometimes to not be selfish. That's hard work."

"Not being selfish?"

"I mean, yeah. Thinking about, like ten other people in this house? Sometimes I think it would be nice if everyone just thought about me for a minute."

"We do."

"And that's the thing. I have to remind myself to calm down and think about that. It stinks."

Henry came around the corner into the porch, holding their robes. "I'll leave again so you two can drop your clothes into the washing machine and put these on. Polly, I've already started your bath."

"You what?" She grinned at Rebecca. "See. That right there. That's what I'm talking about. Madly and desperately."

"You two are so gross."

~~~

Polly dropped into the hot, pulsating water. Henry had also turned on the jets. "How much did you hear?" she asked him.

"Enough. I figured that you knew I was there."

"If not, you'd fallen asleep."

"She's going to be great."

"Yeah. There are going to be more clean bathrooms in her future, but she'll get there. I think we've gotten past the 'I hate you' stage with her."

"I heard Caleb say that to you the other day."

Polly nodded. "Those little ones have so much pain and anger in them. I try not to react, but damn, it hurts the soul to hear those words come out of the mouth of someone I love. I'd like to strike them from their vocabulary."

"Do you think we'll be able to adopt them one of these days?" Henry asked.

Polly sighed as she sank lower into the water. "I hope so. They've become part of the family. Mrs. Tally has spoken with their mother over and over again. She keeps insisting that she's getting her life together, but then she falls apart. JaRon cried and cried the last time we went to visit her in Mitchellville. She's not anyone he knows anymore. We had to have a long talk about being able to love more than one mommy at a time. They don't get it and they don't like it." She snarled. "And she won't tell Marian anything about a sister to the boys. There's no record of the birth and she says that the boys don't know what they're talking about. I hope that little girl is in a safe place."

"Maybe she gave her up for adoption to a family that wanted a child."

"I hope so," Polly said. "That's the only thing that gives me peace. It doesn't feel right, though. If the boys have a sister, they should know her."

He nodded and stretched. "What do you want to do tonight?"

"If everything is okay over at the Waters' house, I think I'd like to just hang out with my family. Maybe let Cat and Hayden go out by themselves. We could play board games with the boys or watch a movie together. I feel like snuggling."

Henry waggled his eyebrows. "Snuggling?"

Polly laughed out loud. "I love you so much, you nut. We can snuggle all you want tonight. After last night, I'll be thankful to land in my own bed at a normal hour with you."

"No dogs."

"Right," she said. "No dogs. They'll sleep with the boys tonight." She looked up. "Sylvie says there is a chance Shelly and Lissa might move into an apartment together. Marta is talking about helping them figure it out."

"Really?"

"Yeah. I don't know. I haven't heard anything. I know that Shelly has been having a great week with Marta, but she needs to talk to us before she makes big plans. Not because she isn't an adult, but because it's the right thing to do. She needs to talk to her father, too."

"Can they afford it?"

"I was thinking of that little apartment at Mrs. Worth's house. That's affordable and she'd keep an eye on them."

"You're wicked."

"I can't help myself. I kind of thought that Shelly would come home after work, but then I realized her father was picking her up tonight for a weekend in Omaha. I also need to talk to Lissa. I want to find out what her thoughts are about staying in Bellingwood."

"How long did you agree to let her stay at the hotel?"

Polly grimaced. "I didn't say. I can't just kick her out on the street again."

"What time do the girls get off work?"

"Not today," Polly said. "I don't have it in me to redirect two young girls today. Monday. I'll work on it Monday." She smiled at him. "Maybe by then, they'll have come up with a plan of their own and all I have to do is help them implement it."

"I was surprised when you didn't do more to 'rescue' Lissa." Henry put air quotes around the word.

Polly nodded. "Me too, but she didn't want that from me. She wanted someone to bail her out of the trouble she'd gotten into, but then she was done." She shrugged. "That's okay. I certainly don't need people to want more help than they need. It doesn't change what I do."

"I love you."

"I love you, too. The water's getting cold."

Henry put his finger in. "Really?"

"I'm pruning." Polly let her head sag. "I'm so tired."

"Are you more tired or hungry?" He stood up and grabbed one of their large bath towels.

"Tired." Polly got up and out of the bathtub and took the towel from him, wrapping it around her body. She peered at herself in the mirror. "Circles under my eyes. Where in the world did those come from?" When she turned around, she realized Henry was gone. "They're like ghosts around here," she muttered and wandered into the bedroom. Polly sat down on the bed and contemplated the clothing choices she had, then glanced at the pillow. While still wearing the towel, she leaned over and dropped her head down, then stuck her feet under the sheet.

"Rebecca collapsed in her bed," Henry said quietly.

Polly didn't have the strength to open her eyes. She barely felt him pull the sheet and blanket up over her shoulders.

CHAPTER TWENTY-FOUR

Breathing deeply with contentment, Polly looked around at her family. They'd had a relaxing evening, just hanging out. The boys were tired, having spent the day with Cat, Marie, and Bill. They'd gone out to see the work at the bed and breakfast, stopped by Elva's stable where she'd spent time with the boys on horseback. They'd gone to Story City to see the carousel and have lunch. After that, they'd landed in Ames at a park with playground equipment. The boys had chased each other, played on the slides and climbing equipment and when they finally got home, they were worn out.

Cat and Hayden were just as exhausted, but when Polly offered them the night off, they'd mustered enough energy to take themselves up to their apartment and crash. They thought they'd go out another night.

Heath's hand was better, but it still hurt him. He'd spent his afternoon helping the construction crews close up for the weekend and he was tired by the time he got home.

All in all, it was a quiet Friday evening at the Sturtz residence.

Polly whipped up a couple of meatloaves and Rebecca helped

her make French fries. After dinner, she sent the boys off to take showers — little boys could be stinky after a long day of playing.

Then it was popcorn and a movie. They were all so weary that she wondered how many of the boys had fallen asleep during the movie, but they would watch it again and again, so she wasn't worried.

JaRon's curly head lay across her lap and she idly stroked his hair. He and his brother had grown much more comfortable around her. Caleb wasn't quite ready to reach out for affection, but more often than not, he allowed her to hug him. He was sitting on the other side of JaRon, close enough to be connected, but far enough away from anyone else who might try to touch him.

Noah was tucked in between Heath and Rebecca, one of his favorite places to be. He adored the big kids.

Rebecca had gotten calls after band let out this afternoon, her friends all wanting to hear about what had happened that day. Kayla had asked if Rebecca wanted to come over that evening, but she'd waved off.

Elijah was draped across Henry. That boy just didn't care about what he looked like when it came to affection. He would grab it any way he could.

"What do you think, Polly?" Henry asked. "Another movie?"

"Only if you're prepared to carry sleeping boys up to their beds."

"We won't fall asleep," Elijah protested. "Please?"

"Please?" JaRon asked, looking up at her with his big brown eyes.

She patted his head. "Stop that. You're trying to melt me."

He nodded.

"I don't care," she said with a shrug. "Tomorrow's Saturday. You all can sleep as late as you want."

Elijah jumped up. "Yay!"

Polly felt her phone buzz in her pocket. Everyone who might need her was right here in this house. She moved until she could reach it and pulled it out. Why was Rachel calling?

"I need to take this," Polly said. She scooted out from under JaRon. "Go ahead and start the movie without me." She walked out of the family room and down to the kitchen while swiping the call open. "Hello?"

"Polly?"

"Yeah. Hi, Rachel. What's going on?" She glanced up at the clock on the kitchen wall. It was only nine o'clock. The way things had been going at their house this evening, it felt more like midnight.

"Are you busy?"

"No. Do you need something?"

"Can you come over to Sycamore House?"

"Right now?"

"Yeah." Rachel's voice grew softer. "Andrew's here."

"At Sycamore House?"

"Yeah. His face is bruised. He's been hurt kinda bad."

"Have you called Sylvie?"

"He won't let me. He totally freaked out when I said I was calling her. I told him I had to call somebody. He agreed that I could call you."

"Me?" Polly could hardly believe that. After what they'd been through, she couldn't imagine that he wanted to see her.

"Where is he?"

"I found him upstairs. I usually walk around the building before locking up at night, just to make sure the lights are off. He was hiding in the bathroom."

"Give me a few minutes. I need to put my shoes on and tell Henry where I'm going. Don't let him leave."

"That's not a problem."

Polly ended the call and shook her head. She'd been talking to Henry earlier that day about how Lissa didn't want anything from Polly except to be bailed out of a problem. She'd offer her help to anyone who needed it, no matter how they responded. Now she had to get past the things that Andrew had said to her. He needed her. He also needed a good swift kick in the pants, but right now, she needed to release that and find her empathy for the boy.

Henry came out of the family room to find her. "Everything okay?"

She beckoned him closer and took him out to the porch. "Andrew's at Sycamore House," she whispered. "Rachel just called. He wants me to go over there. She says he has bruises on his face. He doesn't want his mother."

He stood up straight and rigid. "You don't think that …"

"I don't know what to think," Polly interrupted. "I don't want Rebecca to know what's going on. Just tell her that I had to go out. Rachel had a problem at Sycamore House."

"Send me a text when you know what's happening with the rest of your night. At least we finally know where he is."

Polly held on to his arm as she slipped her feet into a pair of sandals. "I'm sorry to duck out on you."

"No, other people need you." He kissed her lips. "It's good to know that you always come home to me, though."

She rested in his arms. "I'm so tired," she said. "I've spent way too much time worrying about other people's kids."

Henry walked outside with her. The Waters' house was dark and quiet with no cars in the driveway or on the street. Andrea had sent Polly a text earlier that evening telling her that they were spending the night at Louis and Deb's house. She supposed that made sense. This house wasn't yet their home. They hadn't even been there a week yet. Deb and Louis's house was safe and comfortable. She glanced back at her big, towering monstrosity of a house. It was her home. They'd had so many experiences inside those walls. With eleven people living here, they'd claimed nearly every inch of the place as their own.

"You're thinking hard," Henry said. He opened the door of the Suburban.

"Yeah. I love our home."

"Go take care of your boy. We'll hold down the fort for you."

She reached up to kiss him again, climbed in, and pulled the door shut.

Andrew must be truly frightened if he allowed Rachel to call her. He had to know that his mother would love him, no matter what. There was nothing she wouldn't do for those boys. They couldn't make her angry enough to stop caring about them. After what Jason had put Sylvie through his freshman year in high school, Andrew surely couldn't believe that she'd reject him for this behavior. For Pete's sake, she'd been putting up with his attitude all summer.

Polly shook her head as she drove into the back drive of Sycamore House. She looked up to see lights on in what used to be her apartment. Sometimes she missed this place so much. They'd had fun up there. Laughter and fun and growing up. Through all of the days that she'd lived here, Andrew had been a huge part of her life. He was just always there. She thought back to that first day he'd met Obiwan in the auditorium. He'd been such a little boy, yet willing to learn how to behave so he wouldn't frighten the dog. He and that dog had chased each other through this yard so many times.

It wasn't surprising that the place he felt safest was upstairs. There was no space in this building that Andrew didn't know intimately. He was as much a part of it as anyone.

She glanced up at Doug Randall's apartment. Through all the changes, he'd stayed right there, thankful to have a great place to live. My goodness, these kids had grown up. Polly was not a fan. Young and innocent. She preferred them that way.

Polly unlocked the door beside the garage and went inside, then made her way up to the second floor. So many changes. An elevator instead of stairs. It felt strange.

She walked through what had been her bedroom and then her office. It was now storage, with shelves lining the walls. The old media room and dining room had been transformed into a lounge with a large-screen television hanging from one wall and clusters of tables and chairs scattered around. Her kitchen was a delightful bar, used for parties and weddings. The large living room was wide open, a few comfortable benches scattered along the outside edges. Beryl's paintings had been hung on every wall.

"Rachel? Andrew?" she called out.

Rachel came out of what had been Polly and Henry's bedroom.

The three bedrooms were now meeting rooms that could be set up for small wedding parties as well. There was always something going on up here.

"We're in here," Rachel said as she walked out to Polly. "Thanks for coming. I didn't know what I was going to do."

"Thank you. If you want to go home, I can take it from here."

"Are you sure?"

Polly nodded.

"Thanks. Anita and Doug are already at the apartment."

"Are you going out?"

"No. Not tonight. Billy got some new board game he wants to try. We'll probably be up all night anyway, but at least I don't have to go far to get into my bed." Rachel laughed. "I'll talk to you later. I hope this all works out. Everything else is locked up."

"Thanks again." Polly watched her walk through the main room and then turned. She walked through the door and saw Andrew sitting at a table, face down in his crossed arms. "Andrew?"

"Yeah," he said.

"Do you want to talk?"

"Not really."

"You know you can't stay here, right?"

"Yeah. I guess."

She walked toward him and tried to decide where she wanted to sit. She chose the seat right beside him and pulled it out.

He hitched his chair away from her.

Polly had played these games with kids far too often. She hitched her chair closer to him.

He tried once more and she followed him.

Andrew finally looked up. "You aren't going to stop, are you?"

"Nope." Polly caught his chin with her finger before he could drop his head again. "Let me see your face."

He pulled back. "I'll be fine."

"What happened?" She traced a deep bruise and lacerations on his right cheekbone. Blood had dried in his nostrils and his lips were split.

"Would you believe me if I told you I ran into a doorknob?" He tried to laugh, but put his hand over his lips to stop them from turning up.

She shook her head. "Who did this to you?"

"You already know."

"Did he hit you anywhere else?" Sylvie had told them that Anthony had been very careful about not hitting her where it could be seen by anyone else until he'd finally run out of patience.

Andrew shrugged.

"Oh, honey." Polly reached for him. She wanted so badly to hold this boy that she loved so much.

"Don't," he said. "Just don't."

She caught his eye and smiled. "You know that before we're through here tonight, you're going to be in my arms. The sooner you give in to that, the easier this night will go."

"You're always hugging me," he said, a hint of the old Andrew in his face.

"I will always hug you. I've missed you."

"Not yet." He turned away, then stood up.

"Where are you going?"

"I don't know. Nowhere."

Andrew wandered to the back windows that looked out over the creek. "It was easier then, you know."

"When you just had to obey your mom?"

"And you. I knew you wouldn't ever make me do something I shouldn't. I was so naive."

"What do you mean?"

"Just letting you and mom make all my decisions for me. I was safe and I didn't even realize it."

"You don't feel safe now?"

He turned back to her. "No. I don't know what I'm doing anymore. I can't make a good decision. Not one. It's like I want to think for myself, but I don't know who that is, so I make stupid decisions. I hurt people. I hurt Mom." His voice went to practically a whisper. "I hurt you and I hurt Rebecca. All the people who loved me. I just screwed it up so bad."

"You know there's nothing you can do that is so bad it can't be fixed. Forgiveness is kinda what we do around here."

He slowly nodded, still looking out over the back yard. "But it's so difficult getting from here to there."

For the first time, Polly looked at Andrew and saw a young man. Physically he'd grown up so much. Gone ... completely gone was the little boy who had fallen asleep draped around her dog. The child who took utter joy and excitement in exploring her library, in having his very own desk and office below the stairwell, in rushing out that back door with Obiwan, in every new thing that he experienced, had grown into a young man who didn't feel prepared for this new life. He'd tried to do it alone.

She smiled at the memory of a conversation she'd had with Jason when she'd explained that he was part of something bigger. That they all were. Her friends had given her the strength she needed. They'd given her advice and support, and most of all, love. Polly and Sylvie both had hoped that their kids would just absorb that knowledge. Rebecca was intuitive enough to grasp the concept, but she'd also spent hours talking about it with Polly. Andrew and his mother probably hadn't had those conversations.

She stood and walked over to stand beside him. "You aren't alone."

"I know."

"Do you really?"

He shrugged.

Polly slid her hand into his. The little boy's hand that she'd held so many times was now bigger than hers. "You've made some pretty big decisions this summer."

"You mean the ones I've screwed up?"

"Yeah, those."

"How will I ever learn to do the right thing?"

"By talking to the people who love you."

"But they ..." his voice trailed off. "Yeah. I get it."

"But they what?" Polly pressed.

"I know what you all would have said to me. I didn't want to hear it. That was my first mistake, I guess."

"When did you start spending time with Anthony?"

Andrew jerked, but didn't pull his hand away from Polly. "I can't believe you knew that."

"I didn't at first. We all believed you were just trying to test the waters of independence. I don't think I realized until the other day."

"When I was an asshole?"

She smiled up at him. "I'm not going to deny that you were an asshole. Let's be clear."

"It was like two weeks after Jason's graduation party. I didn't want to see him or talk to him, but he called me maybe a couple of times a week, just to talk. He asked me what I was doing this summer and what kinds of things I was interested in. He was so great. Nothing like what Mom or Jason said about him. Then he asked if I'd go to lunch with him. What could it hurt? He picked me up. Mom and Jason weren't around. I knew what they'd say. Both of them hate him. I didn't want to hate my dad. He's my dad, Polly."

"I know," she said quietly.

"Then he was coming down a couple of times a week. He'd let me drive and we went all over the place."

"What did you talk about?"

"My life here and the people I knew. He didn't like Bellingwood. He said it was the worst place he'd ever lived. That people were judgmental and wouldn't let a guy just live his life without getting all up in his business." Andrew turned to her. "You know that's right. You've heard the things people in town say about you."

Polly nodded. She wasn't interrupting him yet.

"I told him about some of the things that bugged me. And he listened to me. Really listened. At least I thought so." He shook his head. "I don't know. It was like all the things that made me a little mad became a big deal, you know? Those were what we talked about. He liked hearing them and told me that I was right to feel the way I felt, that I had a right to be my own person. It made sense. I get tired of being treated like I'm little Andrew Donovan."

"You've grown up a lot," Polly said.

"Not really."

She pulled his hand up and splayed out his fingers, then rested her hand on top of it. "There was a day when your little hand fit in mine. Now, look at it."

"That's just outside stuff. I'm scared all the time, Polly."

"You didn't used to be."

"I know. But now I'm scared about all of these decisions that I have to make alone."

"You don't have to make decisions alone," Polly said. "How have you not watched me be part of a community of friends and family? Yeah. I do a lot of things by myself, but Andrew, I've got more than twenty years on you. That's twenty years of learning things the hard way."

"I have to learn everything the hard way?"

"Nobody likes it, but those are usually the best lessons. Those are the lessons you don't have to learn again and again."

"I've had a lot of time to think tonight."

"Yeah?"

"I totally screwed this summer up. I wish I could go back and start over."

"What have you learned from this?"

"Dad's a bad man," he said, touching his face.

"When did he hit you?"

Andrew turned to her, his eyes suffused with tears. "This afternoon."

"Where were you?"

"He was already tired of having me around. I could tell. We were in Boone. I started walking and I just ended up here."

"You walked up here with a bloody nose?" Polly asked.

"It didn't bleed that long." He huffed. "The only place I could think to get to was Sycamore House. I didn't think about Rachel finding me. I guess it's good she did."

"Do you want a ride home?"

"I'm going to have to face her at some point."

"She loves you so much, Andrew."

"I know. I disappointed her this summer."

"Yeah."

He frowned. "You don't pull any punches, do you?"

"Why should I? You know what you did. You know how you've hurt people. You're going to have to figure out how to fix that. We love you more than you'll ever know. What you believe are immense chasms between you and everyone else? They aren't that big. All you have to do is be honest and loving. Apologize, ask for forgiveness. Those are bridge-builders. The thing is, we love you so much that we don't need you to meet us halfway. All you have to do is start, we're already on our way to you."

"You mean that."

"You know me, Andrew. Of course I do."

He sank onto a cushioned bench beneath the windows. "I'm so sorry. I can't believe I screwed this up." Looking up at her with tear-filled eyes, he pleaded, "Will you forgive me for those things I said?"

"Of course."

"I don't feel like that about you, Polly. I love you like I love my own Mom. You are the best thing that ever happened to our family. I am so sorry. How did I let that hate get inside me?" He pounded on his chest. "It all hurts so much in here. I don't want to be that mean kid."

"You aren't that mean kid, Andrew," she said. She sat down beside him and gathered him into her arms as he sobbed. "I love you. You have always been my boy, my little sweet and wonderful boy."

"I'm so sorry. I hurt you. I hurt Rebecca. Will she ever forgive me?"

"You are her best friend. She misses you."

"How can I fix this?"

"Apologize."

"I've messed up, though," he said, sitting up. "I mean, really bad."

"With Maddy Spotter?"

"Yeah."

"How bad?" Polly asked. "Like we need to get you tested for STDs, bad?"

He rolled his eyes. "I was so mad at everyone and she wanted me. I was never going to do that with Rebecca. We talked about it, you know? We, like, respected yours and my mom's rules about it, but we also thought it would be stupid to do that, just because we are so young. Then, Maddy found out we broke up. She even said that it would piss Rebecca off if we got together. What the heck? I was up for that. Rebecca already hated me."

"She never hated you."

"Well, you know, I thought she did. We never did anything together after we broke up."

"Because you separated yourself from her."

"You're right. This is my fault. It made Maddy really happy. She couldn't wait to tell all her friends that she and I were together. She thought that maybe if Rebecca was mad enough, she'd lose focus. I didn't know how to tell her that when Rebecca got mad enough, she only focused harder. But Maddy was really into it."

"And you?"

His head snapped up. "Oh. I'm making it sound like we, you know, did it. We didn't. At least not all the way. She had this drawer full of condoms. I couldn't believe it. I didn't want to do that with someone who had all of that in her room. Disgusting. Sloppy seconds. Not me."

Polly released tension she didn't know she'd been holding. "You need to lead with that when you talk to your mother and Rebecca."

"Seriously?" he asked. "You guys think I'd do that?" He grimaced. "Of course you did. I've given you every reason to think I would. Man, I'm going to have to fix all of this. It's going to take forever."

"No, it really won't," Polly said. "Remember when Jason was in trouble his freshman year?"

"Yeah."

"How much of that time do you remember?"

"I guess some. Not all of it."

"Trust me, it will be a big deal for a while, but sooner than you think, life will return to normal. The difference for you is that you did it over a summer break instead of while you were in school."

"Mom's going to kill me."

"Not at first," Polly said with a smile. "She's going to be thankful you are safe. She's been worried. Then, she's going to do her best to find your father and have him tossed in jail for kidnapping and beating you."

"I don't want her to do that. I just want to not think of him anymore."

"She'll get there, too. She just needs time. Then she'll kill you."

"How bad?"

"However bad it is, just remember that it's temporary. It won't last forever. You'll face punishment and you'll have to grovel, but she loves you. Are you about ready?"

"Will you come in with me?"

"For just a minute. You need to do this on your own. I am not protecting you from your mother."

"You never have, I guess."

"Where's your cell phone?"

"Dad made me turn it off so no one could trace it. He figured Mom would call the sheriff. Man, he hates Sheriff Merritt. I left it in his glove compartment."

"Can he get into it and find your contacts?"

Andrew shook his head. "No. If he tries, he'll brick it. No one knows my password, not even Rebecca."

"Maybe he'll do the right thing and send it back to you."

"Doubtful." He stood and held out a hand to her. "I'm ready."

Polly stood and pulled him in for another hug. "I told you this was going to happen."

"You got me to hug you twice tonight. That's kind of a record."

CHAPTER TWENTY-FIVE

"Oh, I forgot something. Wait and I'll walk out with you," Sylvie said.

Polly waited at the back door while Sylvie returned to the living room. Though it was late, there were plenty of people still here. Polly was exhausted, though, and wanted nothing more than to go home and sleep. This had been an emotional week.

Lydia and Aaron were here, as was Tab Hudson. Jason and his girlfriend, Mel, were sticking close. She was leaving for college next week and Jason wasn't sure what he'd do without her. His friends, Scar and Kent were both leaving town as well. Scar was off to the University of Iowa and Kent was going to Simpson College down in Indianola. He had another week on the state universities, but Jason was feeling the loss of his closest friends.

Tonight's conversation with Andrew hadn't been easy. There had been the usual amount of tears — buckets-full. Sylvie was livid at Anthony's behavior; Andrew went back and forth between sorrow and shame to attempting justification for his behavior. Fortunately, he generally ended back on the sorrow and shame side of things.

He knew what his father had done to him. They hadn't needed to point it out. The poor kid had recognized most of his father's behavior as it was happening, but it was something he'd never experienced. Not only had he wanted to please the man, but he was trying on some of that behavior for himself, attempting to understand how it might fit into his personality. He'd left with Anthony because he knew that his own actions threatened to halt the freedom he was experiencing. Anthony encouraged the bad behavior, hoping that would draw Andrew closer to him.

Andrew admitted that it was exhausting, trying to keep up with the surly attitude and actions that caused him shame. When he attempted to have a real conversation with his father, Anthony had laughed at him. Then he'd tried to bully his son, calling him names and ridiculing Sylvie and Jason. Andrew had allowed his father to get away with that, knowing that if he protested, it would only bring trouble.

His father hadn't done much drinking around Andrew until today. They'd traveled through Iowa the last couple of days. Anthony wanted to show his youngest son off to a couple of his girlfriends. Andrew hadn't been impressed. When they stopped in Boone to meet up with another girlfriend before heading back to Fort Dodge and his live-in, Anthony took Andrew to the bar where she worked and proceeded to drink until he became loud and mean. Andrew tried to leave and his father insisted he stay. At Andrew's second attempt to leave, Anthony punched the kid twice, announcing that he was embarrassing him. Andrew had taken the punches and crawled off into a corner. The bartender-girlfriend told Andrew that he needed to call someone. Anthony tended to be violent when he was drunk.

Andrew's phone was in the car and Anthony had locked it. There was no way to get to it, so Andrew made a third attempt to leave. That's when Anthony backhanded him and bloodied his nose. The girlfriend and several others pulled Anthony off and told Andrew to get out while he could. Andrew ran. Rather than stop and be caught by his father again, he kept running until he arrived at Sycamore House.

Sylvie wanted her ex-husband arrested. Andrew didn't want to be the cause of that, but Tab took his statement and photographs of his injuries.

It wouldn't be surprising if the man ended up in jail tonight. Especially if he was still in Boone.

There was enough to file a protective order against Anthony. He would no longer be able to have any contact with Andrew.

Most people would have sense enough to stay away, but not that man. He kept coming back, trying to insinuate himself into a family that he had never bothered to care about. What he thought he might gain from this, no one understood.

That's not true. Sylvie understood. For Anthony, it was about power. He couldn't bear that there were people directly connected to him who weren't under his control.

"I'm sorry," Sylvie said. "I just needed to ask Aaron another question."

Polly smiled and opened the door. Padme nosed at her leg. "The dog out or in?"

"She can go out with us."

The evening was still warm and humid, and the cicadas sang.

"Thank you for being there tonight, Polly."

"You know I will do anything for your boys. I love them like they were my own."

"They love you, too." Sylvie walked down the back steps. She nudged a ball off the sidewalk into the yard. Padme jumped up and down, then snatched the ball with her teeth and ran off. "I know I need to have this talk with Andrew, but did he tell you anything about Maddy?"

"He didn't do anything," Polly said. "And I believe him. He said that he wasn't going to be sloppy seconds, and that he was a little freaked out when he saw her drawer full of condoms."

Sylvie clapped both hands against her head. "Thank you," she breathed. "I didn't want to ask him about that in front of everyone. We can have the conversation when it's just the two of us."

"Andrew and Rebecca need to talk sometime," Polly said.

"I know." Sylvie nodded. "But I don't know if they should get back together yet."

Polly shook her head. "I don't think they should, but they've both been miserable. She misses him desperately."

"He misses her too. Maybe he can come over early tomorrow, before we all show up for the party?"

"You're coming?"

"Eliseo would like to. We've been talking quite a bit these last couple of days."

Polly raised her eyebrows. "You have? About what?"

"About not waiting until the boys are grown for us to be together."

"Holy moly," Polly said. "Say what?"

Sylvie swatted at her. "Stop it. When everyone is gone tonight, we're going to speak with the boys about Eliseo moving in here. There are some medical needs for Eliseo that we need to address. Nothing big, but the boys need to understand his limitations. He's never needed to expose them to anyone but me and his sister."

"The burns?"

"Mostly his PTSD. At least he's comfortable around the boys. When Elva and her kids moved into his house, he lived at the barn for the first little bit. He doesn't do change well and needs open space to maintain his calm. We also have to figure out how we're going to live here with three dogs." Sylvie scowled. "Three dogs, Polly. And all three of them are your fault."

"But they're the best-trained dogs in the county."

"Thank goodness for that."

"When is this going to happen?"

"Before Christmas."

When Polly grinned, Sylvie held her hand up. "We're not getting married. He is so afraid of saddling me with his long-term care and I don't know that I'm ready to be married again either. With everything that's happened this week with Anthony, it brings back terrible memories. Eliseo is the nicest, most generous man I know, but I'm terrified, Polly. I don't ever want to be put in a position where I have to run away to protect myself again."

"You won't. You know that in your head."

"But not in my heart. My heart is scared to death."

"Then let your heart tell you when it's ready."

"What if it never does because it's so fickle?"

Polly chuckled. "That's why you have me and the girls."

Sylvie glanced at the back door. "I should probably go in so they can wrap up and get out of here. Thank you for being here for me this week even when you had so many other things going on."

"I need to deal with Lissa tomorrow," Polly said, scratching her head. "The poor girl doesn't have a clue what my expectations are. I feel as if I've just left her there with nothing."

"Marta says she's been friendly with Gayla and Brittany, too. Did Shelly ever call you?"

"No." Polly heaved a sigh. "I'm the one who usually initiates these conversations. I've been so out of my mind the last couple of days, I've let them fall to the wayside. And now she's in Omaha with her dad for the weekend."

Sylvie frowned. "I don't think so. I think that was canceled."

"Great," Polly said. "She didn't tell me about that, either. I hate having these responsibility conversations."

"At least this one's yours and not mine. I get to have two of them with my boys now. I can't tell you how much I'm looking forward to that."

"What are you thinking about with Jason?"

"I don't know for sure yet. I hate to drop an anvil on his head when his friends are moving away, but then again, maybe this is the best time to do it. I understand that he doesn't need to come up with a life-plan tomorrow, but he needs to at least have a plan for the next year. Even if it's to wander around the country and work for food and lodging."

"That would kill you."

"See how desperate I am? He's a great kid, but he needs to focus. Can I send him to you for this conversation?"

Polly shrugged. "Make sure I'm good and grumpy from dealing with the rest of my ragamuffin tribe."

Sylvie pulled Polly into a hug. "Thanks for rescuing my youngest ragamuffin tonight. We'll see you tomorrow. I'm bringing cupcakes and rolls." She chuckled. "Jason's bringing something, too. He's coming as an adult. Andrew can still be my kid, but not Jason. First step, right?"

"You might be pushing it," Polly said with a laugh. "Are you going to make Eliseo bring his own dish?"

"Maybe."

"Okay, I'm outta here. I'm glad your boy is home and things are heading toward normal."

"Thank you again, and Polly?"

"Yeah?" Polly had her hand on the back gate. She turned.

"I love you."

"I love you too, sweetie."

"Padme. Come." Sylvie patted her leg.

The dog sat down in front of the gate beside Polly.

"Padme, come here. Now."

The dog looked up at Polly, big eyes as innocent as could be.

Sylvie strode down the sidewalk. "Like I need one more animal in my life disobeying me."

"You know Eliseo can correct that behavior," Polly said.

"In me or the dog?"

Polly decided to stay quiet as Sylvie put her hand on Padme's collar.

"As soon as you're gone, she'll be at the back door wanting to go inside. Thanks for everything."

By the time Polly got home, the house was dark. They'd left the outside lights on for her, but everything else was closed down. She was surprised that Rebecca wasn't ready to pounce when she walked into the kitchen. She'd sent a text earlier in the evening to let them know that Andrew was home and safe, but she'd ignored the many questioning texts from her daughter that came after that.

Lights and low sounds came from the family room, so Polly walked down the hall. Sure enough, Heath and Rebecca were sprawled out on couches watching one of the latest Avengers movies.

"I'm home," Polly said quietly.

Rebecca sprang up. "It's about time. You have some explaining to do."

"'Splaining," Polly said.

She got a frown from Rebecca. "What?"

"Nothing. It's late. I want to go to bed."

"No. What you want to do is tell me what happened this evening." Rebecca stalked past Polly, walked out to the kitchen and got her phone, then swiped it open and jammed her finger at it. "Home and safe. That's all you told me. Do you not know me? How is that enough?"

"It's all I had time for." Polly laughed as she walked over to the refrigerator. Yes. She could eat everything in there. Her stress from the last few days had washed away and she felt hollow. Not emotionally, but she wanted something to eat. "I'm starving."

Heath walked in. "I could eat. What shall we make?"

"It's gonna have to be fast food. I can't wait much longer. I might shrivel up and die."

"Oh no you don't," Rebecca said, coming around the corner of the island. She stepped between Polly and the refrigerator.

"Move or you die," Polly said.

"Talk or you don't eat."

Polly feinted to the right, and then hip-bumped Rebecca. "Outta my way, little girl, or there will be blood."

Heath came in from the porch, carrying a frozen breakfast pizza. He calmly turned the oven on to pre-heat and unwrapped the package.

Rebecca turned on him. "You cheated."

While she was distracted, Polly pushed her further out of the way and opened the freezer section, then took out a container of frozen cookies. "This is a start. What else?"

Heath pointed at the open refrigerator. "Marie and Cat bought bagels in Ames today. I wouldn't mind having one of those."

"Bagels it is," Polly said. She rummaged until she landed on the zipper lock bag that held a half dozen. She nearly tossed it, but instead, pushed it across the island at him.

"You made me nervous," he said. "I saw it in your eyes. I thought I was going to have to dive for it."

"Whatever. Plain cream cheese?"

"Yeah."

She grinned at Rebecca when she heard footsteps coming down the back stairway. "Looks like we have more company."

"I'm never going to find out what happened," Rebecca whined.

"What's going on in here?" Henry asked as he came around the corner. "You're home."

"And starving. We're having cookies, bagels, and breakfast pizza."

"I'd eat some of that," Hayden said, coming into the kitchen. "Cat will be right down."

Heath heaved a sigh. "Better get another pizza."

"Did any of you hear from Shelly today?" Polly asked.

Henry pursed his lips. "Uh, yeah. I did. I forgot to say something."

"I'm glad you did. What did she say?"

"You were asleep when she stopped by to pick up some things. She said that she'd be back tomorrow. Marta just needed one more night. I thought she was spending the weekend with her dad, but I guess that's off. He had to go somewhere for work and wouldn't get home until late tomorrow. He might stop by here, though. I told her to invite him to the party."

"I'm just so glad she talked to you. I was going to have to have a chat with her about communicating responsibly."

"No. She did good," he said.

Cat came into the kitchen, wearing her pajamas and a loose robe. "Are we having a party?"

"The world is leveling out," Polly said. "People are back where they belong and I'm ready to relax."

"Rebecca said that Andrew was home."

"And safe," Rebecca interrupted. "That's all I was able to tell you because that's all I knew. Someone …" she glared at Polly. "… refuses to give me any more details. Never mind that I used to date the boy. Never mind that he's been my best friend since I moved to Bellingwood. Never mind that I'm the most curious girl in the world. What does she care?"

Henry laughed and wrapped an arm around her shoulders. "You are the most curious girl in the world. It will take you far, but it will drive us nuts. Maybe Polly can't tell you anything more. Did you think of that?"

She rolled her eyes. "Well, no. Why would I think about that? Remember? Curiosity. Can you tell me anything more?"

"He'll be here tomorrow for the party," Polly said. "He's coming early so he can talk to you."

"What does he want to talk to me about?"

"I suspect he plans to apologize. He's been doing a lot of that this evening."

"See," Rebecca said, crumpling the plastic and paper from the frozen pizzas in her hand. "I knew there was more you could tell me." She stalked over to the pantry and threw the trash away. "Do I just need to stand here with my mouth open until you spill a few more tidbits?"

"He's had a rough couple of days. You should wait to hear it from him. It's not my story." Before Rebecca could protest, Polly held her hand up. "No more harassment. You wouldn't want me to tell anyone about the things we talk about. I'm not betraying his confidence, even to you. He's fine. He's home. He's got a lot of things that he needs to deal with and if Andrew wants you to know more, he'll tell you himself."

Rebecca shook her head in disgust. "What good is it living with the one person who knows everything if she has integrity and a conscience? It's not fair, I tell you. It's just not fair."

"Life stinks," Cat agreed.

"How's your hand, Heath?" Polly asked. She reached for it and rubbed her fingers across the bandage.

"Pretty good. Hay looked at it after we got home from work. He cleaned it up and put this new bandage on."

Polly looked at Hayden for confirmation.

"No sign of infection or anything. He's good."

"Does it hurt much?"

Heath shook his head. "Sometimes, but it's fine. It doesn't hurt today as much as it did yesterday."

"You'll still take it easy next week, too," Henry said. "You start classes soon and I want you ready for that."

"I can't believe it's here already," Polly said. "These late night parties are going to have to end."

"Because we're such party animals." Cat moved around them and opened the cupboard door, then took plates out.

Henry scowled. "Real plates?"

"Ummm."

"Just kidding. We have a dishwasher. Polly, do you remember the days when you did most of the dishes by hand?"

"I only had you and Rebecca in the house," Polly said.

"And Jessie," Rebecca said. "She was there, too."

"Yeah. She was. My goodness, that was a while ago. Well, I'm glad to have a nice dishwasher now."

The timer on the stove dinged and Hayden opened the door. He slid the pizzas out onto a cutting board that Heath handed to him and set them on the counter.

Polly looked across the island and caught Henry's eye. He smiled and winked at her.

CHAPTER TWENTY-SIX

Reaching down to pick up a soccer ball that had landed in front of her, Polly tossed it to the side. She couldn't see where it came from and no one seemed to be waiting for it. Their backyard was packed with people. It felt like every single person in Polly's extended family was coming, and their children, too. What better way to introduce the Waters family to Bellingwood?

Lydia had snagged little Theodore Ogden from his mother and Joss's kids were running around the yard, playing with Molly Locke and Elva Johnson's children. The two youngest Waters girls, along with Rose Bright, were doing their best trying to keep Mimi Mikkels on the quilt Joss had laid out on the grass.

"We brought fried chicken!"

Polly looked up and her eyes grew big. "I didn't think you'd be here."

Jeff Lyndsay smiled as he put two trays of chicken pieces on the table. "You were right."

"Well, duh," she said. "About what?" She came around to shake Adam's hand. "I'm glad you're here."

Henry crossed the lawn. "It's good to see you again, Adam."

"What about me?" Jeff asked. "I was friends with you guys first. I bring a new person into your life and you ignore me?"

Polly gave him a quick hug. "We love you best. I promise. Now, why was I right?"

"You told me I shouldn't hide him. I'm done hiding."

"This is a perfect place to unhide him," she said with a grin.

"Adam, let me introduce you to a couple of gearheads," Henry said. "Nate owns a beautiful '62 Impala, and Kirk and his son are restoring a Camaro."

Jeff watched them walk away. "Well, there goes my date."

"You can hang out with me," Polly said.

He frowned at her. "I can make my own way, thank you very much."

"I just thought maybe you needed some comforting."

"We tried to get here early," Sylvie said, coming in with Eliseo and Andrew. "There were a million things going on and I couldn't get out of the house."

"Looking kind of rough there," Jeff said to Andrew. "Girls are gonna dig that."

Andrew grimaced. "Okay. I guess. Is Rebecca here?"

Polly nodded toward the back porch. "She's over there with Kayla and Cilla."

"I better go face the music. How much did you tell her last night?"

"Nothing," Polly said. "In fact, I nearly died because I chose to keep your secrets."

"They really aren't secrets. Everyone is going to know what happened to me."

"Yeah, but it's your story to tell. However, I suspect that Rebecca won't let you go until you tell her every single detail." He started to walk away, but Polly caught up to him. "I want you two to stay outside. I know that your conversation might be intense, but no more private stuff. Got it?"

"What do you mean?" he asked, frowning.

"Henry and I aren't ready to see you two fall back into a relationship. Don't you push her."

"I wouldn't do that."

"Fine. Now you really won't."

She let him go and went back over to stand beside Sylvie.

"What was that?"

"I told him not to push Rebecca into being together again."

"Good," Sylvie said. "We all know how high emotions can make things seem more important than they are. Those two need time to figure out how to be friends again."

"I'm glad you're with me on this," Polly said. "Come on, I want you to meet Andrea."

Andrea, Sal, and Joss were in the gazebo, looking out over the cemetery.

"Andrea," Polly said. "I'd like to introduce you to Sylvie Donovan."

"Ah yes, the other mother who worried this week," Andrea said. "I was considering cages. Would you be interested in investing in one or two? Polly's backyard might be a nice place to hold them. It's pleasant enough back here and they'd be visited by happy children every day."

Sylvie laughed and looked back to find her youngest son. "A cage is a great idea. When he annoys me, I'll put in a request for gruel instead of bread and water."

"Perfection. We take away their blankets if they try to escape."

"And here I wanted a big family," Joss said.

"You have a big family." Sal pointed her finger out across the lawn. "How do you ever keep up with that tribe?"

Joss chuckled. "Shock collars."

Sylvie burst out with laughter. "Oh, thank you. It's been days since I've laughed."

Polly saw Rachel and Billy, Doug and Anita come in, carrying trays. "I'll be right back. I didn't realize they were going to be able to come."

"The wedding was early and there wasn't a dance. It was a light weekend," Sylvie said.

Before Polly could get to them, Cat Harvey stepped up instead. That was interesting. There were plenty of people their age in town, it was just a matter of finding ways for everyone to get to know each other. Now if only Skylar and Stephanie would get here.

Kayla ran over to Polly. "They're on their way."

"Who, honey?"

"Sky and Steph. She just texted me. Sky was making his mother's famous Swedish meatballs and they're almost out of the oven. This is a big party!"

Polly looked around. "Yeah. It is. Kinda fun, isn't it?"

"Andrew made Rebecca cry," Kayla said softly enough that Polly barely heard her.

"Is it bad?"

"No, he said he was sorry to her and then he said he was sorry to me, too. He didn't do anything bad to me, but he said he'd been a jerk. Well, yeah, but it didn't hurt me."

"He's trying to grow up."

"Are you going to let him come over after school again?"

"Don't you think he should if he wants to?"

"Yes!" Kayla said with great enthusiasm. "I missed him, too. I never thought about that, but all three of us have done everything together since I met Rebecca. He's like my brother. I wonder what he thinks about Cilla."

"He'd probably better think that's she's okay. She'll be around, I'm guessing."

"Yeah, she and Rebecca are talking about the first dance this year. They want to rent a limousine and take a bunch of us all at the same time. Cilla says that if we all split it, the cost isn't that bad."

"They do, do they?" Polly said. "That should be interesting."

"I've never ridden in a limo. It would be so cool."

Polly nodded, distracted by the number of people in her yard.

"There's Mr. Greyson," Kayla whispered. "His assistant, Nan? She's so pretty. Do you think they'll ever get married?"

Polly turned and waved at Nan and Grey. "I don't know. Why don't you go back and get more scoop for me on Rebecca, Cilla, and Andrew?"

Kayla giggled. "Stephanie says I am a terrible gossip. But I only tell, like, you and her and Rebecca."

"I think you're just fine." Polly patted the girl's shoulder and walked over to Nan and Grey. "I'm glad you could make it."

"Nan tells me I'm not allowed to be a hermit," Grey said, his hand on Nan's elbow. "Not only is she right, but I thought this would be a perfect group of people for her to meet. There are more here than I expected, though."

"Me too," Polly said. "But it's a good group. Why don't you take her up to the gazebo?"

Grey nodded. "Nan, these are some of the best women in town. A couple of them are the strongest A-type personalities you'll ever meet. Talk about driven. I think you'll fit in just perfectly." He turned back to Polly. "Is Shelly here?"

Polly pointed around to the other side of the house. "She's playing volleyball with some of the kids. Her dad is coming into town tonight. I've invited him to join us."

"Great," he said with a smile. "It will be good to talk to him again."

The gate along the back fence opened as Andy, Len, and Beryl came into the yard.

"Hallooo," Beryl called out. She took a casserole carrier out of Len's hands and walked over to Polly. "I brought a seven-layer salad."

"I see," Polly replied. "Now, you didn't tell me that you made it, you just said that you brought it."

Beryl frowned. "Well, aren't you too smart for your own britches. Do we have enough food for this crowd? You've never had this many people in your back yard. At least not at a party I was invited to attend."

"I think we'll have plenty. Henry and Hayden will fire the grill up in a while."

"Who is that cutie-patootie standing beside our Jeff?" Beryl asked, then she opened her mouth in surprise. "Don't tell me."

"Okay, I won't. His name is Adam."

"I might have to check this one out. He's adorable."

"Funny," Polly said. "That's the exact description I had for him."

"I'll be back later. Are you serving alcohol at this shindig?"

"There's wine and beer inside. We have iced tea, lemonade, and water out here."

"Fine. I'll be good," Beryl grumped. "If I got too liquored up, I might flirt with the wrong man tonight."

Polly shook her head as the woman walked off. "You just never know."

As the evening progressed, more friends and family came in. Stephanie and Skylar arrived and had landed with Tab Hudson, J. J. Ryan, and Jessie. Marie and Bill Sturtz came in with Reuben and Judy Green, as well as Dick and Betty Mercer. Camille and Elise brought bags of chips and ended up in the gazebo with Sal, Joss, and Nan.

"You have quite a large complement of friends," Andrea said, wandering up to her. "Deb is in heaven playing volleyball with the kids and Louis acts like he's found his childhood again talking cars. How do you do this?"

"I just meet people."

"There's more to it than that. I don't know that I've ever had this many friends at one time. Maybe even in a lifetime. And they're all ages, too." She pointed at Beryl. "Who is that woman?"

"Haha," Polly said with a laugh. "That's Beryl Watson. She's the most amazing, talented kook you will ever know."

"What does she do?"

"She's a painter. She teaches my daughter, but her art hangs in galleries around the country."

Andrea frowned in confusion. "Why is she in Bellingwood?"

"She grew up here and never wanted to leave. She travels quite a bit, many of her clients are on the east coast. But she's happiest being close to her friends. The woman is a little wild. You never know what she'll wear from one day to the next and you can never be sure what she'll say, but she is kind and loving." Polly waved at Beryl, who did a small spin in place, then walked toward them.

"Is this the fascinating new neighbor?" Beryl asked. "She's as pretty as her lovely daughter." She poked Polly's side. "Did I get the right person?"

Andrea put her hand out. "Polly was just telling me that you are kind of a ..."

Beryl took Andrea's hand, bowed and lightly brushed her lips across the top of it. "I'm kind of a what?"

"I just have to say it," Andrea said. "A crazy woman."

"Ahhh, my public knows me so well." Beryl dropped the woman's hand, crossed a leg behind her, then swooped her arms out and bowed deeply.

"Never let it be said that I don't know fascinating people." Polly gestured to Beryl.

"What is it that you do all day long?" Beryl asked. "Other than chasing down lost children and moving across the country?"

"I'm a professor."

Polly slowly turned to look at Andrea. "I'm a little embarrassed I didn't ask before. A professor?" She giggled. "I knew you worked from home, but you never said what you did. I didn't want to press, just in case it was something embarrassing."

"Like selling sex toys on the internet embarrassing?" Beryl asked, cackling out loud. "Your UPS driver would love that."

"I didn't know," Polly protested. "And then it got weird because I should have asked when we first met." She laughed. "This is much better. What do you teach?"

"History," Andrea said, caught up in their laughter. "Please be sure to tell my husband what you originally thought. He will love that."

"Do you teach online or what?" Beryl asked.

Andrea nodded. "I taught for years in small colleges near where we were stationed. When Kirk was hurt, I needed more freedom, but I didn't want to stop. I love teaching, so I applied to several online universities and was accepted at two of them. It keeps me quite busy, but it's great fun. I meet students from all over the country and though I don't get the opportunity to spend four years watching them on campus, we enjoy intense conversations and learning experiences. I maintain a strict schedule for myself, but I do have freedom when Kirk and the kids need me to be available." She smiled at Polly. "When the semester begins, I promise that I will cease pestering you during the day. I'll be locked in my study with my eyes crossed from reading too many papers."

"You do bring interesting people into our little group of friends," Beryl said. She waved her arm around the yard. "This tiny little group of friends that you've gathered together. Oh ho, I see that Lydia has finally released the youngest member of the group back to his mother. I believe I shall make myself known now."

As she waltzed across the yard, Andrea shook her head. "I like that woman."

"I knew you would." Polly pointed at the kids on the porch. "How is Cilla today?"

"Better than I expected." Andrea bit her lower lip. "It's interesting. She and her father have spent a great deal of time together since she came home. I understand it. They've both been through a trauma that is hard for an outsider to understand." She stopped and looked at Polly. "Cilla said that you had gone through something similar. Is that right?"

Polly nodded. "Yeah. I'll tell you about it sometime. If she wants to know my story, I'm glad to talk about it. There's nothing to hide. But Kirk and Cilla are talking?"

"More than ever before. It's wonderful for him to have her need him like this. He was more alive yesterday than he has been in a while. I won't say that this is healing for him, but it's good that he sees how important he is to her. It's more than just being her dad now, it's being a sounding board."

"That's wonderful."

"Now I just need to keep her balanced," Andrea said. "She has a tendency to be over dramatic about everything she experiences. She'll blow this thing up if she gets attention for it."

Polly laughed. "I have a daughter just like that. And she's been through some stuff. We had to have a small discussion about over dramatizing her experiences." She looked around. "Hmm. Many of my friends here have been through stuff that you might think would destroy them."

"But the thing is, nearly everyone has," Andrea observed. "If not lately, then long ago. We hide it, we push it away, we do our best to deal with it, and move on." She linked an arm with Polly. "And we're grateful to friends who show up right on time."

Polly pointed across the yard. "Can you explain why men clump together and move off from the crowd? Look at them."

"They're laughing. All of them," Andrea said. "I'm glad Henry has been here for Kirk this week. He was afraid he'd come back to town and no one would remember him, much less care that he was here."

"I'm afraid for the two of them," Polly said with a laugh. "We may never see them if they spend their free time out at Nate's garage."

"I'd be fine with that."

"Yeah, me too. Now, I need to move Henry toward the grill. People will start getting grumpy if we don't feed them soon."

"We don't need no stinking men," Andrea said. "We can grill the meat."

"Yeah? I'm game if you are."

"I just know that if we start it, they'll come running."

Sure enough, when Polly and Andrea walked to the grill, the group of the men who had been standing on the other side of the gazebo made their way over.

"Is it time?" Henry asked.

"It's probably past time," Polly said. "Andrea told me you'd come running if we walked this way. Nice to know you're predictable just because you're men."

"I wouldn't put up with that," Nate said. "Anyone calls me predictable, I walk the other way."

"Really?" Henry asked. "Really?"

Nate laughed out loud. "Yeah. I'm a wuss. Whatever she wants, I do. It isn't like she asks me to run out into the street without my clothes on."

"Where did that come from?" Polly asked.

He shrugged. "Just the weirdest thing I could come up with. So, where's the meat?"

"I need to finish this patio and get those steps in," Polly said. "Here, help me up."

She opened the sliding glass door and with an assist from her husband and Nate, climbed into the kitchen. The temperature was supposed to be pleasant this next week. She was finishing the project no matter what. Polly opened the refrigerator, took out two trays of hamburger patties and walked back to the doors. Hayden took them from her and she returned for packages of hot dogs and brats. There was more in the refrigerator underneath the shed in the back yard, too. There would be plenty of food tonight.

She handed the dogs and brats to Nate, then stood in the doorway and looked out at the gathered group. She'd come so far from those early days at Sycamore House when she worried that she would never know many people. How silly that young woman had been.

Henry came over and held his arms up. "Want some help?"

"No, I was just looking."

"At our family?"

"Yeah. Can you believe it?" She sat down on the edge of the doorway.

Henry sat beside her and took her hand in his. "What's your next big dream?"

"I have everything I want." Polly leaned against him. "I have more than I need. Are you restless?"

He shrugged. "I want to say I'm content. Our kids are happy, our friends are interesting, our businesses are doing well."

"You want a challenge, don't you?" she whispered to him.

"When you asked me to renovate Sycamore House, I had no idea if I could do the work. When you asked me to build a barn in a day, I was terrified, but I couldn't say no. Then we bought the hotel and that was a big deal for me. I learned so much. The coffee shop was a different kind of a challenge. Even renovating this place has been interesting. Now I have good people working at the shop, they don't need me at the bed and breakfast, and the jobs the construction business is doing are fairly routine. Maybe I'm in a professional rut."

"This could be dangerous," Polly said with a grin. "It's only been a little more than five years. You can't do a rut that often or we'll end up rebuilding the entire town."

"I blame you for this."

"That seems like the right thing to do," she said. "Why?"

"I was perfectly satisfied as a laid-back, boring contractor until you showed up. You offered me a different view of the world, one where I could do anything and have a life that was filled with ..." He looked around. "... all of this. I don't want to be laid-back and boring ever again."

"Then I won't let you. We'll dig in and see what we can do next. How about that?"

Henry opened his arms as Elijah and Noah ran toward them. The boys rushed him and allowed him to envelope them.

"Can we eat soon?" Elijah asked. "I'm starving. I've been playing volleyball for hours and my tummy is empty."

"Hot dogs are coming off the grill now," Hayden announced. "Come on up, boys."

The two sidled up to Hayden and Polly grinned. "I would have made them be polite and wait."

"Ahh, they're little kids. Hayden is pulling off enough dogs to feed most of the kids something right off," Henry said. "I love you, you know, even if you do stir my imagination."

JaRon pulled his brother along toward Polly and Henry. Henry opened his arms again and JaRon moved in for a hug. Caleb held back, but Henry caught his shoulder and tugged him closer.

"Did you two play volleyball?" Henry asked.

Caleb nodded. "I played with Elijah. We even won a game."

"That's great."

Hayden turned again. "Come on, boys. I have a couple of hot dogs for you right here."

Polly choked up a little as the boys slowly left Henry's arms. They were becoming part of her family more and more every day.

"They love you so much," she whispered to Henry. "You are such a great dad to those kids."

He shrugged. "You gave me that, too."

"Come on, you guys," Rebecca scolded. "You're sitting back here making eyes at each other when you've got, like a hundred people to socialize with." She winked at Polly. "Best. Day. Ever."

Polly laughed. "You have a lot of those, you know that?"

"We all do," Henry said. He stood and walked over to Rebecca, gave her a quick hug, then mussed her hair. "That's for giving me trouble."

"Did you talk to Andrew?" Polly asked her daughter.

"A little. He said there was more to tell me, but I think he didn't want to say it all in front of Cilla since she'd been through so much. We mostly just listened to her talk. She needed to do that. But he apologized and I think we're okay."

"Good."

Rebecca pulled Polly in so she could whisper in her ear. "And he didn't do anything with Maddy Spotter. I don't have to hate him and I don't have to kill her."

"Then, yay all around," Polly whispered back. "That's probably a better way to start the school year."

Lydia caught Polly's other arm. "You've learned much from me, young Padiwan."

Polly turned in shock. "Young Padiwan?"

"I've been catching up on my movies this summer," Lydia said with a laugh. "You throw a bigger party than I ever did. The student has become the master." She pointed at Sylvie, who was talking to Andrea and Kirk. Eliseo had his hand on Sylvie's lower back. "That's a good idea."

"Which?"

Lydia chuckled. "All of it. I wish those two would decide to move in together. She needs him so badly. When I was at her house the other evening, he was her rock. As things fell apart, she grew stronger the closer she stood to him." She put her hand up. "I know, I know. Not every woman needs a man to give her strength. You don't have to tell me, but Sylvie needs Eliseo."

Polly nodded. "We'll see what happens. I know she loves him."

"I'll be good and quit playing matchmaker, though I'm happy to see Jeff here with someone he's willing to introduce to all of us."

"You can't help yourself," Polly said with a laugh.

Lydia patted Polly's arm. "I'm going to find my husband who lets me get away with my foibles. He probably shouldn't, but he can't help himself either."

Polly watched her walk away and wrapped her arms around herself.

"Miss Polly?" Cilla said.

"Hi there."

"Thank you again."

"You were the strong one who held on until I could find you. I'm proud of you."

"Does it get easier?"

Polly unfolded her arms and put one around Cilla's shoulder. "It did for me. I won't tell their stories, but nearly every person in this group has something in their lives they've had to overcome. Look at them now."

"They're smiling and laughing and having fun."

"Yes they are. You would have a difficult time trying to come up with their stories on your own. They aren't hiding anything, they're just living their lives, stronger now than before. Their friends and family gave them that strength. You have all of that."

"I guess I do. Dad and I talked until late the other night and then again yesterday."

"He loves you very much."

"I know. I'm glad we moved in across the street from you."

"Me too. You're going to have a good year ahead."

Cilla nodded. "Will I ever know all of these people?"

"I promise you. It won't take long. They already love you, you know."

"That's just crazy to think about."

"You have no idea."

THANK YOU FOR READING!

I'm so glad you enjoy these stories about Polly Giller and her friends. There are many ways to stay in touch with Diane and the Bellingwood community.

You can find more details about Sycamore House and Bellingwood at the website: http://nammynools.com/. Be sure to sign up for the monthly newsletter so you don't miss anything.

Join the Bellingwood Facebook page:
https://www.facebook.com/pollygiller
for news about upcoming books, conversations while I'm writing and you're reading, and a continued look at life in a small town.

Diane Greenwood Muir's Amazon Author Page is a great place to watch for new releases.

Follow Diane on Twitter at twitter.com/nammynools for regular updates and notifications.

Recipes and decorating ideas found in the books can often be found on Pinterest at: http://pinterest.com/nammynools/

And, if you are looking for Sycamore House swag, check out Polly's CafePress store: http://www.cafepress.com/sycamorehouse

CPSIA information can be obtained
at www.ICGtesting.com
Printed in the USA
LVHW041733190919
631611LV00011B/951